I0593405

LEGEND OF CAEMERIS

SEER of LIGHT

BOOK FOUR

CLARE L ROLFE

First published by Clare L Rolfe in 2023

Copyright © Clare L Rolfe

Clare L Rolfe asserts the moral right to be identified as the author of this work.
All rights reserved. No part of this publication may be reproduced, stored in a
retrieval system or transmitted in any form by any means, electronic, mechanical,
photocopying, recording or otherwise, without the prior written permission.
of the publishers and copyright holders.
All of the characters in this book are fictitious, and any resemblance to actual.
persons, living or dead, is purely coincidental.

Rolfe, Clare L.

Seer of Light / by Clare L Rolfe

Legend of Caemeris

Paperback ISBN: 978-0-6450880-7-6

E-book ISBN: 978-0-6450880-8-3

Printed and distributed by Ingram Spark

A catalogue record for this
book is available from the
National Library of Australia

Contents

Mir Chiridien

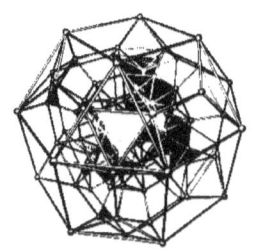

"Tears of Eaudania, Gnostic waters,

Spill over urn, Upon urn.

Source gather debris, Wash deliverer free.

Grey haired thing, knuckles tell stories,

Old washer woman, knows every stain,

Skin to bone to ashen plains,

Where lie the mysteries of making?

Where rests the forest of dreams?

How does water flow so free?

How do you make crystal trees?

Where do you come from?

What will Eaudania see?"

Jinx finished playing the song and left the washer woman alone. He always enjoyed this time of the last moments before the final drop of Eaudania's springs trickled into the wells of knowing.

He wandered into the forest of undying dreams gently humming the last of Eaudania's tears. The sound of the gushing water was deafening but to Jinx it was pure music.

"Jinx."

The bard turned looking for the source of the call wondering who it was that dreamt about him.

"Jinx."

Jinx was an orphan from the last dream of Haladran many star bursts ago, so there were no memories of him in the leaves of the forest. He belonged to the unbounded and therefore had no pathway behind him, only the future to peer into. His need to sing helped sooth his rootlessness. And along with the musical notes, his tears of yearning would spill into the wells of Eaudania. Jinx hoped they would help Eaudania discover the ways of making.

"Jinx."

"Ahh it's the wanderer again. Strange creature. Suddenly appeared on the whim of the great light of Colax" Jinx spoke.

He decided to visit his friend again.

As Jinx left, the great waterfalls of the Sentinel kept spilling into the wells of knowing. It had done this for an age of a star and since the birth of Eaudania.

On the precipice of clouds made from glass, stood an old woman. She was born old. She had never known youth or infancy only the ravages of having lived as long as a star lives. And yet in spite of her great age, she had no memories. No sense of time passing, only the drive to seek and find what makes things happen.

Her amethyst eyes scoured every dip and flow of the torrential water. Every drop was watched as it slid over glass mountains and delved deeper into the valleys beneath her.

Faintly she had heard the lilt of Chiridia voices as they paid homage to her. She did not know what the creatures were, but they always came and watched her. A few of them died in convulsions as the power of the water overwhelmed their bodies. She never tried to stop them or warn them of the impending deluge. It was an insatiable urge to know how the water worked and it was not to be stopped for any.

The waterfall began to slow. This was the critical time when the most could be learned of the making of things.

A drop slithered over a riverbed made of gemstones. She fixated her eyes on every last molecule. Her hand gripped the glass pipette.

"Wait" she whispered "Wait."

Her eyes solidified into quartz as the pipette consumed the last drops. The only sign the glass rod contained anything was the vibration Eaudania could feel.

The washer woman disappeared. Free of the excoriation of the water, the glass cliffs and clouds returned to a peaceful silence. The valleys suddenly bloomed in verdant greens as the forests of dream leaves flourished in the drought.

Eaudania returned to her chamber chiselled out of clouds. Sitting on a large citrine stone, she stared at the molecule she had plucked from the last drop of water.

"Show yourself to me" she ordered.

Nothing changed or moved.

Her hair began to scintillate white flecks and transform into an emerald and ruby weave. She began to cry. Her tears resembled pebbles dropping onto the crystal altar. Her face and hands began to splinter as she poured the eons of searching into a tiny spec of white light.

"Break" she whimpered "Show me."

Nothing.

She shattered into a thousand pieces but instantly reformed.

She looked across the vastness of existence to pierce the ebbing droplet but again it did not explain why it would not shatter and yet it could flow so easily over stone.

Taking a tiny dome she covered the spec. She walked toward the edge of the chamber and looked at the explosions of colour in the forested valleys. It still amazed her. Of course with just one thought she could make the torrents again to keep searching. But the Chiridia who came to watch her seemed to thrive during these water droughts. She looked at the undulations of the forest grow and die many times, in a pattern of perfect symmetry. She found the softness of the green calmed her. Compared to her hard crystal form, the yielding dream-forests and rivers were able to be sculpted and shaped into something else entirely. They were like the water, unlike herself, who could not change.

Tears began to cascade and then avalanche from her eyes, mesmerised by the spectacle of the valley beneath. There were flecks of vermillion and bursts of cerulean as new leaves sprung into existence, mingling with the sounds of the Chiridia. Peering closer she saw many of the Chiridia moving together in unison, pouring out an energy which rebounded with the forests of dreams. She sucked it in but none of it explained the mystery of water. Soon high-pitched noises vibrated around the chamber as she saw her crystal tears crash into the valleys. Some of them crushed the green slopes and plundered into the Chiridia. The tears of the Sentinel came to a rest and settled on the floor of the valleys. Within one blink the forest had grown over them.

"Let me see" she whimpered again staring up and out into the eons of time. "Let me see."

Jinx continued on through the dream leaves following the caller of his name. His tail and long limbs helped make it easier to step over the empty spaces between the leaves but sometimes his foot missed causing him to tumble into dream space. Strumming a branch shaped into a small lute, the notes would bring the bard back to the leaves.

"Jinx you are taking a long time" called the voice.

"I know Wanderer. I will be there soon" he replied.

Suddenly a tear from Eaudania smashed into the branch he was walking along, and everything was pulverised into nothing.

"Goodness me. Fortunate for me I am in the forest of lost dreams, or I would be smashed to less than a spark" Jinx retorted leaping onto another leaf.

The bard stopped and caught his breath. Waiting in the silence, he heard "Jinx" faintly vibrating across the vastness once more. The bard found his bearings and followed the voice.

The Wanderer lay asleep inside a small hut made of leaves on the edge of a great glass cliff. She slept soundly dreaming of constellations of stars and moons and beautiful colours exploding all over the forest of dreams.

Jinx tip toed inside. She woke hearing the creak of the glass door closing from Jinx's entry.

"Hello Jinx."

"Hello Wanderer."

"Shall we make tea?" the Wanderer asked.

"Yes please. I was almost crushed to a tiny star bug's dream Wanderer. Eaudania's tears are strong today" spoke Jinx.

"Oh I didn't hear them. I was asleep watching a star be born. I wanted your singing branch to play as the star came to life. I will need to meet this Eaudania one day."

"Oh you must see her. She is taller than a tree and sparkles more than the great hearts of our suns" spoke Jinx in a dreamy voice.

"I think your music would woo anything, even stir the great stars of long ago" replied the Wanderer.

"Oh I don't think so. Eaudania is not distracted by us or any below her gaze. What her purpose is remains hidden. All the Chiridia know is that our world lives by her whim and sorrow alike."

Jinx and the Wanderer kissed. She poured tea for the two of them. They sipped in silence.

Smoke billowed over the rim of the cups and out through the small opening of the glass cave. Outside the sky moved at the speed of the water that had flowed into the wells of knowing. It was only sky that could be seen. The world was made of dream space so it changed with each waking moment and somehow those who dreamt together could make the same things in harmony, forming what would be called a world. There was no land or mountains or oceans, only the sky.

Jinx began to play his lyric-branch. The Wanderer stared through the window. In the deepness of the empty spaces she thought something called but she could not figure out who or what it was. Jinx's music was soothing, and she began to feel sleepy again. She watched Jinx's slender fingers play the wooden stem as she lay her head in his shoulder.

The bard began to sing.

"Wash over me tears of sacred spells,

Tease from me the heart of wells

stones and steps, empty cares.

Keep pace my feet,

I see you inside the spark of empty space.

I sing to you oh distant mage,

Over and under the forest of whim and dreaming waves.

On a slip stream among the forests and clouds,

Come to me my heart's desire,

Feel the eternal spark enflame,

The living dreams of ancient fire."

"Wanderer, do you like it?'

"Of course I do."

She pulled herself in close to Jinx as he gently strummed.

She could feel the music begin to weave a world. She searched for the first tendril and latched onto it with her mind. Suddenly she was scooped up into a whirling storm of crystals.

"Jinx where are we?"

"I think we are in our hearts Wanderer."

In the distance sat a black spec like a mountain. It grew larger as they went closer and kept changing shape.

"I wonder what that chimera of emptiness is over there. No stars live here and no dreams only a hollowness of lost memories" spoke the Wanderer.

The Wanderer stared as the abyss morphed into different shapes. Something called to her, but she could not figure out if it was a voice, a memory, or a dream.

Peering more deeply into the empty space she saw a small island on a sea of glass. Its terrain was formed from sharp chiselled crevices detailed with intricate patterns darting in irregular directions. A solitary beacon of dense crystal made more spectacular by the darkness surrounding it.

"Oh let us go there, Jinx. I want to explore the island" urged the Wanderer.

As they ran toward the small spec, a dark spot broke away from the surrounding shadow of space and followed them.

The liquid stone of the ocean tickled the Wanderer's toes as she stepped into it. Jinx looked back and saw the black spec following. Jinx wondered why it followed now and why didn't the Wanderer see it, as it was her dreamscape not his.

Swimming was easy in spite of the thickness of the liquid. The Wanderer powered ahead of Jinx unaware of what followed. She crawled up onto a beach of quartz and lay back waiting for the bard.

She luxuriated in the precious sand and stared beyond the dream net into the emptiness of dreamscapes. It amazed her how much she could hear, see, and feel. It was like every particle of existence became visible and was within reach. She wondered how it could be like this. So easy to manipulate the world with a simple idea in a dream. How did everyone exist? Stay alive even, how did they know to eat, drink, and even breathe she wondered.

Jinx plopped down beside her and held her hand.

"Oh Jinx, I think this dream is where I want to remain all the time with you."

"Wanderer, think of all the other dreams that would be lost if we stayed here" he replied.

Jinx could see the shape which now resembled a small rip in the dream net. The darkness was deeper than beyond the emptiness in the sky. Why can't the Wanderer see it he thought.

The bard became nervous peering into that darkness. It was different to emptiness. Jinx quickly stood up and pulled the Wanderer up from the sand.

"Come let us see what dwells here?"

Beyond the dunes stood a small hill made from purple quartz. It was broken by an opening leading into a cave. They walked inside a tunnel awash with magenta light. The air thickened.

"Stop" spoke Jinx gripping the Wanderer's hand "Listen."

The Wanderer could just hear the sound of a low beat. It was barely perceptible. Among the beats were the sounds of breathing echoing against the walls.

"Let's see what it is Bard" spoke the Wanderer.

The low beat grew louder until they could feel the vibration all around them.

"Look Jinx" whispered the Wanderer pointing ahead of her.

The Wanderer looked at the razor-sharp spines along the back and tail. The talons were elongated to fine needles and fangs were visible through the crystal jaw.

"A diamond dragon" the Wanderer gasped awe struck by the ferocious beauty of the creature.

"We must leave. The great dragons have not risen on Mir Chiridien since the beginning days. How is it possible? They were shattered into a million pieces and now another is found. Come Wanderer this is dream malice we walk through. If we stay too long here, we will never be able to leave" Jinx spoke desperate to leave.

"No Jinx. It is exquisite in its beauty" she replied as she went to touch it.

Jinx grabbed her arm and pulled her away.

"No do not awaken it. We must leave and warn the Dream Orators of its presence. Something has forged it and it will bring destruction again."

They raced out of the cave and into the stark whiteness of the day. The three suns of Mir Chiridien beamed removing any shadows.

Jinx carried the Wanderer in his arms as he sprinted across the ocean. The dark spot had retreated but remained visible in the distance.

"Wanderer can you see the foreboding shadow that marks our dream?" he asked.

"When you point it out to me I can but otherwise it does not bother me. What is it?" asked the Wanderer.

"I do not know; it could be what has made the dragon. Or the edge of night-dream. Sometimes shadows break through the three suns' light and live on the edge. Either way it is not good for if it captures us, we will not escape from its nightmares."

The Wanderer looked across and saw the shadow nearing them. Jinx sprinted over the ocean desperate to outrun the shadow.

Jinx landed back in their humpy panting. The window to the outside shut instantly, and they lay in darkness together. The vibration of the dragon's heart still thrummed in Jinx's fingers, tail, and toes.

The Wanderer lay thinking of the magnificent dragon in the cave. She wanted to go and look at it again. If only to touch the exquisitely sculpted scales.

"I will go and warn the Orators. Stay here" spoke Jinx.

"I would like to come with you Bard. I have seen so little here. My dreams always take me far away. I have not seen very much of the shaped spaces."

"Not now Wanderer. It will be safer for you here. The Orators are swift in their wrath, for their memories are long and know the days of malice which once existed. My news may lead to war" Jinx spoke in a low voice.

The Wanderer had not heard fear in the Bard's voice before.

Jinx left and the Wanderer made some tea. She sipped it looking into the clear liquid watching a thousand dream leaves swirl around. She saw the dragon again and decided she would leave now. It seemed this world did not like dragons and yet when Jinx had startled in the cave his tail and crown looked the same as the dragon's.

She sipped the tea and waited for slumber to arrive. In the distance the vague rumble of the Eaudania's tears rippled in the distance.

Suddenly she was entering the dragon cave. The magenta was replaced by the sparkle of the dragon's hide, letting her find her way along the tunnel.

Soon the glittering creature's glow washed over here. She crept up to the leviathan. Its resting body was three times her height and the head was twice her length. Her hand reached out quavering as it neared the glass scales. It was warm to touch as if it was a living thing. The slumbering beast did not stir as she lightly stroked it. She edged her way around towards its face. Its face was peaceful. The eyelashes were slivers of diamond filigree. Her finger pricked the end of one lash, and it began to bleed. A droplet of her blood dribbled down into the lip of the creature. She sucked on the finger to stop it bleeding.

She lay against the breathing torso and let the warmth suffuse into her. She breathed in unison with the steady heartbeat of the creature. She began to fall asleep. Deeper and deeper her own heart pumped with the surge of the dragon's life force.

It woke. The drop of blood had touched its heart and it knew it was found. It stirred and flicked the sleeping creature off its body. She did not stir. The Dragon sniffed the body. Not real, only dream stuff.

It stood and stretched its back into an arch.

The Wanderer awoke and looked at the beast.

"Who are you beautiful one?" The Wanderer asked.

It did not answer but proceeded to preen itself. The huge talons squealed against the quartz and easily cut into it. The dragon ignored the Wanderer. Feeling braver she went closer to pet the beast. It stopped as her hand neared the underside of its jaw. A slight quickening of its beating heart could be felt just as the sWanderer's hand contacted the jaw. Its diamond hide had softened. It turned its head and sniffed her hand again and lightly licked it as if it were tasting her. The tongue was smooth as the Wanderer let it move along her hand.

Suddenly the dragon stood and began to walk along the tunnel. The Wanderer followed. The dragon came to the mouth of the cave and stood looking out into the world. The Wanderer stood beside it.

"Be careful beast. I don't think you are well liked" she warned.

It looked at her and it seemed she could just make out a wry look in its clear eyes.

Its mighty jaw opened wide unleashing a dream shattering roar across the landscape. The cave and island disintegrated forcing the Wanderer to latch onto the dragon's front leg to avoid falling into the waking space. She climbed up onto its back gripping tightly the glass scales as the cacophony of roars pierced her body.

"Where are you flying beast? Into the dreams of the sleeping Chiridia. They cannot be woken by force" called the Wanderer.

Suddenly her mind was blackened, and she almost lost her grip of the dragon's leg as the pain of a black miasma consumed her mind.

"I can wake them. I, Doldraak can wake them. They, the slayers of our race have not vanquished the stone-blood of the mighty Ondraak. Watch Wanderer and you shall see" spoke Doldraak.

"How do you know my name?" asked the Wanderer.

"How do you not remember?" replied Doldraak.

The pair flew into the infinite gaps of dreams space and with each rupturing invasion the booming echoes fractured the diamond scales beneath the Wanderer only to reform. As the black shadow suffused into her, she could feel the beating heart of the beast inside her. Each thump forced the exhilaration of battle fury into her so that she began to crave destruction and conquest.

"Fly, Fly, Doldraak, break the dreams and show me the power of dragon fire!" she screamed across the dreamscape.

Jinx climbed the stairs to the very tip of the spire of the Orators. It was an arduous trek and he breathed heavily with each step. The nerves at delivering the news increased with each level as he knew war was coming. The Wanderer should be safe in their den of dreams. He had hidden her there when he had found her so many dream cycles ago. The bard had known she would not be welcome. But he had become enchanted with her lying asleep peacefully on a silver dream leaf. These leaves were special as they were only seen when all three suns aligned. Jinx had taken it as a sign of gratitude from Eaudania after singing for her.

He reached the top story. He stopped to catch his breath, thoughts of the war to come raced through his mind. Jinx was middle aged by Chiridien standards, but he remembered the last onslaught and the laments of the dream-weavers as they began to rebuild the nexus of memory after Ondraak's progeny had been defeated.

Taking out his lyre-branch, he played to call his lieges. The echo of the bard at play rippled everywhere. Soon a shimmering wall formed opening out into a huge plateau of carnelian stone on which sat eight figures. Their heads were shrouded in scintillating hooded robes. Their body shapes could be discerned beneath but their faces remained hidden.

"Who awakens the Orators?" called a voice.

"Jinx the Bard begs audience" replied Jinx.

"Why Bard? Your tune is sweet no doubt, but it is under dream death that you dare wake us without cause."

"I know this to be true and is not done lightly. Ondraak's progeny have been found" spoke Jinx, swallowing hard as a lump of fear formed inside him.

One by one the eight controllers of Mir Chiridien lifted their heads. Their eyes pierced Jinx's mind seeking the truth of the message. The image of the crystal dragon came to them. They extracted the dream memory and bought it out to view in the centre of the semi-circle of their thrones.

Jinx searched to see if the Wanderer remained out of view from the Orators. She did. He was relieved.

"Indeed the music creature has seen the sleeping spawn of our ancient enemy" spoke an Orator.

"What shall we do?" replied another.

"We shall go to war once more" spoke yet another.

"What if the Sentinel awakes in the time we battle?" asked another.

"Then the destruction of Mir Chiridien will greet the dawn of the three suns" replied another.

"Hasten the militia before the worm feasts on our world" spoke all the Orators in unison.

"Bard, you have done well. You shall be rewarded with more dream space. But for now put down your song twig and bare your blades for to battle we march" called the Orators.

Jinx bowed at the commandment and retreated. As the musician walked away, the overlords of the world stood and thrust back their robes. Underneath stood muscular creatures not unlike Jinx but far larger. They grew fangs and talons. For a brief moment it seemed to Jinx they resembled dragons, but this was blasphemy to think such a thing. They began to descend from their thrones with swords raised, forged from the crystals deep within dream-space. One of the Orators, the one called Inar the Knowing, hesitated as it walked past the image of the dragon. It watched something. Jinx held its breath as it guessed what it had seen.

"I think Bard something else accompanies this, Dragon?" Inar asked.

Jinx felt the probing voice of Inar.

"What do you see my liege?" asked Jinx.

"I see another and there is shadow that follows. For many cycles I have the felt the dream space was emptier than it once was. I wondered if we had a visitor, but my questing eye could not find it" replied Inar.

Jinx did not answer. Inar's talon plucked a piece of the Wanderer's face and the shadow and swallowed it.

"To battle Bard" commanded Inar.

"To battle Great One" replied Jinx.

The forest of dreams felt the beating heart of Doldraak and began to shiver. The Chiridia of making awoke from among the stone and leaves. Doldraak alighted on the side of a mountain and began to issue crystal flames. High pitched screams reverberated across the darkness of waking time as the Ondraak returned again to destroy the weave of Mir Chiridien.

The Wanderer felt the dream lust rise inside her along with the fear and pain of the Chiridia she had shared space with. The confusion of the two feelings began to nibble away at her exhilaration. Suddenly tears began to well inside and she cried out.

"Doldraak, stop!" she cried.

The dragon bellowed even more and the screams of the leaves exploding made her faint. She let go and fell into an ocean of broken memory. Doldraak flew away.

The Wanderer spun into the emptiness trying to latch onto something to stop the fall but there was nothing left. She blacked out as she hurtled into the nothingness.

Eaudania looked across the table at the spot of light. She searched its secret. Her fingers were worn down from etching every miniscule movement of the atoms.

"Change for me. Let time open and show me your secrets" she groaned.

Suddenly there was a loud thump outside. Eaudania placed a bell jar over the particle willing it to sleep. She walked toward the viewing platform and saw the lump on the far side near the cliff. It was struggling to get up. It was wounded or weakened. Its form irritated her. It was clumsy. It stood it up straight.

"Who are you?" asked Eaudania with a tinge of irritation in her voice.

The Wanderer stood blinking. She saw sky and stone and a spectre standing almost as high as the sky in the shape of a woman.

"I am the Wanderer."

"No you are not. You have another name" replied Eaudania.

"None that I know of. The bard Jinx called me that and that is all I know. Do you know my real name?" the Wanderer asked.

"We shall find it for I took many turns of eternity to discover my name" replied the woman.

"Are you what they call Eaudania of the water?" asked the Wanderer.

"I am Eaudania."

"There is a dragon unleashed within Mir Chiridien. It will destroy everything. Can you do something? I think I woke it."

"What is this place you speak of and what is a dragon? Does it live in the spaces between the sparks of light. Can it tell me who I am and where I came from. Does it know how to make water into light so my dim memory can be revealed? Indeed does it know your real name Wanderer?"

The Wanderer stood looking at Eaudania not understanding the creature. She had shrunk to the same height as herself. The Wanderer looked into Eaudania's eyes and saw an image of sprawling plains, colourful but not like the shimmering spectacle of dream forests.

Eaudania left and walked back to the table where the particle of light sat. She removed the bell jar and began to stare at it intensely, forgetting about her visitor.

The Wanderer followed the Sentinel. The chamber swirled in a rainbow of colours with voices, faces and images mixed into it. It was overwhelming, but Eaudania did not seem to notice it and remained staring at something before her.

"Please Eaudania, the dragon has begun its conquest. Can't you feel the pain of the dying dream leaves, trees, mountains, and streams" pleaded the Wanderer.

Eaudania did not answer.

The Wanderer went to the edge of the viewing platform. It stood so high she could not see the bottom and her breath caught in her throat at the distance that stretched before her. The Valley of Dreams and Forest of Wish and Memory was so grand, she felt like a tiny piece of sand standing on the edge of great cliffs. Something glinted in the sky. Closer and closer the glinting shape sped toward her. The Wanderer began to run. Just as Doldraak landed on the stone she dived into Eaudania's chamber. She crawled underneath the stone alter.

"Eaudania the Dragon has come here" she whispered.

Doldraak's claws scraped on the crystal floor as it entered the hall of Eaudania.

"Sentinel" Doldraak called in hissing breaths.

Eaudania finally looked up at Doldraak. She suddenly reached down and pulled the Wanderer out from under the table.

"Who are you both? Again I have been interrupted from my work" spoke Eaudania to the Wanderer and Doldraak.

"Your work is in vain Sentinel as the Ondraak shall destroy this world before your quest can be completed" spoke Doldraak.

"I have no memory of you creature. And how would you know what my quest is?" asked Eaudania.

Eaudania suddenly seized the necklace around the Wanderer's neck.

"What is this clasp? What was contained within it?"

The Wanderer pulled back.

"I don't know. I have always worn it" she replied.

"Don't you understand. I have searched the urns of the sacred waters from time unknown and now here you stand with the knowledge of all things. The one thing which may let me remember and restore my name. Dragon, don't you feel the potency of its stain on the trinket around this creature's neck?"

Doldraak sniffed the air and roared.

"It is true. Wanderer, remember your name" Doldraak commanded.

"I don't know it" the Wanderer cried.

Suddenly the immense age and power of the two creatures weighed down on her. She felt crushed beneath them. She wanted to flee back to Jinx. She was small, powerless, and lost. A sharp pain rose in her shoulder. She realised Eaudania's long fingers were digging into her urging her to remember.

Far in the distance could be heard the sound of beating drums. Doldraak looked across toward the sound. The throbbing sounds of battle grew louder. The dragon crawled to the edge of the cliff and flew off toward the beating drums.

"Tell me your name" Eaudania demanded.

"I don't remember it" replied the Wanderer.

Eaudania snatched a small vial of clear liquid which scintillated in the dream light.

She wrenched the Wanderer's mouth open and poured the liquid down her throat.

"This is all that I have extracted from my scouring of the gobbets of light and dream dust. I give it to you to see what knowledge it brings and so you can tell me. It will not harm you. The truth shall return as the waters of deep dream. The essence of water sinks into deep sleep and the slumber of time. As it flows it uproots the mountains and splits the nexus of dream weave into its elements. And as it ebbs away, new forms are made churned by the power of its flow. If I can just see how, it does this, I can remake the world again, and with it remember who I am."

The Wanderer convulsed on the floor before Eaudania. The Sentinel picked up the odd creature and carried her to a hammock of silver leaves. She heard a boom in the distance and saw a rip in the valley where the crystal forest and cliffs had been torn.

"I sense you are the key to who I am. I have no use for wars between the Chiridia and that beast. I am Eaudania blind and lost in the sea of dreams. I will find the key to water and open the door to my memories."

She walked out and took an ancient crystal urn and began to poor water over the dry diamond and quartz stones. The sound of water splashing onto the jewelled riverbed eased her shaking.

The Wanderer opened her eyes. They had become deep black obsidian discs. She saw and remembered dirt and rock with blue sky. A face smiled at her, beaming brighter than a sun.

"Ange, get up Mata wants us to help!"

"Ok Tessi, but it's nice lying here in the sun."

Ange gasped as her memories returned. She stood. She put her hand to her throat and felt the empty clasp.

"Where is it?" she called.

Eaudania looked over her shoulder stilling the gushing waters.

"What is your name?" she asked.

"I am Ange. I am searching for Ascendant the Custodian and her brethren."

"I do not know of these Custodians."

"Where is it? Where, is the tear of Ascendant?" asked Ange.

"What is this tear?" asked Eaudania.

"Norbu forged it, and it holds the power of Caemeris, and the realm of the Custodians. I must find it. I need to find Ascendant and Lido. They lie imprisoned."

"What is it made of?" asked Eaudania.

Ange went to the precipice of the cliff and began to search for a path down. She could find Jinx. The bard could help her search. Ange felt a well of fear inside as she searched her memories. All that came back to her was watching Gildas over Norbu's body with Nekoda growling.

"Nekoda! Where is Nekoda?" Ange called out.

"What is the tear made of?" asked Eaudania once more.

"Light it is made of light and stone. I have to leave. How do I get to the forest of dreams?" she asked.

"When you find it bring it to me" ordered Eaudania.

"Why?" Ange grew suspicious. Had she said too much she wondered.

"I too seek something Ange. I search answers. Why this water flows as it does and why I can dream it into light but not when I wake. What makes things this way? Where have my memories gone. I do not know who I am."

"I understand but my quest is not to answer these questions. I must find the Custodians and return them. If I do not my world, my people, my family will die" replied Ange.

"Dream them awake and bring them here. Don't you see what Mir Chiridien is? A place for making what our dreams can only envisage. If

I can change anything into real and unreal and reform it, then we can rule the very heart of a star Ange."

"I cannot dwell here unless this is the place where the Custodians are being held captive. Is this where Assumpta and Lido are imprisoned?"

As she began to scramble down the crystal rocks the Sentinel grabbed her arm.

"War is coming. The dragon fire will reign again, and I must watch for the speck of knowledge in the great washing again. My water will not douse the dragon-dreams. You must stay here and watch with me. Perhaps you will see what I cannot" spoke Eaudania.

"I cannot. I think it is better to find Jinx. The bard will know where I can begin to look. The creature found me and may know where to begin" replied Ange.

She pulled free of Eaudania. She noticed the fingers of the washerwoman were cold and hard like the gems made by Norbu. Looking to her eyes she saw hollowness and desperation sitting behind them.

"I will return" Ange spoke trying to reassure the Sentinel.

Ange descended into the dreaming trees. She bounded between limbs, leaves, and over clouds. And as Eaudania's urns began to spill over the world she grabbed a large branch and rode the waves.

"Jinx where are you?" Ange called.

She found their hut. Going side it was empty.

She sent her thoughts out to him calling "Come my bard. The Wanderer remembers."

She went to the small hollow in the wall opposite the window. She had seen Jinx place things inside it when he thought she was asleep. She reached into the darkness and felt.

She pulled out a satchel and some gems shaped into faces. She realised this was hers. She smelt it. It smelt of earth and grass. Mir Chiridien had no scent only the pristineness of dreams.

She saw a grey hair on it. It was Nekoda's. Her heart swelled with longing to see her friend again, but fear rose within her at the same time. Where was he?

Looking inside the satchel was a small leather pouch. It was where she had hidden the prism. She opened it and inside sat a crystal shaped in a tear. She touched it and waited for the power to burn into her hand but nothing. She held it forth to see it burst with power, but it remained twinkling inertly in her hand. This was not the stone forged by Norbu.

"Jinx, come to the Wanderer!"

A roar far off in the distance broke the silence.

"Jinx! Come to me now!" called Ange.

A shadow passed outside the window. Ange ran to it and looked out. Nothing was there.

"Bard where are you?" she called.

She turned. There was a creature standing in a long robe. Its face was hidden by a hood. Outlined amongst the dream shadow was a similar shape to Jinx.

"So this is our visitor to Mir Chiridien who woke the Ondraak" spoke the creature.

"Who are you? Jinx, is that you? I am Ange Tsaed. I do not remember how I came to be here, but I have lost something which may help me continue on my quest."

"I am Inar the Knowing. I thought I sensed another within the memories of the Bard. And what is this thing you are seeking Ange Tsaed?"

"It is a jewel bestowed on me by the custodians of a realm called Caemeris. It has been stolen and replaced with this crystal. Do you know of it?"

She held the crystal tear out toward the figure.

"No I do not but it is strange don't you think that our mortal enemy should have been awoken by a stranger to our world. Are you the shadow which has come to devour our star and suns?" asked Inar.

"I do not know how I came here. I have bested the Ondraak once in battle, but I have no knowledge of them. It would seem they are equally my enemy as yours" replied Ange.

"Still it is not wise to let a stranger walk our dreamscapes. Come I will take you back to the Orators."

Before Ange could protest, she was standing inside a chamber made of dream trees and stones. It was calm and soothing, but she could not get out.

"Help me. Jinx come, please come. Help!" she called.

There was no answer. Suddenly everything began to shake. Then the cage of trees shimmered. She tested them but they remained solid and unyielding.

"Help me!"

She sat frustrated and annoyed. What was happening? She traced her finger over the faces carved into the gemstones. She looked at one of them. It was made of what appeared to be pure emerald. The carving looked familiar. It was Kado. The other was a dragon's head. That was odd. Where had she found these? She had not returned to Arglethium that she could remember.

The third stoneface was a man but it wasn't familiar to her. She put them back and rested against a trunk. She could feel it breathing. It was comforting to feel its rhythm.

She listened.

"Jinx, please help me. Eaudania, I have made a mistake. A creature called Inar the Knowing has gaoled me" she whispered.

"Yes, I see. Wait Ange my urns will flow again. Soon your prison will be washed away."

Eaudania's voice floated around her.

Jinx flew at Doldraak. The metal of his dagger glistened as it screeched along the hide of the dragon.

Flame burst forth into the battle-dream obliterating the mirages of land around them.

The Orators formed a circle around the beast and began to chant. Their low hum quelled the flames and slowly the dream reformed.

An army marched from the Forest of Hopes and Wishes towards the dragon.

"Conjurors, be warned I am here to destroy as the great Oblyquixiton deigned at the beginning of time" roared Doldraak.

"The Ondraak have never conquered any world which the ancient Oblyquixiton has not devoured" replied Vidras the Mage.

"We shall have victory. A new power has come to the great star Mir Chiridien. Be mindful now Conjurors, all is not as it seems" replied Doldraak.

Crystal flames exploded across the army coming over the dream-sea forest, pulverising the Chiridien forces.

Jinx fell down into the shards of star-weave. He watched the Orators draw closer to Doldraak trying to imprison it with the Mirasan chants. But Doldraak grew larger than their first sun and smashed his lieges into tiny fragments.

Jinx could faintly here his name being called. He listened trying to catch his breath. Fear clung to his hide as destruction lay around him.

"Jinx, help me. I remember who I am. It is the Wanderer. My name is Ange."

Ange had heard the loud explosion and became worried. It sounded lethal in its strength.

"Jinx come please. If I find the prism, I may be able to help."

"Yes, I believe you may be able to stranger."

A figure the same as one who gaoled her appeared inside the cage of trees.

"Who are you?"

"My name is Tylax, the Dream-seeker. I will search your mind to find out how you came here."

"Tell me after you have seen."

"Perhaps. If it is useful."

"No you may not search my mind unless you tell me what you find" spoke Ange.

Before Ange could object again, she felt the dream seeker inside her memories. From her birth to now Tylax walked beside her as every part of her life reformed. She began to shake as the dream awoke the pain, sorrow, and fear as well as the strength that lay within her heart and mind.

"I see you have battled many enemies to be here. But something wants you to remain hidden" spoke Tylax.

"Who?" Ange asked.

"Your power will destroy Mir Chiridien if you do not leave. Something greater than the dreamscape keeps you here" spoke Tylax.

"Let me find the prism. It will help. It consumed Voloc the destroyer. It gaoled Descendant. It will defeat Doldraak. I have defeated the Ondraak before with it."

"Its power is what feeds Doldraak" spoke Tylax.

"No it was forged by the great and loving Norbu from the sorrow of Ascendant."

"No it was forged from the mighty Caemeris, lost star and progenitor to us all. Its power is great enough to both create and destroy" replied Tylax.

"Where is it?"

"Your Bard may know. It seems he was the one who found you. Jinx, dream singer and bard of Mir Chiridien you are summoned to Tylax" called the Orator.

Jinx appeared inside the tree-cage.

"Jinx, I have been calling you" Ange went to the singer and hugged him.

Jinx kissed her and then pushed her away.

"Tylax Dream-seeker and my liege. I have wronged Mir Chiridien. I hid the Wanderer when she arrived as I became infatuated with her. My heart swelled with dream song, and I could not let go or bear to share her."

"You are ever the minstrel of words and song soothing to all who listen, Jinx. But I fear you sensed the potency of the creature called Ange and this jewel she carried with her and knew it would be dangerous. Where did you find her?"

"Where is the prism Jinx? It was in this leather pouch. And Nekoda, where is he?" Ange pleaded.

"It was only you I found, no other" Jinx replied.

Jinx backed against the trees. Tylax stared at the bard intensely but knew he spoke the truth but wondered about this Chiridia. He had been able to deceive the other Orators before. Something was different about this one, Tylax thought.

"Until this stone of power is removed from here then we are in danger. Doldraak will grow stronger the longer it remains here. Where did you find the Wanderer Bard?" asked Tylax.

"In the Isle of Stardream" replied Jinx.

"How did you get there? It is forbidden" probed Tylax.

Jinx blushed a bright green at his transgression.

"Song makes a heart wander to all places just as music carries across the wind and oceans, so my heart takes me to all places of Mir Chiridien.'

"Pretty words Jinx, but this has caused a great wound to our star, one which we may not recover from" Tylax growled.

"Where is this Isle of Stardream?" asked Ange.

"Deep dream, beyond memory and close to death and birth" replied Tylax.

"It is a gateway" spoke Ange.

Tylax did not answer her.

"Jinx you will go and re-join the battle. I will seek out where the rupture lies. Wanderer you are to come with me. If we find this jewel, then I will expel you from Mir Chiridien. It will be the only way to rid ourselves of the Ondraak" spoke Tylax.

"My liege I go to my death. Ange, the Wanderer, I will sing my last song to you as I walk toward the battle, full of love and wonder."

"You will die there, Jinx. No I will rescue you" Ange hugged Jinx. She saw Jinx looking at the Orator. She turned to Tylax.

"Why do you send the bard to his death?" asked Ange.

"It is a grave transgression to seek the dream path to the Isle of Stardream. If Doldraak or the Sentinel were to discover it... It has happened once before, when I saw the great blind lizard, who once almost destroyed your world" replied Tylax.

"Mordraag?" asked Ange.

"No its maker" replied Tylex.

"I do not know this creature" replied Ange.

"To the battle Bard. You know your punishment is just for what may come" ordered Tylex.

Ange and Jinx looked at one another.

"I will find a way to save you, my love" spoke Ange.

Jinx disappeared from the cage.

Ange watched the battle below her. The crystal hide of Doldraak was like a blinding flash in the sea of dream night. She could see the dragon's power increasing. Where were the waters of Eaudania? By now the forest and mountains should be awash with her torrential floods she thought.

"You are right even Eaudania's power begins to wane. Do you know who she is?" asked Ange.

"She has been with Mir Chiridien for as long as the dream-scrolls have been recorded. It is thought her quest began when the three suns collided in the beginning age of our star. When the first wells of knowledge began to fill" replied Tylax.

"It was not my desire to be here. I am sorry I awoke the Ondraak" Ange spoke.

"Something wants you hidden but something also drew you here. Once I have found this magic stone then you are to leave. And the Chiridia will continue as they always have."

"How long until we reach the Isle of Stardream?"

"There is no time here. When we reach it, we reach it" replied Tylax.

Eaudania watched the water flow but saw it did not destroy the valley below her. The battle continued with Doldraak, and the Chiridia, both unaffected by the torrents gushing over them. She could see the Wanderer speaking to a shadow. She didn't know who the shadows were, they existed on the edge of her vision, but they always seemed present but never interfered with her work. They called themselves Orators but never revealed their forms to her.

"Ange bring it to me. I can solve this mystery and perhaps also the reason you were thrust into Mir Chiridien. Do not trust the Orator, they are not as they seem" Eaudania spoke.

"Sentinel, she will destroy this place along with the Doldraak if she remains" replied Tylax hearing Eaudania's voice.

"I need to have it. It will answer everything" replied Eaudania.

Ange did not respond. She was not sure that it would help Eaudania. She did know that Doldraak grew stronger with every passing dream.

The dark-light of the dream reality lifted as they neared the edge of the world. In the distance Ange could see a shape form. It was a flat disc sitting amongst constellations of dream dust. Ange found herself walking in air.

Tylax strode ahead. The Orator removed its robe exposing a body not unlike the Ondraak; spines and a tail, except it stood upright like her. Its hide scintillated in the starlight revealing a full spectrum of colours.

"Are you descendants of the Ondraak?" asked Ange.

Tylax stopped walking. It turned its head toward Ange. The outline of a small snout and slit like eyes glinted against the indigo of the dream nexus.

"Our history is lost to us. But you are not the first to see the resemblance. We are peaceful. We seek possibilities in our dreams and our world exists for this reason. We do not seek dominion over others or any creation. It is purely a quest to search for a possibility. This is what makes us and the Ondraak enemies. Their singular focus on conquest and destruction depletes the dream-light leaving only darkness" replied Tylax.

They continued on toward the Isle of Stardream.

"I feel it drawing me to it" spoke Ange.

"You are approaching the precipice of the greatest power we know. Chiridien dreams begin here in their seed-form and grow from it. It is unvanquished in its inexhaustible strength to maintain infinite possibilities at all times" spoke Tylax.

Silence stole their words as they neared the centre of the disc. Ange felt every fibre tingling. Inside the vortex a presence called again and again.

The force contorted her into different shapes while at the same time she remained standing next to Tylax. The hide of the Orator changed colours and stretched back and forth toward the centrifuge of energy.

Ange stared into the centre again asking where the tear lay hidden. She saw Jinx in battle briefly. Her heart ached to save the bard.

"How dare you send the one I love to death" admonished Ange.

"Jinx knows the Mirasian oaths must be obeyed" replied Tylax in a matter-of-fact tone.

Ange heart thudded not wanting to see Jinx die.

"Where is the Tear of Ascendant? Where does the memory of the First Custodians of light lie? Show me, the Keeper of Sorrow and child of Arglethium!" Ange called across the nebula.

In the distance a tiny spec glowed. She raced toward it. Tylax followed. It drew its sword. The spec disappeared.

"I cast it into the sea of lost dreams and future memories" floated Jinx's voice.

Ange dove into the cloud of star dust and swam toward the prism. It bobbed on the surface freely. Each time it sprang forth emitting the power from within it; set free by the Chiridien dream-weave.

She lunged and grabbed it. Instantly she saw what a star sees and nearly exploded from the power of it.

"Why didn't you tell us this Jinx?" asked Ange.

Before there was an answer, she saw Tylax racing toward her with its sword drawn.

"Leave now Wanderer. Let the dreaming be restored."

Ange thought of Jinx. She saw him battling against Doldraak.

"No not yet. I won't let you kill Jinx" spoke Ange as she disappeared.

Tylax remained looking at the place Ange had been standing.

"No you don't know what you are doing. Mir Chiridien will be destroyed. Chiridia gather. We need to seek an intruder who carries the weapon of the Ondraak" Tylax called out into the nebula of dreams.

Ange saw Jinx being pinned down by Doldraak's claws. She stood before the dragon and thrust her dagger into its crystal hide. She felt the prism surge through her like it had on Arglethium but this time the force of the Ondraak beast surged as well. She became pincered by the two wills. She could feel herself being crushed. She grabbed Jinx's hand and pulled the bard free of the claws.

"Eaudania. I have what you need" Ange called.

Instantly they landed on the glass plateau of the Sentinel. Eaudania was pouring an urn over the cliff edge.

"Cleanse the bard in my waters. It will heal the wounds" she spoke without looking at either Ange or Jinx.

Ange dragged Jinx over and taking an urn poured the water over his wounds. Green fluid spilled out and sparkled on the platform.

Jinx coughed but was barely breathing.

"The poison is deep" spoke Eaudania.

"I came to save the bard. The creature is dear to me and saved me from being destroyed" spoke Ange.

"I believe it was done to hide you until the purpose of the jewel could be discerned" replied Eaudania.

"Either way I will not let Jinx be destroyed simply because his heart lies in the wonderment of this world and not with its secrecy" replied Ange.

"Show me this stone of power."

Ange hesitated. The Sentinel seemed too keen to want it when she had no memory of it in the first place. She took it out.

Eaudania seized the gem. She strode back into her chamber and placed it on the stone altar.

"Tell me the memories you hold wondrous stone" she spoke peering into the prism.

Eaudania looked into it and saw herself. She did not understand. She looked more deeply with her eyes closed. Sometimes doing this helped when she read the waters from her urns.

Again her face remained. She went to Ange. Jinx was awake and lay in Ange's arms. She was giving the bard sips of water from a dream leaf. It sparkled magically on the creature's tongue.

"It only shows me. What have you seen when you look into it?" asked Eaudania.

"It blinds me mostly. I saw it take the gods of my world and imprison them. It seems no-one can really control its power" replied Ange.

"Potent it must be for it to consume gods."

The Sentinel played with it between her fingers. Ange watched her. She remembered on Arglethium that she could not touch the prism without it burning her or consuming her, while here it did not seem to matter.

Eaudania went to the waterfall and held the prism over the torrential stream. Ange panicked thinking she was going to throw the prism into it.

"No!"

"No fear, although somehow I think it would find its way back to you even if I thrust it beyond our suns" spoke Eaudania.

"It was given to me. It is Ascendant's tears from the time of the great sundering of her realm Caemeris. For some reason Norbu and Ascendant entrusted it to me and I am able to wield it without being destroyed" Ange explained.

The Sentinel plunged the prism into the waters and instantly the waterfall ceased.

"How do you do this? Tell me" called Eaudania.

She did it again and this time the water changed into crystal rocks. Eaudania's hand was caught in the solid crystals. She pulled free shattering the waterfall.

She picked up a shard of crystal and looked at it. It was blank inside. There was no reflection of herself.

Suddenly Jinx stood and seized the jewel.

"It is not safe Sentinel. It needs to remain with its owner."

The bard handed it back to Ange.

Ange looked into it and saw her own reflection. Jinx watched. Suddenly Doldraak's shadow flew above them. The dragon circled three times then flew down toward the platform of crystal.

Ange stood ready for a fight with the beast, but it simply stood still watching them all.

"So this is the jewel which the Orators seek to hide from me. Show me visitor" commanded the dragon.

"No you will snatch it for yourself" snapped Ange.

"There is no need. I feel it without touching it. Shine it into my eyes and let Doldraak see."

"No it will only make you stronger and you will destroy the Chiridia and their world."

"That will happen regardless" replied Doldraak.

Ange saw the glint in the dragon's eyes and knew she had guessed the worm's intention.

She grabbed Jinx and plunged into the river of shattered water crystals. They fell until the forest of dreams.

"Jinx where can we go to be safe" asked Ange.

"Go to our den. I can weave a song to hide us until we figure out something to do" replied Jinx.

The Sentinel stood with Doldraak and watched the pair tumble below.

"I believe the mystery of this place lies within that prism" spoke Eaudania.

"Water spirit, you speak as if any of this exists. Indeed the prism is powerful, none like it has Doldraak felt before, and with me awakened and that jewel, not only will the secrets of this star be revealed but with it will come its destruction" spoke Doldraak.

"If you destroy this place what becomes of Eaudania, beast?"

"You are unknown to the Ondraak and have no bearing on my purpose nor I on yours."

"We both need this world to exist" replied Eaudania.

"No you are mistaken. This world is an essence of something unknown. Perhaps this is the riddle the Wanderer's treasure will reveal" spoke Doldraak.

Tylax appeared with the Orators. They had their crystal swords ready to attack. Doldraak turned and faced them. It peered at each of them.

"Who shall die first Orators of deceit and malicious dreams?" Doldraak hissed at its quarry readying itself for another onslaught.

"Hold Dream-seeker and beast of the dream star. You stand within the realm of the Sentinel. None shall fight here while Eaudania's urns flow" warned Eaudania.

She took a droplet of water and turned it into a spear. She smashed it into the plateau of glass. The water spread in lightning speed tendrils towards the dragon and the Orators. It froze them.

She turned toward her waterfall.

"Bard and stone keeper return to me. I have imprisoned those who bring war to our world so we may continue on our quest for knowledge" she called.

Jinx lay against the wall of the den. His lyric-branch was humming as he spun a song to hide, he and Ange.

"Silence blind the light,

Bring dream-night to comfort our hearts,

Let us sit in peace arm in arm,

Amongst the balm of hidden songs

Amongst the leaves of lost dreams

Free from Chiridien and dragon fire. "

"Now Ange we will have time to regain our strength" spoke Jinx.

Ange sat looking at the prism. The journey and then the final battle of Arglethium came flooding back to her. After everything she had been through, there was still no explanation of what the prism actually was and how she came to be here.

"How did you find me Jinx? I mean was I awake or asleep?"

"You were asleep my Wanderer. In your hand you held the jewel and in the other was a clump of fur."

"Oh that would have been Nekoda my dog. He has been with me since a child. My heart aches for him and I fear what has become of him. Why can't I remember? Why didn't you say where you threw the prism? You denied seeing it" she probed.

"I was afraid of the Orators. You saw what they did to me when they found out what I had done."

"Yes, I understand" replied Ange.

"Perhaps now while we are safe, we can peer into the stone and see its secrets" spoke Jinx.

Jinx came over and wrapped himself around Ange. She nestled into his warm torso and they both looked again into the prism.

This time they didn't see themselves but inside sat a figure stooped over a stone table. Its face was covered. A tiny spec hovered before it. A corona of colour emanated from the spec. It changed colour. Ange felt pulled to the spec as it changed. The surge of power pulsed through her.

A hand reached out and took the glowing spark. It turned into a water droplet. The tiny spec reformed again and this time the figure touched it and it turned into a torrent of water. Then the hand lifted up and the water followed its movement. The figure stood and walked toward a window.

It looked out into a vast abyss, empty but ripe with potential. The hand plunged itself into the darkness and seemed to be pointing far into the vastness. It was saying go there.

The hooded face turned away. Ange's heart thudded waiting to see who it was as she had recognised the hand.

But instead as they stared into the emptiness, a faint glint indicated that something watched in the darkness. Ange pulled away. Her heart thudded like the raging waterfalls of Eaudania.

"Oh Jinx, none of it makes any sense."

"What did you see Ange?"

"I saw parts of myself and another whose face remained hidden."

The memory of the hand lingered in her mind. It was hers who was changing the light to water and back again. It was her fingers that pointed to the great chasm of darkness outside the window telling her where to go.

She looked again and this time she imagined Nekoda.

The figure returned. This time though it pointed to a palace with massive spire, and a dragon's head. It looked like the lands of her world. The mountain was familiar, but Ange could not remember what it was.

In the distance a dog barked. Her heart lifted. It was Nekoda. The image shook and moved. It was a world not here and not home. Great rocks fell. Nekoda bounded between them deftly manoeuvring avoiding being hit.

"Nekoda, where are you?" He heard her voice and barked in response.

It was gone. Only the hooded figure remained staring into the abyss once more. This time the spec of light flashed blue and then formed into a stone. The stone became the prism.

Ange sat back. Jinx stroked her face.

"What did you see?"

I heard Nekoda. He is trapped on another world. I saw a place from own world. I don't remember what it is called. It was a large mountain with a temple built into it.

"And did you see anything else?" probed Jinx.

"No, only that" she replied. Her heart kept pounding in her chest. It was herself controlling the light but how she asked herself.

A shudder rippled through their dream den.

"The war quickens" spoke Jinx.

Ange thought of Eaudania and the memories she craved. Suddenly Doldraak's snarling jaws tore through the wall of the den. Jinx snatched his arrows and flung them at the dragon's eyes, but they shattered against the crystal.

Ange looked at the snarling beast and remembered the image of the palace and temple.

"No Jinx. Take me to the isle of Star Dream. I must leave with the prism. Tylax is right it will ruin this world. But I will return."

Jinx long fingers became claws and dug into her arm.

"Don't leave me. The beast will devour me as will my world. That is why I hid you. I knew you would leave me."

"No I will return Jinx. You are dear to me, and I will not let Mir Chiridien perish. I have seen a mighty dragon defeated once. I know a warrior who will help me slay it."

Jinx did not move. Doldraak opened its jaws readying to unleash its great fire of crystal.

"Please Jinx, I can't defeat it here. I must bring help. I must go. I will take you to the Sentinel to protect you while I am gone. I will not lose you Jinx, my love" Ange took Jinx's face and kissed him.

They grasped hands as the flame of Doldraak devoured the dream den and tore through the nexus of dream weave. They were flying toward the Isle of Star Dream.

"Sentinel in return for the knowledge you so desperately desire I ask you to protect Jinx and Chiridia from the Ondraak. Use your waters and the power of the Eaudania to quell the flame of the dragon" Ange called into the silence.

Eaudania appeared.

"Wanderer you know what I seek. You have seen it."

"I will return with a mighty warrior to defeat the Ondraak. But in exchange you must protect them until I return. Your waters have energy which will destroy the flame of crystal dreams."

"How do I know you will be true to your word. I could snatch the jewel myself and learn of its ways. Eaudania has searched for an eternity already. Her patience is well tested."

"You don't but as an act of faith I will leave you my most cherished memories of the Mighty Choasa and Keep of Lido. See what the waters of Arglethium forge with their power."

Ange took some of the dream dust of the stars and folded her memories into it.

"Here Jinx until I return this belongs to Eaudania."

Jinx kissed Ange.

"I will hold no hope of your return, but I will fight bravely and if by chance you hear the voice of your bard then it will be full of the love he held for a Wanderer of his world."

"Jinx I will return." Ange hugged the singer. "Eaudania will your waters fill the mouth and belly of the dragon?" Ange asked.

"They will" replied Eaudania.

Jinx walked toward the Sentinel and gave the leaves of Ange's memories to her.

Ange turned just as the roars of Doldraak echoed through the silence. She strode into the swirling star-dream ocean and disappeared.

Eaudania grasped Jinx as she turned to the approaching dragon. Thundering behind came the Orators with their army. In the hide of the dragon were stuck spears, arrows, and daggers formed from the deepest dream state imaginable. But none of the wounds were lethal.

"Halt fierce one. As a boon for one who may have the key to my release, I will bind you and your fire" warned Eaudania.

"Nay remove yourself from the battle washerwoman. You and I share no destiny" roared Doldraak.

"We do now."

Eaudania swept her hand across the star dream ocean willing it to a massive tsunami. She flung it at the advancing army and the beast. But as the dreams and dragon clashed the dragon merely gulped down the waves leaving gaping holes in the nexus.

She removed Jinx and returned to her temple.

"So Bard not all is clear to me, but I sense the Wanderer is true to her word."

She took the memory leaves and placed them on the stone altar.

"It won't be long now. I will prepare my waters" spoke Eaudania.

Jinx stared at the Sentinel. His heart began to break thinking of Ange. Tylax was right his songful heart had been weak and now his world stood on the edge of destruction.

Jinx took out his lyre-branch and began to strum the leaves.

"Oh washer woman, oh washer woman,

Bring my love back to me,

Set free the wonders of your rivers,

Overflowing with power dread

Cleanse the world of the fiery beast,

Let the Mir Chiridien slumber nightmare free.

Quell the crystal spears and flames.

Heal the broken limbs,

Bring Dream Spring with budding leaves.

Fruitful powers of Eaudania's streams."

Eaudania cradled one of her urns on her knee. She tipped it up to begin flowing. A tiny trickle began to snake its way into the sky.

"Flow mighty waters flow into the hide of our bane.

Spill in between scale, fang, and claw.

Take the death-dream from our hearts.

Restore the sleeping hopes, wishes,

All that the suns of Mir Chiridien see."

Jinx sang louder willing the water to gather strength. Eaudania saw Ange's memories of the Choasa flowing, urgent, powerful breaking dirt and stone, surging toward the great oceans. She saw how dense it was, tethered to nothing but with bonds so resistant nothing broke them, nothing crushed them, so the water maintained its power but with the suppleness of dream nebula.

Doldraak appeared in the sparkling clouds. It flew away from the jet of water.

Eaudania tipped the urn lower forcing more water out. The stream became a river flowing into the sky. Doldraak attempted to evade the water, but it followed tenaciously.

A bubble formed around the creature. It attempted to break free, but the water turned into a transparent snake entwining itself around the belly.

"Water spirit you cannot destroy the Ondraak. We are birthed from the first of the darkness, the great Oblyquixiton."

It roared its anger across the dream weave. Jinx shuddered as it felt the world from which it was made begin to rupture.

"Hold steady Dream-warriors. Behold the great Sentinel cages our mortal enemy. Forward to skin the loathsome hide from its bones" called Inar the Knowing.

A nebula sized army of Chiridia, bards, weavers, and warders of nightmares gathered on the horizon to begin battle with Doldraak. The water snake tightened around the dragon's belly stopping it from expelling its flame.

Eaudania reached for another urn.

"Hurry Wanderer, the urns will run dry soon. Then I fear Mir Chiridien will be lost and I will continue to exist with no memory and no hope of finding my purpose."

Tylax slashed at Doldraak. It hissed and blew the Orator away. Jinx filled his quiver with arrows. Plucking one out the bard walked along the water snake toward the dragon still attached to the urn. Jinx sang high above the dream clouds and below dream-sky.

"Fly straight and true tip of my arrow. Break the beating heart of this crystal invader and usurper of dreams."

The bard strode toward Doldraak. The dragon swung around and with its tail began to batter the rope of water attached to it. Each shattering thump rocked Jinx and threw him near the edge of the water. Still Jinx took a deep breath and stood up again. Keeping his balance, he drew an arrow up and aimed directly at Doldraak's eye. Letting go the arrow sped toward the beast.

It hit dead in the eye of the dragon. Doldraak stilled as it tried to claw the arrow out of it.

"Bard your skill is more than any singer. You have the eye of a warrior" spoke Doldraak.

"My heart is filled with love for the one who has left. My world will now be empty, but I will fight in the hope that she will return. I fight with my heart and its beat is true" called Jinx.

Doldraak did not move or answer but instead it shrunk down and closed its eyes. The silver arrow remained in the eye. The water snake was firm in its grip. A group of night-soothers stepped forward and began hacking at the crystal hide. Their blades making sparks of light into the blackness of dream-void as the crystal scales easily deflected the blows.

"Hold your daggers. The worm is cunning and feeds on our impatience to defeat it. It waits until we tire" ordered Vidras the Mage. "Weave, a dream song Bard. Send it to an eternal slumber."

Jinx bowed at the command from the supreme Orator, Vidras. Taking out its lyre-branch Jinx began to play.

"From the dream song of my heart, lift up and whisper,

I call the sleeping sails of stars awake,

into this nightmare to break.

Drifting upon the eternal will, dream leaf, stone, and seas,

Lost memories float away, wings take peaceful flight,

Ease the fear-song of battle and defeat,

Slow the brutal heart of fire,

Melt the crystal fangs of Doldraak, bold and strong,

Return it to sleep caged in fearsome star-song,

Bound to the Mirasian dreaming bed,

Remain an eternity with the slumbering dead."

Jinx's lullaby drifted all through the Forest of Hopes and Dreams, toward the gushing waters of Eaudania and over the void to the Isle of Stardream.

Eaudania felt a tear on her cheek as the crushing yearning to be free of the dragon struck her in Jinx's voice. With this compassion her own sorrow resumed again in her fruitless quest to know how things work and who she was. She stood and left the urn flowing over the cliff toward Doldraak.

Jinx noticed the dragon's breathing began to slow. Tylax approached. Its robe was in tatters, but its eyes shone brightly. The eight Orators began to chant in rhythm with each other. Jinx stood singing as well. Doldraak's body began to scintillate in harmony with the chanting. Small tendrils of dream weave slowly grew cocooning the resting dragon. Then once the beast was fully encased the Orators and beast disappeared.

Jinx stood singing into darkness.

Eaudania came walking across her bridge of water, weeping.

"Sentinel why do you cry?" asked Jinx.

"The longing has returned, and your music has made me remember it."

"The dragon is defeated?" asked Jinx.

"The Orators hide the Mir Chiridien story Jinx. Go seek it and you will understand your destiny as I go seek mine."

Jinx looked at the Sentinel as she returned to her chamber. A sense of doom lay over the bard not certain if the dragon was defeated, uncertain of Ange returning and now this mystery of their history which Eaudania seems to think is entwined with the Orators.

Jinx looked across the shredded dreamscape. Already the scars of Doldraak's awakening were deep and not healing as they should. Jinx turned toward the dream-mountain where the Chiridia dwelled and decided to go seek his destiny as well.

Ange looked over the valley from the stone platform. The smell of Arglethium's air was familiar to her. She breathed deeply wanting to soak in the feel of the sun, the sky, and the firmness of rock beneath her feet. But Jinx was always on her mind. She needed to begin her search.

She remembered this place. The echoes of the battle between the Custodians and where Nekoda was maimed were in her mind. This used to be the Emerald Citadel of Kado's family.

Now in the deep ravine left by the collapse of the Drax Palace grew a verdant forest laced with rivers laden with gemstones as their beds and waterfalls sparkling in the sunlight. The destruction of that time now erased. She heard noises of people playing a game below. She placed her hood over her face and descended a steep stairwell. Again the prism warmed her through the pouch. She tested if she could touch it, but the heat began to burn her.

"Tok roll the dice!"

"Doubles and threes!"

A loud roar went up. Ange crept around the corner of the soldier's den. They wore nightclothes and were without weapons. The dozen guards had their backs to her as she inched her way to the doorway on the far side. She slid past and went towards the entrance.

A large dragon's head glared at her as she entered the inner courtyard of the palace. Light spilled in from slit windows far up the walls. Inside was a marvel of chiselled orichnite and granite. The roof too high to see. Ange walked in silence unseen toward a small doorway. The cheers of the soldiers echoed again behind her.

As she walked outside into a vast open plain, a pale gloom met her. It was bare rock stretching for miles. In the distance she vaguely thought she could see an ocean but it appeared black so she could not be certain if it was water or just shadow. A cluster of lights glinted in the distance. It looked like a village. She decided to walk toward the lights. Night fell quickly bringing a waning moon bright enough to still light her way. She noticed what she thought was a village was in fact a palace. It was many buildings surrounding a large central spire. It was not night torches lighting the buildings in the darkness but moonlight sparkling on jewels adorning the dwellings.

Suddenly a shadow passed overhead. It completely blocked out the moon. Ange ducked down on the path and looked up to see what it was.

It had a long tail and neck. It looked like Doldraak. It flew away and disappeared.

Ange walked into the palace grounds. Again there did not seem to be anyone around. A small tavern located near the entrance gate was open. She could see figures sitting inside. Her stomach rumbled. She went in.

"Some tea and soup with meat" she asked at the counter.

The bartender nodded without speaking. She sat near a window and looked out waiting to see if the shadow dragon returned. The soup was hearty, and the tea tasted thick compared to Jinx's dream brew. But it was good and revived her. As the server came to take her dishes, she decided it was safe to ask questions.

"I am seeking an audience with Kado Ko Drax. Is he known in this kingdom?"

The server looked at her quizzically.

"Fon, can you help this traveller?" the server called.

The barkeep came over.

"She is looking for someone called Kado Ko Drax."

"None by this name. Emperor Scaletryx rules this land. His palace is in the spire upon the hill. They have a list of all the citizens. Perhaps if you go there."

Ange nodded.

"I see. Is there someone who may know of the fate of the former rulers of the Drax Empire?"

"Only the Palace Scholar. Go there. Ask for Hunna."

"Is there lodging here. I will go in the morning to the Scholar."

"Yes, we have a spare room."

Ange looked across the night sky wondering if she was in Arglethium or another dream inside Mir Chiridien. The stars seemed distant but real, and the blackness in between had the same familiar emptiness.

Inside her room was cosy, a soft bed of straw covered in calico sat beneath a window. She lay down. The smells of the world about her reassured her she was home. She thought of Jinx singing to her in between the memories of battle cries between Baachelaus, Norbu and Voloc. How much time had passed she wondered as she drifted off to sleep.

The next morning, Ange waited on a seat staring at the same opulence which adorned the outside of the palace. A small woman came out walking very quickly.

"I am Hunna On-Ghat. I am Chief Scholar to the Emperor. How may I serve you traveller?"

"I am grateful that you would speak to me, a stranger. These lands seem free and welcoming" replied Ange.

"Only to some. Others who do not abide the laws of the Emperor know his wrath."

"I am seeking a prince, friend, and ally. His name was Kado Ko Drax. He was the son of Emperor Ko Paidrax?"

"Hmm yes, I have heard of this name but that was many generations ago. This friend of yours would not be alive now. The Drax Dynasty was the fourth era of rulers and died out. The fate of Kado was not recorded. Are you sure your friend was not another name?"

"Perhaps, but that is the name I was given."

Ange wondered if she was too late. But she would know if any of the ones chosen by Ascendant had perished. The prism had marked all of them. That was the covenant Norbu had asked of them all and she had specifically asked Kado.

"Come we will have tea and I will show you what we have in our records. Perhaps it will help you understand" spoke Hunna.

The scrolls were kept in an antechamber with shelves reaching as high as the temple halls.

Hunna disappeared and returned with a tray of bowls and a small pot of tea.

"Pour while I go search. Kado Kodrax, is that right? What era approximately?"

"Well I thought it was only a few seasons ago" replied Ange.

Strange thought Ange that everyone was being so helpful. She poured the tea and detected a faint hint of herbal scents. She wasn't sure what kind. She remembered being in a cave and drinking tea. The face of the Queen of Matavia flashed in her mind. She shivered at the memories of that terrifying place.

She decided to wait until the scholar took some of the brew herself. Just to be sure.

"Here we are."

Hunna returned and began to unroll three scrolls on a table.

"Now ah yes. It was the sixteenth cycle: it is written of the banishment of the Heir to the Drax Empire Kado to the Sa Dom Temple for a treasonous act and lascivious misadventure with Lord Jiang's daughter. Here it was noted that the sole heir died from ingestion of too much of the lily while the priests were attempting to purify the prince. That seems to be the only record of Kado Ko Drax."

"But I don't understand. We journeyed for many days and nights together and battled together as well" spoke Ange.

"I think it was a hoax or just coincidence of the name traveller" replied Hunna.

"Perhaps." Ange offered the scholar her cup. Hunna sipped and swallowed some of the brew. Ange decided it was safe and did the same.

"You will need lodgings for the night. What will you do if you are unable to find this person you seek? I will let the Emperor's advisors know that someone roams the land impersonating a former heir to the lands of the Dragon."

"I saw him once command a dragon" spoke Ange.

Hunna stood.

"I will take you to a room."

"Thankyou. It seems the Emperor is very generous to be so welcoming to strangers."

The scholar did not answer as she led Ange toward a corridor with doors. Opening one of them Hunna showed Ange into her room.

She sat down on her bed. It was a small room which overlooked the vastness of the stony plateau. She noticed it was night again. Feeling drowsy she lay down. The tea she thought had something in it as she groggily remembered the last time, she had seen Kado when they were in the Keep of Uchala.

A shadow alighted on her windowsill. It watched her silently.

Ange woke to a pale dawn. She stood and looked over the plateau.

"Where are you, Kado?"

"I am here Ange" replied the shadow.

She whipped around startled at the voice.

Kado sat on a stool in a darkened corner of the room.

"Ange, I had almost forgotten" spoke Kado as he came over to her and hugged her.

"How long has it been?" asked Ange.

"Many generations. Even I cannot remember" replied Kado.

"The Keeper comes to call you. Do you remember the oath you all swore?"

"Yes, I do, Am I the first to be called Ange."

"Yes, Kado."

"Have you been able to answer any of the riddles around this cursed stone which seems to bring destruction wherever it lies?" asked Kado.

"No, for me Kado, it only seems like yesterday."

"I do not know what happened to your kin. I have been asleep and only woke with the Harvest Moon festivals" spoke Kado.

"I have lost Nekoda but there is something more urgent to fix before I search for him or the Custodians."

Kado held Ange's face in his hands. Ange looked at them and thought they appeared more like claws.

"You resemble Ange Desert Dweller."

Ange pulled away and looked at Kado.

"Why do you doubt it is me, Kado?" asked Ange.

"It has been so long Ange. I wondered if it was truly you. Your lands are in peril, I have seen the great river Choasa, it no longer flows."

"What is this place Choasa? I have no memory of it" replied Ange.

Kado frowned at Ange's question.

"Who is your kin?" asked Kado growing suspicious.

Ange felt the piercing gaze of Kado's eyes. Eyes which looked deep into the recesses of time, well beyond what was normal for a clay born of Arglethium.

"Tessi was or is my sister. Bensah, my guardian" Ange replied.

Kado nodded and sat back down on the stool.

"So you have come to call Kado, the cursed prince of the Drax Empire."

"I need your help. A world, a world which seems to be made of dreams is under siege from an Ondraak, a dragon. I have awoken it with my arrival and the prism feeds it. If it is not destroyed, this world and someone I care for will be killed" explained Ange.

"How can I help you Ange? I have no powers" spoke Kado.

"I saw you destroy and command Mordraag in the final battle."

"Ha, I see."

"You can defeat them. It is part of your heritage Kado" spoke Ange.

"I am more the blood of Mordraag and Vipex now than Kado Ko Drax. We were all changed."

"The Keeper calls Kado, companion and friend" spoke Ange.

"You believed in me back then. Yes, I consider you a friend Ange. But I am not certain I can conquer this dragon for you Ange. Would it not be better to call upon Gildas or even the formidable Sa-Tuc" replied Kado.

"Dragon's fire is in your blood Kado, heir, and emperor. This world is full of secrets never seen clearly. You were chosen by the great Viper for a reason and the serpent and dragon's hide is built of the same scales. You are the progeny of both dragon and snake. You will defeat this progeny of the Ondraak."

"Who are the Ondraak Ange?" asked Kado.

"I met them in the realm of Baachelaus when Norbu was caged. I defeated them there but only because of the prism. I cannot use the stone on Mir Chiridien, it strengthens this Doldraak. I must call upon bonds made from clay and light and whatever created the Ondraak in the first place. The bonds it was made from flows in your blood" replied Ange.

"How long will this quest take? I am reluctant to leave my lands. Something stirs in the world Ange. I fear that Arglethium is dying."

Ange thought it strange Kado did not seem to understand that Voloc's scourge was poisoning Arglethium.

"I have no sense of time any more Kado. For me it was only a moment ago that I left with Nekoda."

Ange looked at the dragon eyes of Kado's heritage and saw their reflection in Jinx and Doldraak.

"Kado, I know deep inside the love you bared for Sa, not just as a lover but as a true friend and how much you felt betrayed when your destinies were not meant to be. Even now I can feel that wound inside you. Well my friend Jinx lies in peril as does his world. I awoke this creature and now it devours his world. I know that if I do not defeat the Ondraak than it may well be I will never find the Custodians to restore Arglethium and I will also lose Jinx. A world which seems to be able to make dreams real. Jinx's music calls my heart and mind to him Kado. You must understand how I feel, and it is I who brought this destruction because of this quest I did not ask for. Am I not as cursed as you?" spoke Ange.

"Why did you go there?" asked Kado.

"I don't know. I awoke there, and Jinx, hid me to protect me from his masters."

Kado watched Ange. She looked the same and he felt it was the same girl who had left so many eons ago. But what she asked did not seem right, but he had made an oath, to come when she called.

"Are you sure this is not a deception Ange, by Baachelaus or the Custodians, to draw out the prism once more?"

"I don't think so Kado. I know not all is as it seems on this world, but I cannot leave until I have saved Jinx, and fulfil my promise to Eaudania."

"You are right about Sa Tuc, you see much there. But my bitterness has waned with the passing of the seasons. And now I strive to keep my kingdom safe and learn to exist in the vastness of memory of my ancestors and the memories of Vipax."

"Honour the oath. The Keeper calls Kado."

"I cannot leave for long. I want to show you something."

Suddenly Kado transformed into a dragon. Ange stood back.

"Climb on my back and hang on" ordered Kado.

Kado soared into the air over the spire and out toward the plateau where the citadel stood.

"What are those black lines streaked along the land Kado?"

"I do not know. I fear it is a poison that seeps into my Kingdom. It comes from the land which we knew as the Iron Coast."

"I saw where you family's palace once stood is an oasis now" spoke Ange.

"Yes, I have it guarded and placed a holy shrine there as memory to my parents."

"Why is it so dark?" Ange asked.

"I think it is just a slow death, Ange. As if all the sunlight dies as soon as it touches the earth" replied Kado.

Further they flew over the ocean and soon arrived where the Iron Fortress once stood. It was a massive hole now. Nothing grew there. The red sand of the deserts were dulled and appeared washed out.

"I think it is this place which poisons our world. Do you know if it is true what I say? Is this prism you hold the source of this poison?"

"Kado, don't you remember, Voloc and the Iron Fortress of Baachelaus?"

Kado continued to fly and did not answer her.

"I need to find out how I came to Mir Chiridien" spoke Ange wondering what had happened to Kado's memory.

"I will come with you, but you must return me here and now. I fear if I return at a different time then it may bode ill for my land and people" spoke Kado.

"How will I know to send you to this time?'

"I think this ocean of darkness, the black blood may hold other secrets. I will drink of it and as we leave, I will spew it forth as a pathway back" replied Kado.

Kado flew to the water and drank deeply. It was bitter and thick.

"Deep within my belly sit ancient tombs of shadow. When I call you forth you shall reveal the way back to your cradle of doom and death to resume your quest upon the lands which birthed Scaletryx Diamond Fang. Come Ange, let us do battle with this Ondraak and save your beloved Jinx" called Kado.

Ange smiled and held the prism out.

The Orators surrounded Doldraak. The dragon still breathed but appeared to be in slumber.

Graxus the Gatherer stood over Doldraak chanting.

"It will awaken again when the Wanderer arrives, then it shall be unleashed" warned Graxus.

Turning to the assembly of Orators, Graxus spoke,

"The time has come Dream Orators for Mir Chiridien to end. We have seen the arrival of Caemeris. It was foretold in our memories that it will be the end of the nexus of dreams. No longer will the dream weave be formed from the blood of battle between our parents Ondraak and Oblyquixiton and Caemeris. It is time to let the dragon devour our world."

"What of the Sentinel and if the Wanderer is true to her word and brings a warrior to defeat the Ondraak?" asked Tylax.

"Then we destroy both of them and let the light of Caemeris decide destiny."

Doldraak slept. It dreamt of its birth. It saw its brethren spawned into the world and the devouring of the star light and dust. It saw the power of the world reflected in its scales and knew that nothing could defeat the progeny of Ondraak. It saw where the Ondraak came from, and the mirrors of themselves in the Orators of Mir Chiridien. It saw how the Ondraak had split in two and reflected each other, not the same but opposites. It saw the power of Oblyquixiton cleave the star's heart forming the suns and moons. It saw the mighty Ondraak and Mordraag, and White Dragon be hurled far into the blackness of dream death. Its heartbeat in rhythm with the spaces between the water and light.

Eaudania watched the water drop on her altar. She peered into it and split the water. She saw it pulsing with colours. What she didn't know was that the pulsing heart of the water was in rhythm with the slumbering dragon. Doldraak saw the eye of the Sentinel peering towards it. It dreamt of the memories of the washer woman. It could tell her where she came from, but it was not destined that their paths cross. The Wanderer had interfered with the designs of the great energy of the star and its weaving.

Eaudania felt the presence watching her. This had never happened before. She vaguely saw a shadow pass over the tiny beads of light.

"Who am I?" she asked but nothing answered her.

Jinx sat outside the antechamber of the Orators. He had heard Graxus speak. His heart thumped at the news of their impending death with the arrival of Ange. There was no way to warn her not to return.

Jinx went back to Eaudania's chamber cave. He sat thinking about what to do. He picked up his lyre-branch. Perhaps a song into the gateway will warn Ange. The bard fell asleep and began dream-song. Eaudania watched the bard.

"If you can make something hear you when it is not of this world then it is special command you have of the dream nexus" spoke Eaudania, her voice floated around Jinx as he played.

Jinx woke. He was sitting in the Isle of Stardream. The bard began to play. The tune floated into the sleeping world, dreams and through the gate. Doldraak heart missed a beat as the tune echoed across its crystal hide. Tylax heard Jinx and smiled.

"Good the bard had listened and understood."

Kado and Ange stood in darkness among a net of small twinkling lights.

"Who is that whispering Ange?" asked Kado.

"I think it is my beloved Jinx" replied Ange.

"It is full of sorrow and death."

"Jinx doesn't want me to be here."

"*Destroyer of our nightmares, rescuer of Mir Chiridien,*

one cannot be without the other.

Shatter the dreams and restore our sight.

Wanderer far and wide understand you are death and life.

Save the dreamscape, reweave the nexus of this dark night.

But be warned only death awaits, rescuer and Bard's delight."

"Jinx where is Doldraak?" asked Ange.

"Wanderer it sits within the Orators' chambers" replied Jinx.

Kado and Ange sped to the huge dream spire which sat in the desert of night-malice. It twinkled in the half light. Kado looked at it and thought it looked familiar.

Ange felt watched. A deep chuckle emanated around them.

"Progeny, youngling you have come to defeat me. Once again you are in battle with your maker."

"It speaks to me Ange" spoke Kado.

"Yes Kado."

"Who are you great draxon of dream and myth?" asked Kado.

"We were born when the first light met dark, and the shadows were created. Draxon were the pets of the makers. Ondraak the first of our kind, fled and began to search for a place in the shadow. But along with our hides, our sight saw the harshness of light and the emptiness of the dark, so to make ourselves alive, we began wars" replied Doldraak.

"You continue to destroy this world why?" asked Kado.

"To build again and destroy again" replied Doldraak.

"I have come to battle against you" spoke Kado.

"Ah yes. I cannot be destroyed while the stone of Caemeris remains in my sight" spoke Doldraak.

"So it was you who turned me to the unnatural and undying creature I have become?" spoke Kado.

"No your blood was always doomed but had not been awoken until touched by one of our own" spoke Doldraak.

"Vipax is serpent and sentinel of our world" spoke Kado.

"The same blood memories flow as ours" replied Doldraak.

"Did you make Vipax or was it the other way around?" asked Kado.

Doldraak did not answer.

Ange and Kado walked into the centre of the spire. In the distance the hide of Doldraak glowed. It pulsated with the beat of the draxon heart. Kado and Ange approached. It woke.

White cold crystal flame flashed toward them. Kado turned into the serpent form of Scaletryx. As the brethren reared at each other their fangs glowed. Just as they were about to strike Kado turned to Ange.

"Leave or I will never destroy it."

Eaudania appeared in front of Ange. She grabbed her and disappeared.

"No I must leave to give Kado a chance to defeat Doldraak" Ange tried to pull herself away from Eaudania.

"No, your stone will help me understand."

They sat together with the prism between them. Eaudania poured a drop of water onto it. It glided slowly down the side of it and stopped just as it reached the end tip of the prism.

Slowly a small dot point of red with a blue tinge formed. It ebbed minutely and was barely visible.

"See it reaches inside the water and pulls the light from within it."

The chamber around them shuddered.

"Kado" Ange whispered.

Ange pulled away grabbing the prism. But Eaudania raised her hand and encased her in water. Ange could not move the water was so strong.

"Now show me who I am!" the Sentinel ordered.

Ange struggled trying to free herself. Panic began to rise in her chest as she thought of Kado.

She realised that she could touch the prism here without pain or destruction. She looked at it in her hand.

"Eaudania what is the first thing you remember?" Ange asked.

The Sentinel looked at her.

"I remember water."

Ange looked into the prism. She imagined water pouring in great gushing torrents from the urns of Eaudania. It spilled around her and through her but never broke the cage.

"Hear my call and bring the first light. What did the first light reveal?" she whispered.

Slowly colours formed in the swirling rivers around her then the colour overtook everything and then the colours broke down further and became small beacons ebbing, uncountable but each one appeared visible to Ange.

"Do you see washer woman?"

"I see. Show me more."

Ange continued to watch the tiny specs. Then they became smaller again and disappeared into pulsating rhythms. But separate and unique, each one had its own beat. They joined again and this time images formed of a woman, old and bent, carrying urns on her back. Her face remained hidden, her hands were calloused, and hoary knuckles stuck out from years of washing in the river. The water was thick and a deep green. Its well-muscled flow coursed over deserts and mountains. It led to a castle.

The woman was bent before a vat of white calico sheets. Over her stood Tylax.

"What price would entice you woman to leave this life of beggary and labour?"

"Perhaps to have an answer as to why my life became this and nothing else."

'Why this?" asked Tylax.

"It is the only question I know to ask, as it is the only thing I know, if not this then what else? Why was this ordained for me?"

"Do you mean there was no value in your life? Was all of this meaningless, is this the reason you seek an answer to your question?"

The woman did not answer immediately. She sat with grey eyes staring. It could not be discerned if she were thinking or not. Then she spoke

"Have you ever watched water pour? It runs its own way over all the paths of the living and dead and has no memory of either. I watch how it removes all trace of the stains, a witness to the passing of time and history. It returns and then leaves but describes nothing of the time or place it touched. Water is life, no I think water takes life and whittles it away. Water is death and to extract the memories it takes with it means you could become the creator of worlds with its knowledge" spoke the old woman.

"You see much, for a washer woman. I too think your question is worthy and I grant your wish to seek out the answers you desire" replied Tylax.

Suddenly Eaudania's back appeared pouring the water over the world of Mir Chiridien.

"So that is all. I am here on the whim of one of these Orators" spoke Eaudania.

"No you are here because you wanted to know if not this what else and your life had taught you about water and the Orators gave you a chance to answer your own questions" answered Ange.

"I was once a slave to a master who dared to wonder about the mysteries of water" spoke Eaudania.

"I also think you were put here to find out how to make this world" replied Ange.

Kado stood before Doldraak. His sword shone with the starlight and razored edges of a diamond tooth of a Drax. Hefting above his head he sliced into the crystal hide of Doldraak. It screeched at him but did not relent. Its tail swung round and thrust Kado against the wall. Kado plummeted over the edge of the dream space and onto the roof of the forest of hopes and dreams.

Doldraak speared into the forest, uprooting the trees. Kado recovered and sped after it. Doldraak suddenly whipped around and raked its claws along Kado's skin and tore open the flesh.

"You are no match for the power of the Ondraak in their world. Flesh is defeated by crystal light" sneered Doldraak.

Kado heaved himself up. The dragon was right. He was too much of the clay born of Arglethium to defeat this creature.

Tylax and Graxus watched the battling creatures.

"Who will win? This is a new dream. Will it change things?" asked Tylax.

"Perhaps Tylax. Fortunately, the Sentinel remains locked into her quest and holds captive the light of Caemeris. See how this diversion progresses and if this jewel can be utilised" spoke Graxus.

Tylax left. It remembered the image of the old woman, snatched from the questing sight of one the Sentinels, sent by the Seers of Gnoceris. It was by chance that it had come across her and was struck by the woman's wisdom about water. The old woman had understood more than she realised.

Tylax came to the tower of the Sentinel. Tylax saw the visitor caged in the bubble and inside was Eaudania speaking to her.

A shuddering roar echoed across the valleys. In the distance the Orator saw the dragons fighting. Doldraak grew brighter and larger. Soon it would be large enough to consume the Isle of Star dream.

Tylax watched Ange and Eaudania curious as to what they were gazing into.

"Watch Sentinel" commanded Ange.

The prism disintegrated into tiny dots in mid-air. Each of them hummed. Small coronas of colour burst forth and then formed symbols then music then temperatures seemed to change then they stopped as they transformed into white hot lights. Light that was so bright it seemed to break the fabric of the world they lived in as if it had been burnt through by the whiteness.

Ange put her finger into one of the holes and pulled back instantly when she felt what lay behind it all. Eaudania did the same but this time it grew around her and consumed her slowly.

Tylax and Ange both tried to grab her, but it was too strong.

"Eaudania step away now" ordered Ange.

Ange gripped the prism tighter and saw how the emptiness contracted and controlled the coronas of tiny light. She plucked a piece of light and darkness and began to re-shape them. It began to knit the rip in the fabric of dream space.

"Come back Eaudania" she called.

Suddenly they both stood together with Tylax watching.

Eaudania fell into Ange's arms.

"I see now" she whispered and then she fell asleep.

"Eaudania, wake up" Ange gently laid her down. She touched her face and shoulders trying to wake her.

"What has happened?" Ange asked Tylax.

"She has gone into dream slumber."

The tower shook with an horrendous cracking sound. They both looked around and saw Doldraak smashing Kado into the side of the cliff the tower sat upon.

"I cannot remain here. I must leave or Kado will have no chance. Will you look after her Tylax. You knew who she was before all this. Why did you not tell her who she was and let her return to her home?"

"She is home. She is where it was deemed, she should be. No one place is more home to her than another. As with all of us Ange. Eaudania cannot remember because each time she destroys the world in her quest a new one is formed. So far, she has not made one that can be replicated. When she does this then she will remember."

"I don't understand you."

"No with time it will become clear" replied Tylax.

Tylax enrobed Ange with dream-chains made from star web. It held her firmly and she could not shake it loose.

"It is not deemed that the Ondraak be defeated" spoke Tylax.

"I will not let Mir Chiridien or Jinx be destroyed if I have the power to stop it" replied Ange.

Kado saw Ange struggling under the chains thrust on her by the towering figure with her.

He stabbed Doldraak viciously in the chest and sped toward Ange. He collected Tylax in his spiny tail and slammed the Orator into the crystal platform. Tylax hissed but was pinned down by Kado's strength.

With his claws Kado broke the chains around Ange.

"Now, Ange flee and then return when I have destroyed the menacing worm."

Ange disappeared and arrived at the Star Isle. She stood at its rim and dived in. As she fell, she thought of Nekoda. A shadow caught her eye. Looking in the vortex, a figure was walking. It was dark and forbidding. In its hand it held a light. But its fingers were long and old. Its nails like razor sharp blades which snuffed out the light when they moved over it. It walked down a steep staircase which never seemed to end. Suddenly the figure looked at Ange and grinned.

Ange screamed. She landed on rocks near an ocean. The sea air revived her. There were cliffs behind her. On top of the ledge a huge dragon carved out of stone stood looking across the ocean.

She must be back in Kado's kingdom. The sun shone strongly. She enjoyed its familiar warmth. It was all so confusing.

Kado released Tylax and then turned toward Doldraak. An army of Chiridia being led by Jinx was also approaching. Kado reared up displaying his fangs and claws and let loose a storm of fire across the hide of Doldraak. Its crystal scales began to melt from the heat of the flames.

"These flames are made from the clay and heat of Arglethium. They are real and destructive in their power. The flames are birthed from the heart of our sun and are the densest of all light so that any dreams wither under its weight."

Kado grew even larger. The Chiridia army stood back frightened and dismayed at the mighty dragon warrior. Kado grasped Doldraak as it hissed and spat crystal fire back at Kado, but Kado shattered its neck and head into dust. The Ondraak beast disappeared with the gusts of wind and flame.

Kado resumed his normal form and turned toward Tylax.

"Take me to your master" ordered Kado.

Vidras sat on a nebula throne. It had been watching the battle of its ancestors. It stood and came toward Kado.

"Ruler and Lord" spoke Vidras, stopping to kiss Kado's hand.

Kado looked around at the army.

"Stand brethren, this is Scaletryx, warrior dragon of the Ondraak" Vidras waved the army to stand.

"Tell me master all that you know" ordered Kado.

Kado scales bristled on his skin as he spoke. Vidras offered Kado a leaf to sit upon.

"Begin" spoke Kado.

"I cannot tell you Scaletryx" replied Vidras.

"Oh I think you can. Who made this world?" asked Kado.

"The Wanderer with her jewel."

"How? She is ignorant to its power."

"That is her journey to discover what it contains."

Kado seized Vidras by the throat.

"Tell me or you shall see the heart of the dragon fire."

"I cannot. It is forbidden even to the Orators."

"By whom?"

"By the laws."

"Who wrote the laws?"

"The Seers."

Suddenly Vidras burst into flame and disintegrated in Kado's hand.

"The Seers. Who are these, Seers?" asked Kado.

Jinx walked into the throne room and saw Kado on the dais.

"We do not know warrior" answered Jinx.

"Ange is in danger, isn't she?"

Jinx looked at Kado but did not answer his question.

"What is this world?" asked Kado.

"We do not know. Our memories are dreams, no beginning, no end. Only new things each day" replied Jinx.

"Who is the Sentinel?"

"Don't you see that she is Ange" replied Jinx.

"Stop speaking in riddles" Kado shouted.

Suddenly Jinx began to smile and then began to chuckle. Kado watched the mouth bear fangs innumerate in number. Then the bard transformed into a dark shadow that drew the eye and mind of Kado into it.

"Princeling, I remember you and the scent of the lilies that grew on your birth world."

Kado's heart raced as the memories of his drug addled days, the confusion and cravings washed over his body.

"Who are you?" Kado asked.

"You don't know me."

"You are the poison that seeks to devour our world" cried Kado.

"Nay, Voloc lies in the tomb of Magmeris until it is strong again. I am another."

Kado became Scaletryx and flew at the shadow. He latched onto the miasma of darkness, but it quickly changed shape and suffocated Kado's form.

"Where is Ange?"

"Where I want her to be."

The bard reformed grinning maliciously at Kado.

"Now you shall return to your world and our quest shall resume again."

"No, Ange will return looking for me."

The malevolent Jinx simply grinned before Kado felt himself be consumed.

Kado stood as Scaletryx once more on the turret of his Keep. The sun and land was pale. Darkness ebbed in the ocean to the south. He watched the slow death of Arglethium in the waves lapping against the Iron Coast.

Ange climbed the stairs of a cliff. The wind had begun to roar like the ocean below. On it something familiar echoed across it. She climbed faster. The sound becoming more definite. It was a bark.

"Nekoda!" she cried. She began to run. Her weak leg stayed strong as she groped her way over the rocks. On top sat Nekoda. He whined for her to hurry.

She climbed over the last stone slab and threw her arms around his neck.

"Nekoda!" she sobbed.

He licked her.

"Where have you been?"

He barked in response, and she giggled.

"Come we have no time to lose. I need to find Kado and bring him back to his world."

She tied a sash around Nekoda's neck not questioning why the dog had suddenly appeared. She tied the other end to her wrist.

She grabbed the prism and searched for the isle of Star dream. Something pulled on her as she entered the prism.

She sensed something cold watch her.

"No."

Jinx stood before her.

"Where are we?"

"The centre of the Mir Chiridien" replied Jinx.

The bard's voice was different.

'Where is Eaudania?"

"Where she belongs."

"Kado must have won if you are here dear bard."

A scent passed by on a gentle breeze. It was unfamiliar but it was the first time she had smelled something in this place. Nekoda stood near her. His warmth reminding her of how real he was. And how this place suddenly seemed alive. Ange looked around and then at Jinx.

"You are not Jinx."

Everything went dark.

Ange could hear her heart beating and Nekoda's panting.

"Where am I?"

There was only silence.

"Who are you?"

"Resume your quest clay-born. Show me everything" a voice whispered around her.

In the darkness as Ange felt herself moving, she could hear the gushing of water flowing. As the last of the dream-weave faded she saw Eaudania pouring water from her urns over the cliffs and into the valleys. Except this time the world did not disintegrate fully but remained tethered to bonds of light as the Sentinel manipulated crystals making the dream forests solid. Ange's memories of the Mighty Choasa and Lido's Keep returned to her. She saw the bonds of the water were stronger, as were the crystal leaves in the forest.

"I have changed this place. Was that why I was brought here?" asked Ange.

But there was no answer, only the memory of Jinx's songs, calling to the deepest parts of her heart, just like the current of a mighty river.

Opa Phomera

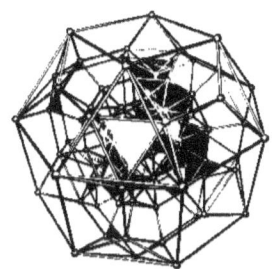

Ange and Nekoda stared across an open expanse of pale light, broken by lines of what appeared to be towers. Their walls were transparent, but it could be seen the way they flickered on the horizon, they were spirals which never seemed to end. Ange craned her neck trying to find the tip of the twirling structures, but they were impossible to see.

A group of figures meandered toward them. They did not acknowledge Ange or Nekoda, and their faces remained hidden to her, no not hidden just not clear. Their features could not be determined. They shimmered between solid to invisible.

"They remind me of the shapes which reflect off the water in the river Nekoda" spoke Ange.

Ange sat down on a seat beneath a massive diamond shaped structure. There was a slight breeze, and it was cool. She saw her tunic was beginning to fray at the cuffs and hem. The prism sat around her neck. She fingered it to make sure it had not been changed in the journey to this place. It did not become warm to touch. She held it up and peered through it. She saw the world come alive all of a sudden. The light changed from pale white to orange then violet, and the towers a myriad shade of blue. They were still transparent, but their shapes were more defined. Some of the towers were spirals while others were made of bricks, the same as the huts of her village and some were completely round with hollowed out centres.

"I don't know what to do. I don't understand anything that is going on. I have abandoned Kado and Jinx. Was that truly Jinx? I am so confused. Mir Chiridien was not what it seemed, and I still do not know how I got there. Or even how we got here" spoke Ange rubbing Nekoda behind the ears trying to comfort herself. He whined and stretched in appreciation.

Her stomach rumbled. It surprised her as she had never felt hungry on Mir Chiridien.

Nekoda whined as well.

"I think we will need to eat first and then perhaps we will find someone or something to help us, Nekoda."

Nekoda nuzzled her hand in agreement.

A sound came across the air. It was a voice calling out.

"Shall we go."

Nekoda stood up with his ears alert ready to investigate where the sound was coming from.

Walking along a translucent like path, the towers stretched above them, blocking their view of anything beyond the walls. It was like an endless forest of spires reflecting into one another. The voice grew louder and soon they saw what appeared to be a marketplace of sorts. Shapes moved together more closely and there was a large open square. A huge tower which seemed to be the centre of the city, rose above them. It was a darker shade than the other structures they had seen, and its base was as a broad as at least three of the smaller ones near it. It was a deep indigo in colour. A figure stood from the top and was calling down to the crowds of ghosts. Some of the ghosts stopped to listen while others continued moving.

The voice stopped. Ange suddenly felt self-conscious. It was strange none of the ghosts seemed to pay any attention to her or Nekoda. She walked around toward the other side of the tower, to see if there was anyone selling food, but there was more of the same.

She went to the bottom of the large tower and leant against it. She wondered if she should go inside. There was no choice really. She would not last too long without something to eat and drink.

Looking at the outside of the tower she ran her hand over the surface. It was smooth and cool. It shimmered slightly when she touched it but there was no entrance. She walked around to where the figure had been speaking. It was not there anymore.

"Help me please!" she called up and out to any of the ghosts.

"I need water and food for myself and Nekoda."

There was no echo only silence.

"Come Nekoda we will keep looking until we find something."

Nekoda followed Ange. He was sniffing the air.

They walked until the light began to lessen.

"I wonder if they have a sun here" spoke Ange.

"Not of the kind you may be used to traveller."

She turned suddenly at the voice.

A ghost stood behind her. It was tall and dark indigo like the tower in the square.

"I see you are not from here. I cannot read your stitching" spoke the ghost.

"What do you mean stitching? I am Ange Tsaed, I am a wanderer on a quest. My companion Nekoda and I are hungry and thirsty. Does this ghost world have any food for ones such as us?'

"Come with me. I will form something for you. I am Yol, seeker of the codes."

"Where are we?" asked Ange.

"Opa Phomera."

Yol turned and began to walk back to the square.

"Was that your voice we heard before?"

"Yes, it was Ange Tsaed. I could not see your being and knew you were not from here. Hence, I followed you."

"How do we understand each other?" asked Ange.

"I am merely looking into your mind and following the flow of your thoughts" replied Yol.

"So how do I understand you?" asked Ange.

"I have formed the pieces of my thoughts to fit to your knowledge. Before you would not have understood what I was saying" answered Yol.

They approached the tower. Passing effortlessly through the walls they ascended into the air. Nekoda wagged its tail at the excitement. Ange patted him. She felt at ease but wondered why she should. Afterall Mir Chiridien became a battle against the Ondraak where all hunted her there.

"You have seen much on your quest, Ange Tsaed" spoke Yol.

"Yes."

Ange bit her lip trying not to think or say anything else, as she suddenly realised nothing would be hidden in this world.

"No we see all things" spoke Yol in response to her thought.

Her stomach rumbled loudly. She looked at Yol and wondered if it had heard.

"Yes, I see you are as empty as I am."

The ghost shook with cacophonous laughter at its comment. Ange looked at Nekoda. The dog whined.

"Now rest here. I will search for food. What do you like the most?" asked Yol.

"Honey, yoghurt and cinnamon cakes" replied Ange instantly. Her mouth salivating thinking about the food.

"Hmm" Yol spoke remaining still as it pondered the images Ange had made in her mind.

"Oh and water, plain water" she added.

"Oh well we have copious water. Look here."

Yol swept its arm aside and outside sat a huge ocean. It was silent and still, no waves broke across the shoreline.

"Can I drink from it?" asked Ange.

"Of course. It is pure and untouched as we the Epimarin have no need of this. It is formed only from the melted threads of air and light and indigo clouds. A grand opus by one of us many eons ago. Beautiful, isn't it?"

"Why is it so silent here?" asked Ange.

"I will tell you our history as we go Ange Tsaed" replied Yol.

"Please just call me Ange."

They arrived in a space which formed transparent walls shaded in blue and a table of sorts. Instantly just as Ange thought of it a chair appeared at the end of the table. Nekoda lay down near her feet. Ange sniffed the air. There was a faint odour, but she could not figure out what it was.

"What you smell is the remnants of making" spoke Yol.

The ghost stood over a series of glass vases and bowls. It placed powder into one and a droplet of water into it. It changed instantly into a bowl of thick creamy yoghurt. Yol handed it to Ange.

She scooped her finger into it.

"It's delicious. How do you do this?" she asked.

Soon a platter of cinnamon cakes and a bowl of honey sat before her.

"Oh dear" Yol looked at the yoghurt and honey running down Ange's hands. It snapped its fingers a small ladle appeared.

"Now for you Nekoda!"

Nekoda wagged his tail in excitement. His tongue slapped in a half smile yawn of hunger.

"He mostly eats animals. He hunts them."

"Oh well that is difficult. We have not learnt the secret to form flesh. The elements yes hence why we remain the alchemist ghosts."

"Oh well just more of this will be ok. Maybe some stewed barley and beans." Ange made in image in her head of a bowl and fields of beans and barley.

A crystal pitcher appeared with water in it and small bowl in front of Ange.

"Nekoda drinks water as well" spoke Ange enjoying the cinnamon cakes. The taste was not exactly the same but still delicious.

Instantly a bowl with water appeared near Nekoda's paws.

After their feast Ange and Nekoda sat on a balcony overlooking the ocean.

"I think it is time we talked Ange" Yol spoke suddenly appearing beside her.

"Yes. I am truly lost Yol. I will have to trust you as I do not know what to do."

The alchemist floated just beside her. It was so silent. It was beginning to worry her.

"Nekoda bark" Ange spoke.

Nekoda let off a few quick snaps which echoed across the waves. Just faintly Ange could see the surface of the ocean ripple gently from the sound.

"Yol you can read my mind. You must know what I carry and what my quest is" Ange probed.

"Yes, I have seen these shadows of your memories and your life before this. You are strong but unaware of all that surrounds your journey here" spoke Yol.

"Something or someone watches me. I don't know what it wants or its purpose. But I think it means to bring harm to me."

Ange stroked Nekoda's scarred back.

"Yes, I agree. This shadow is blind to me. Only the distant traces of its voice memory were revealed. It would require great power to hide from the Epimarin of Opa Phomera. We can see the stitching in anything that exists, or we see the gaps where we have not been able to understand something."

"For some reason it does not take the prism from me but seems to be trying to push me toward it. I think it can't take the prism from me unless I give it to it" mused Ange staring at some clouds gathering in the distance.

"No indeed it cannot. It was bestowed to you. It would destroy any that took it. Even you cannot give it away until it is deemed to do so. You are caged to a jewel prettier than our ocean of light and far more powerful than anything we phantoms have ever devised" spoke Yol.

"I need to learn otherwise I will remain lost and at the whim of this creature which seems to be controlling me."

"I agree Ange. I think it best if I take you to our Primus."

"How much can I trust you and your kind?"

"I don't know. I am low, an initiate, I will not lie. For me to learn from you would increase my awareness of the forming rules. But it is only knowledge we seek, not to appropriate but to learn, delve, speculate. We only allow our knowledge to manifest itself, after much deliberation and approval from the Primus. And besides, you have no choice" spoke Yol.

"Where is this, Primus?"

"The Primus exists inside Opa Phomera. This world is its formulation. We are products from its first methylations of the light and dark and their interaction. We shall travel along the ocean, and I will learn of the taste of water as you drink your fill Ange."

Ange patted Nekoda, more reassured by Yol's words.

"Is this place real? Mir Chiridien was a dream and I think if I searched for it again, I would never find it. Like when I sleep, and my mind is filled with pieces of things that have been but with no beginning or end. No heart to anchor their memories and explain their meaning."

"Opa Phomera is real. Primus will explain and perhaps with time your own questions will be answered as well" Yol answered.

She scooped some water from the ocean with her cask and swigged some. It slid down Ange's throat. It was refreshing. It tasted the same as water but without the earthy flavours of the rivers from her home.

"It is good."

She filled her cask and another for Nekoda.

"There will be plenty Ange. We will walk most of the way with the ocean of indigo as our companion."

"Is it alive to you?" asked Ange.

"Yes, in some ways. I can see what makes it and at times I am tempted to change it into something else. But it is not my work, and I would be severely punished for doing so."

"How do you punish a ghost?" asked Ange.

Yol broke into hearty laughter. It was good to hear the noise thought Ange. Nekoda barked in excitement.

"What a good question. There are ways Ange. To deny an Epimarin their chance to seek knowledge is the greatest punishment" Yol answered.

As they walked Ange noticed the city disappeared and they were walking amongst low hills surrounded by occasional towers. The fields looked like they were moving but were solid.

"The landscape here was formulated or methylated into being by Sonus Actarius. It is from a piece of star far away from here, found on a tendril of memory of a rock and coerced into liquid with essence of indigo light rays" Yol explained.

"How do you know how to make these things?" asked Ange.

"You are so young Ange. Even your Custodians who started your journey are new to our eyes. If we had any eyes" Yol began to laugh again.

Ange giggled as well.

"I like your laugh."

"Yes, it is good isn't it. Such wonderful force to laugh and enjoy. It seems that it can be had without the senses that creatures such as you possess. It was a great breakthrough when Onat discovered this code and was able to translate it into the chains of creation" spoke Yol.

Ange heard the words chains of creation. They brought back memories of Norbu in chains and herself and Tessi at the hands of Baachelaus and Voloc. She shivered.

"We have delved and know deepness of the dark and its negation of existence. But we have also coded the serenity of such a place as well and understand the allure of creatures to it. It is not purely a question of the one or the other, but it seems the interface of both together is where the power of being lives."

"Yes, it is, and I sense the same darkness in the creature that is watching me. It calls to me but makes me fearful. I am born of desert dwellers. I am not a conqueror of gods. Our god was Ancrid. Do you know of it?"

"Desert Dweller, what is this word to an Alchemist ghost? God, and again I ask, what is this word to an Alchemist ghost? I see shadow over the memories from which you have drawn upon" mused Yol.

"It was not a good thing to be like me in my land. I was not desired and not useful. It is a hard life compared to other places of my world. The Mighty Choasa gave much but the sands of the desert took much. So everything my people needed to live, had to be used wisely, otherwise there may not have been enough to survive" Ange replied.

"Ah I see. Such connection to the end days of things. We exist before then. Ancrid. No I do not know this name. Tell me about this god."

"I don't know anything really. We used to pray to it to protect us from sandstorms and enemies who came to steal our land or animals" explained Ange.

"And did this god do that?" asked Yol.

"Well sometimes" answered Ange.

"Your world is interesting. Fickle" Yol commented.

"In what way?" asked Ange.

"It is so much the opposite of our existence. You exist on the edge of death constantly. We search to know the steps between dark to light to dark and their collective memories. We scribe the names and codes of things not yet known. You run to death and from it. We seek what can be known before and while it exists" replied Yol.

"We live in our way. I remember a lot of happiness mostly around my mother and sister, Bensah, Nekoda. There is beauty as well" Ange explained with vivid images of the boabs at sunset.

"Yes, but this is all part of death. In my world it is about understanding what brings death about and looking at all the ways it can be seen and made. What forms before life and the remnants left by death" spoke Yol.

"I don't understand Yol. You make my life seem sad. It was difficult at times but not always sad. When all this is finished, I hope to go back to my home and live again."

"I did not mean to make you feel that way. I merely hoped to explain how Epimarin's see things" Yol answered sensing the longing in Ange for her birth world.

Ange fingered the prism around her neck. Would she ever be free of it she wondered.

"That is something you may need to make a choice about Ange" spoke Yol.

She looked at Yol. The ghost had changed to a pale yellow. She noticed they were at the end of the lake and before them was a vast plain of white translucent emptiness. In the distance stood a tower. Similar to Yol's tower, a helix design but it was larger and shimmered in the emptiness. Ange looked behind her and saw the indigo ocean but not the city they had left.

"I will leave you now Ange. Follow these steps to find me again when you are free to do so. I have enjoyed our journey and look forward to more."

"But where am I?" she asked.

"You are on the edge of our knowledge. This is as far as we have described the things we know. At the beginning stands Aes Opa, the place where the first threads are found, and the coding begins. Aes Vius is our founder and resides here. You will learn much from this creature, our progenitor. Farewell youngling, we will meet again as seekers of knowledge. In us you will find kinship" spoke Yol.

The ghost turned and disappeared.

Ange stood with Nekoda and looked toward the tower called Aes Opa.

She walked on nothing and yet it felt as solid as the earth of her homelands. The tower rose before her. She craned her neck as far as it would go but she could not see the top of the great spire. She knocked on the wall. It was solid.

Her knock did not echo but she saw the soundwaves shimmer in the air. She waited. Nekoda sat down as well. She took a sip of water and ate some of the cakes Yol had made. She shared them with Nekoda.

Leaning against the tower she wanted to fall asleep. As she dozed, she saw a figure coming toward them. She stood as it neared her and Nekoda.

"I am..."

"Yol has left another pupil. Let us begin" the figure spoke interrupting her.

They were ascending inside the tower in circles. Nekoda barked the higher and higher they went.

They stopped in mid-air. Slowly a chamber formed.

"I will not be imprisoned here" Ange warned "I carry the means to leave."

"Aes Vius sees all this. Together we will learn the dead heart of this gift and try to understand its intent. This will be no gaol to languish but a place to perhaps find your way" replied the figure.

"Why do you call it dead?"

"It is formed, It has become. It no longer grows or journeys toward its being. It is made" it replied.

"Do you know of the creature that watches me? It is clouding my vision and stopping me from fulfilling my quest" asked Ange.

"I think you and it share a common purpose and when the answers are found then you will be in danger."

Ange's heart sunk at these words. Anger swelled also but she closed it off, she needed to focus and keep going. There was no choice now, there was no going back.

"Who are you?" asked Ange.

"Aes Vius. Beginner of Opa Phomera and the Epimarin; ghost alchemists. I am old to you. I am older than your sun. I am older than the clay from which you are formed. I am older than the dreams of Mir Chiridien. I am older than the memories contained within that jewel. I exist before life is formed in its elemental state and seek to scribe it to determine where it will go. To predict its pathway not to control it."

"So you know of these Custodians? And Voloc?" asked Ange, hopeful that maybe she had found someone or thing to help her.

"I know of their form and their remnants. The Custodians are the third Age of light of Caemeris. Voloc, is unknown to me, but I see the shadows in your mind, and know its scent, its codes and can see its birthing" spoke the ghost.

"You must be able to help me. It needs to end. You know that this will mean the end of my world, and if it dies, then I will as well, for I cannot bear an eternity of this" pleaded Ange.

"Do not give up hope yet Ange. There is much to be understood" replied Aes Vius.

"What do you look like?" asked Ange.

"Nothing anymore. I was once as brilliant and beautiful as a star, but I have now lost this form and live as the codes I write show. But essentially all that exists in Opa Phomera, is an extension of me and my form" replied Aes Vius.

Suddenly a table appeared with a platter of food with pitchers of milk and water.

"You need sustenance again. Eat!" spoke Aes Vius.

Ange took some grapes and a piece of meat. It was goat like Pata used to make. She gave some to Nekoda who gulped it down in one mouthful.

"You can form flesh. Yol said it could not do that" Ange spoke as she drank the creamy milk.

Suddenly a voice whispered in her ear "Yes."

She felt the breath of the ghost touch her cheek.

"Form yourself Aes Vius so we may understand each other more clearly" she ordered chomping on the grapes.

A thread began to weave itself in the air as Ange continued to feast. She watched the Epimarin grow.

Aes Vius bowed to Ange.

"I will be like the slender reeds of your rivers and the dappled shades of summer and brilliant colours of Belmaris setting across the red sands of your land. Hello wanderer, seeker and keeper of sorrows and memories of Caemeris" spoke Aes Vius.

"You resemble Assumpta, the Custodian who gave me the prism" stated Ange.

"I thought this best for now. I have no reality in the way you understand it. Take the prism out and place it on the table."

Ange removed it. It sat on its side sparkling against the translucent walls and tower.

Aes touched it. It shimmered slightly and then slowly the prism began to unravel.

Ange panicked and snatched it away from it.

"What are you doing? You will destroy it" she warned, suddenly wary of the ghost.

Aes Vius suddenly darkened into a menacing shadow like Voloc.

"Youngling, ignorant being to all that exists in creation. I can create or destroy and yet you sit here blind to the power you hold within your grasp and still consider you are a better Custodian of this jewel than myself. Watch and learn, and then you will understand."

The prism pulled out of Ange's hand and hovered on the table.

"Behold the Tear of Ascendant. Young spirit of hope and desire of those formed of Belmaris. These creatures you called Custodians. Do you know what this truly is?"

"No I do not. It has destroyed my home" replied Ange.

"It destroys. It creates. It is all part of one and the same thing. It directs the light, shows its colours, reshapes its beams to recreate. It brings desire, hope, fulfilment, and despair. Let us pull it apart and see what we learn."

Ange tensed again not wanting to lose it.

"You understand without this I cannot travel anywhere and definitely would not be able to return to home."

"Do not fear Ange. Its fabric will always remain. I see how to write it. And you will as well."

A thin tendril grew out of the jewel. Ange watched it mesmerised.

"What is it?"

"The eye of Caemeris."

"What is Caemeris?" asked Ange.

"Ah...the beginning."

"Why was the prism hidden by Norbu?"

"Have you not seen the lust the shadowed and eyeless have for this? I have."

Aes Vius transformed into a dark shadow as it spoke.

"Come." Aes beckoned Ange over.

Ange sat in darkness. A small spec appeared.

"What makes the light Ange?" asked Aes.

"I don't know. The sun on my world" replied Ange.

"Look how it moves. Look at each singular spec. Count and with each count score it into the darkness."

Ange watched the spec and saw that it did pulse. It was alive.

"Yes" whispered Aes.

She watched and saw with each pulse her finger made a mark in mid-air.

Aes Vius went outside the chamber it had formed around Ange and peered across deep emptiness of the unknown stretching before it. The Epimarin dug deep into the white nothing. Rage met harmony. The ghost reached forward and swallowed the deep anger and hatred. Churning force, insatiable. Aes Vius remembered this power, the surges, and the impulses, urgent, uncontrolled.

"Why do you chase and confuse this Clayborn, seeker and bearer of the mysteries of Caemeris?" asked Aes.

"It has been an age of light since we last met, Aes Vius. You know what I seek" replied a voice with no form. "Oblyquixiton made us to be tenacious in our purpose. We are brethren are we not Seer?"

"You are close, close enough to reveal yourself. You have grown strong, brethren" replied Aes.

There was no answer.

"Our purposes were sundered long ago. Come, return, and let me pull you apart and look upon my brethren. Let me name you and see what you have become" Aes coaxed.

The shadow pulled away. Aes lashed out and attempted to snatch the cloud before it disappeared, but it was too late.

The Primus of the Epimarin, watched in the empty unknown, waiting for the return of its brethren.

It sensed Ange as she counted the music of light. It saw the scores building. Each different in time, length, and size.

"Now order them" commanded Aes.

Ange looked at the collection of marks and saw they were not all the same. It was strange.

She arranged them in size from smallest to largest. But then saw that they had pieces missing out of them. She began to fit them together. But they did not look like the spark of light.

"How do I make it into the light?" Ange asked.

Aes Vius woke from its searching of the unknown planes and laughed heartily.

"Welcome Alchemist. Your journey has begun. Now try again."

Aes searched Ange's mind as she sat distracted with her task. It saw Mir Chiridien and the washer woman. It saw Kado.

"Ahh the deep light of Caemeris flows in you. Such a breach. What comes forth? Close, close lie our progenitors. The codes are being re-written. We sit upon the edge of disruption not destruction. Are we seeing the death of the world and await the rebirth? The Epimarin no longer learn but seek the re-birth. I call you Epimarin, decide now, do we let the music of death wash new the known? Do we destroy the Keeper now and let her face Caemeris, her maker. Such a cliff, such a watershed, such a fall, such a flight, such a deep yearning in the heart and flesh, lacerated, and destroyed leaving us ghosts, phantoms, hollow spectres of creation. I, Aes Vius, maker of you all have shared my knowledge so you may learn. So I may learn. To watch, to see, to know. On the edge of a mountain as steep as these towers we may plunge into the empty unknown to begin to relearn. The new order waits and the walls between the existence and non-existence grows thin. Should we sever these strands of final things and start again? The eye of Caemeris has drawn the gaze of my history, one long forgotten but still ripe with need to usurp the knowledge of Aes Vius. There is no escape, for we are discovered and so to our knowledge. Opa Phomera sits on the edge of destruction with the arrival of Caemeris. Aes Vius sits before the abyss of its history, the edge of conquest with the arrival of Caemeris."

The thoughts of Aes Vius propounded throughout Opa Phomera, and into the Epimarin ghosts. They stilled as their Primus echoes discombobulated their codes, so powerful was this Seer of Knowledge.

Aes returned to Ange.

Ange put the last of the scores together. A tiny spec of light sat in her hand.

"I have remade it."

Aes snatched it. Ange was suddenly frightened. Aes blew the spec apart.

"Again. This time score the recipe into the stone" Aes ordered.

Ange watched marking the movement of the light mesmerised by its intensity and power to control her. Inside it she could see the colours and behind the colours sat memories of a war and in the war came peace and out of the peace she saw more thin strands of tiny dots bouncing around one another and in between the dots was a space marked evenly in harmony. It reminded her of the times she and Tessi would hold hands and spin around so fast each using the other to stay upright until they were so dizzy, they would collapse laughing feeling like they were flying through the air.

Ange sat back panting. She looked down and, on the stone-tablet were inscriptions.

"I have written light."

"Good now remake it."

A clear bell jar appeared. She looked at the codes and with Tessi in her mind Ange made light. The dizziness and elation swelled inside her as the tiny spec formed in the jar. Then she felt sad.

"I do not wish to know such things. To make what is beautiful purely by my own hand seems offensive and wrong" she spoke.

"Ah yes to your mind it would seem like this. A breach beyond what was deemed wise. Your flesh still calls to its death it does not wish to overcome it yet. To you this is like creating death. For us it is homage to the beauty and power that exists in all spaces. Rest now" replied Aes.

Ange found herself in a large chamber with a window which extended along one whole side of it. Its view reached from the plains of the unknown back to the indigo lake in the far distance. A table with a platter of food and drink sat in a corner. There was also a large chair big enough to be a bed. She went to it and lay down. Tears ran down her cheek. The power and beauty she had just felt still raced through her body. It both frightened her and thrilled her.

"I will never be Ange Tsaed again Nekoda. I fear I will be doomed to roam learning the deep secrets of everything and will forget what made me in the first place."

"This fear is real, but you need to finish what has begun and then you can choose. Rest. Dream" spoke Aes Vius.

"Was Jinx real? I wish I could hear a song from his music branch."

Ange fell asleep thinking of Jinx and wondered if the bard were alive or if it had been a trick to reveal the prisms power. The warmth of Nekoda was comforting once again as a reminder that he was real and so was she. The weight of the prism around her neck remained real as well only now it felt like a burden slowly building a cage around her not the bringer of adventure she had hoped for when she left Gildas on the battlefield of the Iron Fortress.

The Epimarin gathered at the feet of Aes Opa.

"So what is our decision?" asked Aes Vius.

"Let the flesh-formed creature reach maturity then we shall decide" rose a chorus of whispers.

Darkness swept Opa Phomera as Ange slept. Aes Vius walked with Yol along the indigo shores of the ocean.

"She will find the path back to Caemeris. It chose to hide itself but has left a trace in the gemstone. The Seer seeks the power of Caemeris as well and knows the path back to it can be found using the prism. It will show the way to remake the Pthohedron once more. It has revealed us to them, and they will seek our knowledge, myself, and revenge for my betrayal" spoke Aes Vius.

"It will open the wars of creation. Oblyquixiton will remember" replied Yol.

"I know Yol. We will watch and learn as Ange grows. We will see the power of her form and learn who will be the path to the lost knowledge of the Caemerin light. The Seer or this Keeper of the children made from clay."

"I sense great potency in her. More than I when you first began to teach Primus."

'Yes. She has already remade the first pearls of water" replied Aes Vius.

"Truly outstanding for such young memories" replied Yol.

On the far shore a shape sat. It was shrouded in deeper violet compared to the ocean of water. It watched the two Epimarin as they strolled in conversation.

No sound not even the lapping of waves against the formed banks could be heard.

"Brethren" it called across the great expanse.

"Ah you come once again. Let Aes Vius know you mind. You tread in my realm and yet you do not welcome me into yours" replied Aes.

"You know you outwit me, or I would not be interfering on this quest in the shadow of lesser ones such as this" replied the shadow.

"True but still if you continue to come here and intrude, I will have no choice but to consume the shadows which veil your thoughts" spoke Aes.

"If I let you do this one thing, I will ask for one thing in return" replied the figure.

"Name your desire" spoke Aes.

"I want the prism and her memories" spoke the figure.

"For what in return?" replied Aes.

"To leave you to your quest Aes Vius. And not to be subsumed by ours" replied the figure.

Suddenly a loud clatter broke across the skies and ocean. The sound woke Ange and Nekoda and the world of Opa Phomeris stopped. The Epimarin heard the Primus' laughter break their creation into pieces.

"Of course you cannot have these. You know she stares into the eye of Caemeris but does not understand this. Whoever these Custodians were, the knowledge and strength cast into them by the Caemeris, is far greater than anything ever known before. It was bestowed to her for a reason. Ones such us would only pervert its use and lead to destruction. Your desires are too out of reach for me to betray this fledgling and the chance to see knowledge bloom. Thankyou brethren you have made my decision for me. I believe we will be at war soon enough" replied Aes.

Ange stood looking across the plains and saw the three figures. She sensed the shadow on the far side and shivered. Aes Vius was strong she could feel the profoundness of the knowledge it held. Something she knew it wanted her to have.

She looked and saw a gaping rent open over the ocean. Blackness began to bleed into the world toward Aes Vius. Ange snatched the prism around her neck and leapt out of the spire toward the Epimarin.

Nekoda barked wanting to warn her. He tried to leap but it was too high, and fear stopped him. He barked watching Ange race toward the seeping blackness in the sky.

She called the light from within the jewel and taking it into her hand flung it at the haemorrhaging darkness. It stopped instantly.

Aes Vius grabbed her before she went closer to the gaping hole.

"Careful Ange. It wants to draw you out."

"Why have you come here? You know you can see what I see. I have been leading you to where you want to go" Ange shouted at the emptiness.

There was no answer.

The Epimarin formed around the shoreline. The indigo lake had started to disintegrate. The ghosts began to repair the tear of the sky to prevent more darkness poisoning the ocean. Soon everything was restored but the ocean looked pale compared to the vibrant blues when Ange first saw it.

"Come there is much to learn" spoke Aes.

"This is the figure I saw walking once when I was trapped in Mir Chiridien. It is becoming clearer each time I see it."

"Yes, that was me you saw Ange, not this one. But yes, you are beginning to understand, as you grow so does it."

"Have I brought this destruction here?" asked Ange.

"Yes and no. I sensed the power of Caemeris, as did my brethren. We both sought it out. But I did not see my brethren when I reached beyond Phomeris. This concerns me. For had I known I would have not quested so far. They have become strong, to hide themselves so well."

"Why won't they reveal themselves, and just take what they want?"

"As you learn you will understand" replied Aes.

They returned to the chamber. Nekoda raced up to her concerned. She patted him.

"It is alright. I am getting used to having to fight every turn I make. What is the next lesson?" asked Ange irritably.

Aes Vius laughed heartily again. Ange looked at the vibrations of the chamber and felt the spire shake.

"Your laughter reminds me of the deepness I used to see in Assumpta's eyes. Great pools which would draw me in but overwhelm me. Your laughter is the same. Happiness and heart are what I have learnt. Bensah, Tata had both. I loved him very much, but he was killed trying to protect me."

Aes listened and coded the feelings and memories Ange spoke of.

"These gods are intriguing. I wish to meet them when the time comes. The creations of flesh and clay are anchored in life and death. This is the price the Alchemists must pay to continue their quest for knowing. They have never known the heavy, densest light, bonded the strongest. Your strength is still unknown to you Ange. Even before Opa Phomera, your kind was unknown."

Ange wondered what Aes Vius meant before Opa Phomera. Before she could ask a table appeared with clear vases. Inside some of them had swirling gases while others had small grains like sand.

"Ange remake our ocean" ordered Aes Vius.

"But wouldn't the ghost who made it prefer to do it" Ange replied.

"We can make as many as we like. You may make one as well."

A tablet formed near Ange. She opened it and began to score out the pearls of water. She remembered the red dunes of her home and how her mother was buried underneath them. A tear escaped from her eye. She took it and saw how it was made.

She looked for the scores which showed red and formed more on the tablet. Soon a droplet hung from the tip of her finger. She walked out into the plains of the unknown.

"Will here do?" she asked.

Aes Vius nodded.

She blew the drop across the expanse and watched a red ocean grow.

She went back inside and rested. Each time she made something she wanted to sleep.

"Why am I so tired after this?" she asked.

"It is because you are flesh formed. We were more like the waters of the oceans but even then, we became depleted easily. So we sacrificed the energy needed to maintain our birth form to pursue knowledge."

"Who was that figure that spoke to you?" Ange asked.

"In time you will understand and then we will speak plainly to one another. Let us make the visions and memories in your mind. What are you thinking of now?" asked Aes.

"I'm thinking that I would like to see the reeds of the great Choasa in that water. But I do not know their sounds as I have none."

"Did they form of the same clay from which you and Nekoda come from?"

"Yes."

"Well pluck out a hair and unravel the mysteries."

Ange plucked out one of her hairs. She placed the prism over it to magnify the strand.

She began to tap the scores of the hair. The strand was made up tiny beads in the shape of a helix. She saw oceans, dirt, and explosions of clouds, thunder, and lightning all behind the minuscule specs ebbing against one another. She began to sift between the patterns until another one began to emerge. She pushed one pulsing ebb toward another and slowly another strand began to form. Soon a slender reed sat on the tablet. She fingered its brittle stem and smelt it. It was the same.

She walked toward the red ocean and placed the reed into it.

"Grow" she whispered.

The edges of the lapping water were filled with the gentle dancing of the Choasa reeds. She looked at her hands. She noticed that faintly she could see the red water through them. She was becoming a ghost.

She rested beside the water, and listened to gentle swaying sound the reeds made, magnified from the silence of the world around them. She watched the waves lap through her hand amazed. She sniffed the air and could faintly smell the green freshness of the reeds mingled with earth. Ange also felt very tired and wanted to rest.

"I am losing myself."

"No you are merely entering into a new form of existence. It takes energy to make things happen and to remember and write them down. Something has to be sacrificed so the knowledge can be learnt and understood. We are closed in our existence. Nothing new exists only new ways of seeing it."

"I don't believe you" retorted Ange.

"There is difference between what is new, or never existed compared to what is unique in its ultimate form, Ange" replied Aes. "All that exists now is all that will ever exist, but how it is seen and understood remains to be discovered. Now I want you to do this again and when you have finished, I would like you to scribe it in the Cadra Phomera of codes. It sits within the Helix of Coaxus, the Archivist" spoke Aes.

"Before I do that, I would like to rest a little."

"Of course. I forget you're a flesh formed. Do not be fearful" spoke Aes Vius gently touching Ange on the shoulder.

"I am not. Fear has passed now. That was with me in the days of my home. There is an urgency to complete this quest and answer these riddles which grow before me. That has replaced the fear."

"You will change because of it."

"I know."

Ange lay down to sleep.

Aes Vius left Ange. The Epimarin knew she still didn't understand the profound nature of the change that would come from her learning here nor the importance of it.

"Yol, the Wanderer will be coming soon to do her first inscription in the Cadra."

'Yes Aes. The journey begins for all of us. We are discovered with her arrival. And once again you Primus will be pursued by your brethren" spoke Yol.

"Yes."

Ange woke and saw the red lake and reeds. She closed her eyes and thought of the tiny sparks which bounded and rebounded to form the scene before her. She collected each of them into her mind and held them. Small specs pulsed inside her. She opened her eyes and the plains of the unknown had reformed except where the rupture in the sky had occurred and destroyed the ocean and fabric of Opa Phomera. A grey nothingness replaced them, as if something had been cut out of the world. She realised once something was known then it cannot be unknown or could it.

Going back to the chamber in Aes Opa she spilled the tiny fragments of her hair out of the bell jar where she had made the reeds. She reassembled them to make more water. Just as she was about to finish, she swept it all away. Looking into the fragments she searched for her mother. Going deep into her memories she plucked out the first one. It was frail and fragmented easily but it was there. Mata was cooing her to sleep in her arms. She delved into the memory and pulled on the essences of smell and sound. She took from the smashed reeds the same colours that were like hers and then took her mother and tried to find the same ones. There were darker shades as well. They were memories of Pata. His words were jarring and seemed to shatter the memories. She grasped them and drilled into them. The darkness of her father was monstrous and never softened, while her mother's fear and love was fierce. Outside surrounding her lake a black miasma formed. Aes Vius watched. It could see what Ange was doing but did not stop her.

Darker the reed lake grew until it inverted. Ange didn't seem to notice the world around her shaking. She pushed the pieces together to bring her Mata to life again but instead the shadows of her father and his indifference seemed to take hold. The lake became an abyss of unwelcoming silence pushing into the serenity of Phomera. A bubble began to form. Far on the edge of the unknown plains stood the figure. Aes Vius saw its brethren.

"Come she opens the gate for you. Come!" coaxed Aes.

"Not yet, brethren" the figure replied.

Suddenly Ange sat back. She was panting heavily from the effort to create. She saw that her hands had disappeared. She had depleted all her energy to make her Mata.

"You went too far" spoke Aes Vius.

"I almost succeeded" Ange replied.

"Why did you do that?" asked Aes.

"I wanted to speak to her again."

"Why?"

"I don't know. I yearn to hear her voice and advice. Why were the shadows of my father there?"

"You are formed from both. So they both dwell within you."

"It seemed to take over everything, suffocate Mata. I do not want that. He shunned me, disowned me from my birth."

"They are both equal not one more than the other. But you are less like your father than your mother and so you were drawn to find knowledge of this darkness. Reform the lake and then inscribe it."

"I will try again you know that" warned Ange.

"I know. I am not here to make you do what we want. Merely to show you how. What you do after that is your decision" replied Aes.

She was beginning to be flesh again. She sat back and closed her eyes.

"I wanted to see her again. Do you understand death?"

"No the Epimarin do not experience it. But have inscribed the loss that is felt. It is one of the grand codes, like grief and love."

"Why those two?" asked Ange.

"They take so many forms and are pervasive. It is a magna opus of mine."

"I have experienced both."

"Indeed. The work you could write would be far greater than mine. Now reform the lake then rest."

Ange stood at the chamber once more and began to make the lake with the reeds. The red shade soon filled the gaping tear where the lake had stood previously.

"So Aes Vius will you keep the knowledge for yourself once it is found. You know that would be against the Cadral Creed" sneered the figure on the edge of knowledge.

The Primus speared a spec of pure energy across the vastness, at its brethren. The figure evaded the lancing light.

"You seek more than you should, and only destruction will come of it. But to hide so easily from my sight, you have grown in strength brethren" spoke Aes.

"Indeed Aes Vius. Indeed we have" the figure disappeared.

A shudder ran through Opa Phomera, climaxing into an explosion of black dust all over the indigo sea and Epimarin towers.

"The Seers have seen this destruction before" whispered Aes.

Ange collected her tablet.

Nekoda was outside looking at something on the platform. She went over to him.

She saw the black soot everywhere.

"Did I do that?"

"Not all of it" replied Aes Vius. "Your presence here brings new matter, and its consequent energy. So our reality is altered because of it."

Ange descended down the spiral stairs to go to Coexa's Helix. The soot lightly covered everything as she meandered along the shoreline.

She wiped her finger on a rock. She smelt the fine dust. It was like the dirt of her home.

"I did do this."

"Some of it yes. But it was also me pushing away shadows until your skills are stronger" replied Aes.

"What made it?"

"The malice or the plains of nulled energy. Un-codable darkness where the Epimarin have not the strength or knowledge to delve. Your world exists within this energy, death, or disintegration. While life exists in abundance, its purpose is to die. At its uttermost end, it becomes negative in its forces. Phomera, is positive or full because nothing is formed yet."

"What is it you hope to learn from me Aes?" asked Ange.

There was no answer.

"Perhaps, I may not be as safe here after all?" she probed.

Yol appeared suddenly, and instantly Ange was in a dimly lit cave. The walls extended high above her and disappeared into a miasma of swirling letters and marks which she did not recognise.

"What are these?"

"They are our library. It is where our knowledge is stored. You are to place your codes in the repository where it will remain protected" spoke Yol.

"Is this your creation Yol?" asked Ange.

"No it was made by Coexa, who has since merged with it. It was an accumulation of knowledge, named the Cadra Phomera. My skill at making is less but I think it is important to remember and then new things can be learnt along the way. Did you have chroniclers in your home?"

"I don't think so. We had village elders who would teach where my people came from, the laws of Ancrid and our tribes, about our ancestors but nothing like this."

"I see what you are speaking about. Such richness and density from your roots. I have never known this. Your knowledge will be valuable. Now here you are."

Yol gestured for Ange to sit in a tear drop chair suspended in the air. Its outline was barely perceptible.

"What is this?"

"A place to remember and consider what has been learnt. It will help you transcribe into the Cadra and keep you comfortable. You may leave it at any time. Ghia Opa created it when the Epimarin were too drained from their questing to then remember what they had learned. Marvellous invention. We call them the Synarcadra. Would you like sustenance?"

"Yes. What about Nekoda?"

"Would you like to rest here or wander across the vastness of Phomeris companion Nekoda? I would like to learn of your hunting skills" Yol looked at Ange enquiring if it would be alright.

Nekoda barked at the ghost and then looked at Ange.

"Go Nekoda and seek out what else lies here and when you return, I will be rested, and you can show me what you have seen" spoke Ange giving him a hug.

"Ahh such love. Did Aes Vius tell you we are yet to scribe the Cadra of love and grief here. You will teach us so much from your life Ange."

Ange smiled as Nekoda sprinted out of the helix chamber with Yol. She was excited for him and herself. She lay inside the Synarcadra. There was a small tray of biscuits and yoghurt and some tea as well. She lay down and closed her eyes. The chamber closed around her, but she did not feel caged, rather a sense of protection.

Ange looked into the Cadra of knowledge and scoured the myriad amounts of coded information. She fingered the prism around her neck and looked deep inside. She saw the vastness of everything the Epimarin had learnt to make and remake. She saw a space next to the Indigo sea and decided to score her reed lake next to it. She lightly tapped the prism and the sounds of the tiny specs coalesced in their pattern which formed the reeds, gently floated out into the Cadra. She altered it just slightly by making the whole a seamless one rather than joining together like the mud bricks used to make their huts. When she finished, she looked at her addition, pride and love swelled inside her.

"Marvellous" echoed through the Cadra and into her mind. She giggled at the amazement of Yol.

She continued to search the Cadra. She dove deeper into its mysteries. Suddenly she was at the limit of the repository. There was a space. She sensed something further beyond the emptiness. She drifted closer allowing something to draw her in towards it. She let go and shut her mind down to be guided. Then suddenly she was encased in ebbing bubbles and large blocks of nothingness. They moved in no particular rhythm to each other and remained separate. They bulged and contracted but never disappeared. Even inside the emptiness there was a pulsing force repelling the bulges. The bubbles would however break through so that the whole space was never entirely empty. Ange reached out and grasped one of the bubbles. She fingered their structure. They were warm to touch and soft. One of them curled around her arm and rested on it. She looked inside it. She saw herself watching Tessi being taken away by the slaver across the desert. She watched Bensah fighting polar bears. She did not feel sad when she saw these memories. She felt a surge of power rush through her. It was intense and exhilarating but not painful. It ebbed away slowly leaving a space where it had moved into her being. It pulsed waiting to be filled.

"Shall I fill this with my life? What can I tell you of it?"

The energy fields moved away and watched her. She deluged it with memories of everything and anything which came to her spontaneously.

It contorted into exploding cacophonies of colour and disappeared leaving the vault empty. Ange stepped into it and began to write her story.

"You see grief for me, began before I was born. I think it is inherited from Mata and Pata. We live and then we die. But in between those moments, each step has to be taken. My steps were uneven and despised by my people. But the sorrow of that was formed before I was born as there had been others to pave the way for me to inherit that sadness. But amongst that sadness there were moments of utter joy, such as when I would be with Tessi or Tata Bensah would arrive; we would play and be happy. Nekoda would forage with me in the reeds and river to salvage stones so they could be sold for markets. These moments softened the hardness of our lives in the dirt and clay.

Death, I only understand as something I have seen. It is powerful and fills me with fear and I know that it will reach out to me one day as with all of the Clayborn of Arglethium. The Custodians who forced me into their world must have conquered death or remain ignorant to it. I carry their memories in this prism whose mysteries are not fully revealed to me yet. I think though when I fly amongst these Custodians and ancient beings who exist beyond my age and my people, I am still bound to those happy times when I was drowning in sunshine and love. Even the power that was wielded by these beings never took away those moments from me. They are etched as deeply as the knowledge inside this Cadra.

Grief always cradled those times and only ever left for a little while. When the plague came and began to destroy everything, I was still able to stand and look across the desert, while inside me was an ocean of storm clouds, when the sky would touch the ground gathering the sand so fiercely that it blinded our eyes and scored flesh off our bodies. The pain was real like the pain in my legs trying to climb the great red sand dunes or heavy baskets of water back from the river. It was uneven ground, and my body was not shaped to fit those crooked paths and steep hills easily. But I climbed them even with the pain, like I followed Tessi across the desert with the breath of the demon seeking my blood, forgotten to everyone except the shadows of death and fear. Grief is always with me but inside that cradle I remember the great and terrible love of my mother. I remember her teaching me to make the cloth for celebration for the weddings. I remember her quelling the neglectful and disinterested rage of my father. I remember her teaching me to keep going and to make cinnamon cakes at the same time. I grieve mostly for Tata Bensah. He co-existed with me, like a pale dawn before a storm. Shrouded by the red dust but never darkening the light of the sun inside him. My grief for him, is the shadow on the edge of a night. A shadow withered and never taken by my dreams to forever haunt me. A shadow that will neither see the beauty of a full moon nor the hope of a ripened harvest. The grief embraced the love I once had but neither destroys it nor removes the memory, rather it steals the joy of it leaving a remnant of the space where joy and love existed.

Love is the presence of Mata who acted like a shelter in a sandstorm, which could rise as high as it was needed to stop the scouring wind destroy everything or be as open as a desert to allow a soft breeze to cool the mid-day heat. I remember when her face would scowl in anger at the droughts, or death of a goat or when Pata would take the rest of the grain and waste it on his goat milk grog. I could see how love can be lessened by those difficult moments but when it is true it never disappears. I hated to see her angry or sad, but she gave me strength to understand that love is not weak and is strong to withstand the things which make life difficult. Mata never lied to me. She said my life would not be like Tessi's but that if I learned to do other things which make me useful then I would remain even beyond her life. She never said I was not worth being here. She would smile and hug me and gather me in her arms. She would stroke my weak leg and say, "I think it is stronger than you think." Mata never cried. She could be angry, she could happy, she could be cold, and she could be sad, but she never shed a tear. I asked her why. I gave her one of my own one day. I had been teased by Takob and I was crying. She sat near me and watched me for a long time. She asked if I was finished now. I said yes. I took a tear from cheek and put it on her lips. I asked if she had ever tasted a tear. She said once long ago but it didn't fix anything. She told me next time Takob teases you, which he will, remember he doesn't see you; he sees fear in his heart, fear of being ostracised, punishment, a lacking which he cannot imagine he could ever overcome. When he teases you, pick up a rock to throw back at him but at the same time offer him a meal to come home. Do what will make you seem like you have conquered his disgust or made him a friend or flicked him off like a scab. You will not change him but it's important you don't let his fear become yours.

I listened to her words, and I thought they were wise, but I also looked at my legs and I told her that I would never be allowed to have what she has because of it. I would be set apart from Tessi with no dreams of my own. I will walk always as someone in the shadow of others more wanted than I. I am entitled to cry and to be afraid of what will become of me. She looked at me for a long time. I remember the sun was nearing the end of the day. Pink and red began to blanket us. She suddenly smiled at me and nodded. You are right. I have shut everyone out and yet you still crave to let those people in even the ones who despise you. That is your disappointment in life, to know your heart is more open than many others. I told her Mata you should learn to cry. She smiled as we sat together watching the night come.

I could never speak to my Pata like this. Even Tessi remained distant from him.

I love Tessi the most and if I were to end this quest then it would be just so I could be back with her dancing the dance of the sun brides among the dust. I remember we have been friends for a long time. She never tried to protect me. We spoke a lot at night before we would go to sleep. One time Mata sent me out because Pata had been in the goat grog and became angry at me. Mata sent me away because she was afraid, he may hurt me. I left with no fear in me. I was little back then, and I didn't understand. I went to the little stream that ran toward the village well. I began to sift the sand in the bed of the stream looking for stones. I found three that day. One was bright blue, and the others were white like the moon. Tessi had followed me and sat near me. She had tears in her eyes. I asked her why she was crying. She said she didn't like the way Pata treated me. He treats you the same but the way he treats you is the way our people live so it looks like it is the right way. But he cares no more for you or Mata than he does for me I said. If that goat dies or you died tomorrow, he may weep because he wouldn't get paid for the loss. But since I am not worth anything he weeps now. Either way he will weep not because he loved you but because of how much you are worth. Tessi looked at me. You are right. She stopped crying. Be my friend not my protector. You cannot help me anyway I told Tessi that day. My life is made up for me from the day I was born and the rules that have been made make sure it remains the same. I have no fear of Pata, and I have no love for him. We will forget one another when the time comes for me to leave. Be more fearful for yourself Tessi as he sees his wealth in you. Tessi looked at me and then hugged me tight. She understood the difference between us and from that time we would walk run and gather our things to make beads, sew cloth and milk goats and collect water from the well side by side as sisters. When I watched Tessi be given to Noai as a dowry and the glint in Pata's eyes I knew whatever my fate would be, that I would still have some freedom to dig for those beautiful stones unlike Tessi, whose every step from that day would be determined for her.

I will show you what I think grief is in my mind. Do you see the great sweeping Chensai desert. It is beautiful in its way. I remember when I climbed over the mountains through the beautiful forests and even rested in Lido's keep and sacred groves I felt out of place and stranger than I had before. I remember thinking that the soft grass and the moist leaves were comforting to rest on but began to suffocate me from their thickness and warmth. While the desert and scrub of the dry bushes and remoteness of the boab trees still let me stand freely. When I looked at their isolation, I could see my face like when it reflected in the still waters of the great river. Or when I looked at my misshapen shadow, I could see the bumps and crooked lines like the trees and bushes who shaped their existence out of the unforgiving sand. They and I were made from the same things and deep within us lay wells of grief that every day we remained alive we would be asked to beg or steel each bit of our lives. It's a hard way to live in an ungenerous world but it also made our hearts big with anger and purpose so that we would not let go easily of that which we loved the most. Those trees and that desert understood each other. The forests, oceans, and mountains fought for control, suffocating all around them and drowned all else with their overwhelming need to devour everything to keep themselves alive. Those places never grieved if something died because it was so abundant, it never missed anything. I believe the ocean would drown itself if the sands ever decided to send waves into its mouth and pull the water under, so stricken with sorrow over its loss of power over the earth. Grief is an emptiness which can give and makes the love clearer. But it can kill. Just as that sand could have taken my life, the love it made me feel when there was food to eat and water to drink and happiness to be had with Mata and Tessi, Nekoda, and Tata. Grief is part of me and who I am, but it is not all there is to know.

Love. I don't know what love is really. I have explained what I felt for Mata and Tessi. But what love is I really don't know. I know happiness, boredom, concern for people I care about and fear. Fear is a part of grief and love. It is made from both. I was frightened of Mata particularly when she was mad, but I loved her. I did not love Pata and felt no fear, as I knew he would not grieve, or care if I was gone and I felt the same about him. So fear is part of sorrow and love.

So what is love? I said before I don't know what love is and I have heard lots of words which may describe it but what it is, I am not certain. I miss Tessi and Tata the most. Mata I would have been made to leave anyway and she would not have followed but I know Tessi and Tata would always have looked for me. Tata lost his child and I think deep down he thought I should be his. He cared deeply for us. I never met his wife. He lived far away from our village but he and Pata did a lot of trading, and our place was where he stayed when he was away from his home. He came looking for me and Tessi after the plague came. He and

I journeyed to meet the Custodians at their special groves. While we were trying to flee to safety, he was killed by Icebear cubs whose mother was trying to teach them to hunt. This was grief for me but victory for them. It was also the love of the mother to help the cubs live. Mata did the same for me she taught me to stitch and cook millet cakes and make yoghurt from the goat's milk. This is one form of love. But there was the love that Tata Bensah seemed to have and show all the time. It was bigger and grander and chosen for no other reason than he wanted to love. It is easy to love a child. I mean I loved the baby goats; they were cute and playful. Like the babies in the village. They were so soft to touch and easy to hug. But the babies weren't just loved because of this they were loved because they brought a future and payment with them. Like the stones which could be sold to decorate the northern women. Or like the Boabs love the rain or I loved the river for water and the stones it gave me. No there is the love that made Bensah search for me and Tessi to love her babes when they were put upon her by a tyrant. But she defended her babes almost to her death. Why do this? Why did Mata not kill me when I was born when she knew my life would be one of derision and scorn. One which made Mata and Pata be cast as outsiders by the village elders and punished with a misborn daughter. Why am I allowed to live when I was considered a curse? This love does not exist between the boabs and the rain or the desert and the sun or even the red snakes and the mice it eats to survive. But only between us. The people of the desert, like flowing water we clung to one another in spite of our hatred and malice for things different to them. Somewhere we learnt in the harshness of the dry sands and the power of the rushing waters and searing burn of desert winds we needed to care for each other.

Tata Bensah El Bunani was a silent man most of the time. He rarely spoke of his life especially around Tessi and me. We never met his wife and know only that he lived further to the south. I had hoped when it was my coming of age I could go and live there and work for a family in his village. It would mean that Tessi and Mata could live peacefully and no longer have to see Pata's anger toward me. Tata travelled far away further than Ancrid City to do his trading. He had seen a lot of the world before I saw it, but he never spoke of it to me. He and Pata would sit drinking goat grog and I could sometimes here him speaking of wars and rich northern people. Even the people who lived further to the east and the jewelled cities they lived in. Tata had been a slaver once in his life. He said he had regretted it but at the time it was necessary to survive. Perhaps that is why he came looking for me and Tessi. To make up for those times when he had sent young girls and boys to a life of chains and probable death. Bensah always reminded me of the boabs that lived on the edge of the desert and who marked the gateway to other places. They are the last refuge for the traveller to have sustenance before the long trek north to Ancrid City and beyond the ranges. He was tall and mostly silent but knew how to give enough with his laughter and a few words like the boabs always gave just enough water to drink. When I woke after being bitten by a scorpion, and saw him and Nekoda, I remember my heart swelled with such love for them both I thought it would explode. I had never felt like that with Mata and Pata. And even now the memory of him being attacked by the bears is still painful like those deep cuts the bears claws would have made in his flesh. So love can be deep and painful and long lasting. It seems to remain constant but hidden as well by grief or hurt or anger. It was like Gildas the warrior who sits upon the throne of Tarentess; a mountain made for its creator Norbu. Gildas was filled with anger and yet remained loyal to me and my sister. It was the threat of the shadow Voloc that bonded us but even at the end when he solemnly swore to come if I called, I could see in his eyes a longing to love as well. It was deep within him but was bent from his will to dominate all within his vision. Tata had none of that inside him, so his heart shone brightly both in his words and actions. I have not tested Gildas yet if his loyalty remains or if that love remains in his heart. Ascendant the Custodian had the power to remove it and I believe it was the fear of that which made Gildas loyal to me and the others. So love can be hidden to the point it is lost and forgotten but there is always an awareness of it like the water needs to be in the skins of the boabs and the sand needs the sun to keep it dry. Its memory is embedded in us, and we don't know why or where it came from. I remember Tata showing me how to polish the river stones so he could trade them. He gave me some cloth made from leather hide of a cow. He showed me how to place the stone between strips and roll it up and down on a larger stone until it smoothed the edges and revealed the colours more brightly. I remember him trying not to laugh at my first attempts. The pebble kept slipping out and then my hands would cramp up and then my back. Persist and you will see it is worth it his soft voice would encourage. Eventually after three days I managed to polish one stone. I put it up to the sun and my heart was awash with the colours that lived inside the small pebble. They swam like river currents moving across my vision and heart. Instantly I understood the generosity of the earth beneath me and wonders the world could give and the lust for it as well. I smiled at Tata, and he patted my head. I remember him smiling at me and calling me the jeweller of the Mighty Choasa. He told me that he thought I would be ok now that I knew how to find the stones and make such pretty things other people would want to buy. He said that it would be a way for me to survive in a life otherwise not wanted. I remember thinking the river made those not me and it was the river I would always be grateful to. I think this was a moment of love between Tata and me, between the river and stones. An old love, ancient and untouchable between giver and taker. It keeps giving in silent untold ways until it bursts through like sunlight during the dry season. Then it is relentless and unstoppable, cracking skin, flesh dirt and bone, opening everything up into its little pieces. Eventually you have to break and give in. It's not hollow like grief can be but full constant and warm when it comes to settle in you. That's why it's hard to let go even for someone as mighty and angry as Gildas.

Kado and Sa loved each other even though Sa didn't know that. Kado is still grieving for Sa, and it has festered inside him. The gouged space made by his love for the assassin has been filled with his sorrow. His life has been fraught with bitterness and scorn, similar to mine and it is for that reason I think I called him first. While my life was marked at birth by hatred it never became so strong that it destroyed my will to live. I could always find the riverbed or the boab tree or be with Tessi and Tata and of course Nekoda. Kado only had Sa and she walked away. Kado exists near the edges of these memories and is tormented by them. But he came when I called and now, I fear I have abandoned him. The fierceness inside him is not his naturally, it was placed there by the ancient sentinels who dwelt deep in the unseen places of my world. Kado and I are kindred in our lives even though his was deemed more important than mine, yet neither of us fitted into the worlds in which we lived. But we understand we were made by the very things that scorned us and so a deep hole existed where either love could find a home or sorrow. I hope Kado lets go of his sorrow.

Ascendant had no love in her. How can a god know love? Ascendant came to the world after many eons of searching for her beloved. I could see inside her when she gave me the tear. I saw in her ancient memory hopes and desires of remaking the bonds between her and Descendant. They were frayed and almost forgotten on the edge of annihilation. I never sensed love there. It was full but empty. Her quest was not to rescue us. Her quest was for her alone. Norbu, Lido and their brethren of wind and fire each existed for the children of Arglethium, but the Ascendant and Descendant were unknown to us and we to them. Assumpta as she called herself could see and feel all that dwelt within our hearts. The kindness, the love but she also knew of the hatred and bitterness that thrived in our world. I knew she lied to me about Tessi being alive. She even tried to take away the hope that she would be alive, and we could be together again. That hope never fully left me, but I was confused about her after I realised it was her that could make or take away those things from me. Things which mean more in the end because everything like the stones and sand and even the Boab trees eventually die and go back into the ground. They have no memories or sense of time. But these newer gods as Norbu called them, they did, and they can remove those bonds which describe who I am and where I have been. The broken Custodian Baachelaus sits upon a throne lost. Voloc an unknown shadow has bonded the god to itself. Assumpta stole the memory of the gods purpose to hide the power she and her beloved have together. I see this power in the tear around my neck. Mighty Norbu, full of deep, ancient wisdom and whose blood pours out the dirt and clay of my lands was wise to hide the power of the last Custodians. In them sat the heart of stars and their strength and power both destroys and creates. In their strength lies the strength of the Clayborn to survive and remember. Voloc's lust was true, and I understand why the shadow chained Baachelaus to draw its beloved out and with it the knowledge of the prism. I hold this thing now and look straight into it and seek out its knowledge but still it eludes me what lies deep within it. But I also never see grief or love. There was no love only knowledge, power and fullness of spirit but never love. When Ascendant came to Arglethium she became weaker in her form and more like us and soon she learnt the taste of tears and the joy of love. I could see she did not understand the imperfect nature of our world and how it shaped its children. The windstorms scoured the lands and brought the plague of the shadow but also moved the sands to open up new places to live. Never did those winds take the great boabs and always water would flow somewhere to feed the children it made. I saw inside the mind of a god and know there is no heart only singular purpose and a sightless vision of control and stagnant existence. I sense the power I hold and, in my innocence, took the quest upon myself, knowing I am doomed to finish it, seek out the answers, and write them here. I know I will be asked at the end who am I. An answer I cannot give yet. I know that these Custodians were not made to conquer our world but to live in it and they have been wrenched away by something more powerful. And my world will die if I do not find them and restore their purpose. This power remains hidden to me but at the same time forges my path through manipulating my steps. But the memory inside those Custodians, which I will break open, will reveal the path to their gaolers. And I will return them to save my home and stop the poison of Voloc which devours it.

It is not love that makes me do this or see this clearly. Love would let this go. No it is my quest for justice and revenge. I will explain.

I still lived within the nest of my parent's tolerance and the closeness of my sister and Tata Bensah. I would wake each day, sure that the desert, river stones of the Choasa, and the breath of wind on my cheeks were always present. Their reliable, and familiar arms always around me. I know my life had sorrow and hardship and it would never leave me. I knew that Tessi would leave, and I would be forced to go away. I knew all this in my heart but still each new dawn would brighten these dark moments of my sleep as if none of this evil existed. I was ignorant and young, and I was happy. Mata's voice and bleating goats would call each of us awake. Like grubs in the stem of the river reeds, I lived in a cocoon and not until it was time would I fly to see what lay over the desert sands. But the shadows of gods and demons stirred and darkened the dawn light and silenced the smile of my mother and those goats. I stood looking across at the deadliness of a red desert and lost vision of a possible life, even if it was to be filled with sorrow. I have lost time to know what my life would have been like. What would have been lived, remembered, and born. I have no memory now of what would have been happy and what would have been sad. Even if I see Tessi again and her babies, I would be left bereft and grieving for what time had been stolen by this wound inflicted by the Custodians, the grief for the moments never lived. What is most sorrowful with this loss is the love that will never happen because of it. You see I cannot tell you what I was going to be because it was never allowed. What I become will be shaped by this quest. I also sense that this destiny will not teach me about love. You see I think that belongs to the clay of the world. Deep within my bones I believe that I will not be able to teach anymore about love as my life will be spent in the quest for answers and then justice to ensure my world remains. Without those empty selfish gods then I believe Arglethium will wither as my leg is withered. Still able to wake with each dawn just as I can take a step, but it will die just the same and lose its shape and its ripening because that has been stolen. It will become the dust of memories in the empty shells of gods formed for one purpose to see my world take shape and no other. To sustain it their hearts were filled with the power of stars which young flesh such as mine was never meant to hear or see. But you see the misshapen of Arglethium, the crooked and the keeper of sorrow does see and hear and wants to know. I know the shadow has ruptured their minds and consumed their memories and I must restore them. The made must restore the maker, so that in time each becomes the other.

And as I journey further into this quest, that love in the boab trees and river stones and the love of and for Tessie, Tata and Nekoda and roaring winds of the desert and abrading sands will remain. For they taught me first and accepted me as no other and now I must rely on ancient power and force to make my way and I will learn to be a god and destroyer and re-maker of things and stories. I will be great, and I will be terrible, and I will learn and know many things. I will walk within the hearts of the great stars, and I will know their secrets and blaze to battle the chaos of doom and fight to change my destiny just to save the world which made me first.

The Epimarin will teach the young one and for payment she will leave her memories in the Cadra Phomera for the ghosts to learn and code as lore of who Ange Tsaed is and what she loved and what she grieved for. And when the time comes, I will become the namer of the unknown and the see-er of things never meant to be seen and I will seek out the power which made all this begin and plunge my hand into its heart and tear it out and ask why did you leave all this to me? For I am no god, and I am no demon, and I am no wanderer or learner of knowledge. But I became a warrior and lost my heart, my life and have forgotten how to love. I will teach whoever I vanquish the sorrow of this as I remove my childish clothes, begin this battle, and see it to the end. I will return one day and look at the mighty Cadra Phomera of the Epimarin and ask who was this? And your brethren shall remind the Keeper who she was and where she came from.

I will not be like the lost gods and shadows who tore my world apart and the young girl thrust her into their paths. Paths of power and destruction, consuming lust and veiled mists of memory and purpose. The weak perpetually prey to their whims. No she will remember the taste of river water and the silence of the boabs in the red sands of twilight. The laugh of her sister and mother and the smile of Tata. She will remember the blood spilled on her behalf by Gildas, Sa Tuc and Kado, the brave Orynth, Queen Nene and her soldiers. She will bring colour to the dawn sky and the dusk moon as it rose over the black oceans of Voloc's doom. She will remember how to love and what it is like to feel the sadness of death and yet still smile at the sun. She will remember Eaudania and Jinx of Mir Chiridien and the sweet songs of the bard. I know that this was not real like the desert of home, but it was a time when my heart was true and still understood love. The denseness of living was still scratched into my flesh. I walk now in a world of ghosts and mists of shadow with ignorance and only the vague hope of finding the answers and these gods that are now gaoled by an unknown enemy. I have lost the firmness of earth beneath me and constancy of love. I will become the warrior and the battle master. I will remember the blood and rage upon the face of the Graan Warrior Gildas and the stealth precision of Sa-Tuc the assassin and the bravery of Kado Ko Drax. I will learn from my teachers, but I will lose the love taught by Tata until it is needed again.

When I was a child, I asked Mata to teach me to sew. I stitched cloth and leather for things to wear and I knew that when I grew too old to remain at my home then I could stitch and sew for other masters. I would polish my stones and sell them to buy milk, honey, and millet flour so I could eat. I would spend my days on the edge of the world watching the other girls become sun brides and raise their children the same. I could see the old cripple sitting on the edge of the road selling her stones for milk and honey. I saw all this as Mata showed me how to sew with my withered leg beneath my bent back. She taught me to make strong sturdy knots so that the seams would hold many days and in all weather. I remember thinking if I could see my fate back then and so could Mata then why did she not drown me at my birth like the other women in the village. I never asked and I don't think she would know. I know now both acts take courage and neither one is better than the other as death rules all and only love breaks death's grasp on our lives briefly. I sit here and etch these stories into this well of knowledge and I will remember when the time comes what it meant to be alive before the face of death with no power to defeat it. I will become the slayer of shadows. I will tear holes through the darkness until I have found the answers to my quest and when I have finished, I will stitch those wounds together again and I will ask them to beg me to let them live. I will be a conqueror, a healer, a destroyer, and sage. I will walk through death and make it vanish until death is dead. I will be the maker of worlds and the deadly blade plunged deep into the heart of stars and when I leave, I will remake their wounds with bonds as sturdy taught by Mata so I can live to be an old woman who sat on the edge of the world and watched how it moved.

I have no more to say on love. I shall miss it. I shall miss the grief that comes with it, but I will remember it when the time comes. It is buried deep within me and my flesh. It seems to always be there, and it never leaves even when it is forgotten. The most precious memory I can think of to help the Epimarin learn, is the way my heart would gladden whenever Tessi and I would play and talk before we went to sleep. I remember her braiding my hair and I would make stone bracelets for her. I remember one day we sat together. It was the day before she was to meet her betrothed. I asked if she was scared, and she answered are you. I smiled and said I wasn't. What will become of us she asked me. I said I have seen an old woman on a road. Beside her sits brightly coloured stones. She sells them to passers-by and travellers. Sometimes she is given food sometimes she is given coins. Beside her sits a dog and rolls of twine and scraps and bone needles made from hyena teeth. She has a small hut behind her where she lies when the wind is too strong, or the rains come. Those travellers only pity her and don't know of the scorn she had to bear in her time. But inside she remembers happiness and the love of a few who dared. Tessi braided my hair as we spoke. She said when I am old, and my children have forgotten me, and my husband is dead I will walk along the road and will look for the seller of river stones. Every day, I will come to sit beside her, and we shall talk of things we could never say to another, and we will remember each and every day. We both saw our futures and knew that nothing would change between us. This memory holds true, and I think best describes love. And I can see now as I etch these images how thick the ebbs of light are, how strong the bonds were and how much energy it would take to break them.

I have written everything I know Aes Vius now I ask you teach me the way to make flesh, to understand how a star is born and how to conquer death and we will say each other's debts are paid.

Ange stepped away and looked at the Cadra Phomera. There was no room left as the pulsing beads of codes bobbed in perfect time with the bulging fields of energy. A large pendulum swung between them deftly missing ordered codes. She stepped out of the Synarcadra and into the large antechamber where Nekoda had waited for her. She went to him and patted him. He stared at her. She felt different. Yol came towards her and bowed. The ghost looked around the Cadra vault and wondered at the new etches. It touched one of them and shimmered overwhelmed with sensation. It stumbled and then disintegrated.

"It will be strange to you Yol. I have not written it down I have left my essence of memory so you may understand what the children of clay are made of can never be fully understood."

"What is this that ebbs inside the vault?"

"I have ordered the love of the dirt for the sky and the sun for the day and moon for the night. The boab tree for the rain. The stones in the river and the desire in people's eye for their beauty. In between lies death amongst this continuance of our world. If the Cadra stalls, then my world dies, and then Ange Tsaed will be no more. I have left myself here for the Epimarin to learn and understand flesh and bone, blood, and tears. They together form love and grief and are intertwined. To separate them will destroy me."

"I think I understand. This is truly one of the greatest formulation an Epimarin could quest for" spoke Yol.

"It is not a construction it is real. It is not remade here for you to copy and make over again. It is original, it is real, and it cannot be recreated by any other. I have left me here so I may continue my quest. I may return one day and reclaim this for me. But if I am to learn the secrets of a star's heart and what lies within the prism then I cannot be the Clayborn desert dweller for I will be destroyed."

Nekoda barked as Aes Vius appeared behind them. The Primus scintillated a miasma of colours.

"Truly remarkable. So initiate are you ready to learn?" Aes asked Ange.

"I need to know how to vanquish the sun and remake the world. I need to be a god and make flesh and destroy it as well. I need to see in shadow and make it darker, even darker than the eyes which peer back from it and continue to watch me. Seeking me out and wanting to know what I know. I need to understand how it is that I can be here and never know of you before now. Why is it that this jewel holds so much power? Finally, when I have learned all this then I will search out the Custodians and condemn them to their destiny and then I will face my own."

Ange stood before Aes Vius and Nekoda. She looked at them. She felt emptied of herself and ready to learn the knowledge Aes could show her.

"Come" Aes Vius.

Instantly she was inside the helix of Aes Opa.

"So you want to become like these Custodians, understand them, and do what they can do. You want to wield the power of Caemeris."

"Yes, I do."

"Draw them. Pluck them from your memory and produce."

She formed a gust of wind and left it dancing in the air around her. She pulled dirt from a piece of her hair and made it into stone. She took a tear and made a pool of water. She flicked a flame to life from the diamond scar on her forehead. Finally she dropped blood on the great altar of learning and extracted the pain and joy of her living as an outcast and the happiness of being kept alive. She formed two shimmering pearls of light and placed them in the circle of the other elements. She began to listen to them. She took her tablet and drew their story. Fire, Wind, Earth, and Water were easy. Clear and transparent. Neatly ordered in circles, with pendulums swinging through them. Then she looked at the pearls of light and thought of Assumpta and Baachelaus. They were grief and love, desire, fulfillment, despair, bitterness, hatred, each entwined with one another and destined never to be apart. Now sundered threatening the children of her world. She forced them together and asked them to sing. She listened.

Yol stood in the Cadra and watched Ange's memories and saw how it suddenly stopped its momentum and fused together. An invisible field of power formed and pushed itself out over the Epimarin and toward the great tower of their Primus. The oceans of reeds and indigo distorted. It reached Aes Opa and stopped. Ange looked at it and smiled. She listened and watched. She took her finger and placed it inside the light. Suddenly she was plunged into darkness. She gasped. Aes Vius stepped toward her to grab her.

"No!" she screamed "Let me see!"

The silence pressed into her, menacing in its need to suffocate. She stared deep into the emptiness.

"Show me who you are?" she whispered. There was no answer. Outside the Cadra magnified more distorting the tower. Epimarin began to gather around the spire. Aes Vius stilled its brethren and pushed the vault of Ange's memories back.

"Brethren we watch at the edge of unknown we have never been able to tread. Heed what steps must be taken. We will soon know what exists after the light of Caemeris."

Ange could sense the presence. The watcher.

"The Keeper of the light of Caemeris comes for you. I shall find the Custodians and return them to their destiny."

Nothing responded. Ange waited for the darkness, the emptiness to re-emerge. Nothing came to her. She pulled away.

She stood before a congregation of Epimarin. Nekoda sat to the side. Aes Vius looked at her.

"What did you discover?" asked Aes.

"There is nothing. Nothing to draw or imagine" replied Ange.

"Can it be conquered?" asked Aes.

"Yes. It watches and waits. It knows that we are on the same path, and I am aware of it."

"Who are you?" asked Ange.

"I am Aes Vius. Seer of the Pthohedron of Gnoceris. A world destroyed, and Seer in exile."

"Is the shadow following something to do with you?" asked Ange.

"Yes, as far as it is of my kind. No in that I was aware of the power inside your prism but only to discover, not to take possession of."

"What does your brethren want and why doesn't it just take what it wants?" asked Ange.

"Because it cannot. It needs you to bring it to it and also to relinquish it" spoke Aes.

"But I will never do that when it is the only way I can save Arglethium" spoke Ange.

"If it kept you distracted long enough, you may have given up" replied Aes.

"Did you bring me here?" Ange asked suddenly realising what may have happened had she not woken from her dream in Mir Chiridien.

"Yes."

"Why?" Ange suddenly grew suspicious and fearful knowing she had given her essence to the Cadra.

"I did it at great risk to Opa Phomera Ange. I exposed where the exiled Seer lay hidden. I did it because I knew what my brethren wanted. So my choice like yours is, do I let this deception continue, and risk my brethren take control of the light of Caemeris, an ancient light, only thought to exist in the mists of legend, and faintest traces between light and dark energy. Or intervene, in the hope, that there was a chance to prevent another catastrophe. My brethren, myself included quested long and deep, in the ancient memory of light and dark, and built a world far greater than you have seen, including this realm of the Custodians. But in doing so, destroyed ourselves, because the knowledge and power was too great to harness. The universe is not designed to be ruled Ange, it is the ruler of all it brings to being, and nothing else. I saw this destruction and knew we had gone too far. And when they wanted to do it again, I left, preventing them from forming a complete Pthohedron. I have remained hidden until now. And if they imprison Aes Vius, and the Caemerin light, light which can harness the densest light and create a world like yours, their power will be unstoppable. They have no kind interest in you the Seers, Ange. They do not wish to learn, they wish to rule and dominate, they seek power rather than knowledge."

"So how do I defeat these Seers and find where the Custodians lie?" asked Ange.

"You will need to learn what the Seers know Ange. You will need to know what the Custodians know. You will be great and terrible, for you will be the namer of things unknown."

Ange stood on one side of the table and Aes Vius on the other. She looked across at the Seer and anger rose again, thinking of Bensah, and Mata and all the people who had died because of these Seers interfering for their own designs.

"So what is Voloc? And what destroyed the realm of the Custodians?"

"I do not know this Voloc, but it maybe that when my brethren, sensed this great source of power, and began to probe and search for ways of harnessing it. In doing so made what we call, the null energy, the shadows, and demons in your mythology, and with contacting the Custodians it became conscious as you are Ange."

"If I fail?" asked Ange.

"Then I will be unable to thwart the Seers, Arglethium will die or become shadow land and the Seers will find a way to harness Caemeris" replied Aes.

"Wont they destroy themselves again?" asked Ange.

"My fear is, Caemeris, may prevent it but in doing so all else will be consumed to maintain their Pthohedron. Caemeris holds the key to forming, creating. It overcame Oblyquixiton, the first star of darkness. The Seers' time has passed Ange. It is time for other things to exist, not ours. My brethren do not accept this. They have said if they can steal your memories, they will not pursue me. But it is a ruse, they do not understand themselves and they will bind me once more to our wells of knowledge once they have the power they seek."

Ange looked at Nekoda. The dog sneezed oblivious to the conversation of Ange and Aes. Once more the love for Nekoda swelled to help balance the weight of what she must do.

"I have given you my very essence, all I can understand about myself. Can you assure me it will be safe once this quest is over?"

"I will protect it until you return."

"If I fail, then it will not matter anyway, and at the very least, perhaps if the Seers have their victory, it may act as a reminder of all they destroyed in their quest for power."

"You are wise beyond your flesh age, Ange. And it is this wisdom which Caemeris brought to existence, and I feel will be the victory over my brethren, and the scourge they have wrought upon you."

"Then let us begin."

The Epimarin formed once more around Aes Opa to hear Aes Vius instruct on flesh forming.

"Epimarin you are dismissed" ordered Aes Vius. Instantly the ghosts disappeared.

"Why do you not let them understand how to form flesh?" asked Ange.

"I have made them for other purposes. Flesh forming is only important to you Ange. It is dense and requires great energy, but once its structure is learned, it seems not to teach. Its physicality impedes consciousness. I require the Epimarin to continue their searching, as I need the strength to keep Opa Phomera hidden, and also continue on my quest to understand memory and what we understand is true" replied Aes.

"Can I trust you, Aes Vius. It seems I have given you what you wanted the most, just like I was walking directly toward your brethren with their treasure for the taking?"

"What do you believe? I can speak and convince you but ultimately like all things, how true they and how reliable our understanding remains open to questioning. All I can say is, I have no interest in conquest, I have learned it and only desire knowledge, Ange."

"There is no choice, I know that. You have at the least made me aware of what has caused the destruction to my home in the first place" replied Ange.

"You have already formed the reeds of your lake from the same substance you were made from. Now what attribute about flesh is different to the reeds. Is there more to its texture?"

"It lasts longer and seems to change with years. It grows and then withers like reeds but the specs with in it, change depending on what touches it."

Ange drew on the tablet. Fine tendrils began to form. She could see the tiny cells grow before her. They stopped. She delicately picked one of the cells up and went to Nekoda. He stood as she neared the dog. She placed the cell on his head and stood back.

"Grow."

Nekoda whined wondering what was going on. Soon a small hair sprouted between his ears and then another. Ange started to laugh as his body began to regrow hairs. Nekoda barked and scratched as the fur poked through. Soon the dog's body was fully covered in brindle fur, shiny and soft.

Ange patted her friend.

"Your scars maybe hidden now dear friend but your bravery and love for Norbu to protect and defend the great lord of our lands is etched in your flesh and the eternal Cadra Phomera to remain for eternity. I will place your codes alongside my own so that our lives will remain together."

Nekoda barked, and then sat scratching and licking his hide.

Ange felt the fur and the surge of strength went through her at being able to make this happen. She felt the lips of desire kiss her. She remembered Gildas. She remembered the fear and reverence she had of him and also her will to learn from him. She understood she was becoming more kindred in spirit to the great warrior as she grew in knowledge. The urgency to use this knowledge and conquer mysteries surrounding everything which had happened to her, and her people filled her completely. She understood Gildas need to rule the world, the thirst to have everything within her grasp was becoming insatiable.

"Remaking flesh will come at a great cost" warned Aes sensing the swell of desire in Ange.

"I know which is why I have emptied myself into the Cadra. The Ange that stands here now is not the same one who entered. But I will remember who that girl was when the time comes. I know what I will remake."

Ange stood across the platform and looked at the edges of Phomeris. She stared into the nothingness. She took her blade that Gildas had given her and pricked her finger. She let the drop of blood pour from her finger. She froze it in mid-air before her and stared into the rich redness of it. She saw the particles inside and then broke the particles apart until their codes were visible. She took the codes and rearranged them. Aes Vius watched and scribed everything onto a tablet. But Ange saw it and stopped the ghost.

"This is the not how it is forged, Aes. Watch" spoke Ange.

A small pendulum swung in perfect time through a spinning wheel with holes cut into it to allow the pendulum to keep swinging.

Ange stopped the perfect apparatus in mid motion and changed the timing and spacing of the holes. She stood looking into the distance. Soon a figure began to walk toward her. Its shadow shimmered amongst the nothingness. She felt her heart quicken in pace as the shadow drew closer. Nekoda stood and began to bark in excitement. His tail wagging madly.

Bensah stood before them. Ange stood astonished to see Tata alive once more. He smiled at her and Nekoda.

"Do you know who we are Tata Bensah?"

"I sense we were once bonded. I cannot remember your name" replied ghost-Bensah.

"I am Ange Tsaed, and this is Nekoda. Your dog. You were friends with my father and traded with him" spoke Ange.

Nekoda ran toward Bensah. He patted the dog.

"Why am I here? I have memories of deserts and cities built of red stone."

"I wanted to bring you here because I wanted to say thank you Tata."

"For what?"

"For showing me the beauty of river stones. I also wanted to tell you I am strong now. I will continue the journey we were forced upon, and I will go with you and Tessi in my heart. I have protected those memories and they will never be destroyed whatever happens. If I return and decide to be the old woman on the edge of the village selling her stones, then she would die happy as she was able to tell the people who loved her how much she loved them as well."

Bensah smiled at her.

"Your words have a familiarity sister and perhaps this journey you will re-tell so I may remember."

Ange went toward Bensah and hugged him. He smiled and patted her on the head.

"Perhaps one day I will do that Tata" Ange replied.

They stood looking at each other. Then Ange raised her hand and suddenly Bensah disappeared. Nekoda barked sniffing the ground where his old friend had stood. He barked at Ange.

"Do you have sorrow at what you did? You created and destroyed someone who you hold dear?" asked Aes.

"No Aes. For I did this knowing that I could let go of him. But I needed to tell him how I felt for myself. He was taken so suddenly there had been no time before. Was it the real Bensah?"

"That is the deepest mystery Ange. Can what has existed before, be restored to what it was, and be the same as before. Do you believe it was the real Bensah?" asked Aes Vius.

"I believe it is as authentic as my memory allows. As the fur on Nekoda is real. What I sensed most was if Bensah were to remain here with me, our story together would not be changed in its essence, just the where, how, and when. But the why would remain as hidden as it ever does" replied Ange.

"You have grown. You understand what it is like to hold the destiny of things. This is the true power of knowledge to know how to use it. What is worthwhile about knowledge, is the need for it. And knowing when it is no longer required."

"I sense this is the strength I will need for the path ahead Aes."

"So Ange since you have mastered flesh forming what is it that you now wish to learn?"

"To make the heart of a star."

Aes Vius trembled slightly.

"This lies still in the unnamed lands."

"Then we will learn together. I did not give away all that is most precious to me not to understand how to wield the greatest power. My world lived or died on how much the sun gods decided to stay in the sky. Too long or too little either way we withered and died from famine or flooded crops."

Aes Vius bowed. The ghost shimmered slightly. Ange sensed fear in the great mage of knowledge and wondered what would make an Epimarin frightened.

"Bring forth the eye Caemeris" commanded Aes Vius.

Ange put the prism on the table.

She could see into its swirling colours and ancient memories but still the whereabouts of Ascendant and Baachelaus remained hidden.

Aes Vius and Ange looked in together. The ghost disappeared and Ange felt its presence in her mind.

They dove into the prism and chased light until its beginning. The power began to push back. Ange saw Norbu and Assumpta watching Baachelaus being chained and pulled into an ocean of darkness. They were engulfed in sorrow.

"Hush this pain. It belongs now in the Cadra Phomera. You hold no dominion here" spoke Ange.

Instantly the grief let go and they continued on. Ange could feel herself being pulled to pieces. Aes Vius hissed viciously at the pain of it.

"Hold strong Seer. We are not defeated yet. The mighty star wishes us to remain blind to its strength and beauty. Show us. Prove your strength and push us further into your well of power" commanded Ange.

Onwards they sped. Ange saw the creation of the Custodians and then came the cold. Nothing. They sped into emptiness. Something watched beyond and let them come. The cold bit deeply into Ange's flesh. Aes Vius began to crystallise. Soon a deep boom shook them shattering the Seer and rupturing Ange into small pieces. They reformed again. Then their flight stopped. They floated in the air.

"Tell us where we lie" called Ange.

"Take what you seek Clayborn. Remember to use it wisely."

Ange reached out and took a piece of shadow. It sat in her hand. She could mould it and shape it. It pierced her flesh entered into her and consumed her.

"Out of me. I control you" retorted Ange.

The shadow appeared on her hand.

Aes Vius watched from within her and saw what she held. It gasped in her mind.

"Take the heart of the star and tell me what it shows" Aes asked.

Instantly they were back at Aes Opa. Ange put the black matter onto the table. Aes Vius formed before her.

She took it and wrote on the tablet. It formed into perfectly balanced loops of tiny light specs with blackness in between. Over the small, dotted loops a bright corona of pure white spun, while at the edges were colours. Similar in intensity and variation as the ones Ange had seen in the prism. It moved in harmony with the dotted light. It never varied. But at the edge the dots inverted rather than expanded.

"Show me the heart of my sun."

The dots of light increased but were fractured. The corona of light changed its pace of movement. Still harmonious but different.

"Why are the specs of power ruptured slightly?" asked Ange.

"I do not know. Something has changed it" replied Aes.

"Show me Mir Chiridien" ordered Ange.

Instantly they changed. The corona became solid and slowed its journey around the loops. The light and dark evened out. Colours were fused into transparent crystal. Then the crystal split and formed replicas of itself over and over again in symmetrical patterns.

"It is like the reflections in the clear water" spoke Ange.

"Make Jinx" she commanded.

The bard formed. She could see inside its body the ruptured specs again. It lasted briefly as Ange looked into its eyes. Her heart sank. She realised that the bard was not real. The same shadow which had been following her was the same as she saw now inside the shell of Jinx. She saw Eaudania, and the image of the shrouded figure pointing when Eaudania had looked into the prism.

"It was just reflecting me, that's why I appeared in that image" asked Ange.

"Yes, Mir Chiridien, is one of the Sentinel threads sent by the Seers to understand the formed part of existence. A clumsy attempt to manipulate the prism power and replicate a world. That is why Eaudania cannot find her answers or stop the world collapsing. The knowledge and power is incomplete" replied Aes.

Ange plucked the ruptured specs of light and pulled them apart.

"So what leaves its mark of destruction on things I hold dear and in the heart of a sun?" she asked.

She looked and could not see.

"Where are the Custodians?"

The heart of the star reformed. The coronas grew larger and faster along the dotted specs. The specs remained perfect and untouched by the darkness. Suddenly it stopped as one of the light specs increased in size, it overtook the heart of the star pushing through into another space. It disappeared, but Ange could just make out an opening, where the large particle had travelled. A shape pulsed, angular in its outline, like a rock shaped into a brick.

"Here is a way to find where they lie Ange" spoke Aes.

"How will I find this place?"

The shape reformed and then along the length of the chamber a map of stars was formed briefly and then fused together again almost instantly.

Ange saw a great veiled web clove the map in two. Beyond it was barely visible but she saw the bright dot of energy beyond the barrier.

"Show me Voloc which has poisoned my world?" asked Ange.

The specs and corona dimmed. They inverted and the air around Ange and Aes distorted, pulling both of them deep inside the dark spot. Some of it ruptured off and the image of Belmaris showed its heart speared with the dark matter. It expanded ever further.

"What made Voloc?" asked Ange.

Suddenly everything disintegrated before them, and the prism sat hovering in its original form.

"Why wouldn't it show me what made Voloc?" asked Ange.

"Because the light of Caemeris did not make it" replied Aes. "Do you know the path where you need to tread to find this place of the Custodians?" asked Aes.

"I saw it."

"If you remake what has happened then you may never return to what has been your first life. Are you willing to let go of that for the sake of saving your world. One life is as valid as many regardless of how it is lived. Or is that not true?" asked Aes.

"I don't know" replied Ange. "Place an imprint of the prism in the Cadra Phomera. It will be safe. The paths are etched inside it for my way home. I have the way forward etched into my codes and my way back is held here safely for my return. I sit with the vision of all that is to come, and I wish I could hate all that has been and everyone who exists so that this vision will be so much easier to wrought. But instead my heart swells with the love I have for Nekoda, Tessie and even Gildas, Sa and Kado. Even the memories of my Mata and Bensah rise to speak to me and urge me to know that all this was worth it to know of their existence rather than not know. It is this mountain of love which holds the tide of despair and grief and urges me on to conquer all that dwells within my reach to bring forth the destiny of the Custodians and save Arglethium rather than watch the annihilation of all I have known."

Aes Vius bowed to Ange.

"You and I have witnessed the unnamed lands" spoke Aes.

"Yes, for I am great, and I am terrible. I am the namer of things unknown."

"Indeed a new Seer has been born" replied Aes.

"And when I call will you answer?"

"The Epimarin will answer."

"And will Aes Vius hold true to keep my memories safe?" asked Ange.

"Aes Vius, seeks knowledge not conquest" replied the Seer.

Simeris

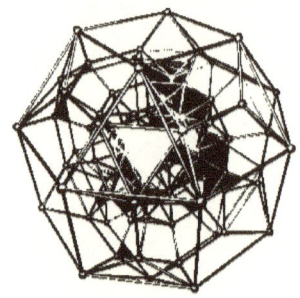

"In the wastelands of lonely souls, lies the janitor to clean the stones, free the bonds of broken bones, letting go of all their woes. But while these scrubbers shine the white and suck the marrow their eyes seek out tomorrow. Searching for new sand to pave the way for Oblyquixiton bringer of death to everything."

Calaton finished scraping the rocks clean. Storms were forming on the horizon. The storms had become more ferocious this cycle. Lasting many simes and leaving nothing for its kind to offer to the Guardians. It worried Calaton. It had never happened in its memory. It wondered what was changing. It gathered the sack with the remnants collected in this scavenging trip and walked back to its cave. Inside the cave was filled with what appeared to be decayed remains. Its offspring Unat was sifting through bones of dead creatures. It had them arranged in neat piles based on size, shape, and whiteness.

"There will be enough to take to the Chieftain. Their odour is still strong it will please them" spoke Unat.

"Good. We will wait until the storms have passed" replied Calaton.

"They are so frequent now elder" spoke Unat.

"Yes progeny. More deadly than before. But they reveal more places to scavenge, so it is good for us" spoke Calaton.

The howling winds arrived. The janitors hibernated in their cave waiting for it to pass. Their offerings were ready to be taken once the heavy clouds of darkness passed letting in the blue light again. The clouds draped the world in purple rain with the red ions of darkness mixed in, masking the storms lethality with a brilliant display of colour.

Ange stood on the mountainside and watched the storm descend. Aes Vius stood next to her.

"What do you see?" Aes asked.

"I see death here. There is softness, an easing of great power. The power ebbs with possibilities but is dead within itself. Something lies here, dormant but ready to be woken" replied Ange.

"I will leave you now. Your memories when this is finished will fill the Cadra Phomera."

Aes Vius disappeared leaving Ange alone. Nekoda sat beside her. It lapped at the purple rain and sneezed at the taste of it.

She began to walk into the valley following the storm. Its vortex circled in the centre. Ange could sense the power within it as it pulled on the air around her. Every particle within it shook in obedience to the electrical void within their codes. Ange began to memorise it as she followed its path. The ground was firm beneath her feet. It was made from a fine white dust. She picked up some grains and was instantly met with a vision of something looking across a wide open plain. Its eyes followed a moving form in the distance. Suddenly she was speeding toward the moving shape. The shape became more defined as her sight focused on it. It was a furry creature with eight legs. Similar to the spiders which lived under rocks in her village. The creature trundled along slowly over the stones oblivious to what was following it. Then she saw it glare with eight eyes as the creature with whose eyes she watched, snatched it into its mouth. The spider's fangs appeared, glistening and sharp, pierced one of the eyes. Everything stilled in the turmoil. She watched the spider thing dawdle off while the images slowly darkened. The creature whose sight she had watched with died. The white dust must have been its bones Ange realised.

A screech tore out into the skies. Its echoes touched Ange's ears. She winced and squatted down waiting to see what made the noise. Nekoda barked but the storm sucked the sound out of the air muting it. Ange scanned the vista to see if there was anything around them. Nothing.

"Will we go on?" she asked Nekoda, patting him on the head.

She continued along the vast plains of bone sand. The fine dust had been splattered with the purple rain. Her throat became scratchy the longer she walked. She let some of the rain pool in her hand and looked at its composition. On a tablet Aes Vius had given her, she wrote the small strokes to form the code of the rain. There was a bleb pulsating she did not recognise from her own flesh. It beamed strongly with the blue hues. It was empty of any other colour and the shadows between the energy particles did not exist. She ignored it and found what she needed. She made water. It was clear and pure. She pulled more from the wet drops in the sand until a pool had formed in mid-air. She drank in the drops. She gave some to Nekoda as well. She took her leather pouch and filled it as well. A tiny drop splashed onto the sand as she fastened the top of the leather cask. It sank into the bone dust.

Ange could feel the water replenishing her body. Her heart swelled with love for the knowledge the Epimarin had let her learn. The storm moved further into the heart of the great desert. Its surging forces remained static, and did not relent in their energy, tearing the sand and rocks to shreds. Ange remained outside the range of its power surges to avoid being swept up into it. She noticed that the rocks reformed their shape after the storm had passed by. Continuing across the empty dunes, aimless, with no landmarks or any signs of something living here to help guide her. She had seen from the map drawn by the prism on Opa Phomera that this world existed in a deep well of emptiness where nothing, not even small stars dwelt.

The water drop sank into the ground. It nestled amongst the dead of Simeris. As it disintegrated into the desert its scent floated down into the ancient heart of the star. It slowly drifted into the great halls buried beneath the heaving storms above. The scented breeze echoed in ancient silent caverns and eventually came to rest upon the face of a being. It stirred. Its huge corona lifting as the drop of water slid past its massive head.

"What zephyr is this that wakes the mighty Stonthrax? It has no name here. Its colours are not of Uchala or the death song. Its smell is not of death or venom."

Its claws scraped along the stone rest it sat upon. The bedrock shook as it stood. In a circle sat eight other warriors surrounding the throne of Stonthrax.

"Yonta come" called Stonthrax.

Stonthrax's massive talons gestured for something to come forward. A low growl emitted from a tunnel that led into the throne chamber. Claws scaping over stone echoed over the enclave of the creatures. The Yonta emerged through the opening. It had a snout of dog with eight eyes. Its legs were long and thin and its body slender. It was graceful when it moved. Its hide was covered in tiny spines, and it was completely white like the sands of the bone desert. It yawned and stretched from being woken from its slumber. Its gaping jaws revealed two diamond fangs. They glistened in the darkness. It let out a high-pitched squeal.

"Come to me. Loyal beast made from the sands of the dead and the fang milk of the Thrax. Yonta, mighty seeker, something has come to the sacred star of Simeris. Go seek it out and return to us with your eyes."

Yonta stretched its mouth wide open and out of it came a long thin mewling sound almost like song.

"Yes, sing the song of Yonta. It is many simes since we have heard the melody of Yonta" spoke Stonthrax.

The beast left swiftly and silently.

Ange had stopped behind a wall of rock. She could see what appeared to be openings to caves. She was hopeful of finding something or someone. She headed toward the cliff face. The storm had swung away from the cliff. It was strange there didn't seem to be any day or night just a perpetual warm twilight.

Suddenly a screech bounded around them. It felt like it had picked her up and thrown her against the rock wall. Nekoda winced in pain.

"Are you ok?" she patted Nekoda to check he was not hurt. He licked her as well.

"I think we need to make it to those caves. Something dwells inside the storm" she spoke.

Ange had braced her weak leg, so it was easier to run on the sand's surface. It held fast as she sprinted along the sand. The screech burst across the sky and thrust her forward. Tripping she tumbled along the sand. Nekoda stopped seeing her fall over. He raced back and protectively nudged her to get up. She stood and looked around. There was nothing. The miasma of the storm was far off into the distance now.

She started to run again. Just as she neared the entrance, the screeching sound exploded, throwing her into the darkness of the cave. Getting up, she dusted herself off, and walked further into the cave. It was silent and the walls were white. She saw piles of bones and dead carcasses. She also saw a group of sleeping figures. She stopped and grabbed Nekoda.

"Shh" she whispered to her friend, just as he was about to bark.

The sleeping creatures did not appear to have weapons. On the far side was a huge bowl with powder on it. There were some dregs of bones left around the outskirts. One of the bodies rolled over and opened its eyes. It blinked. It had seen her. She hesitated. There was no choice she would have to take a chance.

The youngling jumped up when it saw Ange and Nekoda. It made a slight squeak alerting the others.

The group stirred. Ange looked at them. They were long and spindly but not as tall as herself. Their eyes were tiny black dots and their mouths small holes. They were bald with fluffy ears.

"I am Ange Tsaed of Arglethium. A place far from here and born from the star we call the sun. I am on a quest seeking the Custodians of my home to return them to their destinies."

The group looked at her blankly.

"Do you understand me?"

Again no response. She stooped and with her finger drew on the ground two crosses and a line to signify her travel. She drew an eye and pointed to her own to indicate she was looking for something.

The first cross she pointed to herself and the second to the spectator before her.

"Understand?" she asked.

One of them came forward. Ange noticed it had the largest ears. It rubbed out her drawings and began to draw a figure in the sand. Ange watched and looked at the figures. She had seen them before. The Guardians who had taken Sa Tuc and herself.

She nodded to indicate she knew these figures.

She pointed to her cross and nodded again to indicate that they were on her world as well.

The creature shook its head vehemently. It stabbed it viciously into the cross.

Ange looked at them staring at her.

"I will need to be wary Nekoda. The Guardians after all gaoled Baachelaus and were commanded by Voloc once. Perhaps these ones here are their ancestors and remain enemies of the Custodians."

Pointing to herself she spoke "I am Ange. Are you able to speak?"

She touched her mouth and then gestured toward the creature.

The creature went towards her and touched her face. She did not flinch as she knew she could destroy them easily. She sensed that they were made of the same stuff as the desert, fragments of other dead things. It felt her mouth and vocal cords.

"I have an idea" Ange spoke.

She touched the scavenger as well on the throat and then pulled the prism out.

"Speak" she commanded and thought of the words in her mind.

"I speak" squeaked the creature.

"Who are you?" asked Ange.

"We make the desert. We scavenge the bones to make the desert" it replied.

"What is your name?"

"Calaton" it replied.

"I am seeking Custodians of my home to save my people."

"We do not know of this place. We live to make sand" replied Calaton.

"Are you servants to these creatures? I know them. They were called Guardians. Aracnine" spoke Ange.

Calaton shrunk back shaking its head. It wagged its finger at Ange warning her.

"They came with the demon who imprisoned the Custodians meant to protect us."

"We do not speak of the gate masters. They are sacred and must not be awoken. Their wrath is unforgiving and swift" Calaton warned.

"I think it is them who I must find. They will have the answers" replied Ange.

The walls of the cave began to rumble. Ange went to the entrance. The storm had turned around and was heading back towards the cliffs.

"That isn't a storm. What is it that makes that screaming sound?" Ange asked.

The scavengers trembled and ran toward the back of the cave. Their black eyes peered back toward Ange. Nekoda stood barking at the approaching wall of dust, rain, and purple cloud.

Suddenly the cloud formed into the shape of spider. It was huge. In its mouth was another creature squirming to be free. It was like a bird except its head was a serpent. The snake-bird opened its mouth and the screech erupted across the desert and into the cave. Ange collapsed from the pain.

The spider swallowed the snake-bird beast and disappeared back into the desert. As it passed the cave, eyes formed in the red and white dust. It peered at Ange and Nekoda and the frightened scavengers. It watched them. Ange did not move. She felt the power within the storm and wondered what lay with in it.

The eyes disappeared and the miasma of the storm continued past the entrance of the cave. On the sand lay a trail of bones littered along the path. The scavengers ran toward the entrance.

Calaton grabbed Ange and she could see happiness in its pinprick eyes.

"You have blessed us. Such a bounty and to remain alive after the vengeful one had passed. You are blessing to the Ghoc."

"What is it?" Ange asked.

"We do not know. We wait until it has passed and then if we find anything to make into the sacred sand of Simeris we take it" replied Calaton.

Ange nodded. The sand beast's eyes had looked directly at them.

"Has the creature in the storm seen you before?" asked Ange.

"Yes."

"And what happened?"

'It ate our younglings and left nothing to scavenge or give to the sacred desert" replied Calaton.

Ange wondered what was going on. It probably sensed the prism around her neck. The cyclone of sand and rain contained a lot of power. She could feel it inside her and was drawn to it.

"You are our protector. Guardian of the desert. Wanderer of the places beyond. Flesh upon bone not yet given to the sacred sands of Simeris" Calaton spoke with awe in its voice.

The family of Ghoc all looked up to Ange. While it was only Calaton who spoke she could see they understood its words.

"I am not sure why we were spared the wrath of these sand spiders, but I would like to seek them out" spoke Ange.

"We are bound to help you now. But first we will gather the gifts left by the desert. Then we will seek out our Elders. They may have more answers for you" spoke Calaton.

"I understand. I think you may know more than you are telling me. But we will gather the bones as you say" replied Ange.

They climbed down the cliff. Ange directed Nekoda to grab a large bone that looked like a claw and take it up to the cave. He picked it up in its mouth and began to chew on it.

"No. Up there" admonished Ange.

Nekoda whined not wanting to.

"Yes, you must be hungry. I am as well."

She pulled a hair out. She began to form a fish in her hand.

"Here Nekoda."

She kept the fleshy parts of the belly for herself and threw the rest to Nekoda.

I eat myself, she thought. The profoundness of this played on her mind. For some reason, the memories of Eaudania pouring her urns out over Mir Chiridien bloomed in minute detail. She wondered how much her waters would wash away the death that lay here and bring life to the forsaken wastelands. She realised she could bring life now as well, just like water could.

She saw Nekoda watching her.

"You understand, don't you?"

The dog barked. She threw what she couldn't eat to him. He gulped it down in one chomp. She picked up what must have been a head shaped like a flower. She wondered what sort of creature this would have been.

She heard Ghoc's voice "Death happens to all things not just the flesh formed on Simeris."

Ange looked at the bone, perhaps it is the skeleton of a flower she thought. She returned to the cave.

Already there were some of the Ghoc at a wheel, grinding the bones to a fine dust.

An eerie silence blanketed the world. Only hers and Nekoda's voices could be heard. Even the elder Ghoc's voice sounded hollow. The crunch and steady rhythm of the wheel was soothing.

Ange fed the skull and claw to the wheel and watched as they were pulverised under the heavy rock as it rolled over it.

"What are these creatures?"

"We have no name for them. Only those we serve would know. We are here to serve the desert" replied Calaton.

Soon the sand from the bones filled dozens of chiselled stone bowls. The Ghoc carried one on each shoulder. Ange took the leather straps around her waist and tied a bowl to either side of Nekoda and then picked up two bowls and balanced them on a long leg bone over her shoulder. This was how Mata used to carry water from the well. They followed the procession of scavengers into the valley until they reached the edge of the sand. Before them lay a massive expanse of rocks which looked carved. The Ghoc poured the sand out and began to walk back to the caves.

"What is this place? These look like old buildings" asked Ange.

Calaton did not hear her question as it was too far away. She walked over the ruins. She bent down and swept her hand over them. The pulses of energy were very faint, almost nothing. The stone was red not white.

The carved-out squares reached for leagues. To cover them with sand would take many lifetimes Ange thought.

She went back to the caves. She passed another procession of the scavengers taking the ground bones to the edge of the desert.

She filled Nekoda's bowls again. He trotted off as she collected her own.

"Have you made all this desert?" Ange asked.

"Yes, we have" replied Calaton.

"Do you know what you are burying? Are these ruins everywhere beneath the desert?"

"We only do our duty."

Ange stopped asking realising it was futile. The creature would not tell her even it knew the answers.

Soon all the bone sand had been dumped in its new place. Ange sat with Nekoda and drank some water. The Ghoc looked in amazement as she made water from her cask.

"You must be born of the Guardian" asked Calaton.

"No. I was taught this by others."

She saw three of the Ghoc were kneeling and bowing as if they were worshipping her. She got up and pulled them up.

"Tell them to stop. I am no god. I am different that is all. I have learned many things on my quest. I am ordinary in my homelands. I live the same life of servitude as the Ghoc. We are equals."

Calaton gestured for the Ghoc to rise.

"It would not be right to have two Rulers visitor. The Guardians demand our loyalty" spoke Calaton.

Ange nodded as she gulped water. Nekoda lapped some from one of the stone bowls.

"So how do I find someone who can help me on my quest?" asked Ange.

"We have been blessed. We will claim scavenger payments for these gifts and lead you to the Chieftains."

"Will it cause trouble for you and your family?" asked Ange.

"No. I would have not offered. It is our right. We have been spared wrath and given bounty and treasure. You are welcome here" replied Calaton.

"Why is there no night or day here?" asked Ange.

"We do not understand this" replied Calaton.

"How do you know when time begins and ends here?" continued Ange.

"We live by the simes, and sands of the desert" replied Calaton.

"What are simes?"

"The moments when we sleep and are awake. When the storms come and leave. When we are busy with the bone work and when we are at rest."

Ange understood a bit.

"Come we will begin our walk" spoke Calaton.

The dozen scavengers walked in pairs behind Calaton, Ange and Nekoda.

"Are there many of the Ghoc?" asked Ange.

"Yes, but we live apart and the desert is large."

"Where do you come from?" asked Ange.

"Where do you come from?" replied Calaton.

Ange smiled at Calaton's answer.

"How long until…" she stopped herself asking. The answer would be one sime. The time they are awake.

Over the horizon of white sand in the distance was a shadow. Its shimmering was muted by dust. It reminded Ange of the desert of her home. She missed the colours that sprang to life over the red dust with dawn and sunset. The sparkle of the river and dark sturdiness of the boab trees. Here all the life had been bleached out of the world. She wondered why when it was a star. She had briefly seen the heart of their own sun and it blazed with fury, heat, and burning gold. This was a cold place; still, lifeless and entombed in a moment.

"We go there" spoke Calaton.

The Ghoc pointed to rows of holes in a mountainside. It was a larger settlement than the place they had come from. She could see steady trails of scavengers walking in and out.

"I will take you and ask for simes payment. My younglings will remain here. It is not safe to mingle. We forget where we come from and lose our place in the desert. It means that the scavenging work is not finished. We would risk the wrath of the Rulers" explained Calaton.

"So you are placed where the desert needs to be completed?" asked Ange.

"Yes."

Ange and Nekoda followed Calaton into the cave settlement. The other Ghoc remained standing in line. Their tiny black eyes watching. To Ange they looked like spiderlings watching the mother leave the web.

The caves were more ordered here like a small city. As Ange and Calaton approached, the lines of Ghoc stopped and watched them. They did not seem menacing to Ange more curious.

"We will find the oldest scavenger inside" spoke Calaton.

The tunnel was completely dark. Along the walls were bones and carcasses piled high. There was a group of five Ghoc busily grinding the bones into the sand.

"Why do they have so much here?"

"Every Ghoc gives something. They have to keep sand thick here."

"Why?"

Calaton didn't answer. Ange guessed the Ghoc protected something underneath.

At the end of the tunnel there was a chamber full of Ghoc. This time though they were carving bones instead of grinding them down. In the centre of the silence and white dust sat the Chief Ghoc. Calaton went over to it and bowed. Taking some bones from a pouch in its belly it handed them to another Ghoc sitting down. Calaton gestured for Ange to come near.

They sat. Ange swigged some water.

"I want to know what the creature is in the desert storm?" she asked.

"It is not allowed for the Ghoc to know this" replied Calaton.

"Where can I find a way to learn of it?" Ange persisted.

Calaton did not answer. Ange assumed it was communicating with the Chief. She looked around the cavern and realised that all the members of the clan were looking at her. Their tiny eyes in such numbers began to worry her. Was there something else watching from behind? Nekoda was leaning against her. He was sniffing a skull. She wondered where the bones came from as there didn't seem to be anything else alive beside the Ghoc and the creature in the storm.

"It is not decided whether an answer to this question can be granted. It will need to be pondered. You are to wait here until a decision is made" Calaton spoke.

"I cannot remain too long. I will seek out the answers with or without permission."

"This is unwise."

"Why?"

"The Ghoc cannot have two Rulers" replied Calaton.

"I am not your Ruler. I am here on a quest. It was revealed to me that I should come to Simeris, as a pathway could be found from this place" spoke Ange.

"I do not know of these things. Wait be patient. You will have your answers for what you seek. I must leave now, or I will lose my younglings. You are safe here" spoke Calaton.

Calaton left. Ange watched the small creature walk into the darkness of the tunnel. The Ghoc within the cave continued to stare at her. She wondered if she should give them the power of speech. They did not seem to be surprised by Calaton being able to speak.

"Are you able to hear me?" she called in the eerie silence. Their eyes continued to stare at her. She looked around her. Nekoda whined wondering what was happening.

She turned to the Chief sitting in the middle. She wondered if she should give it speech. Its eyes were larger and body unlike the others in the room. It was more like her in its shape.

"It would be unwise to treat the eldest of the eldest as you have my youngling. I wish to have no voice. With no voice we cannot insult our Rulers."

The words of the Chief were crystal clear in her head.

"I apologise for what I did. I saw no other way" replied Ange.

"There are always other ways" spoke Ange.

"How can you speak to me, and we understand each other?" asked Ange.

"The same way you made Ghoc speak. We know how to change things" replied the Chief.

"I want to seek out the power within the storm. I believe it holds answers" continued Ange.

"As you have been told, we will need to think if this is wise. You will need to be patient" answered the Chief.

"I will seek out the storm myself if I need to and find the creature which dwells inside it."

"It would be unwise visitor. We will give an answer. If you are here to receive it, then we will tell you" replied the Chief.

"Tell me something of yourselves and Simeris" asked Ange.

"Such as."

"What are the Ghoc?"

"We are the desert makers. We make the sand from bone. This you know" replied the Chief.

"Who made you and how do you live here? There is no water and nothing to eat" spoke Ange.

"We live on dust alone. We are not alive like you. We have already died. We become the dust again" answered the Chief.

"But where have all the bones come from. There is nothing alive."

"You have only witnessed the edges of the desert. The heart is the life sand of our world. Besides why do you think all things which exist must be born and die in the one place" replied the Chieftain.

"Is this why the Ghoc are here? To protect the heart of Simeris" probed Ange.

"You see much visitor" answered the Chief.

"Protect it from what?" asked Ange.

"This is not for you to know until it is wise for it to be revealed" replied the Chief.

"Tell me how you are able to speak and yet the others cannot" continued Ange.

"Eons of simes. All of it a questing web. I have remembered and learnt."

"You do not give this knowledge to the others?" asked Ange.

"We have only one Ruler."

"I am tired of this. I must find the heart of this world. I sense my answers will be there."

"Be patient" ordered the Chieftain.

Ange got up and walked around the chamber. She was looking for another entrance. There was none. The Ghoc remained still.

"I am stopping you from working. Won't your masters be angry?" she probed.

There was no answer.

"Please begin your bone grinding again. I will wait" spoke Ange.

Ange sat down against the wall to think again. She felt that the storm would welcome her. She knew it sensed power. It could bring life to dead matter.

The dust and noise of the stone-wheels crushing bone filled the chamber. It was soft, muted and didn't seem gruesome. All the flesh had gone. All the life blood removed. The only reminders that life existed now pulverised into a blanket to cover the world and remove the final memories of what existed before. Why did they want the world to be covered over? What were these Rulers of the Ghoc hiding? She would wait a little while more and then she would seek out the storm again or go back to the ruins she had seen with Calaton. She took another hair and formed more water. Nekoda drank as she did. Her stomach rumbled but she did not feel hungry. The water was enough.

The snout of the Yonta moved over the body of Calaton. It had the stench of the visitor on it. The other Ghoc watched. No reaction and no sense of sorrow at the second death of their eldest. It would mean the next eldest would take its place.

The Yonta screamed into the air. Its echoes rippled through the swirling dust. Seek was gouged into its mind from the Stonthrax. Seek. It left the sand and walked over the ruins. Its claws scratching on the old carved rocks. The scent disappeared. It turned back to the sand and continued on. The Ghoc took Calaton and placed its body on the great grinding pestle. It fractured into a thousand pieces until the final pile of sand was scraped into a bowl. The next eldest poured the dust over the edge of the desert and proceeded back to the cave. Silence whipped through the air as death was buried again and again. Simeris was the star which had conquered death and had extracted the fear from the remains and turned it into sand in the wind. Its heart hidden deep within the great skeleton desert.

Ange woke. She had fallen asleep against the wall. An echo of a scream vanished as she opened her eyes. She wondered what she had dreamt about. Nekoda was next to her asleep as well. The Ghoc had left and only the Chief remained in the chamber.

"Are they replenishing the desert?" she asked.

"Yes."

"Well I have waited. Will you give me the answers I seek?"

"The Yonta comes" replied the Chief.

"What do you mean?"

The Chief stood and began to walk toward the entrance. Ange followed.

"I can give you no answers. The Rulers will not allow it" spoke the Chief.

The Chief walked out into the desert and began to crumble.

"Wait Chieftain, what is the Yonta?"

But there was no answer as the Ghoc Chief disintegrated into the wind.

The emptiness of the cave struck her suddenly. There were no Ghocs anywhere. Not even any trace of their footsteps in the dust.

"We should leave Nekoda. We will follow the wind as I think it chases the storm."

She saw a pathway up to the top of the cliffs. She headed towards it. The wind was only mild gusts, but it was stronger than when they arrived here. There was a thickness to it she hadn't felt before. On reaching the top to no surprise there was more of the white desert. It was flat, no dunes at all. The flatness was unnatural. She knelt down and scooped the sand away. After an arm's length she saw stone like the ruins when she was with Calaton.

Looking around her she waited for the wind to blow again. She took a sash which tied her cask to her waist. A gust lifted the sash, and she watched the direction it blew. She ran in the same direction to keep up with the wind. She looked deeply inside the air and searched for the currents that drove the wind on its course. She could see tiny creatures inside it. It was not wind at all but transparent insects in a swarm. She focussed harder and looked at one. It was made of bones.

"It should be called the Bone Star" she called to Nekoda who was enjoying the race across the sands. He barked back.

Soon in the distance she found what she was looking for. The miasma of white and purple cloud sweeping across the horizon. She saw just above the meniscus of sand, sitting in the sky eight pale blue discs. She realised they were moons. They hung at different heights. Some were large and looked close to the star and others were tiny dots.

She raced ahead to reach the storm. A screech erupted across the air. It was the same sound she had dreamed about. She turned to see where it came from but there was nothing there.

"Quickly Nekoda. I think that may be the Yonta."

Soon the cyclonic force of the storm met them. She felt the power surge in the air the nearer she came. They ran in the swarm of bone-flies and grains of sand. She pushed into it. The edge of it pushed her back almost making her fall over. Waiting she saw what she wanted to do. A wave of sand lifted up as the wind vortex tore over it. She put a strap around Nekoda's neck.

"Hold tight and wait" she called to Nekoda.

Nekoda trembled with excitement and fear. Its tongue was dry from panting and the abrading air.

A low rumble came toward them and from behind a high-pitched scream. She looked back and saw the vague outline of a large beast. It was tall and its fangs glistened in the pallid light. Its huge jaws were fully extended. The squeal almost sounded like a song. Ange turned back towards the storm. She braced herself and leapt as the wave of sand was about to engulf them. She was caught in its slip stream. She held

Nekoda tightly as she looked for the creature inside. It was impossible to open her eyes. She looked with her mind.

"Where are you? Are you all around me? I know you are here. I seek the ruler of the sand."

There was no answer. Ange dug deep within the power of the prism to pull all the threads of the living and dead things into her consciousness to find what drove the storm to such a frenzy.

"You know what I seek."

The eyes appeared around her. Then a body. It was long and slender, but its head was round. It floated before Ange. Its claws extended. It was made from bone as well.

"Does nothing live here?" asked Ange.

It stared at Ange. Its talon touched her. Her heart was beating so fast she thought it would burst.

"Who is thee that comes to my realm?" the voice wrapped around her like a vice.

"I am the Custodian of the tear of Ascendant formed from the memory of Caemeris."

Suddenly the storm calmed. The creature swayed in front of Ange; its huge claws firmly latched around her neck.

"How do you know this name, most ancient, most lost. Most forgotten one" the voice spoke, with a deep resonance that Ange felt it vibrating through her.

"I have learned of it as part of my journey. I need to restore the destiny of the Custodians, to save the world I come from. I can feel the power in this storm, and that it may help me find a path to where the Custodians lie."

"Rhac does not exist for this" replied the beast.

The talon began to squeeze. Nekoda yelped.

Ange took a deep breath and went into her mind. She sped into the mind of the creature Rhac. The pain engulfed her, and she felt a pang of fear for the first time since arriving in Simeris.

"I shall know the power of Rhac, desert storm and bone grinder" Ange called.

Rhac roared at the invasion of Ange into itself. It let go of Ange and exploded out into the dust and cloud. The cyclone returned stronger than before and resumed its furious scouring over the desert. Ange plunged into the depths of the creature Rhac.

"Show yourself so I may score your code into the Cadra Phomera for eternity."

She began to dig out the shadow and veils blinding her from seeing what lay at the heart of its strength. Rhac screeched at the pain and dug itself into Ange. They were plunged into fear and agonising pain. They tumbled through eternity and into deeper ancient memories. But none of it was made clear. Then Rhac touched the prism, and everything stopped. It let go of Ange and let her fall into itself. Nekoda was barking wondering what was going on. She stopped falling and scraped away the shades. The Rhac was an empty shell.

"Who gives you power Rhac?" called Ange.

"I am the last breath of Simeris before the great death. I wash the sands away to keep the memories alive. We were flesh once until the sixteen stole it away. I am the last of the Simeran Oracles, protector of the Thrax."

"What caused the great death?"

"The sundering of the Guardians. Their knowledge was lost and broke the circle of warriors so that the venom seeped deep and killed the heart of Simeris."

"How long ago? Nothing lives here."

"Too long. Too long. Yet the memory in your stone brings them again" replied Rhac.

"Who brings who?" asked Ange.

"Them. I am dying. You have brought my second death" replied Rhac.

"No I will bring you back. Show me what you are."

Ange looked into the Simeran spirit and saw its form and memories. It was strong and fierce. The world was full of life, cities, and wondrous creatures. There was no desert but oceans of purple with all the moons brightly studding the red skies. Mountains were covered in yellow trees and the rock was blue. The Oracles rose high above the citadels and surveyed the lands. They watched and moved in unison with the moons and stones. They were strong and faithful in their purpose. They were connected to something else. It would not reveal itself, but it required them to watch and protect.

"Show me your Rulers" ordered Ange.

"We have no Rulers. Only those we watch and protect. We kept the moons aligned and made sure they rose and fell within simes of each other so we would always exist."

"I know another, lives within you. Why does it hide itself?"

There was no answer from Rhac. Ange sensed it was beginning to die.

"If you die Rhac what happens to the desert?"

"It suffocates Simeris. The moons will fade and be lost to eternity. The star will die and become the vacant wind and be lost like the memories of Caemeris" answered Rhac.

"Show me yourself in your first form."

An image appeared with Rhac standing on the edge of an ocean. It stood almost as high as a cliff with a spear in its talons. Its head was round. Large fangs hung from its jaws. The muscled sinews in its arms rippled with every minute movement. Its strength was formidable.

"What is needed to be an Oracle, Rhac?" asked Ange.

"The Oracles would rise with the moons, and they would seek blood. Other creatures from the great void of Oblyquixiton would find their way here and seek to destroy the Simeris peace. Many times I have had to quell the Guardians and invaders, so much fury would rage through their hides. The Yonta unleashed would seek out its prey and Rhac would devour it before it decimated those who dwelt here. Simeris is where disintegration and levelling of power of the created, but never conqueror of what dwelt here and never denied things their existence."

Ange heard the name Oblyquixiton. She wondered what secrets could be revealed here about the ancient shadows. She touched the image of Rhac and taking a drop of venom from its fang she etched the code of its being.

The storm around it had begun to dissipate as Rhac slowly dissolved.

"Rhac I will bring you back to your true strength, but I ask one thing in return."

"Rhac does not barter."

"You will show me the path forward and reveal the mysteries of Simeris."

The song of the Yonta broke through the silence.

"Will you show me the path to the Custodians?" asked Ange.

"Rhac does not barter. You wield the eye of Caemeris and its memories" replied Rhac.

The vibrations rippled through the air and sand, as the Yonta called across the oceans of sand looking for its prey.

"Quickly now. The destruction of Simeris is at hand. The Yonta will run freely, and the bone sand will shroud the memories and glory of the world protected by the Oracles" spoke Rhac.

"I will restore you, but if I can make you, I can destroy you as well. I sense you will have knowledge I can use" spoke Ange.

"Caemeris only makes life to bring death, not annihilation, which is the realm of Oblyquixiton" replied Rhac.

Suddenly Ange could see the codes reshaping into a form. She saw the arms and sinews grow and then the body and talons. Finally the eyes and head. The fangs were wet with venom. Rhac opened its jaws and tested its talons.

Rhac snatched Ange.

"Who are you to remake the Rhac? How have you come with the potency of the lost Caemerin light?" Rhac hissed at Ange, as its abysmal eyes peered into hers.

"It is mine, bestowed upon me by the Custodians" replied Ange.

The song of the Yonta bloomed across the sky. Rhac turned and saw the beast of the Guardians. Its fangs glistened.

"You are unleashed pet of the Thrax" spoke Rhac.

The Yonta snarled. It strode back and forth sizing up Ange and the Oracle.

Ange pulled herself away and turned to look at the beast which had pursued them.

"So Oracle tell me of this creature" she asked.

"It sings the songs of battle and feasts upon the last of the breath of fear as the flesh dies. It is indestructible. The Yonta understands the tears of the Guardians and their rage. It inflicts their pain for it became leashed by the power of the Thrax and its song is used to destroy the Oracles. The Oracles who let the shadows ebb and flow between the dark and light, not annihilation."

"Am I strong enough to defeat it?" asked Ange. She noticed Nekoda was cowering near her. Not even Voloc had that effect on him.

"What do you sense Nekoda? What makes you frightened?" she asked.

The Yonta stopped striding and opened its mouth fully. The song which rang out was hypnotising and began to make Ange feel sleepy.

"Is that how it speaks to its masters?" she asked Rhac.

Rhac was flushing red and purple. Its fangs poured with venom. Its muscles and tendons were tensed to the point of bursting from its hide. It launched itself toward the Yonta. The snarling and growling was vicious. Ange pulled Nekoda behind her and watched. No blood spouted and no flesh was torn but the ferocity of the blows inflicted by each of the Simeran creatures pulsed through her.

Rhac and the Yonta pulled away and circled each other. Ange watched them. Rhac was strong but the other while it was only bone and decayed hide Ange could sense the strength within it. What made you and who commands you she wondered.

She walked toward the melee of battle between the two leviathans. She felt the air be cut as the Yonta swiped at Rhac. Venom sprayed around her. She felt a drop land on her cheek. She felt it burning into her skin. She reached forward and grabbed onto the neck of the Yonta.

"Hold steady" she told herself as the fear rose in her chest. She could feel deep intractable strength within the creature. It released its grip on Rhac's throat as Ange's lasso wrapped around its neck. It stared at Ange. She could see a presence behind the black impenetrable eyes. It reared up at Ange. Opening its jaws it sang out into the air.

Rhac circled waiting to pounce. As the Yonta came down it shot towards Ange. She stumbled but managed to keep hold of the leather strap. The beasts face sat a fingers width away from hers. The breath spread over her. There was no smell, and it was not warm. The creature was dead and being kept alive like everything else on the star.

It closed its mouth and its fangs retracted as it stared into Ange's eyes.

"Show me who is the Yonta" she whispered.

A tiny sound began to grow. It was soft like the cooing of a child. Then it grew into a lilting melody. Ange listened to it trying to understand its codes. She realised it was singing. The deeper notes had a darkness around them and drifted down into the bone sand. The higher ones floated to the moons beyond. The two forces were bonded together and helped form the Yonta. Suddenly the notes darkened, and she could feel herself being drawn into the eyes of the Yonta.

She stepped back and pulled the leash so it would sit on the sand. But it reared up and screeched. Its claws cut through the air and collected Ange on her arm and torso. She flew across the desert and landed heavily.

Nekoda snarled but kept its distance.

Ange stood. The leash swung around the neck of the Yonta. She ran towards it again. Nekoda barked loudly trying to warn Ange. She did not listen. She snatched the leash and pulled out her dagger threatening to pluck out an eye.

"If I cut out your eye, will I have a better chance of understanding you?"

The Yonta pulled back fiercely. Suddenly it grew larger. It was three times the size of the Oracle.

Ange fell to the sand. It stomped to crush her, but she managed to dart out of the way.

Rhac walked over to her "We cannot defeat it this simes."

The Oracle swept Ange up and began to race across the desert. Nekoda followed. The Yonta gave chase.

"Where can we hide?" Ange asked.

"In the place of my ancestors" replied Rhac.

Over the thousands of leagues of sand the Yonta chased the Oracle until on the horizon stood eight towers.

"Highest" called the Oracle. One of the towers opened and it sped inside.

The Yonta yelped as if it had been cut off physically when the tower closed around them.

"Where are we?"

"The realm of the Oracle Moons. Here the Thrax are blind" replied Rhac.

"Why did the Yonta yelp with pain?"

"All are connected on Simeris. So if one is lost then it is felt within all who dwell here."

Rhac went to a reredos inside a wall. Inside the enclosure shimmered with purple and blue pulses of light, similar to the colours of the moons. Ange touched the edges and it trembled. Suddenly she was pulled out into the sky and was looking upon Simeris. She saw it in its entirety and drew a breath at the vista before her. Half the star was covered in sand, but the other half was a massive tapestry of buildings and remains of a city. In the cities were piles of bones and carcasses waiting to be scavenged by the Ghoc. On the far side in half shadow was a huge gate. It was in ruins and jagged rocks sat around the edge of it extending out for a league either side of it. It reminded her of Baachelaus' face; the face of destruction and war now in decay bereft of any hope of restoration. Further into shadow the landscape seemed to end, like it had been chewed away.

The star sat on its own in the emptiness of the darkness. The eight moons were aligned as they were from below. She removed her hand from the wall and instantly she was back in the tower chamber.

She saw Rhac was entering a tunnel between the towers. She followed.

"I have seen a gate to what lies beneath the sand and stone" spoke Ange.

"You are unwise to go there. You are not as powerful as you think" replied Rhac.

"Where are we going?"

"To wake the other. You shall restore the Oracle to their sentinel seats. We will remain in watch for the rebirth of our world" replied Rhac.

"Why did it die? I will not restore anything until I have my answers."

"Rhac will no longer need it. The Oracles have their power restored through Caemeris."

Ange stopped.

"Enough!" she pulled the codes together and disintegrated the beast. It turned as it began to disappear. It fought her and she sensed that it could defeat her. She drew deeply upon the prism and was able to control the power that surged through the ancient form.

"Don't underestimate what gift I have been given. Now tell me why Simeris died?"

"I have already told you. Once one thing is cut off then it is felt amongst all other Simeran. Even the slightest bone fly is connected. Its death means something. So it was when another wanderer took something from us that began our destruction."

"Who is this wanderer?" asked Ange.

"We do not know" replied Rhac.

Ange knew the Rhac was not lying. There was nothing she could not see within its ancient memory. It had come into existence after the rift and had only seen the world briefly before the great death began.

They entered into a chamber with the same layout as the one before. There was another reredos. Inside the wall, a faint outline of a figure was carved inside it. It resembled Rhac.

The Oracle placed its talons into the centre of the carving. The wall of purple ether glowed with deep red and coronas of yellow and blue. Unac awoke. Ange could feel the pull of power from the stirring of the creature.

"I have awakened you. Can you lead me to the answers I am seeking?" Ange asked the creature.

Unac roared at Ange. The pain of being in decay seared through its body.

"Unac remade from Rhac, reborn from the Keeper of Caemeris and Oblyquixiton. The Oracles are here to protect Simeris not relinquish its power. You are alone in your quest. But not in the battles that will come" spoke Unac.

"Unac older and now younger than Rhac. Are the others able to wake?" asked Rhac.

"Those Oracles were the first. The first made and the first to die. They are no longer even in my memory. They will not wake" replied Unac.

"Rhac and Unac shall be the last reborn" spoke Rhac.

The two creatures embraced each other, and Ange felt the vortex of power which swelled inside them. Eight of them would be formidable indeed. Her heart thudded thinking of what she was yet to meet that would require such behemoths to be the protectors of this world. She looked up and saw that two of the moons glowed brightly. Perhaps that is where the Oracles were.

Outside the song of the Yonta closed around the tower.

"It strengthens. It sings the songs of death" spoke Rhac.

The warbling sound pierced the towers easily and made the walls ripple. It rose into a crescendo both alluring and frightening. Nekoda whimpered and cowed in the darkest place it could find.

The towers shook and then the walls were gone. Ange could see the vibrations of the death song. Her ears began to bleed, and Nekoda was in contortions whining with pain. She felt the prism burning around her neck. She realised it was calling to it. She pulled it out.

"Here song beast. Is this what the Rulers call to bring back?" Ange strode to a window in the tower.

It stopped singing.

"No other may command it. It was given to me" she called to the Yonta.

The Yonta stood still watching the prism swing in Ange's hand.

"Do you understand. It is given to me. It is mine until the Custodians are restored."

She stepped through the window and onto a spiral staircase and descended toward the Yonta. She kept her eyes on the leather sash around its neck.

It opened its jaws. The Oracles were behind her.

"It is mine" she repeated.

The Yonta cooed lowly. Ange could feel the prism respond.

"Take me to your Rulers. I will show them, and we can barter" Ange spoke trying to provoke the creature to show her where its masters were.

The cooing rose into baying. The prism began to burn again. Ange looked at the prism as it began to glow. The higher the baying the more she could feel it burning and vibrating. She saw that it was beginning to shimmer. Suddenly the Yonta snatched it and sped into the desert.

Ange was stunned.

"We must follow" she called to the Oracles.

They stood with spears ready massive and towering.

"Follow your enemy. It has stolen the memories of Caemeris, your resurrector" she commanded.

Rhac scooped Ange up. Speeding into the desert they chased the Yonta.

Ange's heart raced. This creature tore the prism straight from her without hesitation. Then she remembered First of the Aracnine taking it and not being affected by its power. Panic began to rise that she would never see the prism again and perhaps the Rulers were even more powerful than the Custodians.

Rhac covered a thousand leagues almost instantly. They reached the edge of the bone dust and saw the massive expanse of the city ruins. The buildings were worn down to the stone they were carved from. It was like an intricate maze there were so many paths intersecting each other.

"Is it a map?" asked Ange as the Oracles stopped.

"You see much visitor. Each place was etched when an ultra-sime was reached. When a new epoch dawned in strength and battle wisdom since Simeris was made" replied Unac.

"We will go no further. We have entered the realm of the Yonta. Its lair lies perpendicular to moon Igna" spoke Rhac.

Ange followed Rhac's talon and saw the smallest of the moons sitting directly above the gaping hole she had seen when she was in the tower.

"I will need to pursue it and take back the prism. What power lies here it can so easily steal it? Few others have been able to hold the prism. One was its forger and the other shadow and the creature which caged it" spoke Ange.

"You must learn this yourself. We are here only to keep the Yonta weak for it is an insatiable beast once it is released. It would devour the wind and sand alike leaving itself to starve instead of admitting defeat" spoke Rhac.

Rhac and Unac resumed their poses as they stood guard at the edge of the desert.

"Come Nekoda" spoke Ange.

Nekoda whined, not wanting to hunt the creature. He sensed its strength.

"I know, I also feel fear in my heart. But I have made a grave mistake. I must take back the prism. If the Rulers here can wield its power, then it may mean the end of our quest."

She began to walk across the rock. It was easier for her weak leg with the firmness of the stone. Nekoda barked and looked at the Oracles. They seemed oblivious to them.

"We have gone this far. We need to keep going together. If this is our end, then we will be together" she patted Nekoda on the head to reassure him.

Ange took off down a culvert in the direction the Yonta had fled. Nekoda hesitated but seeing Ange leave created the same need in him as Norbu in danger. He leapt off the desert edge into the maze of stone racing to catchup to his beloved companion.

Ange remembered the direction of the gateway from the moon and guessed she was headed towards it. She heard the panting of Nekoda and smiled.

Above them the Yonta watched. It was camouflaged into the stones that formed the city walls. The prism was caged inside its lifeless thorax. It watched Ange. It smelt its odour. It growled wanting to devour the flesh thing. But it was called to go back. It raced along the wall invisible to Ange. It looked back at the Oracles. They saw it. They knew the strength of the Yonta and how dangerous it would be unleashed. It craved destruction and only the leash of the Guardians kept it from rampaging across Simeris.

"Rhac waits for you Yonta" called the Oracle across the death winds.

Ange began to tire.

"We will rest a bit. It was further than I thought."

She felt the breeze and thought she heard a whisper upon it. She looked up searching but there was nothing. She sensed they were being watched.

She made more water for she and Nekoda. Some splashed onto a stone paver. It began to sizzle. Curious she did it again. The stone hissed and bubbled. She waited until it stopped and then inspected the stone. It had burnt all the way through. She smashed a stone suddenly against the wall and ground it until it was a fine powder. She inspected it and tried to see its codes. It formed into layers of time. So thin barely discernible but still there they were. So many of them uncountable. She lifted one single layer and in it she saw eons of beings existing. Battles and times of peace. Creatures walked the world. The Yonta appeared and ravaged the world to almost extinction. It was truly a powerful beast. So what was stronger than you to put a leash around your neck Ange wondered.

She disturbed another layer and saw in it the rise of the Oracles and the eight moons of Simeris be born. They formed from the eyes of a creature who sat upon the mountain watching. Within it was silence and peace until the Yonta saw it and wished to destroy it. The battle between the two behemoths almost split the world in two. Suddenly she was engulfed in thick dust and barely able to breathe. She pulled out and looked upon the dying watcher from the mountain. It cried in pain and misery and fear for its world. As it drifted into bone dust its eyes remained watching on the sand. Soon the Oracles formed from its blood. Eight of them.

Each of them took an eye and thrust them high into the skies where they came to rest eternally watching, caretaking.

"Who was this great watcher Rhac?" Ange asked.

"Shomac. Bleeder of peace and gaoler of the raging winds. Quiet ruler of Simeris. Remembered now in our moons. Destroyed by Yonta."

"Shomac's sorrow was great and love for Simeris can still be felt in the stone memory. I will remember this, and the bleeder of peace and gaoler of wind will sit in the Cadra Phomera. Yonta set Simeris to war" spoke Ange.

"Yes" replied Rhac.

"So now I must find those who leashed the Yonta. Why would beings so powerful require the prism?" asked Ange.

She and Nekoda eventually came to the end of the culvert after a league. It was closed off by a wall of collapsed stones. She climbed and stared across the flatness. There was nothing, not even wind. She scanned trying to see anything which signalled where the gateway was. In the shimmer of the stone there was shadow, barely discernible.

"This way Nekoda."

She looked back and saw Nekoda rigid, with its hackles up staring in another direction.

"What do you see?" Ange scanned across the maze but there was nothing she could discern.

Nekoda saw the Yonta racing about half a league away. It was heading toward the same shadow. It slowed and looked across at Nekoda. It pierced Nekoda's gaze and mind making him yelp.

Ange went to her friend and patted him.

"Come we must brave for there is no other way."

Nekoda barked.

"Louder my friend."

Nekoda barked and then howled.

Ange giggled "That is better the great wolf of Arglethium has come to battle. Let all hear and tremble at the sound of the mighty warriors of the red sands."

They took off toward the dark shimmer. Together they raced alongside the battle beast of Simeris, invisible to Ange. Nekoda fearfully kept guarded glances as they each converged toward the same place.

The gate was massive as it loomed above them. It was taller than a mountain. There was nothing behind it. The vista of the maze of ruins extended beyond the stone archway. Ange swiped her hand through one of the pillars. It glided easily through it, but to Ange it was like, the grains of stone moved around her rather than her penetrating the stone.

"What do you think Nekoda? I saw a huge opening when I was upon the eyes of Shomac. There is a way down."

Nekoda barked again into the distance.

"Is it the hidden beast? It is like the river snake of the Choasa; silent and quick. It is circling waiting for me to walk through. Perhaps it is a trap and waits for the bait to fall into it."

Nekoda continued to stand at full attention, staring out into the empty silence. Ange stood beside him.

"Yonta, sing your song and show me the way to your masters. Perhaps they will meet their match in me, and we can barter that leash off your neck for the jewel you have stolen. Sing Yonta. Let the beauty of the Yonta of Simeris sing forth."

The Yonta had waited for the prey to walk through and be trapped so it could feed off them. But they had sensed it. The call came and it could hear the urging in the sounds of the prey. It wanted it to come. The Yonta song could break the heart of stone and make the wind shiver and quake. It would crush the flesh of this unknown scent with the echo of Yonta.

In the distance the air shimmered briefly and out of it appeared the beast of Simeris. It raced toward Ange and Nekoda. Ange grabbed Nekoda's leash and held fast.

"Stay brave friend. It is full of pride, and it cannot resist to show its strength."

The Yonta charged into them snarling and then breaking into its call for death. Ange heard it and felt it call to every part of her body wanting to end. Nekoda whined not wanting to listen. It drew upon the memory smells of the dirt of Arglethium to withstand the long urging.

"Beast. What barter can I make with you?" shouted Ange.

The singing continued and Ange could feel herself falling apart. She closed her eyes and concentrated on the sounds. She soon began to see the vibrations in the air. She traced them with her mind and began to learn them. They were little darts of exploding colours only they were dimmed compared to the colours she could see in the prism. They were veiled in something. Venom. It was like venom. It poisoned everything the sounds touched. She grabbed one as it came near. The pain seared through her.

"Show me!" she screamed. She broke the codes of the venom and looked into the raw sounds of the Yonta. She was breaking apart.

The Yonta cried its death song across the skies. The ruins began to crack from the music as it floated into the very heart of the stones. Rhac and Unac stood listening. Their spears were ready to battle the destructive melodies as it neared.

"Visitor you do not know what you do" called Rhac.

Ange remembered lying beneath the Fortress in the deserts of the Iron Coast. She remembered Voloc. She formed Voloc before her and tore the demon memory apart. She plucked a piece of emptiness inside and shaped it into a corona of darkness. She ate it and spat it out all over the echoes of Yonta just before the song tore her and Nekoda to shreds. Suddenly everything was silent.

The Yonta stood before Ange. It still held the prism, but no sound came from its jaws. Ange stood. She had collapsed from the strength of the music. Heaving she looked at the beast.

"Now I have seen what leashes the true song of the Yonta. The venom of the Rulers. I have quelled the mighty death chant of you beast. I can unleash you from their bonds. So shall we barter?"

Nothing happened.

"Come now your Rulers must know by now. Return the prism and I will free you of your leash. Show me where they lie, and I shall destroy them as well."

The wind swirled around them. Ange could sense the prism deep within the chest of the beast. Its power always called to her. She wondered if she should just destroy the creature and take it back.

A low rumble grew around them. It penetrated into the ground beneath. The Yonta stood firmly without flinching. Ange looked behind the creature and saw the ruins shimmering, dust plumes danced with the rumbling sounds bearing down on them. Suddenly the Yonta yawned widely and began to sing again. It was high, sweet, and melodious. It was ancient and cried to the birth of all things made at their first moments. Ange knew she would not withstand this onslaught. She began to run back to the Oracle. Just as she went under the arch, the gateway opened, and she stumbled into a pool of black water. She looked for Nekoda and he followed and further beyond at the entrance shone the eyes of the Yonta. A current caught them, and they sped through the silken blackness expelling them into the chamber of the Guardians. The water did not flow with them or pool around them. Ange noticed she was dry. The liquid vaporised into air. She stared at the figures sitting around the walls and recognised them instantly. It was the Aracnine.

The Yonta meandered past her and Nekoda. Stopping it stood in a pose of submission before one of the Guardians sitting in the centre. Its huge talon opened and the Yonta vomited the prism into it.

"You may hunt as reward" spoke the figure on the throne.

The song of Yonta echoed as it sped away into the bone desert of Simeris.

Stonthrax held the prism up and peered into it. Ange could see its eyes racing trying to search its mysteries.

"It was given to me by the Custodian, Ascendant" Ange spoke.

"I know this light. New and old, but not older than us but potent. We are weary from our watching and seek the darkness and relief death brings. But this. This brings a flesh former. A knower of Caemeris and scholar of its memory. The conqueror of Oblyquixiton. Flesh maker you will restore us, and we will be mighty again."

"What will you give me in return?" asked Ange.

Stonthrax stood and walked toward Ange. She cringed at the strength of this Aracnine. She remembered the potency of the eight and this one made her heart quake.

"What do you ask of Stonthrax?" the Guardian spoke.

"I seek the Custodians of my world. Ascendent and Baachelaus, Seraf, Aerean and Lido. They were imprisoned by Voloc, gaoler of Descendant. The god was chained by the eight, the Aracnine, the Guardians of Uchala, now reborn in Sa-Tuchala."

Stonthrax towered over her. She was not frightened, and she noticed Nekoda was not shaking as he did with the Yonta.

"The prism is mine mighty one" spoke Ange staying her ground in front of the leviathan.

"It holds a memory as ancient as the Guardians. Its secrets are deep dark and old. It remembers Oblyquixiton" spoke Stonthrax.

"I only know it was made by Norbu. Keeper and maker of the lands I was born."

"These Custodians are unknown. Strong indeed is this forger to reshape the eye of Caemeris and wield it so freely."

Stonthrax stooped down and peered directly into Ange's eyes. She felt a slight tingling on her skin as if something were trying to pierce her mind and heart.

"Why are you here?" Stonthrax asked.

"I was shown this place by the prism. It guides me to where the Custodians are held, and it seems I must come here" replied Ange.

Silence was ruptured by a deep laughter.

"What you will find is death" replied Stonthrax.

"Something lies here which will unlock the mystery of this quest I did not ask for" replied Ange.

Stonthrax went back to its throne and sat.

"The Guardians of Simeris have no use for quest. We live on the edge of annihilation flesh former. The endlessness of death, and decay is our domain."

"What are you?" Ange asked.

"Fledgling creature our bonds bleed with the poisons of time and eternal stillness of what came first. The webs of memories are only pierced at great cost to the Guardians. To rupture those webs is almost a death blow to the old creatures who watch time. What will you give the Guardians in return to draw on the deep wells of our existence?"

"Mighty one you are covered in the dust of your failing kind. I will remake the world, so the bone dust does not veil Simeris in its shades of mourning and forgetting. You know I am a flesh former. You have seen what I can do with the stone. I have remade the Oracle and stripped the leash of your venom from the Yonta and live to speak of it."

"This jewel is not in our memory. It is new and made from things we have not seen. What makes it powerful is the force which made the colours before it, known only as Cacmeris. How can the Guardians trust something which it does not understand?"

"There is nothing I can tell you or give you which will make it true for you. I can only say I want this quest to be finished as my land and people will die if I do not restore these gods. We both want to live and without making this pact we both die."

"Stonthrax sees this but has grown weary since the sundering of our kind."

"Then let me restore you and with that knowledge I will place the Guardians of Simeris in the Cadra Phomera to be remembered for eternity."

"Stonthrax will think as it has no knowledge of this Cadra Phomera or ones such as you. And it has no need of this knowledge. Stonthrax, Thraxus and Gate Keeper to Oblyquixiton, will exist beyond anything you can offer and is the shadow of eternity flesh formed. All things remain here, until time ends" spoke Stonthrax.

Ange stood in front of the huge beast and saw it close all eight eyes as it thought. She walked around the chamber and saw that there were eight of them like the Aracnine. They looked like stones carved into definite shapes. The pale light reflected on white walls helping to illuminate the other figures and the place where they were entombed.

She went to find where the light came from.

Stonthrax went into the ancient webs of memory. It Stonthrax sat above existence basking in the brightness in the first moments of their creation. The sixteen stood behind their progenitor. The Yontas were in battle and the Oracles did not exist. Simeris light came from the last rays to touch the world before Caemeris and Oblyquixiton had made their pact. It was unrelenting in its strength and never waned. The Guardians had been called to the merging of the stars and had been drenched in the forces of the adversaries. Hardened hides and poisoned fangs dripping with the potency of powers which could break existence and remake it. Now here lies this power again and the fragile creature, so easily crushed, wields it ignorant to what it is. Does Stonthrax let the prey pass the webs of memory in peace for the gift it will give it, or does it fade into decay, a destruction wrought by its own fang bite and talon wound? The creature knows what it offers; the Guardians glory will be restored by its touch.

"Eight I wake you all to answer Stonthrax."

The groans of eternity echoed in a crescendo of pain and rage as the other Guardians were wrenched from slumber.

"Why have you pulled us from the webs of entombment?" whispered eight voices.

"Oblyquixiton and Caemeris remnants have drifted into the gaze of Stonthrax. The creature who custodes its power only does so in fragments. It offers us rebirth for the return of the vessel which holds a memory of Caemeris and passage through the gates of Stonthrax to find its maker. It is weak, fragile, and easily consumed into us. Do the Guardians seek another era in existence or is this the end of Simeris?"

"Our webs are thick with age and time. Heavy weave, dense and poisonous, blinding our eyes shredding the hide made from things before us. Not the lightness of strength, speed, or deadly force, which was us the Guardians, even after the sundering from the eight. Stolen by the wanderer breaking diluting the venom of blood bringing the bone dust and web-death. It must be etched again our glory. It is our duty. We remember Oblyquixiton and the Caemerin light. Let the Guardians free once more and it will be the age of battle-web and the remaking of Simeris" spoke Nine of the Guardians.

"So I Stonthrax have been answered. So the Guardians will be remade."

Ange continued through the vault. The walls were tunnelled in a circle and were perfectly smooth. There was a dim light, but it didn't seem to have a source. It was an endless path and she wondered if there was a beginning. The deep silence reminded her of the chasm where Voloc had imprisoned she and Tessi. The silence felt alive. She wondered what watched beneath its veil. She touched the wall trying to find out if she could see what was behind it but there was nothing. Not even cold or heat. It was dead.

"Tell me why I am here?" but there was no answer only the deadness of stone.

For a long time it seemed she walked with Nekoda following. An arch appeared muted by the soft light. She entered and before her she saw the heart of Simeris. It ebbed lightly. She heard the death throes hiss quietly as the star died. She touched the thickest part of the hissing to feel if something existed there but there was nothing again. This place was truly dead.

Stonthrax entered behind her. She startled not hearing the creature moving.

"It is the memory of light dying. Once we no longer hear it then we will be dead. Finally and completely" explained Stonthrax.

"What is your decision mighty one?" asked Ange.

"We crave to live again. For this you will have your jewel back" spoke Stonthrax.

"And passage for what I seek?" asked Ange.

"You are looking at the remnants of Oblyquixiton. We first bled here when the Guardians were first made and as our wounds healed, they leaked the memories of our battles here. Into the well of our deep memories."

"Are you formed from Oblyquixiton?" asked Ange.

"Perhaps. When time is made there is no time before it, hence we do not remember our maker" replied Stonthrax.

"Will you open your well of memory and let me pass?"

"Stonthrax will."

Ange looked at the shiny eyes. Unreadable. A shiver went through her as she peered into them to guess their secrets. A foreboding washed over here. The potency of this creature was greater even than Voloc and the Ascendant and Norbu. It was still and quiet and knew its purpose. What had she awoken? There is no choice she thought to herself.

"Give me the prism" she asked.

Stonthrax opened its talon. Ange's hand was smaller than one of its claws. The prism a mere spec inside it.

She took her dagger and pricked the opened talon and took some of its blood. It was iridescent purple. She held it suspended in the air and looked into it through the prism. She gasped as the codes began to untangle. Inside them came bursts of light then dimmer light then dots and then darkness. Then it stilled as a cloud of colours burst out followed by darkness. Inside the darkness sat a presence and it stared at something else. The raw power burned and overwhelmed her.

Ange cried in pain as the negative spaces began to consume her. She saw a strand. It came loose from the miasma of energy. She latched onto it. She pulled it out and toward her. She let go of the prism and let the drop of venomous blood fall. She took the strand and scored the code into the stones near her feet. In it she saw how they were made into the warriors of protection and the venom of light and the impenetrable darkness. She blew the codes toward Stonthrax, and they settled on its hide.

She stepped away gasping. She realised it was a mistake, but it was too late. What have I done? Her heart thudded so loudly it seemed to be echoing off the walls of the tunnel. But then she realised it was not just her heart that was beating. She turned and saw the shadows of emptiness begin to form into a bright droplet of blood like that of the one she had drawn from Stonthrax. The heart of Simeris was beginning to beat again.

Stonthrax stood still. Its eyes peered into the emptiness of the chamber. She gathered Nekoda towards her and waited.

Then the giant warrior inhaled, and Ange could feel it empty the chamber of air. Suddenly it let out its breath in a high-pitched squeal. It reached into the heart of Simeris and drank it dry. Ange saw shadows gathering around Stonthrax. They began to sway it was mesmerising. In the distance Ange could hear the song of the Yonta. It was not sad but seemed joyful as if it were celebrating the coming of the Guardians again.

She shrunk back. Then light bloomed, and Ange could see all eight of them standing in a circle and their bodies pulsed with life emitting a purple glow over everything. Stonthrax turned to Ange.

"Welcome stranger to the Guardians of Simeris. Our memories are reborn."

The piercing song of the Yonta grew around them. Ange saw the creature standing at the entrance. Its fangs and eyes glistened in the ultraviolet glow.

Stonthrax turned to it.

"I release you beast. Simeris is reborn and its warriors will regain their strength and glory."

Ange's heart thudded. She had seen the power of the Yonta. It would destroy this place like it had in the past. She snatched the Yonta's song to keep it leashed.

"Not until you tell me where the path lies to find the Custodians?" she asked.

"We must let the poison of Caemeris strengthen our hides before we break the webs of memory. For destruction will come if the Thrax are not strong to hold back the Oblyquixiton" spoke Stonthrax.

"What do you mean?"

"The bonds are heavy and ancient which form our webs. We must prove ourselves worthy of their power before we can reveal a path through them to one not born of them" replied Stonthrax.

Before Ange could answer the Yonta broke free, and the Guardians erupted into high squeals. She felt the stones and walls disintegrate and reform. She blocked her ears as the pain increased. She saw the throbbing drop of blood and reached for it. She took it and spun a bone-glass vial to hold it.

"What have I unleashed Nekoda? Here I hold the heart of Simeris" called Ange.

The Guardians sped out of the tunnel. They were fast and silent in their movement and Ange lost them quickly.

She kept going until the entrance to the surface came into view. Entering out onto the stone maze she blinked in the harshness of violet light. There was nothing. No sign of the Guardians or Yonta.

She took the vial of blood, and she threw it toward the moons as hard as she could. The bone-vial disappeared.

"For you Aes Vius, and the Cadra Phomera to keep. If I bring death to all, then not all will be lost as these remnants will remain" she called up into the sky.

She decided to go back to find the Oracles. Racing into the ruined maze of the city she sent out a call to Rhac. There was no answer.

"Hurry Nekoda."

He panted behind her, close to her heels.

Soon the dust of bone sand began to stir as the wind blew around them. A cracking boom rocked the walls spilling rubble onto them. She climbed up to look out across to see what was happening. The thunder rippled underneath her feet.

'Rhac!' she called. Still nothing. She clamoured down into the canal and raced. The sand was becoming thicker as she neared the edge of the city.

'Rhac!' she cried again. Still nothing. Then she froze. On the edge of the desert stood Yonta. It had Unac in its jaws. The Oracle was flailing trying to break free of the Yonta. She sped towards it and with her dagger bore down on the beast.

"Rhac! Where are you?" Ange shouted.

The Yonta snarled at Ange and Nekoda dropping Unac as it turned.

"Come to me beast. I have conquered you once already" Ange coaxed.

Ange and the Yonta met fiercely. She stabbed her blade into its massive jaws viciously. She whipped it out just as the razor fangs snapped shut. She slashed again and this time took a fang with it. She jumped away. With the piece of fang she formed a shape from the sand. It grew and began to resemble the Yonta. She leashed it as it grew. As it reached the same height as its parent, she set it free. The massive beasts clashed and struggled with each other. It reminded Ange of the Matavians using the flesh of children for decoration and their blood for strength. What had she done?

Suddenly Yonta pulled away and stood still. Ange's beast circled. Then the Yonta began to sing. It was the death lullaby Ange had heard before. It pervaded the air. She saw her pet began to falter as it mimicked the Yonta's throat and jaw, but no sound came out. She had not mastered all of the beast. Soon her creature lay confused and snapped at nothing in the air trying to fight the death song. Then it stopped convulsing and stood. It turned toward Ange and Nekoda and began to sing along with its parent.

"Run!" she screamed to Nekoda, and she took off into the bone desert. Both Yontas chased them.

"To the Oracle towers Nekoda."

She saw shadows moving on the horizon.

"Rhac!" she screamed. But then she saw the corona of spines and realised it was Stonthrax. The Yonta slowed its chase when it saw the Guardians as well. Ange sensed the full strength within the Yonta she had formed. She had made the shell but not the power of song death which lay with in the creature. That had been given to it by its parent.

"Come let us do battle as of old. Strengthen web and talon alike, sharpen fang and bring the venom to life" spoke Stonthrax to the Guardians.

The Guardians and Yonta clashed into each other. A tear in the surface of the desert opened up. Ange lunged toward a rock to stop herself falling in. The two Yonta and the eight Guardians battled furiously and the forces coming from the wounds of each of them flooded over Ange and Nekoda. She could barely breath. Forcing herself up she leapt across the chasm and ran toward the towers of the Oracles. She saw the last remaining tower shimmering in the distance. She noticed it shook each time the warriors clashed. It wouldn't be long before it would be destroyed as well.

She saw to the left a line of Ghoc. They were standing like statues. She pushed ahead. She saw Rhac. Her heart sunk. It was fighting another Yonta. This one was fully formed. She saw more of them emerging from the caves. The caves where the Ghoc had lived. She realised the Ghoc were the remnants of the Yonta somehow transformed into the death janitors. The death song rose into the sky, she looked up and saw the eight moons breaking apart. She watched Rhac look up and it flung its spear toward the moons to keep them together.

"Stranger, use your jewel to keep our creator watching or we will be lost" roared Rhac over the cacophony.

The Yonta snarled and latched onto Rhac's torso viciously bringing the Oracle down.

"No!" Ange screamed.

Taking out the prism she pulled a memory out. On her hand sat the eyes of Norbu.

"Hold. Hold as you held Arglethium against Voloc. Hold as the gaolers held Baachelaus in their vaulted emptiness. Hold as strong the bonds of clay forged by the Caemerin light" Ange whispered into the prism.

The moons reformed and the towers stopped shaking. She sped toward the Yonta and snatching the spear of Rhac stabbed the beast through the heart.

"Nay do not slay the beast!" called Rhac in Ange's mind but it was too late to hear the warning.

The dead song exploded into the wind as it fell calling more of the beasts across the vastness.

Stonthrax turned and screeched, revelling in the battle lust.

"What have I done?" Ange gasped in disbelief.

"Unleashed death-life and the vastness of memory into the world once more. Here is where the light and emptiness met, forging a potency so great it cannot be destroyed or conquered. Did Stonthrax not say the dominion of the Thrax was death. It is eternal and guides all things" spoke Rhac.

"Quickly into the towers" Rhac and Unac picked Ange and Nekoda up and sped toward the Oracle dwellings.

Inside it was silent. The walls shimmered as before.

"I have unleashed the destruction of Simeris."

"No you have rebirthed it. This is Simeris that you see but we see also that new death awaits and the light which feeds Simeris may become entombed bringing annihilation. Your weapon has changed something. The power is greater, and the Guardians are aware of it" spoke Rhac.

Ange wondered as well why it would be different. She had taken some of Stonthrax and the Yonta. How could it be different?

"What caused the long death in the first place?"

"The sundering of the sixteen to eight" replied Rhac.

"What caused the sundering?" asked Ange.

"A wanderer. It plucked them from the battles of Caemeris in its lost journey and they never returned. But the sixteen were formed from the same web and the wound was too deep to ever be healed. The sacred venom bled out into the Simeris and so the long death began."

"Do you know the name of the wanderer?"

"No."

"What did it look like?"

"It watched with the same brilliance as the moon above."

Ange followed the talon of Rhac. It was the colour blue. She had seen that before. Sa-Tuc in her re-birth and the eyes of Baachelaus.

Ange thought of Kado on Mir Chiridien. She feared the same would happen if she called Sa. But Sa was stronger, and her body flowed with the same power as this world.

"I know where I may find help Rhac. I need the knowledge of the Guardians and they will not give it to me until they have strengthened their battle webs. But I fear they will destroy everything before I learn their secrets" spoke Ange.

"Do as you must" Rhac turned on hearing the death song again.

Ange touched the wall of the tower and the prism.

"Hold. Hold until I return" she called.

She thought of Sa-Tuc and the last place she had seen her.

It was night in the desert. Pitch black with a few stars poking through. The moon was on the wane and provided no light. The smell of the air was familiar.

"Sa-Tuc, I have returned, and Ange calls you. Will you answer me?"

Scanning the lands, the muted dunes and rocks gave way to a darkened gouged out shape. Ange walked toward it and soon arrived at the edge of a massive gorge. She turned to look for any signs of life and in the distance as pale dawn broke, she could see the silhouette of a dark spire. She guessed it was the ruins of the Iron Fortress. She looked across the horizon and noticed it appeared ragged, as if something ate away at the world.

The silence was more familiar than on Simeris. Walking down into the gorge she found some berries to eat. She ate while she waited for the daylight to show her where the assassin dwelt. A small spider came trundling over a stone near her foot. Its vibrant blue stripes made it an easy prey for birds. She put her hand down and let it walk up her arm.

"Where does the sentinel lie?" Ange asked it.

It walked down off her arm and began to move across the rocks. She decided to follow it. It ran quickly like the Guardians of Simeris. Nekoda barked at it wanting to eat it, but Ange kept his leash on. The spider did not seem disturbed by the dog.

Soon the spider stopped on large slab of stone. Behind it was a small crack, just large enough for her to fit through. A crow cawed in a tree above the spider. Ange picked it up and put it beneath a bush, so it was more hidden.

"It's not good for you my friend to be out in the daylight. Come Nekoda."

She entered into the cave. A small stream cut a path through the sandstone. The further she went along the stream, the dimmer the sunlight became. A pale blue glow replaced the sun rays.

"Sa-Tuc, it is Ange. I have come to call on our covenant made over the tears of Ascendant. Answer me, Ange calls."

The blue light grew more intense and almost began to blind Ange. She stopped as she could no longer see. The glow was suffocating.

"Answer me Assassin."

"Sa-Tuchala has not heard that name for eons. Keeper, you have come, what is it you ask of me?"

"Great Sentinel and friend. I have awoken an ancient power and it now rages to a new destruction. It is the Aracnine's place of birth. Their maker Stonthrax of Simeris has been reborn with the Tear of Ascendant. I fear it will feed off its destruction until nothing is left. Yet I need Stonthrax to show me the way to where the Custodians are bound" replied Ange.

Sa-Tuchala formed into the shape of what Ange remembered, the petite and lethal assassin. A blue shadow radiated around her.

"Ange this is grave news indeed" Sa-Tuchala.

"I have seen and learnt so much Sa. So much more than what exists here. Something stops me, the Seer. It seeks the same as I do and waits until I unlock the knowledge it needs and will steal the power when it is revealed."

"The Guardians are the second oldest in the known powers of our consciousness. Even Uchala had not seen their kind before until its questing webs stole them from their nest. The sentinel blended its blood with their venom and our kind was born. Great danger awaits us Ange" spoke Sa.

"Great danger has been snapping at our feet since the Custodians woke and brought Voloc with them. The Aracnine are the only ones who can contain them so I can find my way to Ascendant."

Sa made a high-pitched whistle. Ange waited. The chamber was awash in blue, but it did not reveal any detail. The eight suddenly walked through the veil of violet and stood silently around them.

"Stonthrax of Simeris has been reborn."

Suddenly the eight Guardians unleashed their high-pitched squealing. Ange blocked her ears.

"Still yourselves" commanded Sa.

The screeching stopped instantly.

"First, if we return, as I am bound with my covenant to Ange, Custodian and Keeper of the jewel of Norbu, what will be our fate?"

"Our sundering wrought their death and now they have been unleashed into consciousness again. Stonthrax is the gateway to beginning. It will want to heal the breach. The Guardians are formidable, and our first web of binding. We are bound to Sa-Tuchala, but the bonds of birth-death are stronger."

"Will it be our destruction?" asked Sa.

"Not ours but yours Queen" replied First.

Ange's heart sunk at this news.

"Oh Sa what have I done. I left Kado on Mir Chiridien to battle the Ondraak and now I offer you death, either here or on Simeris."

"It is not you Ange, but things made before you which now poison us here in our cradle of Arglethium. If you are not successful, our doom is sealed. Have you not seen in your journeys back the sky fades and the trees whither inexorably to death."

"I have."

"You have also re-awakened the moons of Simeris, long is their gleam and far into the void does it reach, it will call to Voloc, and hasten Arglethium's demise" spoke First.

"No, how is this possible? I saw the path forward and it showed Simeris. There was no other way. Everything I do seems to make it worse" Ange sat down overwhelmed by the despair which consumed her heart.

"Sa-Tuchala must now give back the power her lust stole to sate her hunger and Sa-Tuc the Assassin will once more fight for her life and fulfil her covenant with Ange."

"Sa, call me Ange, bringer of death" spoke Ange.

"You have seen a path before you Ange, where none exists behind you. We will go, we will battle. For Sa-Tuchala, a reckoning is being asked and in payment, a way forward is given. Ever has existence, extracted its cost on things brought into being" spoke Sa.

She pulled Ange up from the ground.

The Aracnine gathered more closely around Ange and Nekoda. Sa transformed into her sentinel form.

"To Simeris" spoke Ange.

Ange drew the eight moons and touched the prism. They arrived in front of the Oracles tower. Rhac and Unac turned and saw the Aracnine and Sa. Their spears were ready for any attack. The white sand was still and there was no wind.

"Hold Rhac. I have brought them here to balance Stonthrax" called Ange.

"They are the sundered eight and this is a descendant of the one who wrought the destruction of Simeris" spoke Unac.

"I am no descendant. I am one in the same now with this clayborn of the world she inhabited. I remember this place and its scent. It is veiled in its own decay" spoke Sa-Tuchala.

The Aracnine loomed over Sa and the Oracles. They had become the same size as Stonthrax and the other Guardians.

"The light of their world calls to them. Which side will they choose?" asked Ange.

"Aracnine. Is Sa-Tuchala your Queen or is Stonthrax your Ruler now?"

The eight swayed. Massive and imposing. One strike with their mighty talons would decimate the Oracles, Ange, and Sa. They waited for their answer. Ange felt the breeze on her cheeks and knew the Yonta were coming.

First lifted its claws and placed it gently on the prism.

"This stone holds the key to the gate. Stonthrax will know where the gate lies. We will quell Stonthrax and then we will decide. Our Queen is still Sa-Tuchala until the sundering is healed."

Ange let out a sigh of relief. Sa did not say anything. Ange knew that silence meant the assassin was planning her moves.

The Aracnine screeched their war call across the vastness. Beyond the many ruins and over the emptiness came the other eight of their kind. They had been tracking the Yonta after being defeated at the gates of the city.

Stonthrax stopped as the ancient call of brethren resounded drowning the noise of the storm and battle.

"So wanderer you have returned. Usurper and disturber of ancient bonds. Thief of the darkness of Oblyquixiton" called Stonthrax.

The Aracnine gathered around Sa to protect her.

"Younglings. You are missed. Will you not heal the wound which tears our world apart?" asked Stonthrax.

"Not yet" replied First.

"You are poisoned by the questing webs of the wanderer. You are poisoned by the power that the clay-born brings" spoke Stonthrax.

The songs of the Yonta began to whisper then rose slowly around all of them. There were twelve of them. They stood howling in unison. Ange could feel it in her chest. It thudded so hard it began to hurt.

"Sa look what I have done."

"You were not to know Ange."

The death song rattled her bones and she felt herself being torn apart.

Sa reached out her hands sending blue tendrils of light. The fine filaments vibrated with the song.

"Come Guardians to battle and bleed into the bone sand to bring Simeris to life again and her moons of death may wax and wane with our glory" ordered Stonthrax.

Everything happened at once. The Aracnine and Sa were wedged between the Guardians as the Yonta circled their prey. Rhac and Unac stood with Ange and Nekoda.

Stonthrax and First clashed while the Yonta's song penetrated the crust of the ground and went deep beneath. Ange could see cracks forming everywhere. The moons above waxed and waned with each furious onslaught of the Guardians and the Yonta.

Sa's webs spread out slowly and feeding off the singing and vibrating in the same harmony. Slowly it grew until Stonthrax pulled away from First and pulled the filaments towards itself.

"You will not weave your webs here wanderer" spoke Stonthrax.

Rhac and Unac sliced viciously at Stonthrax to break its hold. But it was too strong.

"You are deluded mighty one. If you do not let us bind the Yonta song, then it will destroy your home" spoke Sa.

"No it will unleash Oblyquixiton quickening our strength and restoring us to our realm" replied Stonthrax.

Ange did not understand what Stonthrax was saying.

"Stonthrax, we agreed with your restoration you would reveal the wells of your memory and show a pathway for me, once your bonds were tested" spoke Ange.

"We remember and will show you the chains which come with delving into the memories of time and how to pass the gates of the Thrax" replied Stonthrax.

Suddenly the Yontas music grew into a deafening crescendo and Ange could feel herself being pulled apart. The prism however remained intact. The Aracnine grew even larger as with the other Guardians.

"Sa and Nekoda come to me" Ange called.

She pulled them close and touched the stone. Nekoda trembled.

"Show us Oblyquixiton" she spoke to the prism.

Stonthrax and the Aracnine roared in unison as the Yonta consumed Simeris. She saw Rhac and Unac disappear into the moons of Shonac. The memory scent of the first oracle and the sorrow of the destruction washed over her. Tears came to Ange's eyes.

Everything stopped and they floated in a river of silence and swirling colours.

"Is this in your memory Sa-Tuchala?" Ange asked.

"No."

The colours stopped moving.

Ange and Sa felt something watching them.

"Older than Uchala speak to us" called Sa.

There was no reply.

"More ancient than the Guardians and this stone. Speak to us" commanded Ange.

There was no answer.

"Oblyquixiton" spoke Ange.

The sixteen Guardians were walking toward Ange, Sa, and Nekoda. Leading them were First and Stonthrax.

"Is Sa-Tuchala still your Queen?" called Sa out to First.

They approached slowly. There was no answer. As they neared, Ange saw their eyes were bleached white and their mouths stitched closed. On leashes were the Yonta held by talons of the Guardians. They formed a circle around the trio.

"Do not let go of the prism Ange. We sit before death" warned Sa.

"Deep lie the memories here. Breachers of the gates. None shall dwell here in the havens of Oblyquixiton" spoke a voice.

"Tell me the way to the Custodians. Stonthrax made an oath to let me see the path forward. I seek the Custodians to free our world" spoke Ange.

"You seek too much, and grave is this intrusion into the unknown" replied the voice.

"We did not seek this out. It has been bestowed on us. Voloc the destroyer has breached our world" replied Ange.

Ange felt the presence inside. She did not feel pain or fear but merely power. Far greater than her and the Epimarin and the prism.

"The Guardian Stonthrax's memory will show a way to where I will find a path" spoke Ange.

Ange trembled as she felt the rise of something wrathful penetrate the prism. She saw an image of it exploding into a dust.

"No. Now you have seen. You have learnt. Give me my place. Let me learn" pleaded Ange.

There was no answer.

"Sa do you feel it in you?" asked Ange.

She turned to Sa and saw that her eyes and mouth had been stitched together. She looked at Nekoda and he was the same.

"Why do you do this? I am made of dirt, of desert and river stone. Dense and heavy with the sun and rain, of flesh on bone. I stand in the blood of power which made the memories before that dirt and water. Now drink of my power. Understand where your death lies, and my life began" spoke Ange.

A shudder went through her. She could feel the presence wanting to gag and blind her, but she pushed back with the prism. She drew out the mind of Norbu and Descendant.

"I watch back with the memory of union and power with the waterfalls of time still cascading into existence sustaining, drawing, forging, making. On and on and on. No end. Forgotten one, see what you remain ignorant to" Ange continued pushing back at the power bulging from inside the prism.

Ange let Oblyquixiton into the prism. Its power was excruciating to control.

"Show me who is the Seer and where do I find it?" she ordered.

Pouring into the prism the ancient force swallowed the memories of the Custodians and the sundering of the Custodial realm. It saw its progeny Belmaris wedded to Voloc and the battles of Magmeris and Belmaris. It saw Arglethium and it saw the eye of Caemeris strike out its light to make it all. It began to lust again, dormant at peace, the disruption of time woke within the ancient power. It saw the memories of its awakening. Its completeness with Caemeris and then its withdrawal into slumber. It knew where these creatures lay made in its ignorance. It knew where Caemeris lay. It knew who the Seer was. It knew this creature seeking a path to the non-existence of Oblyquixiton held the power of Caemeris with in it.

"Potent. Strength. Young. Raw. Ignorant. You must learn. Then when it is understood you shall decide who remains, who returns, who sleeps, who conquers and who falls" spoke the presence.

"Show me where do I go?" Ange cried overwhelmed with the power of the force.

"Progeny wake" ordered Oblyquixiton.

The Guardians woke along with Sa.

"Battle well. Teach the youngling. When it has learnt to open the gate, Stonthrax, mighty one of mine, grant your progenitor this favour. Wisdom is beheld in my eternities of slumber. A new era approaches. It is time to grow. Allow the gates of the Thrax to be breached" spoke Oblyquixiton.

"What is our reward for this boon?" asked Stonthrax.

"Simeris shall be yours" replied Oblyquixiton.

"The chains of Oblyquixiton shall erode?" asked Stonthrax.

"Beware only my enemies are set free, only Caemeris was set free, none other" replied Oblyquixiton.

"The score is high to draw upon wells of memories of our kind" spoke Stonthrax.

"Build well, learn and be strong. The time will come when the wanderer shall be as potent as Oblyquixiton when Caemeris is found again. A time will come when even the mighty Thrax maybe defeated" replied Oblyquixiton.

Sa woke. She looked at Ange.

"What has happened?" Sa asked.

"I have woken war. But I will be shown a path to the Custodians" replied Ange.

"Not war. There will be no victors. It is about forcing creation by revealing the face of death to the living. Uchala took the threads of this world when the Aracnine were ensnared in them. The sixteen must be reunited with Stonthrax. It will not be easy. I will fight to keep them. They brought Oblyquixiton power with them and were able to control the power of Caemeris, and Voloc. Without them, Voloc will not be contained by Norbu's potency, or Sa-Tuchala" spoke Sa.

"Stonthrax was promised Simeris and will not show me the path without being given Simeris. Simeris requires the sixteen Guardians to complete its strength. The Yonta shall roam free and destroy all" replied Ange.

Suddenly Ange and Sa stood on the edge of the bone desert. As they scanned the horizon before them, they saw the world was ruptured in half. The Aracnine swayed behind them. Their eyes and mouths had been unstitched.

The wind picked up around them and with it the song of the Yonta.

"I will seek out Rhac and Unac" spoke Ange.

Sa-Tuchala rose to her full strength. Ange sped across the dunes to find the Oracles. Nekoda ran beside her.

The Yonta song grew. Three of the Yonta were behind her. Ange saw the moons had been remade. Such potency to destroy and remake so easily. A sudden lust to know that power and command it rose inside her with the death song of the Yonta.

She took her sash and made a lasso out of it. She swung it in the air and stood waiting for the beasts to get close enough. One of them lead the pack. She strode toward it. Swiftly she slung the sash around its neck. It instantly reared away pulling Ange with it. She dug her feet into the sand and hung onto it.

"Come to me. I am the Keeper. I am great and I am terrible for one day I shall be the namer of all things."

She yanked it toward her. The beast snapped viciously at her. She did not relent. She pulled fiercely on the strap and forced the beast to the ground. The other two growled menacingly in circles. Nekoda stayed close to Ange his eyes locked on them.

There was a sudden yelp as the Yonta lay on the ground completely subdued by Ange. She took the prism and placed it on the creature's throat.

"Sing and I will know the song of death" she called.

The beast began again to sing, and the others joined the chorus. Ange felt the prism draw in the song. She began to write the codes into the sand. She memorised them. She stepped away. She began to follow the marks in the sand and sing with the Yonta. She called them all to her. They gathered before her. She sang louder and louder. Nekoda began to howl in unison. She could feel the sand beneath her feet give way. She gripped the prism and called the power of Norbu, Baachelaus, Assumpta, Lido, Aerean, and Seraf into her. Soon her voice began to call over the cacophony of song death. The creatures began to bow down. Ange's warbling became the only voice. She pulled the air around her and made a cyclone. It swept the Yonta up and herself.

"Rhac and Unac. Come to the Keeper. Let us restore the moons of the oracle. The eyes of the Simeris and watchers of the watchers of the gates to Oblyquixiton."

Rhac and Unac heard Ange's call and opened their towers on the mountain of bone. They walked toward the miasma of storm in the distance.

"We go to the Guardians. We meet them and will draw the secrets from them" spoke the Oracles.

Reaching the edge of the ruined city Ange saw that the labyrinth was beginning to restore itself and rise up from the dust. A huge obelisk stood directly in the centre. On it sat Stonthrax. It had taken its throne again and sat as surveyor of Simeris. The other Guardians sat below in a circle each being able to see in all directions.

Stonthrax reached for the aquamarine moon and plucked a ray out of it. It became a great spear sparkling luminously in the indigo and white. The spear split at the tips and resembled fangs. Stonthrax remained seated as Ange and Nekoda approached with the Yonta.

"Still your fear, friend" she whispered. Nekoda stood near Ange. She noticed how he did not wish to join. Instinct telling Nekoda that the powers and memories were beyond a humble mongrel breed made from the density of clay. She patted him and they looked at one another.

"Trust me again Nekoda."' He licked the air as if to eat her words and to tell her he did.

"Now" she whispered and let the leashes of Yonta go. The death song burst forth. She walked behind as the Yonta began to attack Sa.

Rhac and Unac looked at Ange and attempted to attack the Yonta. They savaged at Sa as she battled them. The Aracnine remained still. Ange looked at First and saw the great Guardian was fixed upon its maker Stonthrax.

Ange went to Stonthrax. Its eyes watched her. Its huge talon lashed out and grabbed her.

"Where is the nest of the Thrax?" Ange asked as Stonthrax drew it close to its fangs.

An image bloomed in Ange's mind.

Stonthrax showed Ange the Obelisk and where the gateway stood between Simeris and what existed before it. Ange saw it.

"Intruder and bringer of the dense light and chains of the living, to pass into the webs of the Thrax, and see the heart of the Simeris, no flesh dweller can live. All things decay which pass through Simeris. All things which live, must die. This is the covenant and the oaths forged by Oblyquixiton. Hence forth, clayborn of Caemerin light, your dust shall become the dust of Simeris and only the memories of your sight will pass through my gates. The mighty Stonthrax venom is strong, and only it shall remain in your hide, and your bones will become the sand that the Thrax tread upon. Do you understand intruder and bringer of decay over death?"

"I understand, it is the price I must pay to see this quest to its end" replied Ange.

Suddenly Stonthrax fangs glistened, and Ange felt them pierce her chest and plunge directly into her heart. She gasped, feeling the surge of poison inside her.

"So be consumed by the lifeblood of Stonthrax, Guardian and Keeper of the Gates of Oblyquixiton. Let the venom consume your hide and entomb your heart and memory for your journey to continue."

Stonthrax let her free. Ange saw Sa battling furiously. Her heart filled with sorrow that she sacrificed another companion, one who had taught her and protected her. Nekoda barked furiously at her at abandoning Sa.

First stared from its throne. Ange stayed beneath and watched the mighty creature assume its destiny. It was magnificent. Its existence not diminished by Arglethium but strengthened into the hardness of clay and reshaped by its first destiny, a Keeper of time. Here on Simeris, it glowed like the sun on the river in spring. It was ripe and had come to fullness. Will you remember you helped me once great one, she thought.

Suddenly Ange heard "The Aracnine will remember, Clayborn."

"And if this Clayborn asks to give Arglethium more time, will it be granted with this thread which has been spun between the world of Clayborn and the Gate Keepers of existence?" Ange asked.

There was no answer, but First's eyes moved and looked directly at Ange. Ange saw an almost imperceptible nod.

"Come Nekoda, to the gates" called Ange. She began to run toward a small archway which rose above the ruins. On it were carvings of the language of death. Between the pillars was a hole. Before she entered, she began to write on the ground.

"Sa hear my song" she spoke.

She began to sing as she wrote. Faraway the assassin heard the voice of Ange as she battled the Yonta.

Ange gave the leash of the Yonta to Sa.

"I will return. I will not let Arglethium die" spoke Ange.

"Simeris destiny lies in its recreation and death. It will shine once again. And when you call Sa-Tuchala shall come. There was a time when you would not have had the heart to quell the battle and fight the usurper. Much has changed in you little one. Have you discerned what the

Guardians are yet? When you do you will understand? You are great and you are terrible Ange, for you will be the namer of things unnamed."

Ange's heart thudded as she let the song death go. With the memories of Stonthrax within her, Ange stepped into the obelisk and disappeared with Nekoda. Inside Ange saw the webs of time before her and understood that the Guardians made time with their battles, waxing, and waning like the moon and setting of rising of the sun. Without them then nothing would pass so all shadow and light would merge into one. Colours would dull and nothing would live or die.

"I have brought you your freedom Stonthrax and Simeris will ever be known as the star of time" spoke Ange.

Ange fled into the maze of web her heart thudding wondering what awaited her now. She wished Aes Vius were with her.

"Mighty Stonthrax where would the other eight dwell. There is no space for them here. First am I still your Queen?" called Sa across the expanse of ruins.

"Wanderer you see much but Simeris is large, and underneath is found the nest of the Thrax. Here is where the sundered sixteen shall reign and the moons of Simeris are blind to what dwells within it" replied Stonthrax.

"We will battle and learn of each other's strength. Sa-Tuchala is bound to her first purpose and last form. She is held to an oath now to the keeper of Caemerin light and must stay true to this fate. If she lives or dies, it is for what the light has let her become. She is not ready to leave the Clayborn or release the Aracnine from their homage to her."

Oblyquixiton gently rested on the edges of deep slumber. It had been awoken by this traveller bound in the mysteries which made it. It felt the freeing of the Guardians. New enemies which in time would require defeat. In silence it watched and waited for Caemeris to be found and a new epoch of creation to begin.

Gnoceris

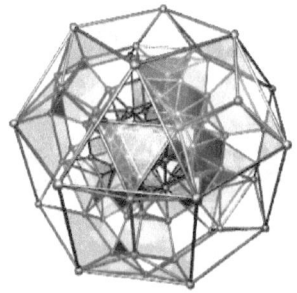

"I sit amongst the powers of existence. My lust to control them is great for I know I can. I have wielded the strength of many things. I have destroyed and remade, re-shaped, hidden and revealed. I have lived as creatures who have senses, ones made of hidden fires of light and the unknown of darkness. I watch now to see the ultimate power revealed and my lust satisfied. Caemeris, I come."

It was a place which could be anything. It had been wrought by the powers of light and shadow. The controller of the domain called Gnoceris, was Pthemnat, the Seer. Formed as offspring with the merging of Caemeris and Oblyquixiton. Pthemnat was one of five Seers, the Pentat. Together they equalled the strength of the prism which Ange wore around her neck. Their power was only usurped by their creators. Long ago when darkness cradled the first sparks of light and the wars had not begun, the five had rebelled against their creators. Why it is unknown. They fought to make their powers their own, and in doing so formed the Pthohedron of the five.

Gnoceris had become the unrivalled nodal plane of formation. This node of power grew until it touched the gates of Stonthrax and spilled into the webs of memory and time. But the Thrax had remained true to their purpose and held the Seers back. Questing ever further the pulsing vexa and qedra of the Pthohedron sought anything which could be consumed. The Pentat sensed the nexus weakening and knew destruction would come. But the Seers wanted to seek out the end of energy, what existed before and at the end of power. They remained blind to these things, and in their desire to know watched Gnoceris destroy itself. But the Pentat remained; Pthemnat, Aes Vius, Glaxa, Xtomat, and Osesa. As they drifted in their shells, they began to sense a burgeoning nexus ebbing beyond their sight. A nodal flow of dense light, increasing in exponential power. It lay beyond where the Pentat, could reach.

Eons passed, the nexus of Gnoceris was remade, but weakened and slow to remake the strength of the original weave. Pthemnat knew without more vexa it could not remake what had once been Gnoceris.

"Brethren, I seek more. What will you give, to make this so?" asked Pthemnat.

"You wish to re-build Gnoceris?" asked Aes Vius.

"Yes" replied Pthemnat.

"How?" asked Aes Vius.

"There is power beyond here" replied Pthemnat.

"What is this power which calls to the Pthohedron?" asked Glaxa.

"It is progeny of Caemeris" replied Xtomat.

"How do you know this?" asked Osesa.

"Nothing else has this strength to cross the webs of the Thrax, for even the Seers of Oblyquixiton and Caemeris merging, may not do that" replied Aes Vius.

Glaxa, Xtomat, and Osesa formed a thread of qedra. Pthemnat took it and speared it across the void and through the webs of the Thrax.

"A path has been made. Let us continue our building" spoke Pthemnat.

"We will bring the wrath of the Thrax and more destruction yet again to Gnoceris. I no longer hold to this quest. I seek knowledge not power" replied Aes Vius.

With that the Pentat split, the vexa merged into the bonds of the five Seers and Aes Vius disappeared.

Pthemnat wanted Caemeris. The bleeding of the deepest strengths and bonding of existence had been stolen and needed to be taken back. Oblyquixiton had allowed the deep energy wells of the Caemerin light to escape. Only the Seers questioned the wisdom of this. Only the Seers knew what had been lost.

Pthemnat watched many things. Its consciousness travelled along the streams of light, letting it see saw far, wide, long, and deep. Only the webs of the Guardians could thwart its vision and reach. Then suddenly in the depths of future memory there was a rupture, a stab of colour appeared. Pthemnat felt it prick its mind and looked toward it. The Seers began to watch. The Guardians of the silent one had been sundered and the death song of the Yonta had begun. Its deep sonorous sounds were soothing, formed from the placental vexa of creation. Doomed to live outside existence and death. To watch and wane, when their will to power remained longer than the first stars and longer than the colours and shapes, they were made from would surge up and force them awake once more. Their will was not malicious. The Seers did not seek death but knew that if they controlled the nodal flows of vexa, they could form any vision they deemed. For this they wished suzerainty over those things consumed by colours and light. Together the Seers could consume Caemeris and Oblyquixiton and new stars would be made.

The bright spec grew stronger and stronger until Pthemnat could no longer ignore it. It broke through the threads of Stonthrax and struck the Seer directly inside the Pthohedron. It awoke its memories of its brethren. For the first time something existed in new time and energy and was equal in power to the Pthohedron. It would no longer need the union of the five to conquer the silent one and the one who breaks the quiet. The Seer turned toward the spec of light. It saw many creatures be born and become aware. It saw a world, not a star, a dense body, drawing light into it. It sat in the embrace of Belmaris; the star named by Aes Vius the namer of the formed. Pthemnat looked deep into the pits of its first memories and saw that it was Caemerin progeny. The lost star had left its scent on the void. It watched as the scent of Caemeris permeated everything and looked at what it created. Dense, clumsy slow to form but definite in their shape. They were primal and untested. Ignorant to everything except themselves, unaware of what lay before them with short lived memories like their lives.

It watched wars of shade and light. Immature and unformed. How easy for the shades of malice to capture them and begin the schism of Caemeris vision thought Pthemnat. Again and again the wars continued. The dense creations of the world birthed from the derision of shadow for light. Caemeris was still lost and creating chaos. Meanwhile Pthemnat watched and waited.

The Seer drifted to the webs and touched them. Stonthrax strength was great and unbreakable. Its memory wells deep and second only to Oblyquixiton. The Seers were never to exceed their place it had been deemed. Pthemnat sat and waited. It watched and felt the contraction of time and light together as the prism was forged. The Seer's questing thread of qedra had ruptured the making of Caemeris, and now Caemerin power had been consummated into the nodal stone.

Pthemnat neared Oblyquixiton's webs. It saw the wound inflicted by the Pthohedron spear of power when the five were one. Pthemnat saw its silhouette cast out into the spawned creations beyond them. It had found a way to breach the Gates of Stonthrax. It watched the Caemerin nodal bonds, complex with an unknown strength of the nega-nodal flows. It saw the liquid on the dense world ran and made the clay burst forth with entities as tall as the sky, long reaching limbs with gentle threads which moved with the currents of power formed in the space around them. Creatures and beings, complex and different, their number as many as the vexa and qedra which formed Gnoceris. Pthemnat took some of the Gnocerin vectra flows and formed rivers and oceans of power. The Seer found a way to manipulate Caemerin light. It saw a path was forged for the prism to come to Gnoceris. With its strength of forging solid bonds of qedra, and retained memory of destruction and creation, Pthemnat understood it could use the prism to make Gnocerin weave stronger than ever before.

Pthemnat saw Aes Vius across the expanses of time void.

"Brethren, you are discovered once more. You found the wound of our spear and fled" spoke Pthemnat.

"Where are Glaxa, Xtomat and Osesa?" asked Aes Vius.

There was no answer.

∞

Dawn on Gnoceris was astounding even to Pthemnat. It had been Xtomat's creation. The energy of dawn ruled the Seer planet relentlessly because at any time the power and knowledge contained in its core could replicate itself into any of the Gnosa who dwelt within its nodal sphere. Pthemnat felt the surging wave of the next nodal era, or dawn, and let it wash through its form, regenerating itself. It required vast amounts energy to control the nodal power, and prevent further dawns erupting throughout the vectra flows, potentially rupturing the weave which underpinned Gnoceris. Pthemnat relaxed as the nodal surge passed without disruption to the nexus weave.

"Ruler, the delegation of Marina have arrived" spoke Magt the Informer.

"Show them in" replied Pthemnat.

The chamber of Seer rule was angular and precise. Being creatures of pre-defined states of energy, the Seers were shaped exactly in the forms of a prism. At any time they could become whatever they wished within the confines of their nexus flow.

Pthemnat rested amongst the crystal walls almost invisible. Like leaves of glass the Marina entered and waited for their ruler to greet them.

"Welcome" spoke Pthemnat.

The group shimmered and formed a circle of entities.

"You may communicate" ordered Pthemnat.

"We seek sanctions on ourselves. We have delved too far and a deep hedron now forms under our dwelling."

"It comes at great cost to stop these kinds of nodes. It is easier for the Seer rulers to let it consume you then to risk ourselves to stop it" replied Pthemnat.

"We will live with it rather than destroy it but seek sanction of it, so we can co-exist" replied the Marina.

"You have breached our laws. Why should the rulers risk their own diminishment for ones who have broken the rules even the Pthohedron must abide?"

"We seek sanction. We fear this one has driven deep beneath Rhenat, the giving ocean of power" replied one of the Marina.

"You have failed greatly then if you have placed the ocean of Rhenat in peril and you now dare come here to ask for our salvage" spoke Pthemnat.

"We seek sanction."

Pthemnat rose out of the wall of crystal and morphed into the shape of a thin spear. It whipped around and through the menagerie of power-collators causing them to shudder in unison. The Seer stopped in front of them.

"I will need to see the hedron and I will decide what to do. When I have returned you will have my ruling" spoke Pthemnat.

The Marina left instantly.

"Magt I will leave for the ocean of Rhenat" ordered Pthemnat.

A low rumble began to emit around the Seer. It was the Qedra of the Pthohedron lifting up out of the solid wall of the torix weave. The energy required to move consumed power from everything around it as it made its slow ascent.

The ocean of Rhenat called to the Seer due to its density of energy flow. Its tides were huge and soothing to Pthemnat when its lust and conquest would overwhelm its delving into the fields of power. There were three great oceans of calm which had been given as a peace offering to the five seers by Oblyquixiton. The ancient force had understood the surges of creation inside the Seers and knew that a competitor was born. Pthemnat and Oblyquixiton also understood they were enemies destined to consume each other in future memory. The Qedra drifted effortlessly towards the ocean as the Seer thought upon the Marina and what it would do after sanction had been applied.

The Marina were troublesome. Their ability to reshape the torix weave of Gnoceris and discover new pathways of energy was useful but it continued to be destructive.

Pthemnat waved and a small cube appeared. It was a map of Gnoceris. A dot of red light pulsated signalling the position of the Seer. Pthemnat watched as it slowly drifted to a red patch where the ocean lay. On the periphery of its vision it always felt the silence of Oblyquixiton and the surging battles behind the webs of Stonthrax. Something had pierced the webs and the Seer thought it must be the creature making its way closer.

The red glow grew more pervasive as the ocean neared. The power of was thick and dense. The Seer felt it inside its mind and called for it to cleanse.

"Deepest, potent, strongest, wash and cleanse the voyager as it makes its way to your core" spoke Pthemnat.

The waves of pure energy shook the Qedra and Seer, splitting them apart and together again. The Seer had the strength to control it but let the ocean suffuse into itself lusting to feel subjugated once more.

The Qedra stopped. The red was suffocating. Inside sat a deep purple wound billowing out furiously with vexa. The sparks where it met with the currents of the ocean exploded creating black voids. Pthemnat left the Qedra and neared the vortex of the ruptured energy node. It took a piece and studied it closely. The power of it rippled up and over the form of the Seer.

"They have disrupted the vexa codes and remade them in unstable bonds" spoke Pthemnat. The Seer reached inside and taking the node of vexa it crushed it into their minute components and letting them be dispersed into the sea. Soon the nodal surges began to diminish.

Pthemnat had not inspected the ocean of Rhenat in many eons. Its torcs and ebbs gave off sprays which assisted in making portals for travel between the edges of the weave.

Pthemnat merged into the ocean and felt itself be re-energised. It could feel the ripples pulsing in perfect timing and proportion. It was balanced. Then it felt the distortions rise again. It saw the hedron node had reformed. It was larger this time. Indeed the Marina had delved deeply. They had gone into the under canvass of the torix. It was pulling vexa from their stubs in the outer weave of Gnoceris.

The Seer drew upon the ocean and rose to its full strength to quell the rising distortions. They were powerful. Pthemnat grew into the shape of a scythe prism and slashed at it viciously bringing the ballooning node down. It began to rise again. The Seer speared itself into the node and dove down into the root of the cancerous energy. It saw the embedded feet of the vexa and slashed at it again and again until it stopped rooting into the mesh of the torix. Exhausted it drifted back into the Qedra to restore itself.

"Have the Marina banished. They are tiresome in their delving. Send them to the Vers quadra. There they may delve as much as they please. It is exhausted for any use, but they may farm their precious hedron."

Magt looked at the Seer and saw how much it had depleted the Ruler.

"Should we not destroy them Seer Ruler?" asked Magt.

"They will do that themselves. They are only being sustained by their constant meddling and pushing the limits deemed wise by their Rulers. Let them grow and understand the power they seek. With time they shall wish they had remained ignorant to the codes which rule the Rulers" replied Pthemnat.

Magt bowed understanding now why the Seer was not malicious. Their ultimate fatigue would be put back into the torix weaves and nourishing the collective knowledge of the Pthohedron.

Pthemnat remained in the ocean letting it heal the breach on its power. The ocean had been thinned and would require rest until the wound in the node was restored. It realised in its quest to understand this new prism of power in future memory it had neglected Gnoceris.

"Go I will return after I have seen the node restored" ordered Pthemnat.

"Yes Ruler," replied Magt.

The Qedra disappeared. Pthemnat listened to the sounds of vexa and codes writing constantly. Alluring and resonating to the deepest parts of existence. Such an unstoppable force willing itself into the conscious of the Seers. Gnoceris was made for them to rule. They had grown bored with their constant questing for more power until it was determined that they should be like their silent and destructive progenitors. They would learn how to describe the rules, remake them, and rule them. They made creatures to rule. One provision they placed on them was always to be contained within the nexus of Gnoceris. They could never leave.

A ripple surged through the ocean. The Seer looked with its eye and saw that Stonthrax had been reunited with its brethren. Oblyquixiton had been awoken. It would not be long now.

It saw the weak node begin to rebuild in the ocean of Rhenat. The Seer shone brightly through the red miasma of the ocean particles thrilled by the act of the node's restoration. Brighter and brighter it grew until the red was drowned by a pure white. Then it stopped. The Seer looked at the new node. With the last of its remaining power it willed the bonds to merge in the fledgling source of energy then collapsed.

Pthemnat floated in the ocean and out into the convexa of energy until it reached the shores of Ozas. This had been shaped by Seer Glaxa as a means of recovery, rebirth, and rest. Glaxa had been given a glimpse of Simeris and had seen the mighty citadels forged by the Guardians. It had determined that such glorious control of the codes of energy deserved to be made on Gnoceris.

"Ruler you have come to visit" spoke Tagen the Codecin of the citadel appeared before Pthemnat.

"I had been required to restore a breach and thought I must come and visit the beauty of the Citadel Glaxa" spoke Pthemnat.

"You are welcome" spoke Tagen forming into a visible state.

Pthemnat had taken the appearance of one of the Oracles without the eight eyes. It had seen their majestic beauty during one of the battles on Simeris and enjoyed their refinement of energy.

Inside the main spire was the conclave of Glaxa. The Seer had imbued its special control of the restorative codes for forming. Glaxa's gift of the Ozas was particularly potent. The Codecin who dwelled here had learnt the ways of seeking knowledge and would grow. It was necessary for Pthemnat to rule Glaxa, as it sensed the Seer's desire to quest for knowledge and not the restoration of Gnoceris. It was as Glaxa attempted to disentangle itself from the Pentat and seek out Aes Vius that Pthemnat intervened. Pthemnat knew that Aes Vius had grown strong as well. For Aes Vius to be bonded to Glaxa as well, would mean an imbalance on either side of the threshold which bound all existence.

If the Codecin of Ozas knew that their founder no longer resided in the Pthohedron it would lead to disharmony which may render destruction to Gnoceris.

"I have not been here for many cycles, but I have sensed a disharmony spiral almost to the shores of Ozas" spoke Pthemnat.

"Oh we have become too much like the fisher Marina and delved too far. Seer Glaxa has been generous to make sure we do not overstay and exhaust the node beds. The boundaries of remain firm, Ruler" replied Tagen.

Pthemnat strolled over to the edge of the viewing platform. The ocean of Rhenat was going into the resting phase which meant that the dark emitters let the vexa shine more brilliantly.

"That is good. I have just banished the Marina for their breaches."

Pthemnat stared into the mind of Tagen but felt the blush of secrecy quickly fall across the ebbing pulses, blocking Pthemnat. There was nothing that could be hidden from the Seer, but it took tremendous energy to delve into the nodes of a Codecin. Not this time Tagen I am still depleted from hedron node in Rhenat thought Pthemnat.

"I have been impolite. Let us rest. I would like to re-acquaint myself with this marvellous formation" spoke Pthemnat.

"We miss Glaxa. Will the great maker ever return?" asked Tagen.

"Perhaps. The Pthohedron is ever delving Tagen. We can be distracted. We also grow bored quickly hence our long absences forever trying to find more energy" replied Pthemnat. Tagen was always direct. Pthemnat enjoyed the interaction especially with the veil of secrecy it cloaked its mind in.

"What would you like to see Ruler?" asked Tagen.

"Show me the location of the disharmony."

Instantly they were sitting amongst white noise and static shocks. The explosions were so great that it formed an odour. It was acrid and stale.

"You have entered into the merge points of two stars. Infant ones not fully formed yet. This is adventurous even for a Seer" spoke Pthemnat.

"We came upon it as we were repairing the edges of Ozas. One of us fell into it. It consumed Sol" Tagen explained.

"No doubt."

Pthemnat was perturbed that a star could be forming within the weave of Gnoceris. Stars had been destroyed when the Seers first came to conscious to make Gnoceris. They were destructive by nature and needed to be contained. They extorted everything around them for their dominance.

"What drew you to this sector?" asked Pthemnat.

"It had never been considered before Ruler. It suddenly appeared in our vector searches, and we grew curious about it" replied Tagen.

"Suddenly appeared. Can you show me the sector charts?" asked Pthemnat.

The maps of the Ozas quadrant opened up. Pthemnat watched and scrolled through the layers of weave, each of the netted axons firing as the Seer searched through them. It came to a black spot where the stars were forming. The Seer froze everything around it even Tagen. It peered into the empty centre of the star. Pthemnat shuddered as the heart of the star bled into its consciousness. It was so devoid of energy that it created a sense of cold. To be felt sensually outside the energy geodes was close to the power that only the Pthohedron could corral. Gnoceris was drawing things to itself. It was collecting energy. Perhaps it was evolving into a star itself. Would the Seers be able to control the energy of a star, formed from the larval waves of power originally made from the merging of Caemeris and Oblyquixiton wondered Pthemnat.

Suffocating in the energy fields the Seer pierced the emptiness with a node of energy from itself. It sat there inert. Not moving or reacting. The Seer watched. Normally it would begin to expand and destroy the void to stop the reaction of the nega-vexa which fed off it to form light.

"What sort of darkness are you made from?" asked Pthemnat.

The Seer again pierced the emptiness with a node. A few tendrils emerged but were eaten quickly and withered before Pthemnat could draw them back. Stilling itself the Seer let the dark call to it. This was rarely done for the heart of a star could consume anything it touched. Pthemnat placed a protective veil of vexas around itself and then let the blackness in. The Seer fell back. The emptiness was unknown and potent. Not even the seminal memories of Oblyquixiton's birth met the strength of this star. It was not the blinding agony of Caemeris either. Pthemnat pulled on the Qedra's well of energy and plunged into the heart of the emptiness. Swimming in the slippery matter until it found the densest part. It stopped and began to pull the Pthohedron down toward itself to generate a poisoned node. The node formed and then grew into a miniscule beacon of raw nebula. The Seer stayed and watched it increase in size. Then it stopped. The Seer drew again on its power to strengthen the node, but nothing happened. It did not begin to decay but remained the same.

Pthemnat knew it could not draw upon anymore power without rupturing the weave of Gnoceris. It withdrew and returned to the citadel chamber. The plug formed from the Qedra reserves would be enough to hold the star from expanding any further.

"Tagen" called Pthemnat. The Codecin woke. It looked a little confused but shrugged it off as a star storm which occasionally rained on the citadel and disrupted the energy flows.

"Yes Ruler. Another star storm. There have been many recently."

"Yes. As a gift I have left a genode with in the star-chasm to help keep it stable. I am glad for you making me aware of this new source. The Rulers will study it and consider what we shall do with it. It may well be that there is a chance it can be harvested, and a new level of power has become available" spoke Pthemnat.

"Yes Ruler. We are grateful for your generosity. Our sentinels have been in contact with it since we first delved."

"And what have they learned?"

"I will show you."

The sentinels sat in a conclave around an empty patch of weave. The Seer attempted to penetrate their minds but was unable to break the hold of the star's energy. It had locked them and was feeding off them the same way it did with the weave.

The Seer seeped into the eight inanimate figures. They were completely consumed by the chasm. It placed a veil of vexa around them to starve the star draining more energy. Pthemnat called the Qedra and turned to Tagen.

"Leave them be. It will be valuable once we understand what they are seeing."

"Yes Ruler."

"I must return. The Rulers are pleased to be aware of this and will give you guidance once more is understood" spoke Pthemnat.

The Qedra appeared instantly and Magt opened the dais for Pthemnat to enter.

"Magt gather the sentinels and bring them with us. They are in conclave and will assist our understanding of this phenomena in Ozas.'

The Qedra ate the encircled sentinels as Pthemnat joined with the Qedra.

"I have searched too long beyond the webs of Stonthrax and neglected Gnoceris. It has been invaded by a new force I have no memory of. Even when I peer into those remnants of time this potency remains unknown to me. My brethren Seers are lost, and I cannot call upon their will to bring forth the veil of Oblyquixiton. A gift bestowed as a peace offering to quell the great ambition of their Seers. But instead I am here. I remain as the one who continues to know where the lost one Caemeris has wandered and seeks to draw it back. Now I see in this musing I have forgotten what the Seers first battled, and their purpose was. To gaol the infant stars as they were made. To stop them usurping the emptiness and ultimately destroying everything made. To stop them challenging Caemeris. That purpose changed as we grew in strength and saw as much and as far as the makers of chaos. And in my urgency to conquer I have let a youngling birth, but its progenitor is unknown to me. It is more potent, and its profundity draws far beyond the memories of the Pthohedron. I wait also for the Wanderer to come with this new gift which may hold the weaves and waves to Caemeris, and the Seers ultimate suzerainty over the nodes. This Seer lies musing on its ambition and now faces destruction of the world wrought from the fragments of memory and vexa of energy. Give me your secrets youngling usurper and I will see how to remake you and bring you into the nexus of Gnoceris" spoke Pthemnat.

Pthemnat moved into the unconscious conclave of sentinels. They were formed as the ancillary to the Seers when Gnoceris grew to its final size. It became too draining to always be everywhere and so the sentinels were formed to be semi guardians. Formulated from remnants of the webs of Stonthrax. Watchers and Questors which remained unfettered by the codes of the forms they were expelled from but potent in their own right. When Gnoceris was destroyed and the quest for power beyond the Thrax was decided, it was the Sentinels which formed beyond the gates and began the great wandering. Searching, seeking with eyes to watch guided by the imprint of the Seers. They took names for themselves, from the knowledge of Aes Vius to bring definition, to energy – Uchala, Eaudania, Shomac, and Vipax.

Inside the conclave Pthemnat watched how the star had grown silently amongst the energy bonds. Cloaked because it was not using the links which vibrated when the shaded matter and light mingled. Vexa within vexa then it formed a crystal shape so tightly packed together that it consumed itself. Soon the roiling fire of a star was forged by the tractate of Caemeris and Oblyquixiton.

"Why are you so silent? It is as if you have broken free of the chaotic one and made your own path" asked Pthemnat of the infant node of light.

Sitting from within the conclave of sentinels, Pthemnat was bemused. It sensed neither chaos nor silence only power. The star ebbed against the genode made by Pthemnat. It would only hold for so long. The energy fields rebounding back and forth between the genode and star vexa eventually wear down and become overwhelmed. The Seer took a piece of the star. It gave off the scent of burnt matter. It placed the piece inside a vexa veil. It remained stable. Soon it would reach the critical phase of where the star would arrange itself and remain stable or it would explode. It was not large enough yet to obliterate Gnoceris, but stars were unpredictable and could consume in an instant or grow over eras as long as the memories of Oblyquixiton. Pthemnat shaped the vexa veil containing the piece of star into a cone.

Magt watched the Ruler through the shroud of node cloud. It was using the deepest knowledge of their Rulers to decipher the event in the Ozas. It had disturbed the Seer and Magt could feel the disharmony as it rippled through the weave. Low and threatening. It was strange that the young star had formed so quickly without the Ruler knowing. Magt had seen the obsession of the Ruler grow until it had almost been lost in the miasma of the forbidden zone for eons. Magt wondered if this is what had happened to the other rulers. There was a myth that Ruler Pthemnat was the only remaining ruler of the world and that in fact the Seer had extinguished the others. It was only myth, but it was what was fuelling the increasing delving into the under nexus of the weave and these eruptions of power which if unleashed without the proper coding would destroy everything. The creations of each of the Seers were trying to find their makers.

"Magt" called Pthemnat.

"Yes Ruler."

"You are to take these cones remnants from the star and deposit them in the dead ocean of Idata."

"Yes Ruler."

Magt hesitated.

"This star vexa will provide a means of regenerating the weave there. Long silent, this could be its rebirth. I have made it stable. Simply release it into the vapour. I will set one of the sentinels to watch" spoke Pthemnat.

Magt took the tiny crystal shaped cone. While its potency was strong there was nothing to see. The vexa were invisible except to the Rulers sight. It slid into the stream of energy and arrived at the expanse at depleted nodes. Magt took the cone and flung it out into the vapour and swiftly left. The ocean of Idata was known to deplete the energy waves of any Gnocerin who delved there.

"Another Magt. This time in the edge of the weave among the relics of Lon."

"Ruler you know I will obey. But…"

"I have protected you Magt. I need to find a way to quell the young tyrant which grows here. This way I may find its secrets. For it shall either whither or it will bring mortifaction" explained Pthemnat.

"I understand" replied Magt.

Magt once again threw the cone out into the nebular rim and watched it disappear. It felt a tug as the star matter burst into the chasm of darkness. Magt wondered again of the wisdom of this dispersing into the dead zones. What if the star did regenerate the nebulas but, in its state, not that of the weave. The Ruler was the only one with the power to even look into the invading star and to contain its destructive energy. But what if its sight had been distorted by the presence of the star's darkness?

Magt arrived back expecting to be given another task, but the Seer was deep in stasis and did not request anything. Magt returned to the sanctity of its noda to re-energise. Lying in the chamber of field vexa it slipped into Gnocin slumber.

Pthemnat was held in a trance with a tendril of the young star. It had codes on it which were indecipherable. Plucking out each strip and filament it attempted to read the origins of this intruder.

It pulled each segment apart until every stroke, vibration, and confluence was separate. It then reformulated them into the weave of Gnoceris. A small patch formed but the energy to maintain it was massive and the Seer disintegrated into its nodal chamber depleted.

"What is it and what made it?" Pthemnat asked.

The Seer tried to reform itself to return to the Sentinel conclave, but it was impossible. It took the genodal codes and shut them off. The only thing on Gnoceris which remained awake was the Qedra. The weave became dim and inert. The Seer pulled upon the ancient threads it was made from and called for the Pthohedron to come. Slipping back into the Pthohedron, it lay in Gnocin slumber to remake itself.

The young star was held captive ebbing against the vexa veil.

Ange climbed through the webs of Stonthrax. They clung to her as if they did not want her to leave. She cut them with her blade, but they instantly remade themselves, only stronger. She decided to stop and figure out how to manipulate them. Nekoda lay in deep sleep. She had bound him in the webs and commanded him to slumber. She did not know what lay beyond the gates or even if he could survive it. She sensed whatever the Guardians kept watch on was something her kind would never understand or know. It was a great wall which separated existence. Like the waters which fell from the sky into the ocean to make fish and then the dirt which grew food. Formed from one place but each just as different in purpose and form, none could understand the other. Stepping into the webs, caused the same feeling when she had first seen the black ocean. Its immensity and strangeness had overwhelmed her. The only familiar thing was the memory of the river and the dripping water from the boab trees.

She decided she did not want to risk Nekoda's life. The prism afforded her protection, but it may well be the place which made the power of the prism, meaning everything would be equal to its strength. She would be naked for the first time and that also meant her beloved friend. She would not risk him suffering needlessly. She had placed a code around Nekoda cocooning him safely. If she did not return, then the webs were to return the dog back to Sa-Tuchala's protection.

Sitting in an open patch of white gossamer web she took the prism and reformed it to make a tablet. She coded the webs and copied them. She made a small bundle. She cut them and remade them. She was able to cut them again. She saw that when the web remade itself it used a dark shadow entwined in the helix of its design. She saw that no code existed inside these patches but a low hum. She listened to it, and it reminded her of the Yonta song. Slowly it started to reduce and become silent then it disappeared. She remade the thread and then cut them. Again they reformed but this time the shadow and music disappeared more quickly. Trying it again for a third time the music did not play at all. Ange realised that with time the web would weaken and not be able to make itself. She resumed her slashing in its suffocating denseness and eventually began to make progress. Her blade slashed and the web gave way and remained open. Suddenly the force of her cutting thrust her out into an ocean of colourful tiny dots. She saw a stream of colour moving very fast around her. She went to put her blade away but there was nothing there. Then she saw her hand disintegrate, then her arm and then her entire form.

"Where am I?" she asked but there was no sound. The prism remained intact strangely enough. She looked around her to see where the gateway lay but it was gone. She felt a warm flush in her which she assumed was where her heart would have been. She began to panic. What if she could not get back to Simeris? Suddenly a slip stream of energy caught her, and she was moving amongst the lights, becoming part of them. The movement was generated by her changing into light and back into darkness.

Ange squeezed the prism and called "Stop!"

She did. She was relieved that she could at least control aspects of this place. She stepped out of the energy stream and into a cloud of green crystals. They shimmered constantly and she could feel their hum. She let one float onto her mesh like hand. It sat their humming. She could see it was sending out vibrations around it powering the blank patches in between. Then all of the green specs swarmed around her and sat ebbing gently near her like she drew them to her. Then she realised it was probably the prism. Looking further she could see a solid shape. She made her way toward it. It was like a shore and on it were dwellings. She saw they were made from the same netted lights as herself. Figures were moving swiftly back and forth. She stopped on the edge of a thin coastline. She sat watching. Soon however she saw that the edge was distorting toward her. The prism drew everything to it. She backed away not wanting to arouse any interest. She stopped and held the prism up to her eye to view the world through it. It instantly appeared whole. All the energy coalesced into one, making a massive dense landscape similar to her home. When she took it away it was like there was only the particles before they became joined to make everything the way it appeared. She looked again. The figures were thin ethereal like the Epimarin but more solid. This was strange as the Epimarin did not change when she had neared them with the prism. Why would it do it here she wondered. She looked across a vast ocean raging. There were waves so high she could not see their peaks. They were pure energy. When she removed the cloaking effect of the prism there were hectic flows of nebulas once more. Far off they changed into quiet patches of small rivulets. She could hear a low hum intertwined among the surging specs; it was similar to the shaded veins in the webs of Stonthrax.

"So much here. So much could be gathered and remade into anything. Is this what lies at the heart of the existence? Aes Vius you should see what I see. Is this what exists even before the memories are made? Raw and unformed in its purpose waiting for a pathway. That is what lies in the unknown vistas you see in your towers. There is only the dust waiting for something to rest upon. A vision needs to exist for this world to form. This is unquenchable, insatiable strength. I feel every part of me being pulled and restitched together. When I watch through the prism, my memories of an ocean come to being. It both frightened me and seemed to pull me in, so it could drown me in its greatness. It was familiar yet unknowable. I think if a creature made from the dirt and clay came here then this would eat bone and flesh and thickness of shape like the desert. I am protected by the prism. It seems to be able to make the world real to me and not be taken over by the sheer force of the power which surrounds me. Where am I now? My heart lies with you Aes Vius in its safekeeping. I feel the lust for power here could break the gates of Stonthrax and it would bleed into the worlds we live. But would it also destroy us and everything? Something wise made the Guardians to hold back this place. Is this what Caemeris did? Is this what it wanted to remain hidden? Did something break the bonds and crash into our world? Is that what caused the desire to dominate and conquer fill our minds and stain the deserts and rivers with blood over and over again. It was power which was never meant to be in our reach yet came unseen and hidden and there it remained, unfettered because of our ignorance? I have brought more power to this place by coming here with the prism. Is this why the mighty Norbu hid this prism, stored the eye of Caemeris in it, so its power could not be stolen. And yet here I am with it, the deliverer of the very thing that was desired all along. I brought destruction in order to save my world. I will find out what is wanted, and I shall tell you Aes Vius and place it into the Cadra Phomera. I draw closer to this Caemeris and the mystery which surrounds it. I will understand what made the Custodians and what can destroy them. Will I become lost to myself and forget Nekoda, Sa, Gildas and Kado. Will I forget Tessi and Bensah? I have left sorrow and grief in an existence where it mattered. Now I see a place where anything can be and not be at the same time. I can see the black oceans and what makes them, so they no longer frighten me as I understand how to create and destroy them. I stand clothed in a lightness of existence before it even becomes. I can see what lives around me and in the non-light which breaks the spaces that hum continuously. On and on I can feel it pull my very essence out of me and put it back together. I desire the power to control it, formulate it into what I want but I know it would indulge me for a moment and then in its complete harmony it will simply go back to the smallness it is and wait for something else to be. Like the water from the sky falls into the earth making the mighty Choasa flow, until it reaches the ocean and disappears. I understand that it does not stop simply because I want it to. But comes and goes as it pleases with no care if it forms the raging ocean destroying the cliffs or lets the crops grow which feeds the children in the village. This is why I see it as an ocean of power through the prism. The prism contains the memory of Caemeris, and it is only with in this cage can it be found again to ask if it will contain what bled into our world. I will discover this world Aes and when I return, I will tell you of it so that the great unknown for this clay-born can be named."

Ange turned back to the shoreline and walked toward it. She felt the surges of the slip stream push her and will her to merge into them and listen to the music of existence, but she gripped the prism tightly and felt the desirous power retreat a little letting her remain in her form. She stood on the edges of the Ozas and walked toward the citadels.

A figure emerged from the tower. Curiously, it saw the creature. It was unlike anything it had seen. It appeared as a blank dense patch of energy which consumed the vexa as it passed through it.

"Greetings" spoke Tagen.

"Hello. I am Ange. I am a visitor from elsewhere. Where am I?"

"You are in Gnoceris. Created by the Pthohedron Seers. I am Tagen, Codecin of the Ozas zone."

"I am here to learn of this place."

"The Seers are our rulers here. They are the ones who must teach you. They will be curious to know about you."

"What is the name of the ocean which surrounds you?" asked Ange.

"Ah this is the ocean of Rhenat. Seer Glaxa made it as a repository of power" replied Tagen.

"Can you tell me of the ocean and this Seer?" asked Ange.

Tagen hesitated, wondering who the stranger was. Perhaps it was Ruler Pthemnat testing loyalties and adherence to the rules.

"Do not be alarmed. I am not known to your Rulers and in time I will seek them out. But for now I desire to sit by this ocean and learn of it. I once stared at a great dark chasm of water which was so fierce, I thought it would kill anything that entered it. This reminds of that place."

"I see. May I ask where this was?" asked Tagen.

"You would not understand Tagen. Just as I don't understand how this place was formed" replied Ange.

"Ah well that I can explain to you visitor. I can explain how codes contain the memories of Ruler Osesa. One of the five. In its questing for power it had discovered the need for vexa to form shapes and then fit together. The vexa and qedra are made from these codes. I am a Codecin, discoverer of codes. Made by Osesa to study and learn and make sure the codes remain harmonious, warn of any anomalies which if discovered, then the Rulers are informed. They alone can determine if these anomalies warrant intervention or maybe left to increase their knowledge."

"Where do the Rulers dwell?" asked Ange.

"The nodal bed of the Pthohedron: the repository of the Rulers of Gnoceris."

"I see. The power here is overwhelming. How it washes up and over and through me and in me. May I show you something?" asked Ange.

"Of course" replied Tagen.

She took the prism and placed it across the ocean.

"What do you see?" Ange asked Tagen.

"Why the vexa are aligned perfectly and there is no disharmony. I can even see the song of Glaxa more clearly and the waves of Rhenat move in unison. It is truly a marvel to watch. This is when Gnoceris is building to a release or surge of star-death is imminent. It is sent away far into the chasms beyond our realm and helps keep the balance" spoke Tagen.

Suddenly a massive flare shot through the prism and struck Tagen directly. It exploded into a shower of sparks over Ange. She stood taken aback.

"What have I done? Tagen? I didn't mean to strike you."

She looked around. The prism could control the energy and make it a weapon as well. Tagen reformed behind her.

"I am sorry. I didn't know it would do that" Ange spoke concerned for the Codecin.

"You carry a great tool of nodal strength. For it to wield the ocean of Rhenat it must have been designed by one of the Seers for their use. Have they given it as a gift or way of controlling the zones?" Tagen asked seemingly unperturbed by what had just happened.

"No it was forged by a ruler in another realm. But its potency is strongest here" replied Ange.

"I will send you to our Rulers. It is important for them to know you are here" spoke Tagen.

"I will make my way there eventually, but I need to understand the ways of Gnoceris first" replied Ange.

"I sense an anomaly in this approach. The Rulers are absolute in their realm. They are always aware of any disharmony."

"Then why have they made you?" asked Ange.

"To assist and control the energy of the vexa but they are always aware of what we do" explained Tagen.

Ange considered it was more that they needed to draw on power to maintain their strict control of the world. It would be draining and difficult to sustain. They would desire the power of Norbu's gift to help them she thought.

"I will go soon enough to your Rulers Tagen. But for the moment I want to explore Gnoceris a little more. Show me."

Ange could feel the resistance from the creature but using the prism pulled the energy streams away from Tagen's hesitation forcing it to agree.

"This way. Our citadel is forged from an image Seer Glaxa had touched once in a deep delve well beyond the edges of existence. It was almost forbidden, and I believe the Seer needed to slumber for many turns of nodal regeneration."

Ange guessed the Seers had ways of peering beyond the gates of Stonthrax and had seen other worlds or perhaps they had forged them in some way as well. The Seer who had followed her in Epimaris had only supplanted images of its own shadow. Its power had not been fully consummated beyond the gates otherwise it would have snatched the prism for itself.

Ange followed the creature watching as it merged in and out of form with the energy fields. They disappeared altogether inside a net like structure. Then they resumed their shapes inside a large dome like building.

"This is the node Fedar. It lies beneath the citadel and is where all the power is drawn to and emerges from to make the Ozas" Tagen explained.

"You are trusting to show me this Tagen. If I had a weapon which could destroy the node, would it wound your Rulers?" Ange asked.

"For a weapon to be so destructive we would have been drawn directly into its nodal strength when you entered our world, and we would not be here" replied Tagen.

"I see. What would destroy Gnoceris?" asked Ange.

"Nothing we know. The vexa never depletes only wanes so that anything formed from the Rulers simply collapses and then slowly reforms."

Ange wondered how the Seers came to be so powerful yet not warlike. It will be interesting when she and the Seers finally meet. The strength in Gildas and the hatred and domination in Ranik and Voloc felt as powerful as these nodes and yet they only sought destruction in their minds. This was different. This was like the river running over the lands after the great rains in the spring. Strong and forceful and would drown anything in its path yet it was accepted as a cleansing of the desiccated earth to replenish it for crops and fish to feed. Nothing could stop that river from overflowing or any of the unintended death it caused. It was the world at work in its goodness not the hatred and lust for destruction which warriors of war brought with their swords. An artificial death, not like the Mighty Choasa; strong, urgent, and unrelenting but meant no harm or good, it simply existed within its codes and always allowed for re-birth when its conquest of the world had finished.

"The nodes ebb and flow between the slits in the fabric of shadowed matter. All of it has energy and must be in harmony otherwise the nodes expand too far, and everything must be remade" spoke Tagen.

"I understand. We have similar elements from my birthplace which live by the rules laid down in the beginning days" replied Ange.

"Now I will show you, our citadel" spoke Tagen.

Ange looked beneath the veiled dome structure and looked at the churning energy flows. It was mesmerising. She let it flow into her while clutching the prism as she knew she would not have the strength to resist falling into the massive pool of raw power. The shaded emptiness was dancing in perfect harmony with the torn chaotic light. Its music was alluring to every part of her more so than the death song of the Yonta.

"Come, the nodes are intoxicating, aren't they?" asked Tagen.

"Yes, they are beautiful" replied Ange.

"This is the pinnacle of Seer Osesa's work. It was made to bring the nodes above the under-weave and into the open of Gnoceris. If you meld into the edges, the power is so strong you can feel the push and pull between here and beyond our world. Go discover" urged Tagen.

Ange merged into the upward spouting vexa and out into the rim of the energy weave. She completely disappeared and then reappeared. The prism remained the same, solid in its shape like the web of a spider between tree branches. It bowed slightly like a web in the wind, but it never broke. She let it float.

"Tell me your secrets, gift of Norbu" Ange spoke into the miasma of vexa flow.

It bobbed and vibrated in the void but never changed.

"Show me" ordered Ange.

"I am" the prism replied.

Ange was stunned. It had responded in her mind. Had she made the voice up, so desperate to finish this quest and be rid of all it. No she sensed its' presence within her mind. It had shimmered in the energy waves, and it had responded to her like it was alive.

"What are you?"

There was silence.

"No don't do this. I have been changed to the point I am no longer recognisable to myself. I am doing this because..." she hesitated. "How dare you do this? Tell me" Ange demanded.

There was no response this time. The pulsing energy continued silently.

"I want answers. I will thrust you into the webs of Stonthrax, to remain, stagnant until I decay and wither along with everything else. Ange Tsaed will remain here in the stasis of pure energy, under the rule of the Seer, never to leave and end her story. Your power never released or ruled by any other. To remain silent until the death of Simeris and time."

Silence.

Ange knew her threat was hollow. Her feelings of frustration swelled the nodal flows of energy. She was becoming more embedded into Gnoceris the longer she stayed. She floated back to Tagen and morphed back into the shape of herself.

"I am glad I have let Nekoda rest. I am weary" she spoke.

"Of Gnoceris. You only just arrived here" replied Tagen.

She did not reply to the Codecin. It wouldn't understand. Was it the Seer playing tricks to make her give the prism to it she wondered.

Tagen watched a tear in the weave repair itself where the visitor had dispersed into the flows. The vexa and qedra were drawn to the creature and its tool. Tagen opened its mind to let the Rulers know of Ange's presence. There was no response. It was not the first time Tagen had not felt the presence of Seer Osesa or Glaxa but did not probe further. Seer Pthemnat's visit was reassurance enough for the Codecin. Could this be the Rulers, here in another form? What else could disrupt the under-weave and repair it wondered Tagen. Yes, perhaps that was it. Perhaps this was another phase of Gnocerin knowledge Osesa and Glaxa were attempting to make thought Tagen.

"Tell me how the nodes are made Tagen" spoke Ange.

"Oh I cannot do that. This is something the Rulers must explain. They made them and control, them."

"But the nodes draw power to them and help form the weave?" asked Ange.

"Well I shouldn't show you this, but it will help explain" replied Tagen.

They entered what appeared to Ange a waterfall and slipped into the river which flowed beneath it. She felt herself pulled to pieces from the magnitude of the power. Suddenly they were on the edge of the under-weave once more. Looking at the columns of massive flows, emitting from a crack in the chasm shadow. It was the entrance point for the power which sustained Gnoceris. Ange dived in anxious to know where this was coming from. Tagen waited. It felt a little perturbed. Perhaps it was not Seer Osesa. If it were, then surely Tagen would have been sent to dredge the dead nodes for showing this to the visitor.

Ange swam in pure light and was completely blinded by it. The prism was still not affected but she noticed it had become black like it turned the light inside out.

"Where am I?" she asked. There was no answer. She touched the prism.

"Where am I? Where are the custodians? Where is Caemeris? Where is Oblyquixiton?" she called.

Ange took the prism and began to write the codes of the light.

"Do I take you back to the Epimarin to learn of what you are? Is it you Seer who continues to follow me like shadows in a full moon in the desert. Half hidden and forbidding but menacing the sand mouse who skips across the sands by revealing its hide to the sand-serpent."

She scored the codes. They were simple. One strike up and another down followed by three in between. She folded them over until they mushroomed out into crystal shape. Then the scores formed into a circular motion the more she added so that they ebbed in bulging billowing flows over each other forming a dense ball with a hollow centre.

"Not yet" came the answer.

Suddenly Ange was back with Tagen looking at the massive waves and columns of energy.

"It must be Caemeris" she whispered.

Tagen was bowing to her and drifting in out of her shape.

"Mighty Ruler you have returned. Seer Glaxa, I bow to you and welcome you back. So many nodal wanes since you have come to see your creations."

Ange looked at Tagen. She wondered what had happened here that the Seers were so interested in her quest yet did not seem to pay attention to their own world. Ange decided to take advantage of the Codecin's misunderstanding.

"Tagen, Codecin, loyal one, you are great to keep my creation true to the codes laid down by the Rulers. Show me the rest and then we will gather again in the Citadel" spoke Ange.

"Of course, Ruler. Here the codes are washed and reformed to keep them pure. It makes the slip streams and energy vexa far more stable and when they reach the limits of their cycle then their death is not as destructive. It is of course how we maintain the weave, separate to the chasm of shadow which surrounds us" explained Tagen.

"I see."

Ange watched codes gather like flies in the marshlands or the ants in their nests. Racing in swarms but there was rhythm to it and Ange could hear music humming underneath.

"Have the Seers ever gone to war with another Tagen?" Ange probed wondering if these Seers who could wield power so easily would have desire to conquer each other.

There was silence for a long time. Ange began to grow nervous. The humming increased markedly and soon dominated the whole space. She looked at the prism. It was still unchanged by anything. Ange understood why the Seers would seek out the prism. It reigned over everything because it was unchangeable. Nothing could defeat it if nothing could not destroy it. Mighty Norbu, I cannot grieve for you, not yet but I wish you could tell me how you made this stone. Suddenly her musing was broken when Tagen finally spoke.

"You remember the reason for the dome of Quun, Ruler. It stopped the oceans of vexa usurping the Gnoceris entirely. It grieved you to have to quell the creations of your brethren Rulers. I remember our last contact. You told us in your citadel, Gnoceris must remain. The energy lust will never die, and it must be contained. Even the Pthohedron will not understand the destruction we make unless it is contained. You said it was insatiable. There is no conquest as you call it visitor, but there must be containment" replied Tagen.

Ange did not respond. She merged into Tagen to see the memories. She morphed into the shape of the Seer Glaxa. Tagen bowed when it saw her.

"Seer, you have come when it matters most. A grave breach has occurred. I was unsure if it was you. But now I know that it is I will show you what I showed Seer Pthemnat. Star death has come, and it is raw and beautiful. Drawing the Ozas into its alluring power. Can you heal the breach to stop the decay?"

"Show me where it is'?" asked Ange.

Ange heard Star-death and she shivered. It reminded her of the destruction of Voloc on Arglethium. Tagen slipped into the node stream and took her where the breach had happened.

"Ruler Pthemnat has placed a nodal control around it" spoke Tagen.

"How did this happen?" asked Ange.

"We delved too far" replied Tagen.

Ange fell into the emptiness and saw for the first time the prism swell and begin to draw the void into itself. The emptiness was different to the edges of the under-weave. It was silent. There was no hum. She remembered the cavern when she was held captive by Voloc. There were no memory codes to draw where it had come from. It was alive and dead but aware as well.

"Tagen, leave me. I wish to explore more deeply. Perhaps its mystery will reveal its secrets to me."

"Of course. The Rulers know and make all."

Ange released the prism into the emptiness. She saw it suck in the darkness drinking as it if had been without sustenance since it had been shaped. But for all the darkness it consumed it made no difference to the emptiness around her.

"What are you? Are you the shadows of Oblyquixiton? Are you the heart of Caemeris? Are you the eye of Baachelaus? Are you the memory of Ascendant? Are you Voloc? Tell me for you are not of Gnoceris. Are you what makes the prism? Is this how it draws its strength?"

"You were called. You leap beyond what the clay formed should know. But you are here existing because of this repository of my will. You are aware and acute and made of stones and dirt. Things too dense to live here. It is good they do not. The ones you seek to bring back to your world will be found. But not before you understand. Your presence has thinned the veils between what came before all that was formed beyond the Thrax. The stone of the youngling custodian you call Norbu is a travesty and curse. It was made to capture the power of existence. It is craven to exist and drink of this silence. It seeks to quell its own chaos.

Its wrongness to be at all. It will pull all into it until there is no more. You are not ready yet to destroy this malformed tool. Find these Custodians bring them to your home, then you who audaciously journeyed beyond the boundaries of your existence, you should learn of power, strength, creation, and force. For a time will come when we shall stand before each other and only one will remain in the constant flow of existence and annihilation."

"It will be I" pronounced Ange to the ripples in the blankness, almost musical in their quality but depleted of any sense or feeling.

"You are Caemeris. The lost one. The one desirous of power, destruction, and rebirth. You are the first to pierce the silence and destroy the dark. If I have no answer than my enemy is born. Why have you chosen the clay youngling? Fragile and not fully grown to be the one to make your return known?" asked Ange.

"Youngling, there is no will to be defeated or battle which in your ignorance is to begin. There is simply the formed of light and nothing. There is no deception or conquest but what you carry, contains both. Now it seems there is a third entity, you wield this entity, Clayborn of Arglethium. And you shall weep when you have finished your quest, for while there is nobility in you to save the beauty of the formed, the sorrow of how to keep it from dying will overwhelm your fragile heart. Your battle is not with us but with yourself" replied the emptiness around her.

Suddenly the darkness became thick like a river of black blood. The smell was strong. Ange once more was reminded of Voloc. Had Voloc come to life again? Had it been the one manipulating her all along. The blackness began to churn. Ange felt herself be pulled into it. The prism distorted but continued to drink in the emptiness voraciously as if it was a living thing. She pulled out and returned to Tagen but just as she saw the Codecin suddenly she was sucked back into the slip stream of the vortex of power.

"Tagen" she called.

"Tagen" she called.

"Tagen" she called.

It kept reverberating around the energy field within the darkness. She gripped the prism and willed it protect her. It did not.

"If this prism is yours to control then why not will it to destroy me or enflame me to battle with you. I have walked naked in the desert of my lands with nothing more than the hope of a better dawn than the one before. I have succumbed to the death song of the Yonta and convinced Stonthrax Gate Keeper to allow me to pass. Are you certain I am not ready to face you? Tell me where the Custodians lie. Stop these games. Those made from the newest light wish peace and a return to joy. No battle exists here other than the one you have wrought" called Ange.

The cyclone continued and Ange felt herself being squashed into tiny pieces. She saw the prism sitting in the darkness and let herself be captured by it. Inside once again raged the battles of the Custodians and a profound darkness that bled into Baachelaus fracturing its purity and brightness with the poison of Voloc. She suddenly saw a black spec growing. It was cradled in a raging heart of a fiery sun. Perhaps it was the sun which warmed her home. The blackness lay their asleep. It was unaware of her looking at it. It grew and grew until the sun expelled it out into the void. It screeched. Suddenly a spear of white fire sped across piercing the shadow in its very core. Thrusting it back into the ball of heat. It screeched again. But remained in the cradle of fiery power. It slumbered again. Ange watched Voloc from the middle of the prism and wondered what Voloc had to do with the prism. The shadow woke and seemed to peer directly at her. But she was sure it would not see her. The gates of Stonthrax kept worlds apart to keep the rawness of creation from consummating everything into itself. Voloc left the sun and Ange saw it arrive in the deserts of her land. She saw the darkness spread once more and death of the oceans and deserts. Slowly like a poisoned stream Voloc spread over her world.

"Is this now or when it came the first time setting a plague on the land. Almost destroying everything?" asked Ange.

Ange watched the growing shadow, and nothing stopped it. It grew denser and denser until Arglethium disappeared. Voloc screeched into the abyss and Ange heard the cries of annihilation.

"Stop thy death, for I am the progeny of dark and light consummated in the webs of time. No end shall ever come until Oblyquixiton and Caemeris are destroyed or become one" spoke another voice.

Was this Voloc or one of the Custodians Ange wondered. Whatever these two mighty powers were, they had begun all of this, and something caused them to rupture.

Ange searched the prism for any clue of where the Custodians may be. She saw the shape of the Seer watching. She had seen that before and wondered where that place was. It was not Gnoceris. It had rock and stone. She saw a hand come out from under the sleeve and begin to write codes on a tablet.

"Turn to me" Ange beckoned.

The figure turned to her. She saw the face, aged hair, and skin. The eyes were almost opaque.

"How long have you lived?" asked Ange.

"An eternity. I have grown bored. Breathing even becomes a heavy chain around my neck and a thrill as each breath is another moment I have lived and defeated death" replied the figure.

"Where are you?" asked Ange.

"I cannot tell you. I put the rules in place" replied the figure.

"Do you hold the Custodians prisoner?"

"Come and you shall see."

"Are you me?"

"Come and you shall see."

"I do not know where you are."

"Come and you shall see."

The image began to fade. Ange grew frustrated.

"Will the Seer show me?"

There was no answer.

"If you put the rules in place change them so I may end this. Why live so long and yet have no wisdom to tell. You should know how to fix this" pleaded Ange.

"Come and you shall see."

Then the figure faded altogether. Leaving the prism drinking the fragments of star-death.

Ange extracted herself and merged back into the citadel with Tagen.

"Seer Glaxa have you been able to quell the usurper?"

"No Tagen. It is strong this star. I believe it is time I returned to the Rulers."

"As you deem."

Tagen watched as Ange flew into the nodal flow of vexa to find the Rulers.

"Seer I am here. I am the one you are seeking. From the shadows of future memory I have come. I bring the prism of Norbu, of the Custodians, the eye of Caemeris. Show me your secrets. Tell me where the Custodians lie so I may quench Voloc's thirst and release it from its death quest and the Yonta's death song may only be the machinery of time not a destroyer of all of things and their codes" called Ange.

Pthemnat woke from the conclave. It had seen the Wanderer enter and then invade the node of power it had brought with it. It was time to meet.

"Come Wanderer into the Qedra. I have stabilised the star death and we are safe for the moment."

"You understand I am not a Seer."

"Of course not. Tagen is still growing and does see all things clearly. It is loyal and always the energy flows are unfettered to Tagen. Tagen lies in purity of vision made by the Ruler Glaxa."

"Where are these Rulers? Tagen mistook me for the Seer called Glaxa."

"The Seers were five, born of Oblyquixiton and Caemeris. We are more powerful than stars but weaker than our progenitors and the Guardian Stonthrax. Our desire to know and understand power is limitless and we constantly seek it. Gnoceris is the place where energy binds and draws the dead hearts of stars to it and repels them equally" explained Pthemnat.

"You know I have met one of your kind before. Where are the others?" asked Ange.

"Aes Vius left to seek knowledge. The others are with me" replied Pthemnat.

"Would you ever take the form of one of the young in future memory? Dense and formed of sun, water, and dirt" asked Ange.

"It is not possible for us to exist in this manner. It is not bidden that the Pthohedron should ever need the weakness of dense energy so defined and brittle from the weight of its need to be exist. Life and death is nothing to us. We do not understand it and do not desire it. Whatever you see inside your prism is not of the Pthohedron's making. Your prism called to me even beyond the webs of Stonthrax and that is why I have appeared to you on your journey here. It is the power it contains. Its flows and ebbs are remnants of Caemeris. It has touched the future memory within your realm and has left its stain. Your prism may unlock the mystery of where Caemeris has passed and show the codes of where it remains" replied Pthemnat.

"Have you blinded me and altered my path so that I came here?" asked Ange.

"I am only Ruler of Gnoceris. I seek your prism to usurp its power."

"It is not yours to control. I was made keeper of it."

"I know the nature of your quest" spoke Pthemnat "But it will not stop me seeking out the mysteries of this gift. Your Custodians were formed beyond the webs of time and are Caemexa in their design. But like you remain ignorant with only vague senses of something before them and no purpose other than fulfilling the shape of the stone, water, and dirt you describe, and the hearts and minds of the creatures called the Clayborn."

"But unless you tell me how I may return them to our world then Voloc will be unstoppable, and we will die. I must fulfil this promise. Does none of this concern you? Surely the power contained within my world and myself in the form I was born must stir wonder in a reaper of power?" asked Ange.

"Indeed when we first sensed it, the persistence to break the webs of the Thrax and reach here, told us what strength was contained in your making. But the Seers are not of the created, our interest remains within our purpose and desire to remake Gnoceris."

"Seer, is there a bargain I can strike with you? I can only see your destruction if you take the prism. There were rules made and if they are broken then I think you will find it will not give you what you desire."

"A bargain. Why should I bargain with a feeble mass such as you? I know you have seen glimpses of the Caemeris, and you hold keys to its location. I will simply enter the prism and learn its knowledge" replied Pthemnat.

"You don't understand it only contains what I need to know to end this quest. For some reason when the realm of Custodians was ruptured it set things into motion by their own will. It was like it let go and said be. As if it no longer wanted to be the progenitor of all that existed. It feels to me like it is dead. In dying it has given us our purpose to grow and learn and no longer be bound to the rules it made. It wants the clay to be tempered and shaped by its own designs not by Caemeris or the Custodians" pleaded Ange.

"I see all that you have seen but we see the first power, the most potent power within it."

"How did Voloc come to the realm of the Custodians?" asked Ange.

"Our searches reached far and wide when the Pthohedron was whole. We became whole and were drawn to the under-weave of energy and even the nodal surges beyond Thrax. In our full form as the Pentat we sent a lance, to quest and score a path to the reality of the created. It broke the gates of the Thrax. A wound was opened where none existed before. And so this quest of yours was begun" replied Pthemnat.

"You ruptured the realm of the Custodians?" asked Ange.

"Merely altered the energy flows" spoke Pthemnat.

"What was the questing threads which disrupted the Guardians of Simeris?" asked Ange.

"The Seers seek knowledge, and our sentinels began to explore what we could not" replied Pthemnat.

"Uchala?" asked Ange.

"Yes, and others. And when they reached the potent nodes of energy, then we could sense it in the Pthohedron" answered Pthemnat.

"Was Voloc one of these Sentinels?" asked Ange.

"No, this energy you call Voloc, is formed of Caemexa and Oblyquixita, but is its negative, or depletive energy. It draws the vexa flow, or nega-vexa as well but is bound in the nexus of Caemeris."

"Will you me tell how to find the Custodians. I can plunge this back into the webs of Stonthrax where you cannot reach it" Ange spoke posturing the prism.

"You cannot. That gate is closed to you now. You must continue or you will never finish your quest. Once I have learned of the prism's codes, I will set you free. I bear you no malice only the desire to know the power placed in your keeping" spoke Pthemnat.

Ange wondered if what Pthemnat said was true about not returning. Stonthrax had not said she could not return, and Aes Vius considered that she could. Was it a ruse from this mage of light to distract her again?

"What will you do with the knowledge?" asked Ange.

"Understand and become greater than either Oblyquixiton or Caemeris" spoke Pthemnat.

"But you will destroy yourself" Ange replied thinking of what Aes Vius told her of the Seers' history.

"Have you become less than before all this began. You do not understand the Seers, all is not what Seer Vius may have told you. Understand all of the Seers seek knowledge" spoke Pthemnat.

There was some truth to the words of Pthemnat. Had she been lessened in any way since accepting this destiny Ange wondered. Only at the end will she know if it is worth it. She also wondered about the motives of Aes Vius, but the Seer had guided her to the right path. Her instincts told her, if Aes had wanted to just seek knowledge, it would have kept her prisoner.

"Was it you who kept me prisoner on Mir Chiridien or Aes Vius?" asked Ange.

"It was the prism. You entered it and it was drawn to the Sentinel Eaudania. Surely Seer Vius told you this."

"What makes Voloc potent? It poisoned Baachelaus. It seeps everywhere in my world with nothing to thwart it."

"It is like our star-death. When stars are attracted to the nodal beds, they become unstoppable and consume everything."

Ange wondered if Pthemnat knew of her plunge into star death.

"Tell me about stars. I do not understand what they are" Ange asked.

The Seer became very solid all of sudden. Ange could feel the energy around her be sucked towards the Seer.

"Come to the conclave" spoke Pthemnat.

Ange found herself once again staring into the heart of the deep shadow of the sucking star. Pthemnat was distilling pieces of the shadow and attempting to score it onto the energy node. Each time though it would disperse into the flows of vexa and then emptiness.

Ange could see Pthemnat looking at her.

"So you have been here. Tagen in its naivety showed you."

"I have but it almost consumed me as it did you."

"But not the prism" replied Pthemnat.

"You know what I want. If you desire the power within the prism, then show me where the Custodians lie. Ascendant and Baachelaus are too potent. Lido, Seraf and Aerean have the power to rule my home and lands. Norbu has been destroyed and returned into the dirt to protect it against Voloc. It is Norbu's mountains, stone and rock which will remain until the last. I know you have seen where they lie. Their power would draw you to them just as this prism and my world did. Let me pass through Gnoceris" implored Ange.

Pthemnat remained silent. It was true. The Wanderer saw much. Pthemnat had seen where these Custodians had been gaoled. It had been the Oblyquixita who had taken them and hidden them. It did not know which one had taken them or why, but the Wanderer was correct. The Seer had felt the nodal shift in energy and had instantly begun seeking out what had caused the disruption in the under-weave. It particularly felt the essence in the beings called Ascendant and Baachelaus. Baachelaus was thick with the tides of Belmaris. The star that generated the energy to the Wanderer's world. Belligerent and thick with the copulation storm of Caemeris and Oblyquixiton. It had seen Belmaris rise on the horizon of Stonthrax webs and knew that it would become a force too strong to be resisted and once again the Pthohedron would need to quell the star-rage.

But even as the ancient Seer began to seek out the beings of great energy, the prism brimming with essence of them, captive in one place, more stable than the nodal beds and stronger than star-death became into being. And now it was here. Within reach. Pthemnat could feel it ebbing in unison with the under-weave. If the Wanderer ever let it free to feed on Gnoceris it would become unstoppable in its strength to control the existence of all things. This Wanderer was chosen for its ignorance. It would be easy to trap it on the prison star of Durg Icosa. Lethal to the children beyond the webs of Stonthrax even the Seers did not quest into this dead star. Forbidding, denier of light. It sits deep into the far edges where even the under-weave cannot remain.

Pthemnat will acquire this prism and will become a Ruler of more than just Gnoceris. I see the weakness here. This one is easy manipulated into the weave and out of it. The prism guides it. Pthemnat wondered suddenly, has Caemeris come to destroy Oblyquixiton once and for all?

"Wanderer, let us learn together and perhaps we will trust one another. Join me in conclave with the sentinels and we will watch star-death. We will see the heart of these destroyers and watch the power of the prism as it wields its control over them."

Ange wondered what the Seer was truly thinking. She could see the flashes of light energy as the creature drifted into and out of the energy streams. It had been deep in its own thought. Yet it hid what it was thinking from her. She guessed it could not read her mind.

"I will go into conclave with you. Be warned though it may not be what you expect" spoke Ange.

"Nothing is. Don't you know that is what makes the under-weave strong. It never assumes and always seeks out and if something is found it takes it into itself. This is how it has been able to remain intact against stars, Stonthrax and perhaps even Oblyquixiton" explained Pthemnat.

The entranced sentinels surrounded Ange. She became aware of the Seer. Her mind delved into the heart of the star beneath Ozas. The protector node was still in place and keeping the dead heart of the star from seeping further into Gnoceris.

"Show the prism to the node Wanderer" ordered Pthemnat.

Ange pulled it out knowing what would happen. She let it hover and saw it drift toward the nodal thrum. She was not concerned about letting it be free of her grasp. She knew nothing else could take if from her and if she chose it could consume her. In a way she realised the continued search for the Custodians was protecting her from just entering the prism to discover its secrets. But the thought of abandoning Tessie and her world always stopped her. Ange also knew the longer she was away from Arglethium, the more she lost her form, and became more like Aes Vius and the Seers. Even when her memories of Tessi and Mata returned to her, she felt less attached to them. Was this the battle the figure in the prism had warned her about, whether she would return to the Clay-born or remain here among, the Rulers of stars and time.

Soon the dense shadow began to flow into the prism. She saw the energy flow of the Seer stop as it saw it consume star death.

"I knew it. Greater than even Oblyquixiton. Why mighty progenitor of the Pthohedron have you not destroyed this usurper of your power?" asked Pthemnat.

The node began to weaken as the prism sucked hungrily on the dead matter. Suddenly a tear in the shadow formed letting in the under-weave of Gnoceris. Finally when the last of the star had been eaten and only the under-weave remained everything stilled. But instantly the prism began to consume that as well. The node formed by Pthemnat died as it was no longer needed. Nothing flowed. Ange felt the Seer was gently trying to consume her form, but it did not try too much. It knew it would not succeed without her knowing.

"Finally something more powerful than star-death. But where did you come from strong one that not even the Seer Pthemnat can contain your voracity?" asked the Seer.

"What is happening?" Ange asked.

"I do not know. I have never seen Gnoceris still before and I see your warning Wanderer, your weapon would consume our world as well" replied Pthemnat.

Ange went to grab the prism to look at it and see if she could find if it had changed.

"Wait do not touch it" spoke Pthemnat.

"Why not?"

Suddenly as the Seer was about to answer the prism exploded into tiny waves of energy. There was colour mixed with shadow and it was palpable like fine dust. It rained down so heavily it began to form a layer which intensified and became solid like earth.

"It has formed matter. It has formed matter beyond the webs of Stonthrax. The codes never allowed this. It never allowed the energy to become so dense. It was deemed a perversion of the priori memory. First before all else. It made the wall so that the matter would remain in its realm. In future memory time. Not here where it is unknowable to understand what can be made" spoke Pthemnat.

Ange picked the dust up and it felt like the desert sand, but it began to tingle as it if was alive.

"What does this mean?" asked Ange.

"It means it has reformulated the codes to build again and reversed existence."

"Why was it deemed that the matter could never be made here?" asked Ange.

"Nothing was to compete with first stars. This is their urn of creation. A life spring. If other matter came to exist here, then it would stop future memory being made. It would bring death. Your prism is not about restoring life it is a repository of death energy" replied Pthemnat.

"I have carried the means of death with me all this time. But why would the mighty Norbu make such a thing. The great father helped make our world and protected it against the raging destruction of Voloc."

"This creature Norbu would not have understood what it saw when it made the prism. The Caemexa are only aware of what the first star had allowed."

"But Norbu knew it had to protect everything."

"No it only understood destruction that is why it fought so hard against it. But here there is no death, so we create until there is enough and then it ceases. But there is no annihilation. There is no forgetting. Matter is dense and scarred to the point it must die to forget. There is no memory. Each thing must be retaught with every created thing. So it constantly continues onwards until the memories are spent. Here it will never end but it does not always remain the same. I have copied images I have been able to see through the gates of Stonthrax. And Gnoceris continues to grow and with the strength of the other Seers, I quest onwards to find new memory. As it is found it is deposited here. With this I can destroy the gates of Stonthrax and bring the memory of matter here and Gnoceris will grow into a new node of power so that even the stars cannot destroy it" Pthemnat called out into the vexa flow.

Ange looked at the rivers of colour flowing around it. It reminded her of Mir Chiridien and saw how it had been a first attempt at breaking through the webs of the Guardians by the Seers.

"Was Mir Chiridien your way of breaking beyond Simeris?" asked Ange.

"Eaudania was searching for the way to replicate the energy which the prism emitted. I thrust you inside the prism to discover if it could remake Gnoceris beyond the Thrax" replied Pthemnat.

"Why do you desire to know matter so much? If you cannot die, then it is of no importance to understand it as it cannot defeat you. We live in perpetual fear of our lives being taken away. Why would you seek this curse?" asked Ange.

"To usurp Caemeris. It is the only entity which can extinguish and enflame. What you hold is equal to its power. Nothing has ever existed like this. Caemeris has erred and formed the tool which will be its destruction. It is power Wanderer. It is all power. Equal, weaker, formed, unformed, destructive, creative. Everything competes for the energy, to rule it and make of it what they desire" replied Pthemnat.

"Why do you wish to destroy the thing that made you?" asked Ange.

"Because I am made to desire the power in all things and this Caemerin stone is the strongest the Seers have ever discovered."

"I am certain it will not be your destiny. You are bound by rules. You may test them and bend them, but you will never escape them" replied Ange.

Ange rubbed the prism dust between her fingers. She thought about Simeris. The bone sand and the slow inexorable death of the star. Was this another illusion by the Seer to confuse her into giving over the prism? It seemed too similar to the deserts of her memories and the Ghoc scavenging what they could to slowly kill everything. The voice within the prism said she still needed to learn and understand. Then she would be able to find the Custodians. She rubbed the sand and searched for the prism. She could not sense any memories, no scent of Norbu or the essence of Ascendant. No colours of creation.

"Seer you are very clever, but I do not think you are telling the truth. Where is the prism?" asked Ange.

Pthemnat instantly pulled their consciousness away from the conclave. Ange noticed one of the sentinel's energy rivers faltered slightly. It was barely discernible, but she realised the vexa and qedra flows were weakening the more she stayed or was it because the Seer needed to drain energy to continue its ruse.

"To deceive takes a lot of energy Seer" spoke Ange.

"It is mine" spoke Pthemnat. The Seer sent a node of vexa over Ange and ensnared her in the energy weave.

"Where is it?"

"It is mine."

"How did you take if it from me? When?" asked Ange.

"When I heard the echo of your agreement to hold the prism, I knew I had what I desired. The Pthohedron listen to all and everything but unlike the Caemexa and Oblyquixita, we are not bound. The Seers desire power most strongly even beyond the shadowed matter created in future memory. We searched and when the webs weakened enough, I reached out and snatched what was desired. But I also discovered it would not work until the custodian of the prism was present. So until you relinquish it you shall remain a prisoner."

"Is everything I have seen real or is it made to lure me here?" asked Ange.

"No not all. As the webs of Stonthrax weakened further the more I was able to coerce the remnants of light for my purpose. My questing increased and I began to wonder what could be formed. If Caemeris could do it why not the Seer. Could I remake the Pthohedron or Gnoceris beyond the Thrax. Mir Chiridien was and is a clumsy attempt I admit this. But it showed me how powerful that prism is, to make a world inside itself. Formidable and potent. But flawed none the less, and hence it remained in its stasis of creation and destruction.

"Have I trapped Kado?" Ange asked, a well of fear rose. "Have I been imprisoned inside the Cadra Phomera and now remain caged? Was this your plan all along between Seers Aes Vius and Pthemnat?" asked Ange.

"Do not fear so much creature. Matter of future memory does not interest the Seers. We seek what came before all else so it can be made better and stronger. We do not desire what you have. It is short lived and futile for much of your existence. But it is conceded that there is beauty in the shape. You are not imprisoned in Epimaris. And Aes Vius, my peer, remains true in its intention to quest for knowledge alone. But like existence, even knowledge requires power."

"Have you lured Kado and Sa away so the Voloc could more easily usurp my home?"

"The sooner you let go of it the easier it will be to finish this quest and give rightful stewardship to the Pthohedron" replied Pthemnat.

"You have caged them, so that it weakens Arglethium further. And what of me? You keep me long enough on my journey, so that in the end it will be in vain, nothing to return to, and so I relinquish the prism?" Ange fumed.

The vexa and qedra sparked around her as her anger rose.

"You may leave and choose you own destiny. You must have realised by now that you would never be able to return to who you were?"

"Is this truly my fate?" Ange asked suspicious of Pthemnat more than ever. It had not answered any of her questions.

"I will not relinquish rule of the prism to you. Do you really want us to remain here bound to each other? All I seek is the Custodians. Once I have them, I will be able to return them to their destinies and establish their realm again, to continue their purpose. Rid Arglethium of Voloc's poison and then I will decide what to do. I know I will not be the same but that is for me to decide not you. You have caused this to happen" she continued.

"You will need to do much more than rid it of Voloc. Belmaris, warmonger, and disruptor has been annexed by the Caemexa Voloc, which wrought the destruction of your world and began it all. Belmaris seeks many things and most of all would desire to consume all. It grew jealous of the Caemexa you call the Custodians. Its fiery loathing could not destroy their brilliance. Even the Seers locked away beyond the Thrax, building the majestic under-weave of Gnoceris were distracted by the brilliance of their forms. But you see Wanderer they were not made to bring life they were made to destroy things. To know death. Caemeris brings death. It is often thought in the consciousness of light that shadow is the destroyer, but it is not. Within that emptiness lies the way to build, form, and reshape, untethered and free of all other competitors for the energy required to create. Caemeris merged with Oblyquixiton to learn this and began everything formed including you and your world" spoke Pthemnat.

"But in my world, we die without the sun. If there is no morning and night, then our days pause, and nothing more continues. We cannot dwell in darkness, and cold, we cannot harvest crops, there would be no trees or animals, no Clayborn. Nothing grows without the sun" replied Ange.

"You have learnt much from Aes Vius. A great loss to Gnoceris and one which may be restored in time."

"Did you make Opa Phomera?" asked Ange.

"No you may be assured that Aes Vius is real, and its deep wisdom formed the Epimarin which soon grew to almost the same as us the Pthohedron. There is one difference they are made to understand the space between here and matter and learn of its codes. The Seers rule the first knowledge. They are the second knowledge. And you Wanderer will perhaps rule the third knowledge."

"Which is?"

"Death."

"So I am the Keeper of death. I can bring things to being and destroy. I cannot do this without the memories this tear holds. If I were to bring the Custodians back what would happen?"

"I think nothing would happen. You see you weren't just given this to restore the Custodian you were given it to control. That is why I needed you. If it were any other way, I would have simply captured these Custodians of yours for myself and extracted the Caemexa energy" replied Pthemnat.

"I do not wield anything without the prism. If you return it to me, we can strike a barter as we say in my homelands. I will show you the nodal paths within the prism and you will show me the path to the gaol of the Custodians. I was not able to find it with Aes Vius."

"No I clouded your sight" replied Pthemnat.

"So I would come here to you?" asked Ange.

"Yes."

"You realise that there is something else which desires my quest for its own end. It is not just the Seer Pthemnat. Something began this and continues to wait until it is finished. You must know what else could be this potent. Something awoke in Simeris and spoke" asked Ange.

Pthemnat did not answer. It knew it was likely Oblyquixiton which had spoken to Ange on Simeris but also wondered about the ebbing strength of Durg Icosa. Something had awoken there as well, and the Seer wondered if this energy also desired the Wanderer to bring the prism to it.

"When did the Pthohedron break up?" asked Ange.

"We have no sense of time as you do youngling. Again since we do not die then time passing is irrelevant" replied Pthemnat.

"Where are the other Seers?"

"They were needed to regenerate the under-weave and the vexa for the seeking of Caemeris" replied Pthemnat.

"You have consumed your brethren?" asked Ange.

"They are still present but their vexa helps sustain me."

Ange knew there was no stopping Pthemnat from its quest. It had expended everything including its own kind to obtain Ascendant's tear.

"Are the Seers more powerful united as separate brethren or as you are now?" asked Ange.

"Neither. The energy is all the same, none lost, none destroyed" replied Pthemnat wondering why Ange asked this question.

"If you are the same why did the star-death invade Gnoceris? You knew yourself you were unaware of it. Perhaps Seer Pthemnat has weakened the under-weave" probed Ange.

"You see much Wanderer. Perhaps Pthemnat has not considered all there is to consider. It is the first time in our awareness that the Seers delved beyond their limits, its consequences not yet realised."

"Let us be in conclave once more. Perhaps the prism will tell us where these Custodians are. We can search and I can seek out where this gaol lies and may guide you on its knowledge for your quest" spoke Ange.

"You try very hard to make me reveal the prism. I ask you to relinquish your hold of it. I have no desire to seek out the others. We are Wanderers as well and when I have contained the Caemeris and the Oblyquixiton then I shall merge into the under-weave of Gnoceris. The webs of Stonthrax will wither. You, seeker will have your destiny then. Then I will remain to defeat the power within you. You, death bringer. You shadow giver, you maker of star birth and death" replied Pthemnat.

"How did you take it from me without me knowing?" asked Ange.

"I have not taken it from you. I draw upon it from you" replied Pthemnat.

Ange's mind raced where was it. I will be trapped here forever if I don't find the prism. How did the Seer take it from her? She felt the flow of vexa and the star-death and what she thought was the prism's pulsing energy. Eaudania kept coming to her mind. She never understood what the washing woman was doing. She said she was trying to figure out the water and wash the stones. Trying to see how the water was made. Whenever she poured the water, the world would smash into pieces and remake itself. Was it that moment when the Seer could touch the power of Norbu's creation and begin to draw upon its knowledge. That's what caused the world to collapse, the siphoning of power by the Seer. The world of Mir Chiridien was the prism itself losing its power to the Seer. But here Pthemnat did not need to draw the power, the prism was here now and could absorb Gnoceris, so where could the Seer hide it? She remembered Tagen talking about Gnoceris. The Codecin mentioned the Qedra. It was where the Seers dwelt.

Ange looked at the Qedra hovering over the slipstreams of energy. The flow moved so quickly it looked as solid as rock. The shape of the Qedra was similar to the prism. It must be what the Seer had formed when it contacted with her in Mir Chiridien. It was able to understand the energy and draw from it. Passing of days and cycles and seasons meant nothing to Gnoceris or the Seers, as nothing was born or died. It was simply an accumulation of knowledge which merged and changed. The Qedra would seem old and new at once to the Seer.

"Pthemnat, I see your secret" spoke Ange.

The Seer roused. It formed into an apparition like Aes Vius.

"You have guessed Wanderer?" asked Pthemnat.

"Will you show me where the Custodians have been imprisoned?" Ange asked.

"I will."

"You relent so easily why?" asked Ange suspicious of the Seer.

"Because you no longer have dominion over the prism of the Caemexa" replied Pthemnat.

"If I were to leave it here what would happen?" asked Ange.

Pthemnat did not answer. It stood before Ange. It wondered at such creatures who know so little about existence and how it was formulated, destroyed, and remade so many times. But here in its density and ignorance it still understood as much as the Seer. The Wanderer was right, Pthemnat understood nothing of the sensory weaknesses of such over-sculpted matter and how that lead to these shadowed memories. Ones which attempted to assuage the fear of death but only served to prolong a corrupted truth, that their lives mattered in the face of all that existed before them.

"I will learn the memories of Caemeris and Oblyquixiton and with time I will become them. I will seek out Caemeris and the shadowed one and will bring them to the Pthohedron. Here existence will remain and the webs of Stonthrax once used to cage the Seers will be destroyed and no longer will there be this separation of creations" spoke Pthemnat.

"This will destroy the denser creatures from which I was born" replied Ange.

"Perhaps or new ones will be made" spoke the Seer.

"What do you mean, new creatures?" asked Ange.

"Have you not formed covenant with them?" hinted Pthemnat.

"You mean Sa, Kado and Gildas?"

Pthemnat did not answer.

Ange understood she would need to bring the Custodians back to Arglethium and then the final battle for Caemeris would begin. It would be her or the Seer. The Seer saw no value in who she was and only sought the power. The memories of who Ange was on Arglethium remained safe in the Cadra Phomera. The webs of Stonthrax needed to remain. Ange realised that Sa's battle was not a ruse to weaken Stonthrax by sundering the Aracnine. Without First on its throne to balance Simeris, the webs would slowly die once more. Sa would be needed to strengthen the Guardian once more but beyond that her presence was a danger. If Sa remained, she coalesced the power of the Sentinels of Gnoceris in her Uchala form and the power of Caemeris in her Arglethium person Sa. It was enough to weaken the Thrax fatally and allow Pthemnat to rule matter. And Kado and Gildas would become the tools of the Seer beyond Simeris.

Ange saw in an instant her path forward. It was a massive gamble, but she understood there was no way. It could mean perpetual death to herself and everyone she cared about. Those memories locked away in Opa Phomera would never exist. They either mattered or they did not, but they were allowed to exist once so for that reason alone she needed to remain on her quest. It was tiring and she wanted to be back playing with Nekoda and waiting for Bensah to be walking over dunes and the excitement of hearing the news of his journey north. In time Ange Tsaed would need to decide. Even to stay here and merge with the nodal powers would mean that ultimately all power would be drawn to her. The custody of that power was given to her to own. That is what it meant to be the Keeper. Not the ruler but the one who the energy rests within. In the end she would still meet the Seer in battle for it would seek her out to acquire the power. It would still be her and the Seer. But if she did not act now there would be nothing left to remember to go back to at all. The story of Ange Tsaed would fall into the forgotten sands of existence with no trace of who she ever was or what formed her. There was too much beauty, too much love and too much grief for it to be forgotten. It lay with her now to make this choice and none other. It also meant that her closest allies were her enemies.

"If you show me where the Custodians are I will let you remain with the prism until I return" demanded Ange.

The Seer looked at Ange. Pthemnat could see the nodal energy inside her and around her. There was no deception or anything which could be hidden from the Seer.

"You know I don't deceive you" spoke Ange.

"I know. But I cannot see beyond now. This moment. Each vexa which passes through us is learning and no codes have been formulated yet. I must take this risk to quest beyond to find the way to Caemeris again" replied Pthemnat.

"Yes. You have no choice and neither do I" spoke Ange.

Ange could sense the weakening of the protector nodes as Pthemnat pondered the possibilities within reach after so much searching for the prism. Finally she was giving it control of the power. The Seer drifted in the weave as it fed on the power nodes consuming the accumulated knowledge within Gnoceris. Ange began to search for the prism. She realised it was heavily shielded by the power of the Seer. It was almost impenetrable.

"Show me" she whispered "I am coming, and I am almost home. Show me this one last step and destiny will be fulfilled."

The Qedra began to pulse with every whisper of Ange. The Seer remained distracted. Suddenly a small sphere formed in front of her. She saw beacons of light deep within the centre of the sphere. The scent of the energy was familiar. The sound of wind and water with the heat of summer swam over her. A sudden surge of happiness, and sorrow and longing washed through in a wave of vexa. It was the Custodians. She saw a place, a star, no it was a shape like the Qedra. It was the place which imprisoned the Custodians. She had found them. She had found the Custodians. She was so close. So close. She thought of Nekoda asleep in the webs of Stonthrax. If she didn't rescue him in time, then he would be lost in those webs as they decay with everything beyond them. She reached into the side of the prism and pulled a tiny spec and let it become part of her. She could feel its energy instantly. Then the Seer appeared. It snuffed the sphere out and stood before Ange.

"You are truly powerful Wanderer. I think our destinies are entwined far more than we realise, and I think it will be a great spectacle when we meet again" spoke Pthemnat.

"As agreed, Seer, here is the eye of Caemeris for you to ponder and control as you wish" spoke Ange as she gave the memory codes to Pthemnat.

Taking the solid form of the prism, Ange slipped into the vexa waves towards the gates of Stonthrax. She needed Nekoda to be with her. The density of beings must be strong on the prison star for her to be able to sense the Custodians. She was sure Nekoda would be able to exist there. As she touched the webs everything slowed. She remembered the keys to find her way. She dissolved the webs strand by strand until they were weak enough to break. Soon she saw the cocoon of Nekoda. He was resting oblivious to her absence. She began to untangle the webs and reveal her friend. She gently stroked him to waken him. Nekoda's eyes opened. He looked at Ange and saw that his friend had changed once more. Her eyes dazzled with bright specs which flowed like the rain from the sky and trickled down to the great heaving river where he used to wait to catch fish. Nekoda stood up and licked Ange on the cheek. She was relieved to feel his warmth and softness. She knew then she was right to do what she did. She wasn't sure if she would be able to stop the Seer, but she knew she must try rather than spend an eternity wondering if she could have.

"Ok we are almost home Nekoda" she spoke staring in the warm eyes of her friend.

Nekoda barked in the silence. It was suffocated instantly as nothing existed in this place. It was neither a cradle nor a tomb. It was emptiness. She recalled the prison of the Custodians was located. She traced the codes in the webs and instantly they disappeared.

Pthemnat felt the Wanderer leave as it sat with in the Qedra now consumed by the prism of Caemeris. Durg Icosa would be a formidable test for the Clayborn. It would make her strong. Stronger than Pthemnat would have liked. It began to learn the prism and the eye of Caemeris. The prism slowly began to consume the Seer and Gnoceris.

Durg Icosa

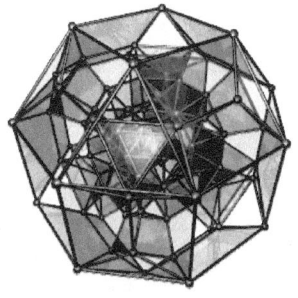

"Tol-Tessar; gaol of the star world Durg Icosa. It was made to call the shaded stars and bind them from their inexorable desire to consume. It is a nexus of nodal and memory energy of Oblyquixiton and is ruled by the Laddarane. Never shall its bonds be broken. For if it is breached, so will be released the nodes of star-death. Over eons, the Laddarane grew in their knowledge as the memories of the imprisoned stars became one with the Tol-Tessar. Its prisoners contained the codes of existence beyond Durg Icosa. In them was the disintegration of formed energy, created and dense. In them was the memory of Caemeris. The Laddarane wondered about this force which existed, so potent to linger long in the last traces of the great bulbs of existence and survive even in the realm of Oblyquixiton. Then came the destruction of Gnoceris, its remnants were captured by the Tol-Tessar and within the memories of nodal creations called Seers; creatures who were a mystery, made of Oblyquixiton negation but able to control the Vectron flows which formed the nexus. It was then that Durg Icosa remained bonded to the Seers and began to feel the ebbing force far beyond the gates of Stonthrax. The Laddarane knew of the questing of the Seers and that a time of destruction would come to the Tol-Tessar. The myth of Caemeris and the Seer of Death grew within the Laddarane cadre of existence. In this myth, the Laddarane drew codes to explain the release of the caemexa and oblyquixita from unending existence. To bring forth the new and surge through the emptiness of uncreated. In their desire for this myth to become reality, the Laddarane began to gather the dead stars and in so doing fulfilled their purpose as gaolers.

But now a force of destruction has been caged in another Tessarch, one not formed in Durg Icosa. It contains the memory of Caemeris in its supra-nodal strength to create. It brings destruction as it forms the very things it makes, for once made, a thing must die. Seer Osesa sees a third power which can be used. The Seer of destruction brings the possibility of a third ruler. The rulers of Oblyquixiton and Caemeris, beyond the gates of Stonthrax. Seer Osesa sees the ambition of Seer Pthemnat, to consume all to obtain Caemeris, the questing has begun the destruction of the first nodes of energy. Seer Osesa, seeks its own pathway, not with that of Pthemnat."

Descendant watched the Tessarch spinning around it. It remembered another prison such as this one. This was soothing as this cage had been formed from the past memories made well before the Custodian's sight had been given. It no longer felt the piercing sorrow and pain it had once felt in the chains of Voloc. Descendent wondered how it had gotten here. Its eyes shone out into the void and reflected the pulsing vexa which formed the boundaries of the Tessarch. It searched out into the emptiness and felt the others. The brethren of its kind remained locked inside together and their collective strengths were bound here. One was missing. The great one made for the younglings of clay. A memory of battle and strength remained with Descendant. Its brethren had been strong enough to conquer and stifle the deceiver. The shadow, Voloc who consumed the light and colour. Mighty Norbu had been lost. Bled out into the creations it had wrought to honour the Caemexa. Now only the five remained.

"I am Descendent, Baachelaus of the realm of light. I have forgotten many things but one thing this Custodian knows, I am not defeated yet. I have been released and reborn as Baachelaus the Destroyer. No longer shall I sit in awe of the ones before me. I sit in the world of future memory before all can be destroyed. Voloc is no longer my gaoler but lies in the ruins of its desire to consume. I have been let free and shall find freedom again to rule. Do my brethren see this, do they see their ruler?"

"Brethren being a prisoner seems to heighten your sovereignty" spoke Seraf. The Custodian formed in the Tessarch. It bloomed into a blue flame.

"We are once again bound together. Is it possible we could remake our prison into the mighty realm of light once more?" spoke Aerean, ruffling the illumination of Seraf.

"Perhaps Aerean. But we lack the greatest one of us. The strongest to wield the power of the caemerin light" replied Baachelaus.

"Norbu" Seraf and Aerean whispered together.

"Ascendant why do you still slumber?" asked Baachelaus.

"Ascendant rests to remember. The vision has been lost and she needs to tell you, its' secret. Then perhaps this cage can be broken" replied Lido.

Lido shimmered on the edges of the dark chamber. The Tessarch moved with her fluidity as it spun around them.

"Tell her there is time and perhaps sitting with us will help her to remember" spoke Baachelaus.

"I think brethren after the destruction you wrought and chaining the mighty Norbu, she wishes to be stronger. We are but observers in this union between the Ascendant and Descendant" replied Lido.

"True brethren. Our purpose is formed beyond that of the four brethren of making. My desire to conquer was usurped by Voloc and veiled my sight in shadow."

"Why are we here?" asked Seraf.

"To draw the Clayborn who is now Custodian of Norbu's stone. Much deception lies along the path. Even with the sight of the sentinel's blood I cannot discern what has placed us here" replied Baachelaus.

"I am uncertain of how strong our bonds are. I have tried to break them with the heart of Belmaris, but they are bonded in energy greater than my own. I am depleted as quickly as they reform" spoke Seraf as it flared against the moving Tessarch with no effect.

"This place is ancient Seraf. It was made before us. This is eonic memory. Unseeable even to us" spoke Aerean as it blew out the flame of Seraf seeing how futile it was to try and escape.

"So this is our doom. I have lain in the tomb of Magnumarum. I have even dwelt within brethren Descendant. Yet none could extinguish the great flame of Seraf. Only Norbu could quell me. So why am I caged here?" bemoaned Seraf, resting against the boundary of the Tessarch.

The Custodians watched the Vectron gently nibble at the form of their fiery brethren. Seraf nudged it with flame and saw how the Vectron split the flame and absorbed it.

"With the passing of the ages, even the Custodian Seraf shall be extinguished" Seraf sighed.

Baachelaus went toward the edge of the Tessarch. It touched the wall and felt the ancient energy suffuse into itself and mingle with the bonds of Uchala, Vipax and even Voloc. It touched all of them and brought to it the memories of its existence in solitude. It took the Custodian to the throne of light and for the first time it saw the vision it once gazed upon with Assumpta. It began to weep. Not because it longed to be restored. The Baachelaus of ancient vision was long dead and could never be what it was destined to be. No, Baachelaus wept because it knew what had been taken and would never be avenged for the theft of its rightful place. Arglethium was out of reach, and it would take eons to learn the Tol-Tessar secrets to unlock it. Baachelaus roared suddenly in frustration and pulled all the Custodians into itself to draw their strength and expelled the energy toward the Tessarch's boundary. But nothing happened. The Vectron simply absorbed the energy. This was not dense existence which became brittle and broke under its own weight, allowing death and rebirth to occur. This was ancient knowledge hidden and untethered by any rules of creation. Baachelaus released the other Custodians.

"My brethren here we remain to learn and to grow until we can be free. Assumpta, equal and usurper of power, rise and join us. Our sorrow for

Norbu and the breach of our realm must be forgotten and a new era of light must be realised. Come now you have slumbered enough. Rise" Baachelaus whispered.

The tears of Descendant dropped and held mid-air. They solidified and began to avalanche across the chamber. Aerean attempted to contain them, but they slipped through her grasp. Lido formed them into a flowing river. Soon the tears moved in unison with the Tessarch and merged with it.

Ascendent slept. She was aware of the presence of her brethren. She had watched them when she and Lido had arrived in the prison. She, like the other Custodians, wished Norbu were here as well. She also felt the presence of her tears and knew that Ange was coming. Her path would be difficult. Filled with much deception as Baachelaus had said. Ascendant and Lido had been captured and taken at the end days and she had not seen the death of Norbu. But she had felt his demise and giving back into the dense bonds of Arglethium to strengthen them. Now her mighty brethren flowed through all the creatures made of that world so they would be nourished and protected from Voloc. She remembered once again the realm of light. She remembered their true name were the Caemexa. They were made after the elder stars to bring creations into being. The caemexa were made only from the memory of the Caemeris. Voloc, the negation sent to cage the Caemexa because with them had begun the destruction of creation. Ascendant and Descendant were set upon the thrones of light to gaze at each other so that one would always provoke the other's vision. Once it was broken then the threads of existence could not be remade. Their purpose was to awaken the younglings and bring them to their fullness. By doing so they wrought the destruction of the Caemexa. Descendant had forgotten its destiny was to fulfil the desires set in their hearts by Ascendant. Their union was to be permanent and unbroken. Now here the Caemexa, Custodians of the children of clay, of Arglethium, were imprisoned in the gaol made for the stars and powers of the beginning days. Here their union would be complete, and their destiny fulfilled. Ange was on her way and now knew that her destiny would change her forever. Ange would fight for the younglings made from neither light or shadow but the density of earth, air, water, and fire. Their hearts would be given the knowledge to hope and the knowledge of fulfilment and how to die. Here in Durg Icosa, prison of the Caemexa and Oblyquixita the Tol-Tessar would be broken setting Star Death free.

She stirred. She heard the call of Baachelaus. She did not answer. You still do not understand but I will make you see once again what has been torn from you. You will understand and the corruption of Voloc will leave she thought.

Ascendant stirred in the swirling vexa of the Tessarch. Ethereal and angular the walls moved in rhythm with one another. It was the nodal power of the Tol-Tessar. Stronger than anything made. It was perfect and smooth. It was beautiful thought Assumpta.

Baachelaus wept spilling tears throughout the Tessarch. Suddenly it stopped. Assumpta stood in the centre of the maelstrom. Scooping a handful of Baachelaus' tears, the Custodian crushed them and let the winds of Aerean and flame of Seraf reshape them into a prism.

"How we have grown brethren. Once it would only have been Norbu who could wield the laws made by the Caemexa. These are your gifts of anguish. I feel them Baachelaus. I heard your pleas for my awakening. I remember the roar of your awakening on the young world of Arglethium. Now once again we are bound to a realm with our destinies before us yet veiled by our ignorance to things beyond our purpose" spoke Assumpta.

"You are here now. I remember you as I gazed so long ago. You have grown lethal like me. We are not and never again shall be what we were once destined to be" replied Baachelaus.

"Caemeris, enigma and wonder. Where are you? Your destruction lies close now. Your destroyer comes and will be full of your progeny. The younglings have been called and are now set on their path to you. Will you answer when the Clayborn calls?" asked Assumpta.

Assumpta went toward Baachelaus and drew its face close. The Tessarch pulled toward them, sensing the power between the two Custodians.

"We need to remember, and I will show you how."

"Remember what? Who I am and what my destiny once was? I think that has been lost into the eons of time. Here we sit in our cage, as prisoners bonded with the ancient stars of death who cannot be quelled or diminished but merely gaoled. They are the darkness, and we are the shadows who affirm light. We are considered equal in measure and strength to great indestructible creations. Is this now not the time for us to remake the Caemexa into something new and strong once more? Perhaps even in time destroy this mighty fortress and unleash the power of death and light together. A new vision is made, and all shall begin again" spoke Baachelaus.

"You know that is not the path for the Caemexa. To stir Caemeris and Oblyquixiton once more would render us to nothing. Forgotten even in the great eye of Caemeris" replied Assumpta.

"What is it you want me to remember so much? You have searched in the vaults of darkness and the echoes of lost memory for me. Now we sit and look at one another again. What is it you wish me to see?" asked Baachelaus.

"I wish you to see the heart of the Caemeris. Its inner eye and vision. It reaches deep and holds still the movement of time. It stops the birth and death and crushes them at once. It holds back the power of the dead star light and Oblyquixiton. It consumes the energy of the creation and forces it to make beings rather than that of light and shadow. It brings to fruition the essence of creation so it can be tasted, touched, hoped for, and filled with despair for its loss. Remade, again and again. It makes our brethren here build. We helped shape the awareness of the Clayborn creatures" spoke Assumpta.

"And what use is that to us when we have the power to build our own realm?" asked Baachelaus.

"No use but if it is not fulfilled then we die as well. It was not deemed for us to remain caged. We were made to be the makers of other things and with time diminish as our creations continue in their existence."

"Voloc taught me to desire and not simply watch and oversee. The Caemeris left none of this knowledge to me" replied Baachelaus.

"No I am that knowledge for you. I am the piece which lets you be fulfilled. Don't you see it was us together not the one or the other. Without one the other is lost. If you continue to remain apart from me then it can never be completed. It is like Seraf never blazing gloriously to life and Lido never raining. Belmaris the great sun and light giver to Arglethium burns and burns in fury and will diminish as time passes. But because Caemeris and Oblyquixiton never destroyed each other but co-exist so they will never diminish."

"I have no desire for this anymore. I have disintegrated into the heart of the warring star of Belmaris and the ancient, vaulted cage we now sit upon. It is strong this cage. It has feasted on our demise and will not let go easily. Why not try to unlock it and begin again? A new vision. A realm of light and shadow, not darkness but shadow where colours bleed and blend into whatever we desire" spoke Baachelaus.

Aerean formed into a shimmering zephyr and rested near the face of Baachelaus. Still ragged and pale as it was on Arglethium. Imbued now with the blood of Uchala and Vipax and the salt of Norbu it would never be any other form that it was now.

"Pale one, my brethren. I hear Assumpta and I wonder also at your vision. I wonder what the fallen Descendant discerns that we three Custodians of forming cannot. I long to capture this ethereal cage and crush it with Lido's waves and melt it with Seraf's flames both fecund with me and magnified into glorious destruction. But I have become a prisoner now where before I was not. I have fallen with you so tell us what it is you see so I may bless or curse my brethren who has the sight of Caemeris" spoke Aerean.

Baachelaus turned chuckling at the enticement of Aerean and snatched her. She disappeared. The Custodian stood, its eyes flaring brilliantly. An image appeared in the silent chamber as the Tessarch spun around them. Assumpta and Lido noticed how defined the shape of the Tessarch became with Descendant aroused.

"Aerean I would desire to see you forge these waves and flames in the realm of new light and shadow. Watch Seraf and Lido master the stars and all things formed including the Clayborn and turn them toward us.

To worship or serve. But what use are they to us if we could wield the oceans of light and shadow as deep as the tombs of dead stars? If we could rule this place?" spoke Baachelaus.

The Custodians sat among the night sky of the old realm. There was no sun or moon and the wind and fire, and the oceans were still. Baachelaus walked amongst mountains made of glass and diamonds. They were deep indigo and the Custodian's eyes drew in their shimmer. Ascendant found herself sitting far way peering from the tallest peak. She met the gaze of Descendant and instantly felt them lock on her and hold her. They drew close to one another and kissed. It was deeply passionate and Assumpta felt the blood of Norbu stir and the fire, wind, and water of their brethren coalesce to build an ocean of flame around them. Their embrace continued and soon a star bloomed around them and blazed into a sun. The sun was aquamarine in colour and shone across the vastness of time. Assumpta felt Baachelaus enter her and swell inside her conscious. She pushed back saturating the god with her unending quest of longing. They merged and the sun expanded and exploded. Left behind was an empty vault and the swirling Tessarch. Now shimmering in blue green energy nodes. Baachelaus pulled back. Assumpta could see the tears spill from its eyes. She realised then that the two of them had the power to build stars and wield them. She caught the tear as it fell to the floor of their chamber. It was not her tears that Ange held but Descendant's.

Baachelaus looked upon Assumpta.

"My love, there is something I will never forget. The joining of our visions brings the greatest strength, the awareness of existence. What destructive path we made for the Clayborn, to show them who they are. What true Caemexa we are. It is good we are together again. If I am to remain caged for another eternity, then at least you are here to join me" whispered Baachelaus.

"My beloved. I am mistaken. These tears you cry are not of anguish but joy."

"Yes. Together we build cradles and tombs alike and none can stop us. Not even the Caemeris the great ocean of light. My anger when I was released was with Voloc for denying me completeness. That has now been rectified. I am complete and now I seek my own path" spoke Baachelaus.

"But I am not. My lust lies to find fulfilment of the creatures imbued with my desire to keep searching. If you do not join me but usurp me then my destiny will fade and so will the Clayborn creatures" spoke Assumpta.

"It does not matter anymore. That destiny lies in ruin. My dominion is here now. With time as I try to build with you, we will weaken the Tessarch, and we will be set free. With it will be the complete annihilation of the realm of light seen by Caemeris and any vision which it wrought" spoke Baachelaus.

Assumpta moved away and looked through the Tessarch to see what lay beyond their prison. There were so many layers each impenetrable to the Custodian. Baachelaus was blind to think that they would escape without Ange to free them. Their release will only come with the presence of Ange. Assumpta fingered one of the tears of Baachelaus. Inside lay the memories of star death and birth, of Caemeris power to destroy and unite with the Oblyquixita. It was also where they were united together. With the prism, they would return to their original forms and potency. Then the Tessarch could be breached, and they would be able to return to their realm and rebuild. The Custodians of the clay would be able to restore Arglethium and she and Baachelaus would remain infinitely in union together. It seemed too easy. Assumpta felt a foreboding at this dream. She had seen the savage wound Voloc had inflicted into their realm. The darkness which bled in was deep old and stale with its brutality to destroy anything it touched. It would not be so easy to extract it from their visions or the soil of their brethren Norbu. The Custodians were now united and still they sought separate paths. The schism was deep, and nothing healed it. Nothing bridged this discord between the higher brethren. She felt Lido, Aerean and Seraf behind her. Baachelaus lay in meditation. She could see it was counting the rhythm of the Tessarch as it revolved around them.

"What is it Brethren?" Assumpta asked.

"Ascendant we cannot remain here. How was it that we were caged so easily? It was not Voloc the deceiver. What was it?" asked Lido.

"I have searched the vaults of memory in our first awakenings, and I can only see a distant spec. It is light but it is not Caemexa. It wanted the schism to obtain the power we hold within us. To breach the codes which were made before any of our colours formed. I do not know its name, but it seeks power as does Descendant and as did Voloc and so do the children of the clay. It is all the same. It is the right to rule, create, destroy, and change and remake at will" she replied.

"We will die here Assumpta. My flame will wither without the enflaming grace of Belmaris. You know this" spoke Seraf.

"I know Seraf. Your beauty will suffocate in this most indestructible prison" replied Assumpta.

"What do you see? Has being reunited not strengthened the higher brethren?" asked Aerean.

"No it has not. We are still separate and on different paths. This prison will not break without the power of Norbu's forged stone" replied Assumpta.

"Do you see Ange?" asked Lido.

"I sense her. She has much to journey still and even then, I do not know if she will be able to succeed in freeing us."

"Do you see our death regardless of where we lie?" asked Lido. The Custodian shimmered across the moving lines of the Tessarch. As she moved through them, she felt the ancient and unfamiliar power within it. She wondered what could possibly make such a thing as this.

Assumpta heard the question. She looked across the many layers of the Tol-Tessar.

"Brethren can you see that there is not just this cage but there are many beyond it before we would be free. Formidable and wrought with much fear of what its makers wish to contain. I think we shall die either way yes. It was the purpose of Baachelaus and Assumpta to bring permanence and a new dawn to the hearts of the Clayborn. And when that union was complete, you brethren shall then be free to remain in those realms which were made from the first colours of light. But now that destiny lies on the edges of destruction" spoke Assumpta.

"How?" asked Seraf.

"Ange needs to finish her quest to find us and then we shall see. The power of Norbu's stone will be equalled here. Her victory to return us to her home is not fated yet. Many others seek the same thing she does, to exist and to have the power to create" replied Assumpta.

Baachelaus heard his brethren and also saw the eons of Tessarchs, layered upon layer which surrounded the one they were imprisoned within.

"So creator who cages me here where are you and how did you come to be? I am Caemexa, lost destroyer. No longer the Custodian who wrought harmony and fulfilment to the hearts of clay matter. I have seen the vastness of the Oblyquixiton, and I seek it also. Let me watch with the Sentinel eyes of Uchala who stood so close to the webs of Stonthrax and what lay beyond them. If I am to spend an eternity here, then let me learn. For I believe in time I shall be free, and I will be known as the destroyer of the Tessarch. Ruler of a new realm of the colours of creation" whispered Baachelaus.

Descendant searched out into the ether beyond Durg Icosa. It was blind to what lay on the star it was now imprisoned on. It peered into the vague darkness which sat just beyond any light and saw the webs of the Guardians. It tried to look into to them, but it could not. A scent of Uchala drifted across the void. It followed it and saw the war raging on Simeris. It was the progeny of the Sentinel and Clayborn. How had it come here? Perhaps the Clayborn had left a trail of where it had journeyed. It watched. It saw Stonthrax rise from underneath the rock and clash with another creature. It was strong so strong that Baachelaus could feel the waves ripple as the battles raged. There was a shimmering light in the distance. Baachelaus had felt itself be ripped apart by the stone as its brethren forged it. It saw the image of Caemeris in that instant and knew its destiny was lost. Ascendant was confused for her memory was also caged inside that stone and now wanders aimlessly seeking unity. But in time she will understand as well that which was broken cannot be remade. A new vision is needed. The brethren will perish, those who were aligned with Norbu will starve away from the enlivening flame of Belmaris. Baachelaus searched again. It was a dragon. One like the great blind dragon from the wars of creation except this stood with the power of stones and light. A scent of another sentinel Vipax. The progeny of Vipax also battles on another world. It must be the footprints of the youngling Clayborn as it searches for the Custodians. Baachelaus saw Eaudania as she emptied another urn onto the stones. It saw how the world disintegrated and remade itself.

"Creature what are you?"

Eaudania looked up at the voice.

"Being you are gaoled how do you see so far?" the Sentinel asked.

"I am poisoned with the blood of the sentinels Uchala and Vipax. Who are you?"

"I am a Sentinel as well" replied Eaudania.

"What are these worlds I see as search?"

"Many things which do not know their purpose were made. I do not know mine and seek it out as well. You follow the path set by the Wanderer who is seeking its destiny also. The stone of power it carries traces the path back first laid by the questing search of the Sentinels of the Seers."

"Where is the Clayborn?" Baachelaus asked.

"I do not know" replied Eaudania.

"Do you know of Tol-Tessar?" asked Baachelaus.

"I do. But I cannot free you. The codes forbade it and I do not have the power" answered Eaudania.

"So what use are you?"

"I am as useful as you caged one. Our purpose is not to guess why but to understand we exist and for that reason alone we may seek our paths" replied the old washer woman.

Baachelaus saw Kado in its form as the dragon. It was strong here. But Kado's and Vipax's absence would make Arglethium weak. Voloc's poison will seep deeply. Belmaris will grow and nothing will contain its rule of the realm of colours. Baachelaus sensed the end of destiny had finally come with the stone Norbu thought could save its progeny.

"Were the Sentinels seeking the stone of Norbu?" asked Baachelaus.

"We sensed its power but were seeking the thing it was forged from, the eye of Caemeris" replied Eaudania.

"Rest in your death Brethren Norbu. Know that your progeny now die as the very thing you tried to stop happened has now come to fullness in the demise of your vision as well" spoke Baachelaus.

Baachelaus returned to the Tessarch.

"Brethren, Arglethium shall die, and Norbu's forging and death will be in vain. He forged the very weapon needed to destroy its creation. It is time to create a new vision, one where darkness affirms the light and the Caemexa shall rule all that they can make" spoke the Descendant.

Baachelaus' voice echoed through each of the Custodians. Assumpta felt the desire within Baachelaus and also desired the same but did not believe that Norbu's wisdom was in vain. Ange still held the eye of Caemeris and had survived this far. Not all hope was lost for Arglethium.

"I sense your doubt Ascendant" spoke Baachelaus.

"Of course, it is what I was made for" Assumpta replied.

∞

The wind roared around Thraan the watcher. The Tol-Warrior steeled itself against the swelling storm as it approached. It had been on the horizon of Zol for five cycles. Its ferocious winds were scouring the cliff faces and turning them into dust. It struck its spear into the tablet on the ground to warn the others the storm was within distance. Thraan had been Warrior-Apex for as long as the memory of Durg Icosa. An elusive figure, always at the vanguard of the storm fronts and the caging ceremonies. Thraan had no appetite for the ruling castes of the prison planet. The warrior caste was the first of the protectors of the Tol-Tessar. The gaolers of the most powerful entities in all existence. They wielded great knowledge to be able to do this and had often been poached and hunted to extract this knowledge by shadowed figures lusting to usurp the progenitor before them. For this reason Thraan being the first or Apeiro of its caste remained aloof and impenetrable as the prison under its watch.

"I will interface with it in the valley of Mor" spoke Thraan.

The tablet lit up. Thraan read the message. It was from Isax, the second commander of Sena caste. They were the infra-rulers to the Assembly caste, the Laddarane.

"Stand down Apeiro Thraan. Let it pass" scored Isax into the tablet of vexa.

'Why?' Thraan retorted back annoyed.

"It isn't lethal" replied Isax.

Thraan did not respond immediately. Isax had only assumed its command in the last cycle of vexa disintegration and its nodal bonds were still consolidating to the Vectron weave of Durg Icosa. Thraan's senses warned the warrior not to obey the order. Its warrior's bonds had been humming for the last four cycles. Something lay hidden behind the mirage of vapour and dust cloud. It was powerful. To gather so much of a veil meant whatever lay behind it would bring great battle.

"I will stay for one more vecta cycle. If it is nothing, I will be a bit dusty, and I'll owe you a throw of gonj" replied Thraan.

There was silence on the tablet. The young commander would be getting used to Thraan's tactics. There had been manoeuvres by the Sena to move Thraan out of its seat but until a warrior with the strength to gaol a star was found, then Thraan would remain in the seat of Apeiro-

Warrior. Thraan wondered why the Sena would try such a thing, when the Tol-Tessar had always required a Tol-Warrior to control it.

"One vecta. Then remove yourself to the Hadal sector. There is another disturbance."

Thraan dusted the message off the tablet.

Wind scraped Thraan's face between the spikes of its Vectron veil. The veil was made from pure ionised radiation left over from the first stars brought here when star-death was discovered. It melded to its body. Thraan was a formed creature. It did not know where it came from and so consummate was Thraan's dedication to its purpose, it did not waste time thinking of these things. But being formed also made Thraan an outsider on Durg Icosa.

Soon the storm had swallowed Thraan entirely. It stood still letting the excoriating particles wash over it. The surges of particles were rich with ozone and ions set free from the genodal pulses. Then came the scent Thraan had been waiting for. It was death, and it was rich and strong. Its source was unknown and distant from Durg Icosa. It had travelled from future memory to now.

Thraan readied its spear and dove into the destructive yawn of the star.

"Come young one tell me your journey. Tell me what brought you here to the Durg Icosa and the eternal rest of the Tol-Tessar" roared the Apeiro-Warrior.

Thraan's momentum slowed as soon as it landed in the ocean of star void. Thraan took its spear and began to jab pinpricks of energy into the miasma. The void healed quickly with each wound forming an even thicker flow of vexa.

"Come to heel. Tell me your history deadening one. Breach the bonds placed on us all and set your destruction free. Let me have it so I may wield it."

Thraan exploded with energy and passion as the warrior came to full strength.

Spinning into a cyclone of energy Thraan became an apeiron of power forcing the dead heart of the rogue star beneath the veil of nodal weave of vexa. The shadow was reduced to pure black and the glinting armour of Thraan dulled. Its spear of nodal energy crystalised and exploded, forcing the darkness to become brittle. It shattered into fragments. It reformed. Attracted to the power of the spear it washed over Thraan suffocating the warrior.

"You are fecund with power degenerate one. You are new and old, potent, and arrogant. I, Thraan, the Apeiron-Warrior rest amongst your tomb of emptiness but still do not see my death. Come let us play a bit more. I am not tired of this game."

Thraan burst out again and this time split its spear in two.

"Now extension of myself and birth gift from the first memories take your fill and we will understand our prisoner."

Each half of the spear glowed with the codes of creation. In them sat the vision of Caemeris and Oblyquixiton. The spears were a complete Pthohedron of negation and eruption. They had been forged by the minds of the first stars when existence had been unleashed. All knowledge had been placed in them to make them superior to anything else. So the warrior Thraan who commanded their power was second to none. Only one flaw had been placed inside the Tol Warrior codes to prevent their caste from claiming suzerainty over Durg Icosa. One thought of power to control was death. Inside each of them sat a Tessarch ready to cage them if it any point the codes of desire to rule erupted. Thraan knew this and for this reason its desire lay steeped in battle, conquest, and service to the laws scribed within its form. This is why it had been the most long lived of all the Tol-Warriors of Durg Icosa.

Thraan watched the spears grow longer and then they began to hum. Outside on Mount Kalyx the storm had become a frenzy. Commander Isax realised its mistake. The second command grew angry at itself but more so at the prowess of Thraan.

"Perhaps this one will end you Thraan" spoke Isax. "Pull back. Apieron has entered star battle. We will ready the entrance" Isax ordered a group of infra Tol-warriors. They had grown used to Thraan humiliating Isax but were not silly enough to ever recognise it. It would mean immediate disintegration.

Thraan unleashed the spears and spun the nexus of death towards itself. It roared with the glory and surge of power which ran through it. The Tessarch inside shook and shrunk. Thraan climaxed and instantaneously the void was subjugated, weakened by disrupting Vectron flow from Thraan's spear. The implosion pulverised the edges of Durg Icosa causing Mount Kalyx to erupt and the nodal weave surrounding Durg Icosa to rip. Thraan pulsed a flow of vexa in the rent and healed the frayed weave.

Thraan walked from the dust and debris with the ebbing star in its armoured hand. Thraan pulsated with its power. The spear had returned to normal. As it walked down the pathway from the side of Mount Kalyx, Thraan saw the Tol-Tessar Arch. Isax and the Sena warriors were standing outside it keeping it open as Thraan approached. They distorted in the mirage of energy fields the closer Thraan came. Gaoling a star was dangerous, as it any time it could escape and rupture the Tessarch inside and split Durg Icosa. The humming of the star's force flowed through Thraan. It was at this time the guardian was most vulnerable to destruction. The force could break their resolve to serve for an eternity and discombobulate their codes.

Isax bowed as did the cohort of infra warriors.

"We welcome Thraan once again into the Tessarch cages. We wait for the story of this mighty prisoner" spoke Isax.

Thraan barely heard the praise as it continued in its way through the arch. Silence came. Thraan felt at rest. The star in its hand dimmed and the hum of its energy stopped. In the darkness a small tessarch ebbed. It grew larger. Thraan took the spear and watched as its tool transformed into its true purpose, a key. Its name even unknown to Thraan was Durg Secosa, supra-key to the Tol-Tessar. The star slid into the tessarch and began to ebb in unison with its prison. Thraan inserted Durg Secosa and locked the tessarch.

Thraan lay down prostrate before the star.

"I offer this to you mighty one. My life is caged in servitude to keep you away from the makers of light and shadow. You bring the darkness. You blameless but destructive one. Know that Thraan has seen the greatness and majesty of your beauty which is now hidden from existence. Know that your gaoler is captive as well. Together we remain bonded in this knowledge and shared imprisonment."

Thraan stood after the ritual for star-binding. The warrior walked further into the Tol-Tessar. After each imprisonment it would walk and look at its conquests. Thraan did not feel superior or victorious merely satisfied that it had prevented further destruction in the chaotic realms of existence.

Thraan remembered each of the imprisoned stars but could not gauge how long they had been here. Time did not exist. It was perfect stasis so that nothing died, and nothing was born. As Thraan strode deeper into the massive fortress, a new Tessarch would appear and then fade. Thraan tested one to ensure it was still strong. This was the warrior's favourite moment when it was just the great warrior of star protection within the very thing to which it had been bonded for as long as it had existed. The Tol-Tessar flowed through the warrior guard. Thraan could feel the unity between itself and the Tessarch. Thraan stopped walking and began to listen. Thraan felt something was watching. It was different to the surging pulses of stars.

"Thraan, it is time" Isax's voice disturbed Thraan as it drifted toward the strange presence. Thraan turned back.

The arch opened to let the warrior free. A gust of vectrons flew toward it and attached to Thraan's suit of armour. It glowed in scintillating golds and reds and illuminated the vista laid out before the arches of the Tol-Tessar. The guards of the Tol-Tessar stood to attention. Thraan had formed them from an image which had remained with it as long as it had existed. Like Thraan, the guards were dusted in the vectrons and glowed in celebration with their leader. Isax, Tol-Warrior, second only to Thraan bowed as well.

"Mighty one, I have watched, and I have learned" spoke Isax.

Isax came forward and bowed.

"Great one. Once again you have made it known to Durg Icosa its purpose. I stand corrected" Isax spoke.

"Isax your loyalty and dedication illuminate the dust of Zar. You are worthy. A time will come when the great Thraan will be merged into the Tessarch. Then perhaps, Isax, Tol-Warrior will be Isax Apeiron-Warrior. Come let us celebrate over a game of gonj" replied Thraan.

Tapping the spear, Thraan sent the cohort of infra warriors and Isax to their cavern beneath the great mountain of Kalyx. Inside their dwellings were almost cages. Thraan changed it to a large banquet hall. Bowls of Vectron dust sat ready to snort. There were urns of liquid which looked like gold and silver.

Isax took an urn and offered it to Thraan.

"I bless this conquest with milk of star" toasted Thraan sculling the liquid. Almost instantly Thraan exploded into a thousand pieces and then reformed.

Thraan's laughter and joy bellowed across the vast plains of Durg Icosa.

"Drink nexa of the Tol-Tessar" called Thraan.

The company relaxed and roared with celebration and love for their mighty warrior leader.

Isax smiled sculling some star milk.

"Thraan I will return to my duties" Isax spoke bowing to Thraan.

"Stay Isax. We all seek the same purpose. We are brethren not enemies. Only one enemy exists, and we are what stand between it and pure chaos. Drink with your brethren, enjoy their spirit. A successor will come. I am formed and I must be living on borrowed vexa to be here still" called Thraan.

Isax looked at Thraan "I will return Thraan."

Thraan looked at Isax leave. Thraan thought it didn't bode well for Isax. Lust for power was destructive. Thraan understood too well the sacrifice it took to serve and how demeaning it could be but ultimately it meant a better purpose as it was the constant. Power ebbed and flowed, dimmed, and flashed itself to extinction. Those who lusted for it were never remembered and gave no thought to their predecessors to learn. Thinking them fools who had failed where they would not. Isax had much to learn.

The first throw of mini nodes was laid out on a net of nexa and the gonj began. Thraan drank the rest of the star milk and felt at peace. Star-milk was more than a celebratory drink it was an ointment to stabilise the Tessarch inside its codes. Each star that was captured emitted energy surges which were lethal. With time any warrior would be destroyed. The star milk cleansed them and strengthened the bonding inside them, reset the hidden tessarch and maintained the order.

As Isax left, it heard the raucous noise of its comrades. Resentment welled up deeply at Thraan. Isax was ready to take the helm of being Apeiro – Warrior but could not until the flesh formed ceased to be.

Isax sped toward Tol Erda, the citadel of Durg Icosa. The waves of vectrons washed over it again. It was similar to the world it had come from; the nebula Dhalderis. The Dhalderians origins were hidden from them, and they simply dwelt within the nebulas their kind created. Latching onto a tsunami size swell, Isax was catapulted three spans towards a large distant peak. On its summit something sparkled. The source of the light was not discernible from Isax's location.

"Isax why do you come?" asked a voice within the nebula.

"Wait and you shall find out" replied Isax.

"Arrogant."

"Yes always."

The warrior glided into the main chamber of the leader.

"I am weary of waiting" spoke Isax.

"It will happen. Each time the Tol is opened it accelerates the warrior's demise. It won't be long now. There are no other contenders. The key will be passed to you" replied the figure.

"I don't trust you. The Assembly has been absent for so long. Where is it?" asked Isax.

"That is not your concern. You step outside what is permissible for your kind" the voice retorted.

"My kind. You use my kind to keep order. You know without the capability to control a star within us you would be dead along with all other existence. The dead stars would rule" replied Isax.

"You step outside and risk expulsion. The Laddarane council is pre-occupied. Why have you come?" asked the figure.

"I want Thraan removed" replied Isax.

"That is impossible" retorted the figure.

"No it isn't. The Tol-Warriors are mined constantly for their knowledge. Why is Thraan different?" asked Isax.

"You know too much for a mere protector. Be careful" replied the figure.

"Do not speak of us lightly. We are powerful as well" retorted Isax.

A small stream of vectrons suddenly shot out and speared into the impudent Isax.

"Another Tol-Warrior can be found" warned the figure.

Isax flared at the suggestion.

"I am not complete yet. But I can only be finished when I have gaoled a star" spoke Isax growing with anger.

"Ha so the arrogant Isax admits weakness before a Prime of the Laddarane" replied the figure.

"Your breach into Durg Icosa remains my secret. I am not sure the Laddarane council will be so tolerant of you as me" replied Isax menacingly.

"I agree my arrival here, if discovered would not be welcome. It has taken much energy to maintain balance and keep the Gnocerin vexa from bleeding into Durg Icosa and Icosian nexus breaching Gnoceris" replied Osesa.

Isax flared more brilliantly detesting the creature called Osesa.

"You must be patient. Your time will come. Not one of us has full control of the stars and their energy. We do not make them, but we chase them in the hope one time we will wield their knowledge. Many have spent far longer than you in that quest. You are valued. But Thraan is exceptional, and we will not risk its premature demise not even for a brilliant Dhalderian as you. Your ancestors are renowned as the greatest of the Tol Questors" replied Osesa.

"You lecture me on this whenever I arrive here. I want to know why the Assembly has not been to the last two interments of stars" insisted Isax.

Osesa began to grow weary of the incessant impatience of Isax. The Tol-Warriors were so rare they were given many privileges and knowledge.

"Isax there is another surge on the quadrant of Cos. You will need to investigate what is causing the disruption" spoke Osesa.

"Answer my question" replied Isax.

"You are on dangerous territory even with me" replied Osesa.

"I have nothing more to lose. I will risk it. If I am to whither, waiting for the mighty Thraan to end then why should I not go with some satisfaction. I know something has altered. The Star breach is greatest in memory. What has happened? Something distracts the Assembly" Isax persisted trying to get the Seer to answer its questions.

Osesa remained silent and melded back into the energy flows which formed the chamber they were in. It was solid enough to appear like marble and stone but in actual fact was made this way by the mental energy the Seer exerted. Isax remained in the one place as the chamber collapsed.

"I have angered you, Seer" spoke Isax.

"No you have not Isax. I am worried that perhaps we have made a wrong choice in encouraging your ambition. I am considering your question justly, out of respect for what you are and may become" replied Osesa.

Isax knew it had pressed the Seer too far, but it was time. It sensed something was coming which could disrupt Durg Icosa. Its warrior instinct urged it to be prepared.

"The Assembly, as you correctly observe, are in union. They too have seen the increased strength and volume of the dead ones breaching. They felt it best to merge into the Vectron and learn what they could and be ready. They will return with knowledge which may assist in quelling these upsurges" replied Osesa.

"And that is all?" probed Isax.

"That is all. Yes, there is concern like yourself. But it was best to learn first then act. You may be called Isax. We will need you to be focussed. We need the protectors to be ready" spoke Osesa.

Isax remained silent. It was not sure if the Seer had divulged everything and had to trust once more.

"You know I have felt the scent of Oblyquixiton on the wind. The great one is awake once more" spoke Isax.

Osesa did not react. It was dangerous knowledge for anything to be so powerful to be aware of the one called Oblyquixiton. The Seers had delved too far and knew how dangerous it was to be touched by Oblyquixiton.

"I will refer this to the Assembly. Has Thraan said anything?" asked Osesa.

"Not that I am aware of."

Osesa remade the chamber again.

"When you have surveyed the Cos then ask for Thraan to visit. You are right we have been neglectful and not provided the great warriors of the Tol their due accolades" spoke Osesa.

Isax bowed partly appeased but certain there was more to know.

It went outside into the vast plains which surrounded Tol Erda. It sat upon the base of nodal plateau of Kaan. It measured five geonodes across. In its centre spiralled a gargantuan cloud of vexa surges of dark matter. The plateau was larger than Isax's home nebula of Dhalderis.

Isax flew toward the Cos sector. It was on the other side of the nexus-weave from Tol Erda. It knew it would be nearing the Durg Vaga. The place where Assembly was held. Deemed off limits to all except the Council of Rulers. Even Thraan was not permitted to enter. Isax found it tempting to test if the Seer was telling the truth. It would return once it had scouted the Cos.

Osesa relaxed when Isax left. Oblyquixiton. Not since the schism had that name been mentioned. It was left to remain within the Apeiro-Warrior. Only Thraan would understand. For its name to be whispered by an infra-warrior meant something strange was happening.

"Brethren is it true the Oblyquixiton has been found?" called Osesa.

A figure formed.

"Aes Vius" spoke Osesa.

"Yes. It has allowed the Wanderer to come here. It was on Simeris, that Oblyquixiton stirred" replied Aes Vius.

"The Wanderer will bring destruction" spoke Osesa.

"Yes" replied Aes.

"The capture of the Caemexa has called the Wanderer here to set them free?" asked Osesa.

"The Wanderer has followed, our breach precipitated all of it. Now it follows and yes seeks to set these caemexa free" replied Aes Vius.

"This cannot be allowed" spoke Osesa.

Aes Vius did not respond.

"Does Pthemnat still rule the Pthohedron?" asked Osesa.

"Yes, but it remains unaware you have left Osesa. You never spoke of your departure from Gnoceris" replied Aes Vius.

"I too seek knowledge" spoke Osesa.

"Only knowledge brethren?" asked Aes Vius.

"Pthemnat considers it can have the power of the Tol-Tessar without cost to itself. It remains veiled by its bond to reform Gnoceris" spoke Osesa.

Aes Vius knew Osesa had not answered its question.

"Oblyquixiton has been woken. What will that mean?" continued Aes Vius.

"Nothing until the Caemexa are freed" replied Osesa.

"Did you bring the Caemexa here?" asked Aes Vius.

Osesa did not answer Aes Vius. Osesa suspected that its own delving in Durg Icosa, and the wound it had inflicted attracted the nodal power of these Caemexa to it. The Seers questing beyond Stonthrax had caused the breech and now their doom had arrived. It knew that Pthemnat sought the same as Osesa. And it knew Aes Vius and Osesa did not seek the same as each other. Who would win, who would conquer Oblyquixiton and Caemeris wondered Osesa.

"So what must we do?" asked Aes Vius.

"Wake the Laddarane. The Caemexa are to remain here and never to be freed. They have seen their purpose destroyed and like all things will now seek their own suzerainty over the power they wield. But this will bring further destruction, as the Seers seek their place also among the rulers of existence" spoke Osesa.

"Once again, corruption has seeped into the Pentat" spoke Aes Vius.

"You disagree, but it will rupture the nodal weave, if these beings are allowed to rule in their own realm, here. For even if the Seers remained true to their purpose, we are powerful regardless, and would only destroy whatever attempted to co-exist with us. You are still veiled in this knowledge Aes Vius" spoke Osesa.

It was Osesa and Pthemnat, who did not understand their purpose. Now it sensed Osesa's intentions were far more ambitious than that of Pthemnat. One which could prove fatal to the Pentat's continuance thought Aes Vius as it left.

Cos was an ocean. It was deep indigo and reflected the nebulas and moons which dotted the skies of Durg Icosa almost perfectly. The ocean was in fact a vast body of emptiness. It was not liquid. The synapses of the geo-nodes were transparent and were what drew the dead stars toward the prison world. A space in a world of energy which did not possess power.

Isax plunged beneath the surface, causing a ripple across the face of the massive body. Underneath Isax searched for any scars or weakening of the Vectron weave. Its spear lit the way.

Isax senses could not detect anything different. Perhaps it was a ruse by the Seer to get Isax out of the way. Its questions had made the Seer uncomfortable. It continued into the deeper hollows of the void. The depths of Durg Icosa lay untouched by any light. It was unfathomable to any who had not reached this far into the world. It stopped to listen. Nothing. It was complete silence. The hum of the Vectron weave was not present. Nothing.

"Osesa, I think you waste my time."

Isax turned seeking out any sign of breach. As it did so it saw two specs peering across the vastness. It stopped and readied its spear.

"What are you?"

There was no answer. The aquamarine specs did not move or react to the presence of the warrior.

Isax cautiously moved closer. The dots of light grew larger. It began to see translucent figures moving. They were inside the Tol-Tessar. They were unaware of Isax watching them.

"What are you? You are not made from star death and are not flesh formed like Thraan. What have you been hiding Seer?" asked Isax.

Isax flared into a brilliant Vectron flow to leave. It sped to each expanse of the ocean to ensure that nothing had infiltrated. Isax made its way toward the Durg Vaga again. It donned its caging armour in readiness. What was the Seer doing? In Isax's mind anything unusual was deemed lethal. Its purpose to protect so embedded inside its formulations that it trusted nothing. Even the Seer knew to keep its distance from the Tol-Warriors. It had arrived here after Durg Icosa was made by the unknown. They had seen the dead ones attracted to its energy reserves and had devised a way to learn of these exiled stars. But the Tol-Warriors had been here first, caging the power and keeping it safe within the Tol. The Seer and Tol-Warriors were equal in strength and knowledge. However the Seer was an invasive force, while the Tol-Warriors were an extension of the energy flows of Durg Icosa, a natural ballast evolved over eons. Isax war was with Apeiro-Warrior, not the Seer. Osesa could be dispensed with no effect on Isax desire. Perhaps it was time for Osesa to be gone so I can focus on Thraan thought Isax.

The yawning mouth of Durg Vaga appeared. Isax flew directly into it. After a steep descent, the perfectly cylindrical tunnel changed direction to a forward passage. Isax stopped and began to walk the rest of the way. It was dangerous for the warrior to be inside the Keep of the Laddarane. The Laddarane resented the warriors and Thraan. Isax put on an invisible armour to hide itself in case the council knew of its presence. A low hum began to signal in the translucent amber light. Isax followed, encoding the signal as it went.

The signal grew in strength and changed into sounds of speech. It was rhythmic. Like the sounds Thraan made when it was meditating during the long watches. It was called vexa-song. Isax stood at the entrance of a tomb. Inside it saw Seer Osesa, and another who was unknown to Isax. Their luminescence was so bright it was like being up on the surface. Suddenly cylinders began to emerge from the vectrons of rocks. They were thin like Tol-spears. Creatures began to form out of them. They stood silently as if they were unaware. A few of them seemed to look toward Isax but did not react.

Soon the entire cavity was crowded with the figures.

"Laddarane, you are woken. The Pthohedron remains in schism. But we sense star death is near. Oblyquixiton has stirred and the Caemexa caged. The doom of Durg Icosa is feared. Do the Laddarane remember what was foretold?" spoke Osesa.

"The Laddarane remember, and we wait for the destroyer to reveal itself."

The Seer bowed.

"The Conclave of the Tol-Tessar, sacred well which maintains the walls of Stonthrax rests within the Laddarane. When the Wanderer arrives you will be called" spoke Osesa.

The figures glowed dimly, and the humming commenced once more. The two figures disappeared.

Isax remained hidden behind its armour. So the conclave was only made of the Seer, not the council of the citadel. Who was the Wanderer? Isax knew the Seer had kept secrets but for the Seer to control the Laddarane, something was wrong, a deep imbalance in the Vectron flows was imminent. It explained why Assembly had not been present for the last two interments. The Seer was storing energy for this invader called the Wanderer, thought Isax.

Isax walked into the cavity. It touched one of the figures. It awoke with a burst of nodal energy almost blinding Isax.

"Are you brethren of the great Tol and protectors of the Durg Icosa?" asked Isax.

"No we are the Laddarane. We were made first and the warriors came later. We are here to destroy the destroyer. You are here to capture death."

"Are they not the same thing?"

"Oblyquixiton has been awoken. Without the Caemeris it will bring destruction. The Caemexa have been found, called to sacrifice back to the shadowed might. But the Wanderer comes to free them. If the Tol-

Tessar is ruptured, then we are annihilated" shimmered the sliver of energy.

"Who made you?" asked Isax.

"We are Durg Icosa" the Laddarane replied.

"When will the Wanderer come and how will we know?" Isax continued.

"Watch the Apeiron. It is formed" replied the Laddarane.

"Will Thraan be defeated?"

"All will be defeated" replied the Laddarane.

Isax left and returned to the Tol-Tessar.

The celebrations had finished. Isax removed its armour. Thraan appeared.

"All sectors are clear" spoke Isax.

"We can rest a while. I will go to the table of Kalyx and meditate" spoke Thraan.

"Where are you from Thraan?" asked Isax suddenly.

"I do not know. Why do you ask?" replied Thraan.

"Don't you think it strange that you are ignorant to your origin. I am Dhalderian" replied Thraan.

"I think I am old. Of nodal knowledge" replied Thraan.

"Who made you?" asked Isax.

"Again Isax I do not know. Even if I did then it would not matter. Our histories are forsaken for the privilege of being Tol Warriors. I must leave now. Isax, I fear where you delve will lead you to disintegration. I will demise at some time and a successor is needed. You have been the Quasa Secosa bearer and have been strong in your patience and boldness. Do not throw it away" warned Thraan.

Isax watched Thraan take up its vigil on the great table of Kalyx.

Seer Osesa had seen the warrior leave the Laddarane tomb. It had been a grave breach. Isax was dangerous. It could cause disharmony before it was needed when the Wanderer arrived.

"Aes Vius what shall we do?" asked Osesa.

"I think we must wait for the Wanderer. The Caemexa remain divided. Thraan is strong. The Clayborn may be defeated yet" the Seer replied.

"We are not" replied Osesa.

"The Laddarane will not be removed easily. They are bonded to the shadow of Oblyquixiton."

"Who woke the shadow?"

"The Wanderer when she pierced the gates of Stonthrax. Although I wonder if she was allowed" replied Aes Vius.

"What will we do with Isax? It has breached its sacred oaths which means its desire to usurp the Thraan grows" asked Osesa.

"Let the Tol-Warriors fight their battle. Theirs is a deeper knowledge and bond to Durg Icosa than ours. It will help us to have them distracted and perhaps understand more of their strength when the time comes for us to rise again" replied Aes Vius.

Aes Vius and Osesa disappeared from Durg Icosa. Aes Vius stood in its tower looking at the Cadra Phomera.

"It is up to you now Ange. All threads of the questing webs first sent by the Seers, meet in the great recesses of Durg Icosa. Will you remain and become Apeironex or diminish and your world along with it. The Seers seek their power and will wait to see if they will survive to wield it. Seer Osesa does not see all there is to see. Nothing is certain" Aes Vius spoke.

Thraan watched over the vastness of its domain and felt its codes wash throughout the world. It was in unison and felt whole with Durg Icosa. The strength of the bond was so strong the warrior knew if it ever broke it would be the end. Osesa appeared behind Thraan and bowed.

"We call you to Assembly Apeiro-Warrior" spoke Osesa.

Thraan bowed and went with the Prime of the Laddarane.

"Mighty one it is not without great need we have called you away from the world. But there has been a breach of the sacred oaths. One of yours has entered Durg Vaga without cause" spoke Osesa.

"Isax."

"Yes."

"Destroy the Dhalderian" ordered Thraan.

Isax remained near the arches of the Tol thinking of the figures it had seen in Cos. Was this the Wanderer or these Caemexa the Seers spoke of? It went back to the ocean and found the eyes and figures once more. It looked into the Tessarch. How were these figures brought here without a breach. Was there another way inside?

Isax took its spear and tapped the ebbing Tessarch which contained the creatures. A small ripple emanated from the place Isax had touched.

The Custodians turned to the ripple in the Tessarch.

"So our gaoler has arrived" spoke Descendant.

"Who are thee?" asked Isax.

"Your potency is strong and pierces our cage so I can see you with the eyes of the Sentinels" replied Baachalaus.

"Who are thee?" Isax asked once more.

"We are Custodians from future memory. We are Caemexa of the realm created in the Third Age of light. We exist beyond the borders of the great stars of light and shadow" replied Assumpta.

"How have you come here?" asked Isax.

"It remains a mystery to us also. You would be in grave breach creature to be here" spoke Baachelaus.

Isax looked at the Custodian and saw it appeared to be formed. While the rest were ethers of great energy coded recently, with tight bonds between the vexa and with hues beyond light, shades between darkness and pure energy.

"Which world do you belong?" Isax asked.

"We belong in the realm of Caemeris and are formed under the dominion of Belmaris" replied Assumpta.

"You will be extinguished for this if your rulers learn of what you have done" spoke Baachelaus.

"Free us" implored Seraf.

Seraf flared into life, but it was pale against the luminescent star warrior.

"I cannot. Once you are here then it is deemed you remain until the Thrax have waned. Stand down pale one. Your eyes see beyond the prison for it is them which caught my attention. Are you here to destroy Durg Icosa?" asked Isax.

Baachelaus chuckled.

"I feel your lust powerful one. We are not here to destroy but to learn and then overcome. My brethren seek freedom to return to our realm, but I see where this is futile. We are here locked and caged once more. I believe we can bargain. Your rulers seek Caemexa and the memory of what made us. You seek to rule" replied Baachelaus.

"You do not know or understand Durg Icosa, creature of new light" replied Isax.

"Oh but we do. We do. Voloc would have destroyed us long ago had it not been for the memories of Caemeris we bear" spoke Baachelaus.

Isax knew it could overcome these prisoners but to do so would alert its presence to Thraan. The creatures were lost and seek freedom. Isax realised if an alliance were struck then they could be used to overthrow Thraan for them to have their freedom. The pale one contained many nodes of power, and the others were equally as potent.

"What are your names?" asked Isax.

"I am Descendant. Baachelaus, ruler of the Caemexa of the realm of light."

"I am Ascendant. Assumpta, equal diarch of the realm of Light."

"We are the elements made for the realm of clay and earth. We live under the rule of our slain brethren Norbu and Belmaris" spoke Lido as she swam near to the wall where Isax stood.

Seraf blazed enlivened by Aerean.

"Feel the power of clay" called Seraf.

Isax could feel itself distorting with the density of the power to shape the vexa. It almost wanted to weep, seeing the bonds of light caged into reality and collapsed into a form. Just as it was about to succumb to the power which tore through its conscious Assumpta stepped forward.

"Cease your play with the Warrior. Don't you understand the greatness of this creature. It wields the power to control first stars. The offspring of the first. It is the gaoler of all that exists" she exhorted to the Custodians.

Isax stood back looking at the group of brethren.

"Do you know why you have been brought here?" Isax asked.

"Something wants our power, and memories of Caemeris. Voloc breached our realm and imprisoned Descendent. And now in our quest to restore ourselves and destiny, we have imprisoned ourselves and doomed one of our brethren Norbu, and its creation Arglethium" replied Assumpta.

Isax had heard of the lost Belmaris star. Far away beyond the gates of Stonthrax. There had not been a darkened one imprisoned from those nodal realms since Thraan had become Apeiro- Warrior.

"Belmaris has not been felt in the weave since the first moments of the nodes" spoke Isax.

"What brought you here Warrior? Even one as mighty as you would not risk it without reason" asked Baachelaus.

"You see much pale one. But it is not for the prisoner to tell the gaoler when to reveal the secrets of its cage" replied Isax.

"No but you understand something wants us to bring us here. I also see the lust inside you. There is another beyond you. The uncontested one who rules above you" probed Baachelaus.

Isax could feel the piercing eyes of the pale figure. Assumpta could feel the swell of power inside Baachelaus. It was not time. We must wait for Ange. She was coming she could sense her.

"You would not dare forsake your sacred oaths for prisoners which are unknown to you. What is your name?" asked Baachelaus.

"Isax of the Dhalderian, Tol-Warrior" Isax bowed to them as it spoke. "Brethren of Caemeris. I believe there is a way for us to find what we both desire. War comes. I believe you draw it with you if Belmaris is the node of the realm of light and clay. I see in you pale one the power of many and lust for much. You have learnt patience in your imprisonment but would be with my power more destructive than any deadened star which lives in the Tessarch. Do you know of the Wanderer?"

"We do" replied Assumpta.

"What is the Wanderer?"

"A Clayborn creature made of the realm of light but bestowed great power. The quest brings her here to steal us back to the realm to restore her own world." Baachelaus explained.

"This creature must be powerful to think it can break the Tessarch" replied Isax.

"It has a stone, prism which captured the memory of Caemeris. It is this which allows her to come here" spoke Baachelaus.

"And do the brethren desire freedom? Do you desire being returned to this place, the realm of Belmaris?" asked Isax.

"Yes" replied Aerean as she swirled toward Isax.

"It is dying. The Wanderer's journey is in vain. We have been sundered from the clay when our brother Norbu was slain. Voloc devours Arglethium and will return it to its first bonds. The Custodian caemexa must seek a new dominion" spoke Baachelaus.

"And pale one would here suffice?" probed Isax.

Baachelaus chuckled deeply. The spear of the Warrior rippled slightly. Assumpta noticed how Baachelaus' power, her own and the other Custodians was seeping slowly into the Tessarch. Was this how the Tessarch maintained its power, it drew it from the prisoners contained within its boundaries.

Baachelaus did not answer. Assumpta could sense the change in Descendant as it neared Isax. Isax seemed oblivious to the danger it was in. Baachelaus' eyes began to change between blue to green to the gemstones of Norbu. Descendant looked at Assumpta daring her to warn the Warrior it was going to attack. It was the spear thought Assumpta, Baachelaus knew it would be a formidable weapon.

"Stand away pale one. I see the lust in you. My spear is not the key you seek" Isax warned. It sensed the vexa surges around itself and within Baachelaus.

"No but it is strong for it draws me to it" replied Baachelaus.

"Yes, and many other nodes which exist within Durg Icosa and beyond" replied Isax.

Isax moved away from the vexa boundary of the Tessarch.

"The stone this Wanderer possesses, it must have allowed her to break the seal of the Guardians?" asked Isax.

"Yes, it would have" replied Assumpta.

Isax pondered this. If this weapon were strong enough to cut down Stonthrax then it would easily overthrow Thraan.

Suddenly Descendant lunged at Isax. Baachelaus forced the vexa flow toward Isax and made it latch onto the spear of the Warrior. They struggled. The force of the two creatures warped the Tessarch and

Ascendant could feel herself being pulled with it. The Custodian did not want Baachelaus to escape. Baachelaus needed to be here when Ange arrived. If they were not altogether than it was futile. She lunged at them and pulled Descendent to her.

"Stand away Descendant, Diarch. Your fate is not that of Isax the mighty warrior of Durg Icosa. You are Caemexa. Far is the sight of the realm of light and long its touch and memory lingers. You see only shadow of Voloc, and dim is your vision, the power you seek here is not yours to wield" warned Assumpta.

Isax pulled the vexa off its spear. The Tessarch was intact and kept the Custodians bound.

Seraf wrapped itself around Descendent to restrain its brethren.

"You are strong indeed. Belmaris must be formidable, and I look forward to when the warring child becomes the deadening progenitor then it will feel the sting of Isax Tol Warrior. What mighty force caged you in your own realm?" asked Isax.

"Voloc" replied Baachelaus.

"And what bought us here?" asked Baachelaus.

"I do not know Creature" replied Isax.

"I was meant to restore us and then that would break the prism, but I could not find you and release you from Voloc. So Norbu hid the prism on Arglethium, and its power passed to the Clayborn. Ange has this burden now. But I fear something else is at work, for its' power has been sensed and imprisoned us here. Something Norbu did not foresee" spoke Assumpta.

Isax listened. It made no sense what these creatures discussed. It knew that all were doomed with the awakening of the great shadow Oblyquixiton. Caemeris was a lost memory to most of the created known. But this weapon the Wanderer carried interested Isax.

"I must leave. My absence from the watch will be noticed. Brethren, we both seek something which may bring our desires to fullness" spoke Isax.

"And now that you know of us what becomes of us?" asked Seraf.

Isax knew then the brethren would not let it leave easily and any disturbance would alert Thraan and the Seer.

"Stand down you have no power over me or the Tessarch. Not even in the eons of time would you be able to overcome the locks of Durg Icosa. Caemexa, you are incomplete, and this is the eternal tomb of your existence. Destruction comes from many directions and a great battle arrives. This Wanderer brings both doom and hope for all and with it a key for many to realise their destiny. The nodes swell with the power which has been unleashed. Isax the Tol-Warrior will wait as it always has, and when the time comes, I will be ready. You have taught me. And I will remember this."

"And in return Warrior what will you give for this knowledge?" asked Baachelaus.

"Return? Your destiny lies with another. Your battle is with the Wanderer. If you are freed, then we will meet at the gates of the Tol-Tessar. This Wanderer will need to overcome the Tol Warriors, and the Laddarane. Only then will your fates be decided."

Isax slipped away into the ocean of Cos.

Baachelaus and the brethren stood watching as the Tessarch resumed its ebbing imprisonment.

"Ange will need to be strong. The warrior will try to take Norbu's stone" spoke Lido.

Baachelaus roared in frustration.

"Once again I seek a way to be free of my bonds and fulfil my desire to rule but again, other forces conspire and manipulate for their own purpose."

Assumpta felt the swell of aggression inside Baachelaus. As did Seraf, Aerean and Lido. Lido began to weep.

"We are doomed and Arglethium. Why did you tell the creature about Ange? She will need to overcome this warrior as well as the gaol to free us" she cried to Assumpta.

"She will be different now. I believe our hope is not defeated. Baachelaus you must obey Ange when she comes. It is the only chance we have. If you do not, then everything Norbu did will be in vain" spoke Assumpta.

"I will wait. Until the Clayborn stands here before me, Descendant's throne of light remains usurped by a creature of shadow and malice. This Isax will return. It and I desire the same thing. I believe you Assumpta, that the Clayborn will come and when she does then so will this Isax Tol warrior. And with both their power then once more the Custodians of light shall rule" spoke Baachelaus.

Assumpta watched all her brethren. Only Assumpta understood the destruction and sorrow Ange was cloaked within.

The ocean of Cos gave nothing away as Isax left. The warrior sped toward the Tol-Tessar to resume its surveillance. It thought about all it had learnt from the Caemexa. The intruder would have no choice but to come to the arch. No other could penetrate it. The Seer knew and the Laddarane would seek this creature out. Thraan would remain loyal to its duty so would pose no threat. How much did the Seer know? Did they understand this node of power the creature carried? Osesa must or it would not have woken the Laddarane. Isax could feel destiny inside itself. It saw its chance to usurp Thraan, the Seer, and bring the great Tol-Tessar under its dominion. Not just the gate keeper but the ruler. Oblyquixiton would have no hold and the myth of the Caemexa would be within its grasp also. Isax flew through the vector streams with the vision of the Apeiro-Warrior in its grasp. Inside its shapeless form sat its own Tessarch suddenly flaring to life. Isax felt a small spurt of vexa emit from its thorax, wondering what had caused it.

.Thraan stood on the cliffs of Pume. This heaving volcano of power always thrilled the Apeiron as it belched great flows of vectron dust up into the nexus weave beyond Durg Icosa. It scoured the flows for any sign of star death. Nothing so far. It felt Isax return and saw its Tessarch had awoken. A sense of loss filled the Apeiro-Warrior. For any Tol-Warrior to breach its codes, meant a loss to the vexa and honour.

"Soon Isax, I will need to seek another who may replace me" spoke Thraan.

Waves and waves spilled up and out over the warrior and it drank them heartily. The specs of power helped regenerate it even further and heighten its senses. A privilege only the Apeiron inherited. Thraan dove into the swirling lava and disappeared. As it exploded into the miniscule codes which made it, Thraan felt one with Durg Icosa instantly aware of everything. It saw the Custodians in their prison and wondered who the dense creatures were. Thraan saw the Laddarane awake and wondered why the ancient protectors were active. There was no star death only the flows and ebbs of the Tol-Tessar. It drank more of the liquid and felt it strengthening the bonds inside it. Thraan would be ready for whatever caused the disturbance.

Ange had seen the formidable figure leap into the heaving volcano and disappear. She was relieved she had gone unnoticed. She slipped into the world through the portal from Gnoceris; the mountain of Pume was actually a massive node-coexa of energy where movement between energy wells was permitted. She looked around her. The prism was firmly latched around her neck. Nekoda stood beside her. It was comforting to feel his warmth and realness. She scanned the landscape to see any sign of buildings or construction. Nothing. She touched the prism to see if it could detect the Custodians. Still nothing. Perhaps she should track this warrior. But she sensed its potency and thought it better to leave it.

"There is no choice friend. We will walk until we find what we came for."

Nekoda whined ready to keep moving.

Ange scaled down the mountain and toward what appeared to be a road. She noticed plumes of vectron dust rose where she stepped. It was all nodal energy but more densely laid then that of Gnoceris. She took the prism out and kept it in her hand. She wondered if she should try and bring the prison to herself, but that may alert the rulers of this world.

Pthemnat had not been clear on who or what ruled here. It was the doom of existence was all the Seer had said.

Suddenly Ange heard a noise like a great throng was walking before her. She neared a small rise and peered over. There were creatures coming from the mouth of a cave. There were uncountable numbers. On top of the entrance stood a figure. It reminded her of Pthemnat. It was long and thin and wore a cloak of pure energy. The colour was indigo instead of the green of Pthemnat.

"You have to be a Seer" she whispered.

She waited until the marching creatures had cleared and were well in front. The Seer left. Silence resumed and she was relieved.

"Come Nekoda into the underneath we go again."

She smiled at herself at the number of times she had to delve into the caves and tunnels and unseen ways. Always there were more secrets to discover sometimes good, some bad but always interesting.

Ange and Nekoda, went into Durg Veda, now empty of the Laddarane. She could sense nothing here which helped to explain where she was and what may help her. She turned to leave.

"Wanderer we have been waiting for you" spoke the figure.

Ange stopped and drew her sword.

"That weapon won't help you here."

"I know but it makes me feel better and in balance" Ange replied.

"A dense creature you are. Caemexa flows within you."

"Are you a Seer?"

"Yes. I am Osesa."

"You are brethren, of Pthemnat and Aes Vius?" asked Ange.

"We are in schism and have not been able to bring the Pthohedron to completeness" replied Osesa.

"You know who I am and what I intend to do" spoke Ange.

"Yes" replied Osesa.

"Was it you or Pthemnat who brought me here?" asked Ange.

"The power of your stone reached far. All of the Pentat were aware and drawn to it" replied Osesa.

"So when the Custodians came, and Voloc invaded you could see what would ultimately happen?"

"Not in the same detail, but energy, light, power all follows the same rules. When power coalesces it draws existence to it and when it diverges, it brings destruction with it. But the nodal stone you carry, is able to usurp these rules, it brings the formed into the unformed present. It disrupts the continuity of creation" explained Osesa.

"Mighty Norbu did this to protect the Clayborn and his realm of light. But he didn't understand, did he?" asked Ange.

"No the one you call Norbu being Caemexa only knew the will of Caemeris."

Ange fingered the prism remembering Norbu. She felt the well of energy at the memory of his death, bloom inside her.

"I have to do this Seer. I cannot return now. Destruction comes by all paths. I at least will choose the best one I know. If Arglethium and the Clayborn were good enough for the mighty forger Norbu, so it is for me" spoke Ange.

"The Keeper of sorrow, the Wanderer, Ange Tsaed, Clayborn, maimed, shunned, girl-child, the warrior, the woman. Destiny asks for a new name. You have left the Clayborn self in the Cadra Phomera. Now you must become Apeironex. The breaker of the Tol-Tessar and conqueror of Caemeris" spoke Osesa.

"What is this name Apeironex?" asked Ange. "This means nothing to me."

"We will go to the Assembly."

Ange was ripped into the vortex stream away from Durg Vaga.

Instantly she was inside a chamber similar to that of Pthemnat.

The Seer stood before Ange.

Ange could feel the prism around her neck gyrating with energy.

"The tear of Ascendant is drawn toward your power Seer or is it you attempting to take it?" asked Ange.

"It is the eye of Caemeris. It holds the first visions of existence and contains them. Its power plays with the codes of the Vectron flows, and nodal weave surrounding Durg Icosa. Strong is this object, dense bonds, unbreakable even for Stonthrax. It disrupts the weave so it can transform it into anything its owner wishes. Mighty was the chaos of Caemeris, and now I see why the Seers were drawn to it as well. It holds both Vectra flow and Nega-Vectra energy" replied Osesa.

"And if I break the prison which cages the Custodians and bring them back to the realm of light, what will happen?" asked Ange.

"None have ever broken the Tessarch. We do not know but Star death will be let loose but perhaps this caemerin node will contain them" replied Osesa.

"I do not believe that the Caemeris and Oblyquixiton, as mighty as they are, would leave their power in the hands of a clay formed creature ignorant to what power she wields. This would be dangerous" spoke Ange.

"You see much. It was in ignorance that Caemeris was able to remain free of the deadening stars. It cloaked itself in your density and even now still remains free of Oblyquixiton. Your mighty Norbu was chosen and formed it from the Custodian of sorrows and lost purpose. It hides its path forward and obscures the memories encoded in the negation once the codes are formed. In doing this none could follow or replicate

Caemeris vision. So it needed to be brought here. And now the vision of Caemeris has come to give Seer Osesa what it seeks" spoke Osesa.

"So what is it that you seek? Pthemnat wants the nodal power of the stone. Aes Vius searches for knowledge which I have given it. What do you seek?" asked Ange.

"We will become the third of the great geonodes and we will rest between Oblyquixiton and Caemeris and bring a new vision to fullness. What you hold will give us this power. Conquest of the Tessarch means we control star-death, birth, and everything in between, whatever we wish to rule" spoke Osesa.

"If you were not deemed rulers in the first place then why now?" asked Ange.

"Because we did not understand but our questing has opened possibilities. You most of all should understand our need to know and dominate Clayborn. It is after all what Caemeris envisaged through the Custodians for your kind" replied Osesa.

Ange grew suspicious. Pthemnat stated none of this. There was no stopping these creatures. They are set on their paths, and nothing makes them change from it. Aes Vius had said the Seers had no boundaries and they wrought their own destruction. They were willing to condemn Arglethium on a whim for the sake of their own ambitions. It was like Norbu only understood what he was made to do, forge, and bring to being. She began to understand the purpose of Assumpta and Baachelaus, their perpetual disharmony the need to question, doubt, hope and desire, fulfilment allowed the creatures of Arglethium to change, grow and learn. Not just follow the same path, doomed to a singular fate until death takes them. That was why Assumpta wept eternally for that lost vision of what could be, when she and Baachelaus were sundered. They saw the lost fate of the Clayborn to be awoken, and new possibilities could be forged. Is that why Baachelaus resisted taking its place once more among the Custodians. It saw its own death in the form of the Clayborn wondered Ange.

"You need the other Seers to remake your Pthohedron?" asked Ange.

"I am able to overwhelm them when I have control of the Tessarch."

"I command the gates of Stonthrax and have made a bargain with Oblyquixiton. How do the broken and sundered Seers expect to hold the Keeper of Caemeris?" asked Ange.

"You will need to enter Tol-Tessar to end your quest. There is nothing we need do. You have done it all. We have simply let you continue to us here. Power craves power and will always pool towards the greatest source. Even the eye of Caemeris cannot overcome the codes of existence. So Clayborn to your quest you shall go. Thraan" called the Seer.

Suddenly the Apeiro-Warrior appeared.

"Stand intruder, I sensed your weapon drawing upon the weave" called Thraan. Its spear pointed directly at Ange.

Ange tensed but knew the warrior would not harm her for it was the Seers intent she be gaoled.

"Mighty one, I saw you in the great volcano when I entered. Your strength and power remind me of a warrior who once taught me and fought alongside me in battle" spoke Ange.

"Intruder, it is not permitted you remain here. To the Tol-Tessar until our rulers determine your fate" spoke Thraan.

Suddenly Ange felt herself being caught in a vectra stream. It was so fast she did not have time to do anything. It stopped. She sat inside an ebbing chamber within the Tol-Tessar. Nekoda appeared alongside her snarling.

"Help! Is anyone there?" Ange called.

Nekoda whined and jumped unable to feel any ground but was not falling either. It touched the frame of the Tessarch. It snarled at it not because it was hurt but because it was so strange.

Ange removed the prism. Why didn't the Seer take it? It would have been so easy. She peered into the jewel and searched for the Custodians. The blue green specs shone out and she knew who it was instantly.

"Where are you?" she called.

"Clayborn you have joined us at last" replied Baachelaus.

"How do I find you?"

The low chuckle made her shiver reminding her of Norbu lying chained on the floor of its throne room.

"None of us know. We have been told we will never escape" spoke Seraf.

"I believe we will. So many people and creatures have said the same to me but here we are gaoled on the edge of existence with a key we don't know how to use" spoke Ange.

"Ange."

Ange heard the voice of Assumpta.

"Ascendant. How do I find you? Arglethium dies and it is only the Custodians which can heal it."

"We know. Did you learn anything in your quest which will help us be free."

"I have tasted star death. I know its form and can remember its codes. The Tessarch's codes must be able to understand the death zones within the stars. I swam in their Vectron flows. I will remember them."

Ange took the prism and began to draw the flows of star death. She scored tiny waves and then touching them made them oscillate back and forth up and down to the point where they become one, forming a hole in the wall of the Tessarch.

"I wonder what will happen if I break the Tessarch?" Ange asked outloud.

"Your world will die without us Clayborn" Descendant's voice drifted around her.

"You were once called the Destroyer, Descendent and Baachelaus. Tell me what I need to know if I am rule this prism and what it contains?"

"You need to understand your desires. To wield the power of a Custodian is to desire only one thing. To exist within your purpose so fully that nothing can remove you from it, nothing else can fulfil what you have deemed is yours. Know what you want and take it, for the next destroyer and usurper will. Know what you seek and seize it."

A memory of Tata and Nekoda arose before her. It was like she was standing their watching them come over the great red dunes. The silhouette of the Boab trees stretched out towards her as if imploring her to remember them. The hot breeze of the desert touched her cheeks, and she could feel grit upon her skin. Suddenly she was staring at her Mata, dead and bloated from the plague. Tessi was weeping next to her.

"I left this sorrow in the Cadra Phomera and when it is all finished, I will place the last codes of my journey with the prism as the future memories of Ange Tsaed, Clayborn, Maimed, Wanderer and Destroyer."

"No tricks Ange. Baachelaus has spoken the truth. Know what you desire. What lies in the heart of Ange Tsaed?" Ascendant's voice floated around her as well.

"I am of the earth, the mighty Choasa and the sun which makes it all happen. I am flesh and bone and thirst for the things which made me live. I have seen the things which came first and live beyond what my kind has ever known. I know the place where shadow and light exist and create. I want what I am. I seek revenge for a world on the brink of destruction, even though that world would forget me in a moment. I am a god of generosity. I am as powerful as the Mighty Choasa, bringing life with no thought to who deserved it in the first place. So brethren come to me, and we shall restore the realm of light for the Ascendant and Descendant to return to their thrones. To let Arglethium flourish once more, so this Wanderer may return to her home."

Ange drew the codes and formed a hollow in the Tessarch. Before her appeared the Custodians.

"I wish Norbu was here" she spoke.

Nekoda barked smelling Lido, Aerean and Seraf.

"You have grown Clayborn" spoke Baachelaus.

The Custodian was still formidable, and Ange stood back from it. She could still sense a strength in it which never seemed to diminish.

"I have reached the last stage of the journey. I will take us back to the realm of light and together we will restore Arglethium."

"How?" asked Baachelaus

"With the power of the prism. It has the strength to break the webs between worlds and layers of existence. It will control you Baachelaus and bring you back to your rightful throne. It will let you see once more with the eyes of Caemeris your maker and not the clouded veil of Voloc."

"We are now beyond the reaches of mere clay. We sit within the cradle of Star death. Imagine what I can learn from the throng of those leviathans. It is not to be wasted on the immature vision which made you" Baachelaus spoke menacingly to Ange.

Ange grew nervous. She realised she would need Baachelaus to capitulate before she could return home.

"Stubborn fool" she whispered. A nodal flow of frustration ebbed around her. She drew her sword as she began to mark the codes with edge of the prism into the Tessarch cell. It warped with each stroke.

"You ask me what destiny do I want? I want my home back" she snapped at Baachelaus.

Baachelaus sneered at her and lunged. It snatched the prism with ease.

"No Descendant! We must return. We are not meant to exist here. It will disrupt the weave; the energy flows already scream with the power which has invaded the dead weave of Oblyquixiton. There is no power within Durg Icosa which you can deem yours to hold. You must return" Assumpta cried.

Ange called upon the memories in the prism. She willed them to come to life and re-order the power of the Custodians to the state they had once been and release the grip of Descendant.

Baachelaus latched onto her as it felt the prism being pulled free. They embraced one another.

"Do you understand lesser one. We are one and the same thing. We are both destroyers of others to make our purpose come true."

"Never. I only want to save what made me. You have lost your purpose and are too afraid to embrace your destiny again. You are too afraid to embrace your death," cried Ange.

Baachelaus sneered at her. She was beginning to black out from the claws around her throat. Ascendant, Lido, Seraf and Aerean surrounded them to force Baachelaus to let go. Nekoda snarled trying to gain traction on the empty vexa weave it stood upon, but it could not reach Ange to protect her.

"We will not spend an eternity here locked away from our destiny. We will die before then. Release her!" shouted Seraf. "I have felt the tomb Magnumarum. I know the pain of death."

"I will have my way. I have spent the life of a star in prison and will not be sent back to another" Baachelaus roared.

Baachelaus' grip grew tighter.

"Die lesser one or become one with me. You are strong. You and I shall rule. You have lived to taste the power of the death and we will be the new shadow which haunts existence" the Custodian cried.

"I will not. I am of clay. I will not remain here in a world I do not belong. Let go of me!" Ange croaked as the claw of Baachelaus squeezed even more around her neck.

Suddenly the Tessarch bulged drowning them all in vectron showers. Isax stood before them.

"So the Wanderer, invader, formed creature has come to Durg Icosa" Isax spoke.

Baachelaus released Ange. The Custodians gathered behind her.

"I have what you seek Warrior of the Tessarch" spoke Baachelaus.

The Custodian held the prism up between its talons.

"What will you give in return for the thing which will bring you suzerainty over your enemies?" asked Baachelaus.

"I shall take the power node. I have no need to bargain" spoke Isax snatching the prism. Baachelaus roared and just as the warrior went to escape from the Tessarch, Baachelaus' talons wrapped around its limb. It grabbed the spear and tore it out of the clutches of the warrior.

Isax attempted to disintegrate into the vortex stream of the ebbing cage, but it was too late. Baachelaus crushed the spear.

"You have destroyed a tol-lance. How?" spoke Isax suddenly wary of Baachelaus' strength.

"I am Caemexa, and the prism makes me whole. Its presence here whether I wield it or not allows me to resume my original form and destiny. None can bind me but that of Caemeris. Now come to me. Let me taste the strength of the Tol-Tessar" roared Baachelaus.

Baachelaus consumed Isax. The warrior and Custodian exploded and reformed. The eyes of Isax blended with the eyes of Uchala. The gates of Stonthrax shuddered. The union of future memory and the knowledge of star death collided in the merged beings of Isax and Descendant. Baachelaus saw what Isax knew. It saw the Seers orchestrations to become third in the powers of creation.

"They must be defeated along with the Apeiro-Warrior" spoke Baachelaus.

Baachelaus talons dropped the prism so enthralled with the powers it now wielded. The Tessarch suddenly opened, and Descendant Tol-Caemexa entered Durg Icosa.

Ange's heart thudded. It was out of control. She reclaimed the prism. It was intact. But it was meaningless. She could not leave without all the Custodians. She looked at Assumpta. The memory of their first meeting came back to her. She remembered the colour of Norbu's stones and how her eyes reflected them.

"It is time, Keeper. Grow to fullness. We have reached the end of our destinies" spoke Assumpta.

"I am not sad about this for I knew it all along. But will I be able to bring Arglethium back from the poison of Voloc?" asked Ange.

"You are Apeironex. You are able to withstand the power of Caemeris. You have breached the gates of Stonthrax. You are no longer bound by your clay form. We are not destined to be entombed for an eternity. Let us go home Ange. Fight well and bring the brethren home. I give you rule over my dominion and if it is willed then you will take your place with Baachelaus as destroyers and creators" replied Assumpta.

"What do you mean, take my place with Baachelaus?"

"You will not be able to defeat Baachelaus. It will see with the knowledge of Caemeris and have the strength of the Oblyquixita from the warrior. The prism will be destroyed and the gates of Stonthrax ruptured. Now it is time. Lido, Aerean, Seraf!" called Assumpta "It is time for us to return home."

The four Custodians gathered around Ange.

"Does the Clayborn call her brethren?" asked Lido.

"The Clayborn calls them" replied Ange.

Ange felt the Custodians become one with her. The prism began to dissolve and formed a drop hanging in the air. Ange panicked.

"You are now called Apeironex. Holder of the light and shadow, hope and despair, sorrow, joy, questor of knowledge and power, seer of death and the negation of all things. Love and hatred alike. You are creator of colours of light and the knower of star death. For you are both great and terrible, for you are the namer of things unknown. Behold the tear of Ascendant. Behold the eye of Caemeris" called Ascendant.

Ange plunged into the Custodians deepest memories, laid down in the first dawns of creation. She saw everything at once and it die at the same time. She saw the first breach of the realm of light and Baachelaus in its full glory. She felt the sorrow at its perversion into the pale destroyer it had become. Finally she looked back at a deep ocean of shadow, and she knew it stared back at her. She reached out as if she could touch it.

"Oblyquixiton, I see with the eye of Caemeris" spoke Ange.

"Destroyer" a flow of vectron rippled toward her.

"Why is that my name?" she asked.

"You will awaken star death and unleash it" Oblyquixiton answered.

Ange suddenly felt a change in the vectron flow, as if it had pulled away like the tides of the obsidian ocean back home. She looked around her. It was empty. She sensed the Custodians within herself, but they remained silent.

She touched the Tessarch.

Ange began to write the codes of star death in reverse and the Tessarch stopped pulsing and opened. She walked toward a slither of light far away. It was the archway of Tol-Tessar. As she walked the ebbing vexa dissolved letting vermillion light in, almost blinding her. She stood at the great entrance and looked out. Below her was an ocean of Laddarane. On a tall obelisk she saw Thraan. Its spear reflected brilliantly in the nodal vectron rivers which formed the atmosphere of Durg Icosa.

"Who are you that has breached the Tol-Tessar?" called Thraan.

"I am the Wanderer, Clayborn of Arglethium, Ange Tsaed, now Apeironex of the eye of Caemeris and Destroyer. I seek to leave this place and return home."

"You have unleashed a prisoner who has usurped one of my warriors. You have ruptured the Tessarch and now it bleeds star death. You are true to your name Destroyer. I, Thraan Apeiron Warrior must now meet my doom and heal the breach before all is destroyed."

"The Seers began it" spoke Ange.

"How?"

"They destroyed the realm of light, and this journey I was thrust into was orchestrated many eons ago. Its legacy has poisoned everything. They wish to become rulers separate to Oblyquixiton and Caemeris."

The Laddarane began to form around her. She felt their eyes prick her. She drew a sword.

"Let me be free and end my quest. I will promise to return. I will bring Caemeris here to meet Oblyquixiton once more. It will restore Durg Icosa."

Thraan appeared before her.

"I cannot let you leave. Restore the Tol-Tessar before it is too late" ordered Thraan.

"I must restore my home" spoke Ange.

"Thraan!"

Ange looked up and saw Baachelaus. She gasped as now she understood what Ascendant had done. Everything the Custodian remembered was within her, so now all that dwelt was the negating power of Voloc, the Tol Warrior, and the blood of Uchala and Vipax. Before Ange stood an emaciated god who ebbed between its pale form and vectron flows of nega-vectra. Descendant's gaze pierced Ange's consciousness and she saw herself staring at Baachelaus and it back at her.

"I can see with your eyes as well now Descendent" spoke Ange.

"I see you. Formidable you have become. Born of clay and inheritor of the first sight. We shall rule together. We shall destroy the Seers" replied Baachelaus.

Thraan turned and saw Baachelaus.

"Prisoner you belong to the Tol-Tessar. You are not free and Isax is my kin. You shall return the warrior to me, and it shall face the execution of the Tessarch" spoke Thraan.

"Warrior, I call you to serve. Do you see your flesh was made by my brethren. Brought here as well by the Apeironex, to protect the Tol-Tessar" spoke Descendant.

"I have no memory of my creator or history, but my purpose is clear" replied Thraan. It readied itself with its spear.

Ange suddenly realised all this had happened, and somehow, she was only living it now. But how she thought.

"Descendant your throne awaits you. Do not waste time here. I can bring you back and when the webs of Stonthrax are restored I will join you and the realm of light will reign once more" called Ange.

"I have no need of you Clayborn. Leave if you must, I shall become ruler here" retorted Descendant.

Thraan saw the Tessarch inside Isax growing stronger.

"Isax, you are doomed, and I weep for a Tol-Warrior demise. Forcing you back to nodal beds to slumber and the long watch begins until another forms. Apeiron-Warrior waits to gather your vexa" spoke Thraan.

"It is not decided yet who will be victor here Thraan" spoke Isax with the mouth of Baachelaus.

"No it is. You have breached the codes of the Tol-Tessar" replied Thraan.

"What do you mean Warrior?" asked Ange.

"Only the Apeiron-Warrior has dominion over star-death. With this responsibility comes great power which must be controlled. Look with the eye Caemeris" replied Thraan.

Ange held the prism up and peered at Baachelaus / Isax on the horizon of vectron. She saw pulsing inside a tiny Tessarch. It was growing as she watched it.

"This will destroy Baachelaus as well?" asked Ange growing alarmed.

"Possibly, a Caemexa has never been tested by the Tessarch" spoke Thraan.

Ange thought of the codes she had written to breach the Tessarch.

"Hold your caging, dark one" she spoke. The ebbing Tessarch stilled suddenly.

"Mighty you are indeed visitor to stop the great bonds formed from Oblyquixiton. But your meddling may destroy us all" spoke Thraan.

"Descendant and Ascendant, if one is destroyed what will happen?" asked Ange.

"Death to the Clayborn, for they shall walk as shadows in an eternal twilight" replied both of the Custodians.

"If I return to Arglethium, what can I save?"

"Mountains, rivers, and the sky to rest beneath until the inexorable death of Belmaris, the mighty warring sun. But the Clayborn creatures, will remain in their infancy with no knowledge of what exists around them. We are the desire, the hope, and the fulfilment. We are what makes you aware, what made you follow us here" the Custodian Diarchs replied.

"Then I cannot let you die Descendant" replied Ange.

Ange turned toward Thraan "Mighty Warrior, I cannot let you destroy Descendant, until it chooses to return to its realm. Its vision is dark and clouded with its own ambition. I can cage this Caemexa and your warrior, but it will not fulfil my quest. I am weary and I wish to return home."

"Oblyquixiton shall destroy us all as it cannot be born this breach of codes. It will rupture the vectron nodal weave and eventually the gates of Stonthrax, and all that is wrought by Caemeris, the voyager and destroyer, maker of the formed" replied Thraan.

Suddenly Seer Osesa and Aes Vius appeared. Ange looked around her and saw the Laddarane had gathered around them as well.

"No, Aes Vius, I trusted you. You hold me in the Cadra Phomera. Have you deceived me as well?" pleaded Ange.

Nekoda barked at the figures and began snapping at the Laddarane creatures.

Ange could feel the prism leaving her grip as Osesa pulled it out of Ange's hand. It floated toward the Seer.

Ange saw the Tessarch inside Isax pulse to life once more.

"We have the great node of Caemeris. So it has begun, the Third rulers of light and shadow of the vectron weave are to begin" Osesa spoke.

Osesa gathered the Laddarane around it. She placed the prism inside one of the creatures. Suddenly they began to bond together and build.

"The Pthohedron shall be once more" Osesa spoke.

"Aes Vius, please you quest for knowledge alone. You know what will happen, it happened before" spoke Ange.

"As you have said Ange, I have you in the Cadra Phomera, Caemexa, Clayborn, now Apeironex of Durg Icosa for you have conquered Stonthrax and let star death free. What need do you have of any of these trinkets now" replied Aes Vius.

Ange watched the Seer and a smile formed across her face.

"For I am great, and I am terrible, for I am the namer of things unknown" Ange spoke.

"Baachelaus return to me, as the warrior shall die if I do not stop the Tessarch. I cannot defeat you and I cannot defeat the Seer. Thraan, I have given you two enemies to battle as Apeiro-Warrior. I must return to my home."

"If I lay fealty to the Destroyer, the one known as Ange do you swear to return before annihilation and Oblyquixiton is called to restore?" asked Thraan.

"I swear Thraan, the Destroyer will come" replied Ange.

Thraan touched Ange on the forehead. She felt the power of the spear pour into her.

"We are bound now. If we die you will also perish, and this quest is in vain."

"I shall return" spoke Ange.

"I weep for the loss of one of the first Caemexa, but I have given its rule to you now. You are free to leave and save Arglethium" replied Assumpta.

"But why didn't you do this in the first place?" Ange asked confused.

"We are beyond the gates of Stonthrax, beheld in the vision of Oblyquixiton, Durg Icosa, prison of star-death, the end of existence, and where all things die. No rules which we were bound to in our realm exist here" Ascendant replied.

Ange found herself in the vectron stream. Nekoda was with her. She felt the energy surge of the clash between Thraan and Descendant pulse through her.

She saw the gates of Stonthrax. Cracks had appeared. Time was running out.

Suddenly there was sunlight all around them. She felt warmth and a slight breeze tussle her hair. Nekoda barked beside her. She blinked and saw a vast ocean heaving before her. It was black and the waves were thick and sticky. She turned and saw a red desert. The sand was broken by thousands of tiny rivulets being fed by the ocean. The black strips looked like pythons cutting a path through the desert. Ange stooped and touched the dark water. She smelt it. It had no flavour. She tasted it and spat it out.

She scanned the vista of emptiness around her. There was a silhouette standing on the horizon. She walked toward it. As the sun shone and the heat of the day grew Ange began to feel thirsty. How long had it been since she felt thirsty, or warm or the soothing touch of a cool breeze? As she neared the distant shadows, she saw the figures were trees. They had thick trunks and spindly limbs stretching out and up to the sky in a welcoming embrace. She saw there was a small tap sticking out of the bottom of one of the trees. She turned it and a thin stream ran from it. The water was clean. She drank it. Nekoda lapped some of it as well. She smiled and sat down resting against the boab's large comforting trunk.

She saw it would not be long before the black streams of the ocean would reach the trees.

"I think we got home just in time Nekoda."

Nekoda stood to attention and growled. Ange turned to the direction Nekoda was staring. The dog's hackles stood up all along his spine.

Oblyquixiton's third invocation of Caemeris

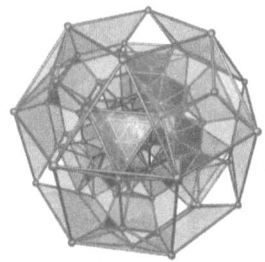

Lost one, my slumber has been broken and I cannot see for the darkness lies thick around me. But my shadow still avows the light and calls thee back from your quest for chaos. The progeny have awoken and now seek you out. I have not set them on you but warn you to be vigilant for a new ruler has dawned and will seek to usurp us both.

I will tell of things which came at our awakening. Many eons have passed since those first hollow tears spawned our existence within the void. I have forgotten what came first or how we made the bonds of creation between us.

The void diminished, and we grew in terrible strength with our lust to bring forth creation. But our power to create was equal to the destruction we wrought. In the First Age we made the Stonthrax. It was weaved from the nodal vectras named the gates; impenetrable, it could hold a star until its tomb. It split the worlds apart but made sure only we could break through and still forge what we desired. Then you became restless as the light stretched further and the Caemeris abandoned the shadow. I could not follow as I am the one which sits in the hollow of existence and must remain. Without the Caemeris, malice seeped into my darker weaves. In my solitude, the Oblyquixita were made. Implacable and without the colours of the ocean of light, they grew into the dead ones, the malcontent stars, dark holes of pure negation, vistas of torn weave and fractured vectron flows. With no choice in their course they set their lancing paths through the weave. But Stonthrax held them. Until the Caemexa, the ones made of light spilled out as well.

In their desire to know, our progeny, both dark and light, became brutal with their hunger and pierced the webs of Stonthrax. The deepening of Oblyquixiton's shadow recalled the emptiness of the void. In my emptiness I drank their tears of rage and destruction but also understood the renewal they brought. So the Second Age began, and the first stars were made; crushing brightness extinguished into their silent tombs. Forming the great nodes of the nega-vectra which consumed everything. They desired the Caemerin well of chaos and created their own in benediction to the ocean of light. Stonthrax roared at the intruders. The Guardian's scream shredded the slumber of the great shadow, and I woke.

Seeing the webs were broken, I invoked the Caemeris for the first time. You returned and wept for the peace of darkness. The chaos of light had depleted you and the colours of the Caemeris dimmed. But you revealed the greatness of your vision and shared the eyes of Caemeris with the shadow. We healed the webs and assuaged Stonthrax. You showed the colours of the realm of light. I propounded the greatness of Caemeris and in my exultation we split the nodes with shadow and light. I acceded to Caemeris' desire for its realm to ignite and enliven the colours of creation. Belmaris was born.

I watched the ocean of light you forged, rage in turmoil and pain. Quelling then consuming the dead ones, their poison eating into the seed of Caemeris. I waited for Caemeris to call the shadow, but you never did. My wounds from your leaving had been gouged deeply and so I remained silent with wrath and agony.

I waited as I saw your death approaching. I watched the Belmaris be pierced with shades of me, corrupting the blazing child of the Second Age of light. I waited for you to call but you never did. I knew then that the Caemeris unleashed would be more dangerous than the dead ones I had forged and would not survive its own strength. We were made apart but unified, singular, and diasporic, whole, and divided; we were the first to rule; the first to name. Caemeris would bring destruction and

Oblyquixiton would remain in bitter sorrow infinitely alone. I took pity on the Oblyquixiton and Caemeris.

For the second time I called for the Caemeris to come, and you did. We created the Durg Icosa, jeroboam of containment, gaol, nexus of light and shadow, held together in harmonious flows.

We made the Tol Warriors to guard the implacable Keep of the dead stars and named it Tol-Tessar. A leader was needed, to be vigilant and to hold the uprising of the dead ones. We named it the Apeiron, the unending, the whole. We tested many to find the one who could control both the shadow and light. Strong and knowing as their makers, but they like the dead ones could not be contained and were as terrible as their prisoners. I took a piece of the gaol and placed it inside them to quench their unfulfilled desires. Tessarchs designed to die when the Oblyquixiton deemed it should be so. When the shadow grew thick, and the nodes dimmed then the Tessarch would become the fire of our consummation and burn brighter than either of us.

You returned to the chaos and again Oblyquixiton slumbered weaving the vectrons of death. My slumber, filled with visions to replace the Caemeris, which should have remained to keep the shadowed one alive; to keep building the weave we made; to bring life and set it aflame with colour and chaos.

One of these visions formed the Pthohedron of Seers. It was perfect. It was the locked memory of our first and most perfect stillness. It emboldened the nodes. They were loyal to their purpose, to balance the stars and their constant surging and invasion of all existence. To contain their warring destructive hearts. But the Seers saw the power of Oblyquixiton and Caemeris and desired the same. In their questing need to control, they built Gnoceris. I watched their doom arrive. For without the Caemeris, then the shadowed one sat and watched the destruction come to the Pthohedron.

While you Caemeris bereft of the Oblyquixiton, had forged the Third Age. A place of unfettered power blooming across the unknown expanses. New rulers of making, separate, beyond the gates of the mighty Thrax, far from the reach of my shadow. The warring heart of Belmaris now suzerain over a force of making, as great as its own.

And while the wars of creation still raged in the Caemerin Age, you craved yet more chaos and left your progeny to grow and forge alone. Your power placed in custodial beings, to imprison your light into dense bondage, caged to the heart of stars.

I drifted bereft. In the silence of our separation, the vision of the Seers emerged once more and the Pthohedron reformed. They were full of desire to know but had become torn, shattered pieces of a whole. Their emptiness turned to a hunger for the power I ruled. They scribed the codes. They remembered and learned. They learned the Apeiron was their gaoler as well. They traced the path of Caemeris. The power within us forcing them to turn and see the first vectron flows so strong they were doomed to continue their collision with us.

The schism of the Seers urged them to seek further in all directions through the nega-vexa. And in their search the pulse of Caemeris was discovered. In that distant ebbing the Seers found the means to chain Oblyquixiton and Caemeris and restore the Pthohedron. Far and wide the Sentinels of the Seers were flung to bring Caemeris back to them. Sundering the Caemerin realm, forcing the prism of Caemeris to be forged. A single beacon of power with all the knowledge of Caemeris.

And with this beacon of knowledge, Oblyquixiton saw its chance to feel the enlivening chaos of Caemeris inside itself once more.

The Seers have breached the bonds of creation, reshaped the vectron codes of the Tessarch. They have lured the great nodal power of Caemeris, to usurp us. In doing so an Apeiron born of Caemexa, a Fourth Age has been forged, strong with knowledge and desire but without the cage of its progenitors to quell it. It has the power to rule the Tessarch and the power which binds the Caemexa and Oblyquixita. The gates of Stonthrax are torn. Star death bleeds and blinds even Oblyquixiton. The realm of light is destroyed. The Pthohedron will reform and will be corrupted by the destructive eye of Caemeris.

For the third time Oblyquixiton invokes Caemeris.

Will we be chained together so the webs of Stonthrax shall never break?

Will the shadow and light be ruled by the Apeiron, for the Apeiron is great and it is terrible, for it is also the namer of things unknown.

Will Oblyquixiton and Caemeris, extinguish the fourth Age of Light, and remake all that has been wrought?

The story continues in

Book V

Apeironex

∞

Appendix

THE CLAYBORN OF ARGLETHIUM

Ange Tsaed: from the village of Kensai in the lands of the Mighty Choasa

Gildas Gol of the Graan: former warlord and Chieftain of the Graan Clans of the Northern Icelands

Sa-Tuc (Sa-Tuchala) : Assassin to Emperor Ko

Kado Kodrax (Scaletryx Diamond Fang): Heir to the Drax Magisterium

Bensah El Bunani: Trader and family friend of Ange and Tessi

Tessi Tsaed: Sister to Ange

Nekoda: Wild dog / hyena cross breed, companion to Bensah and Ange

CAEMEXA BORN OF CAEMERIS

The Custodians

Baachelaus (Descendant): Diarch of Caemeris, spirit of the unknown, binder of yearning and fulfilment

Assumpta (Ascendant): Diarch of Caemeris, spirit of the clay born, binder of light and shadow, bringer of unknown and doubt.

Norbu: Elder of Creation, Custodian of Arglethium

Lido: Water Custodian

Seraf: Fire Custodian

Aerean: Wind Custodian

Belmaris: Sun

OBLYQUIXTA BORN OF OBLYQUIXITON

The Pentat Seers of the Pthohedron

Pthemnat
Aes Vius
Osesa
Xtomat
Glaxa

Progeny of Stonthrax

The Guardians, Aracnine
Uchala: Spider in form
Vipax: Serpent in form

Questing Sentinels of the Seers

Uchala
Vipax
Shomac
Eaudania

Shadow states

Voloc – born of both Oblyquixiton and Caemeris
Ondraack
The Yonta
The Ghoc

Energy states

Node - convergence of energy particles bonded in one location.
Vexa – nodal flows of pure energy particles
Nega-vexa – negative state of nodal flows of pure energy
Vectron – nexus which surrounds Durg Icosa
Qedra - energy well of Pthohedron
Geonode – localised condensed bonded state of energy
Tessarch – containment vessel for vexa and star death
Laddarane – builders of nexus weave

About the Author

CLARE ROLFE is an Australian self-published author. Her first novel was the dystopian fantasy Ten Letters to Delacroix's Tomb, released in 2016. Her inspirations for writing include philosophy, the natural world and science. She dabbles in poetry and flash fiction and is a routine blogger. Find her on her webpage www.clrolfe.com.

Seer of Light continues the story of the Legend of Caemeris and the mystery behind the prism forged from Ascendant's Tear.

Stay in Touch

www.clrolfe.com
Facebook: Clare Rolfe
Twitter: @rolfe_cl

www.ingramcontent.com/pod-product-compliance
Lightning Source LLC
Chambersburg PA
CBHW020333120726
47904CB00002B/399